When the past is your enemy,
all you have is the present. . .

MALICE

Books by Danielle Steel

DANIELLE STEEL

MALICE

A Dell Book

Published by
Dell Publishing
a division of
Bantam Doubleday Dell Publishing Group, Inc.
1540 Broadway
New York, New York 10036

ISBN: 0-440-22323-7

Reprinted by arrangement with Delacorte Press

Printed in the United States of America

Published simultaneously in Canada

June 1997

10 9 8 7 6 5 4 3 2 1

OPM

To my extraordinary, loving,
and very remarkable children,
Beatrix, Trevor, Todd,
Nick, Samantha, Victoria,
Vanessa, Maxx, and Zara.
You make my life worth living,
you are all that has made
my life worthwhile.
You are my life and my heart.
With all my thanks and love,
and apologies for the pain
I may have brought you
with this wicked thing
called "fame."
I love you so very, very much,

d.s.

Chapter 1

The sounds of the organ music drifted up to the Wedgwood blue sky. Birds sang in the trees, and in the distance, a child called out to a friend on a lazy summer morning. The voices inside the church rose in powerful unison, as they sang the familiar hymns that Grace had sung with her family since childhood. But this morning, she couldn't sing anything. She could barely move, as she stood, staring straight ahead at her mother's casket.

Everyone knew Ellen Adams had been a good mother, a good wife, a respected citizen until she died. She had taught school before Grace was born, and she would have liked to have had more children, but it just hadn't happened. Her health had always been frail, and at thirty-eight she had gotten cancer. The cancer started in her uterus, and after a hysterectomy, she'd had both chemotherapy and radiation. But the cancer spread to her lungs anyway, and her lymph nodes, and eventually her bones. It had been a four-and-a-half-year battle. And now, at forty-two, she was gone.

She had died at home, and Grace had taken care of her single-handedly until the last two months when her father had finally had to hire two nurses to help her. But Grace still sat next to her bedside for hours

when she came home from school. And at night, it was
Grace who went to her when she called out in pain,
helped her turn, carried her to the bathroom, or gave
her medication. The nurses only worked in the daytime. Her father didn't want them there at night, and
everyone realized he had a hard time accepting just
how sick his wife was. And now he stood in the pew
next to Grace and cried like a baby.

John Adams was a handsome man. He was forty-
six, and one of the best attorneys in Watseka, and
surely the most loved. He had studied at the University
of Illinois after serving in the Second World War, and
then came home to Watseka, a hundred miles south of
Chicago. It was a small, immaculately kept town, filled
with profoundly decent people. And he handled all
their legal needs, and listened to all their problems. He
went through their divorces with them, or battles over
property, bringing peace to warring members of families. He was always fair, and everyone liked him for it.
He handled personal injury, and claims against the
State, he wrote wills, and helped with adoptions. Other
than the town's most popular medical practitioner,
who was a friend of his too, John Adams was one of the
most loved and respected men in Watseka.

John Adams had been the town's football star as a
young man, and he had gone on to play in college.
Even as a boy, people had been crazy about him. His
parents had died in a car accident when he was sixteen,
and his grandparents had all died years before that,
and families literally argued over who was going to invite him to live with them until he finished high school.
He was always such a nice guy and so helpful. In the
end, he had stayed with two different families, and
both of them loved him dearly.

He knew practically everyone in town by name, and there were more than a few divorcées and young widows who had had an eye on him ever since Ellen had been so sick in the last few years. But he never gave them the time of day, except to be friendly, or ask about their kids. He had never had a roving eye, which was another nice thing people always said about him. "And Lord knows he has a right to," one of the older men who knew him well always said, "with Ellen so sick and all, you'd think he would start to look around . . . but not John . . . he's a right decent husband." He was decent and kind, and fair, and successful. The cases he handled were small, but he had an amazing number of clients. And even his law partner, Frank Wills, teased him occasionally, wanting to know why everyone asked for John, before they'd ask for Frank. He was everyone's favorite.

"What do you do, offer them free groceries for a year behind my back?" Frank always teased. He wasn't the lawyer John was, but he was a good researcher, and good with contracts, with minute attention to detail. It was Frank who went over all the contracts with a fine-tooth comb. But it was always John who got all the glory, whom they asked for when they called, whom clients had heard about from miles away in other towns. Frank was an unimpressive little man, without John's charm or good looks, but they worked well together and had known each other since college. Frank stood several rows back in the church now, feeling sorry for John, and his daughter.

John would be all right, Frank knew, he'd land on his feet, just like he always did, and although he insisted now that he wasn't interested, Frank was betting that his partner would be remarried in a year. But it was Grace who looked absolutely distraught, and shattered, as she stared straight ahead at the banks of flowers at the altar. She was a pretty girl, or she would have been, if she'd allowed herself to be. At seventeen, she was lean and tall, with graceful shoulders and long thin arms, beautiful long legs, and a tiny waist and full bust. But she always hid her figure in baggy clothes, and long loose sweaters she bought at the Salvation Army. John Adams was by no means a rich man, but he could have bought her better than that, if she'd wanted. But unlike other girls her age, Grace had no interest in clothes, or boys, and if anything, she seemed to diminish her looks, rather than enhance them. She wore no makeup at all, and she wore her long coppery auburn hair straight down her back, with long bangs that hid her big cornflower-blue eyes. She never seemed to look straight at anyone, or be inclined to engage them in conversation. Most people were surprised by how pretty she was, if they really looked at her, but if you didn't look twice, you never noticed her at all. Even today, she was wearing an old dreary black dress of her mother's. It hung like a sack on her, and she looked thirty years old, with her hair tied back in a tight bun, and her face deathly pale as she stood beside her father.

"Poor kid," Frank's secretary whispered, as Grace walked slowly back down the aisle, next to her father, behind her mother's casket. Poor John . . . poor Ellen . . . poor people. They'd been through so much.

People commented from time to time on how shy Grace was, and how uncommunicative. There had been a rumor a few years back that she might even be retarded, but anyone who had ever gone to school with her knew that that was a lie. She was brighter than

most of them, she just didn't say much. She was a solitary soul, and it was only once in a while that someone
in school would see her talking to someone, or laughing in a corridor, but then she would hurry away again,
as though she was frightened to come out and be
among them. She wasn't crazy, her classmates knew,
but she wasn't friendly either. It was odd too, considering how sociable her parents were. But Grace never
had been. Even as a small child, she had always been
solitary, and somewhat lonely. And more than once as
a child, she had had to go home from school with a
bad attack of asthma.

John and Grace stood out in the noon sun for a
little while, shaking hands with friends, thanking them
for being there, embracing them, and more than ever,
Grace looked wooden and removed as she greeted
them. It was as though her body was there, but her
mind and soul were elsewhere. And in her dreary too-
big dress, she looked more pathetic than ever.

Her father commented on the way she looked on
the way to the cemetery. Even her shoes looked worn.
She had taken a pair of her mother's black high heels,
but they were out of style, and they looked as though
her mother had gotten plenty of use from them before
she got sick. It was almost as though Grace wanted to
be closer to her now, by wearing her mother's clothes,
it was like camouflage, or protective coloring, but it
wasn't flattering on a girl her age, and her father said
so. She looked a lot like her mother, actually, people
always commented on it, except that her mother had
been more robust before she'd been taken ill, and her
dress was at least three sizes too big for Grace's lithe
figure.

"Couldn't you have worn something decent for a

change?'' her father asked with a look of irritation as they drove to St. Mary's Cemetery on the outskirts of town, with three-dozen cars behind them. He was a respected man, and he had a reputation to uphold. It looked strange for a man like him to have an only child who dressed like an orphan.

"Mama never let me wear black. And I thought . . . I thought I should . . ." She looked at him defenselessly, sitting miserably in the corner of the old limousine the funeral home had provided for the occasion. It was a Cadillac, and some of the kids had rented it for the senior prom two months before, but Grace hadn't wanted to go, and no one had asked her. With her mother so sick, she had barely even wanted to go to graduation. But she had, of course, and she had shown her mother the diploma as soon as she got home. She had been accepted at the University of Illinois, but had deferred it for a year, so she could continue taking care of her mother. Her father wanted it that way too, he felt that Ellen preferred Grace's loving touch to that of her nurses, and he had pretty much told Grace that he expected her to stay, and not leave for school in September. She hadn't argued with him. She knew there was no point. There was never any point arguing with him. He always got what he wanted. He was used to it. He had been too good-looking and too successful for too long, it had always worked for him, and he expected things to stay that way. Always. Particularly with his own family. Grace understood that. And so had Ellen.

"Is everything ready at the house?" he asked, glancing at her, and she nodded. For all her shyness and reticence, she ran a home beautifully, and had since she was thirteen. In the past four years, she had done everything for her mother.

"It's fine," she said quietly. She had set everything out on the buffet before they left for church. And the rest was covered, on big platters in the refrigerator. People had been bringing them food for days. And Grace had cooked a turkey and a roast the night before. Mrs. Johnson had brought them a ham, and there were salads, and casseroles, some sausages, two plates of hors d'oeuvres, and lots of fresh vegetables, and every imaginable kind of cake and pastry. Their kitchen looked like a bake sale at the state fair, there was plenty for everyone. She was sure that they were going to be seeing well over a hundred people, maybe even twice that many, out of respect for John and what he meant to the people of Watseka.

People's kindness had been staggering. The sheer number of floral arrangements alone had surpassed anything they'd ever seen at the funeral home. "It's like royalty," old Mr. Peabody had said when he handed the guest book full of signatures to her father.

"She was a rare woman," John said quietly, and now, thinking of her, he glanced over at his daughter. She was such a beautiful girl, and so determined not to show it. That was just the way she was, he accepted it, and it was easier not to argue about it. She was good about other things, and she had been a godsend for him during all the years of her mother's illness. It was going to be strange for both of them now, but in a way, he had to admit, it was going to be easier now too. Ellen had been so sick for so long, and in so much pain, it was inhuman.

He looked out the window as they drove along, and then back at his only daughter. "I was just thinking about how odd it's going to be now without your mama . . . but maybe . . ." He wasn't sure how to say it without upsetting her more than he meant to, ". . . maybe easier for both of us. She suffered so much, poor thing," he sighed, and Grace said nothing. She knew her mother's suffering better than anyone, better even than he did.

The ceremony at the cemetery was brief, their minister said a few words about Ellen and her family, and read from Proverbs and Psalms at the graveside, and then they all drove back to the Adamses' home. A crowd of a hundred and fifty friends squeezed into the small neat house. It was painted white, with dark green shutters and a picket fence. There were daisy bushes in the front yard, and a small rose garden her mother had loved just outside her kitchen windows.

The babble of their friends sounded almost like a cocktail party, and Frank Wills held court in the living room, while John stood outside with friends in the hot July sunshine. Grace served lemonade and iced tea, and her father had brought out some wine, and even the huge crowd scarcely made a dent in all the food she served. It was four o'clock when the last guests finally left, and Grace walked around the house with a tray, picking up all their dishes.

"We've got good friends," her father said with a warm smile. He was proud of the people who cared about them. He had done a lot for many of them over the years, and now they were there, in their hour of need, for him, and his daughter. He watched Grace moving quietly around the living room, and he realized how alone they were now. Ellen was gone, the nurses were gone, there was no one left except just the two of them. Yet he was not a man to dwell on his misfortunes.

"I'll go outside and see if there are any glasses out there," he said helpfully, and he came back half an hour later with a trayful of plates and glasses, his jacket over his arm, and his tie loosened. If she'd been aware of such things, she would have seen that her father looked more handsome than ever. Others had noticed it. He had lost some weight in the last few weeks, understandably, and he looked as trim as a young man, and in the sunlight it was difficult to see if his hair was gray or sandy. In fact, it was both, and his eyes were the same bright blue as his daughter's.

"You must be tired," he said to her, and she shrugged as she loaded glasses and plates into the dishwasher. There was a lump in her throat and she was trying not to cry. It had been an awful day for her . . . an awful year . . . an awful four years. . . . Sometimes she wished she could disappear into a little puddle of water. But she knew she couldn't. There was always another day, another year, another duty to perform. She wished that they had buried her that day, instead of her mother. And as she stared unhappily at the dirty plates she was loading mechanically into the racks, she felt her father standing beside her. "Want some help?"

"I'm okay," she said softly. "Do you want dinner, Dad?"

"I don't think I could eat another thing. Why don't you just forget it. You've had a long day. Why don't you just relax for a while?" She nodded, and went back to loading the dishes. He disappeared into the back of the house, to his bedroom, and it was an hour later when she had finally finished. All the food was put away, and the kitchen looked impeccable. The dishes were in the machine, and the living room looked tidy and spotless. She was well organized and she bustled through the house straightening furniture and pictures. It was a way of keeping her mind off everything that had happened.

When she went to her room, her father's door was closed, and she thought she could hear him talking on the phone. She wondered if he was going out, as she closed her own door, and lay on her bed with all her clothes on. She'd gotten food on the black dress by then, and she'd splashed it with soap and water when she did the dishes. Her hair felt like string, her mouth like cotton, her heart like lead. She closed her eyes, as she lay there miserably, and two little rivers of tears flowed from the outer corners of her eyes to her ears.

"Why, Mama? Why . . . why did you leave me? . . ." It was the final betrayal, the final abandonment. What would she do now? Who would help her? The only good thing was that she could leave and go to college in September. Maybe. If they'd still take her. And if her father would let her. But there was no reason to stay here now. There was every reason to leave, which was all she wanted.

She heard her father open his door and go out into the hall. He called her name, and she didn't answer him. She was too tired to speak to anyone, even him, as she lay on her bed, crying for her mother. Then she heard his bedroom door close again, and it was a long time before she finally got up, and walked into her bathroom. It was her only luxury, having her own bathroom. Her mother had let her paint it pink, in the little three-bedroom house her mother had been so proud of. They had wanted the third bedroom for the son they'd planned to have, but the baby had never come, and her mother had used it as a sewing room for as long as Grace could remember.

She ran a hot bath almost to the edge of the tub, and she went to lock her bedroom door, before she took off her mother's tired black dress, and let it fall to the floor around her feet, after she kicked her mother's shoes off.

She let herself slowly into the tub, and closed her eyes as she lay there. She was totally unaware of how beautiful she was, how long and slender her legs, how graceful her hips, or how appealing her breasts were. She saw none of it, and wouldn't have cared. She just lay there with her eyes closed and let her mind drift. It was as though her head were filled with sand. There were no images, no people she wanted to see in her mind's eye, nothing she wanted to do, or be. She just wanted to hang in space and think of absolutely nothing.

She knew she'd been there for a long time when the water had grown cold, and she heard her father knocking on the door to her bedroom. "What are you doing in there, Gracie? Are you okay?"

"I'm fine," she shouted from the tub, roused from her trancelike state. It was growing dark outside, and she hadn't bothered to turn the lights on.

"Come on out. You'll be lonely."

"I'm fine." Her voice was a monotone, her eyes distant, keeping everyone far from the place where she really lived, deep in her own soul, where no one could find her or hurt her.

She could hear him still standing outside her door, urging her to come out and talk to him, and she told him she'd be out in a few minutes. She dried herself off, and put on a pair of jeans and a T-shirt. And over that, she put on one of her baggy sweaters, in spite of the heat. And when she was all dressed again, she unlocked the door, and went back to unload the dishwasher in the kitchen. He was standing there, looking out at her mother's roses, and he turned when Grace came into the room, and smiled at her.

"Want to go outside and sit for a while? It's a nice night. You could do this later."

"It's okay. I might as well get it done." He shrugged and helped himself to a beer, and then he walked outside and sat down on the kitchen steps and watched the fireflies in the distance. She knew it was pretty outside, but she didn't want to look at it, didn't want to remember this night, or anything about it. Just like she didn't want to remember the day her mother died or the pitiful way she'd begged Grace to be good to her father. That was all she'd cared about . . . him . . . all that ever mattered to her was making him happy.

When the dishes were put away, Grace went back to her room again, and lay down on the bed, without turning on the light. She still couldn't get used to the silence. She kept waiting to hear her voice, for the past two days she kept listening for her, as though she'd been sleeping, but would wake up in pain at any moment. But there was no pain for Ellen Adams now, there never would be again. She was at peace at last. And all they had left was the silence.

Grace put her nightgown on at ten o'clock, and left her jeans in a pile on the floor, with her sweater and T-shirt. She locked her door, and went to bed. There was nothing else to do. She didn't want to read or watch T-V, the chores were done, there was no one she had to take care of. She just wanted to go to sleep and forget everything that had happened . . . the funeral . . . the things people had said . . . the smell of the flowers . . . the words of their minister at the graveside. No one knew her mother anyway, no one knew any of them, just as they didn't know her, and didn't really care. All they wanted and knew were their own illusions.

"Gracie . . ." She heard her father knock softly on the door. "Gracie . . . honey, are you awake?" She heard him, but she didn't answer. What was there to say? How much they missed her? How much she had meant to them? Why bother? It wouldn't bring her back anyway. Nothing would. Grace just lay in bed in the dark, in her old pink nylon nightgown.

She heard him try the doorknob then, and she didn't stir. She had locked the door. She always did. At school the other girls made fun of her for being so modest. She locked the doors everywhere. Then she could be sure of being alone, and not being bothered. "Gracie?" He was still standing there, determined not to let her grieve alone, his voice sounded gentle and warm, as she stared at the door, and refused to answer. "Come on, baby . . . let me in, and we'll talk . . . we're both hurting right now . . . come on, honey . . . let me help you." She didn't stir, and this time he rattled the doorknob. "Honey, don't make me force the door, you know I can. Now come on, let me in."

"I can't. I'm sick," she lied. She looked beautiful and pale in the moonlight, her white face and arms like marble, but he couldn't see them.

"You're not sick." He knew her better than that. As he talked to her, he was unbuttoning his shirt. He was tired too, but he didn't want her locked up alone in her room, with her grief. That's what he was there for. "Gracie!" His tone was growing firm, and she sat up in bed and stared at the door, almost as though she could see him beyond it, and this time she looked frightened.

"Don't come in, Dad." There was a tremor in her voice, as she looked at the door. It was as though she knew he was all-powerful, and she feared him. "Dad, don't." She could hear him forcing the door, as she put her feet on the floor, and sat on the edge of the bed, waiting to see if he could force it. But she heard him walk away then, and she sat shaking on the edge of the bed. She knew him too well. He never gave up on anything that easily, and she knew he wouldn't now.

A moment later, he was back, and she heard an implement of some kind jimmy the lock, and an instant later, he was standing in her room, bare-chested and barefoot, with only his trousers on, and a look of annoyance.

"You don't need to do that. It's just the two of us now. You know I'm not going to hurt you."

"I know . . . I . . . I couldn't help it . . . I'm sorry, Dad . . ."

"That's better." He walked to where she sat, and looked down at her sternly. "There's no point in your being miserable in here. Why don't you come on into my room and we'll talk for a while." He looked fatherly, and disappointed by her constant reticence, and as she looked up at him, he could see that she was shaking.

"I can't . . . I . . . I have a headache."

"Come on." He leaned down and grabbed her by the arm, and pulled her from where she sat. "We'll talk in my room."

"I don't want to . . . I . . . *no!*" she snapped at him, and pulled her arm out of his hand. "I *can't!*" she shouted at him, and this time he looked angry. He wasn't going to play these games with her anymore. Not now. And not tonight. There was no point, and no need. She knew what her mother had said to her. His eyes burned into hers as he looked down at her, and grabbed her harder.

"Yes, you can, and you're going to, dammit. I told you to come into my room."

"Dad, please . . ." Her voice was a thin whine, as he dragged her from the bed, and she followed him unwillingly into his bedroom. "Please, Mom . . ." She could feel her chest tighten and hear the beginnings of a wheeze as she begged him.

"You heard what your mother said when she died," he spat the words angrily at her. "You know what she told you . . ."

"I don't care." It was the first time in her entire life that she had defied him. In the past, she had whimpered and cried, but she had never fought him as she did now, she had begged, but never argued. This was new for her, and he didn't like it. "Mom isn't here now," she said, shaking from head to foot, as she stared at him, trying to dredge something from her very soul that had never been there before, the courage to fight her father.

"No, she isn't, is she?" He smiled. "That's the point, Grace. We don't have to hide anymore, you and I. We can do whatever we want. It's our life now . . . our time . . . and no one ever has to know it. . . ." He advanced toward her with eyes that glittered at her, as she took a step backwards, and he grabbed both her arms, and then an instant later, with a single gesture, he tore the pink nylon nightgown in half, right off her shoulders. "There . . . that's better . . . isn't it . . . we don't need this anymore . . . we don't need anything . . . all I need is you, little Gracie . . . all I need is my baby who loves me so much, and whom I love. . . ." With a single hand, he dropped his trousers and stepped out of them, along with his shorts, and he stood naked and erect before her.

"Dad . . . please . . ." It was a long, sad gasp of grief and shame, as she hung her head, and looked away from him, at the sight of him that was all too familiar. "Dad, I can't . . ." Tears slid down her cheeks. He didn't understand. She had done it for her, because her mother had begged her. She had done it for years, since she was thirteen . . . since just after her mother got sick, and had the first operation. Before that, he had beaten her, and Grace had listened to it, night after night, in her bedroom, sobbing, and listening to them, and in the morning, her mother would try to explain the bruises, talking about how she had fallen, or walked right into the bathroom door, or slipped, but it was no secret. They all knew. No one would have believed John Adams capable of it, but he was, and a great deal more. He would have beaten Grace, too, except that Ellen never let him. Instead, she had offered herself up, time after time, for his beatings, and told Grace to lock the door to her room.

Twice, Ellen had miscarried because of the beatings, the last time at six months, and after that, there had been no more children. The beatings had been brutal and terrifying, but subtle enough that the bruises could always be hidden or explained, as long as Ellen was willing to do it, and she was. She had loved him ever since high school, he was the best-looking boy in town, and she knew she was lucky to have him. Her parents had been dirt-poor, and she hadn't even finished high school. She was a beautiful girl, but she knew that without John, she didn't have a chance in the world. That was what he told her, and she believed him. Her own father had beaten her too, and at first what John did, didn't seem so unusual or so awful. But it got worse over the years, and at times he threatened to leave her because she was so worthless. He made her do anything he wanted just so he wouldn't leave her. And as Grace grew up and grew more beautiful each day, it was easy to see what he wanted, what would be required of her, if she really wanted to keep him. And once Ellen got sick, and the radiation and chemotherapy changed her so dramatically, deep penetration was no longer possible. He told her bluntly then that if she expected to stay married to him something would have to be worked out to keep him happy. It was obvious that she couldn't keep him happy anymore, couldn't give him what he wanted. But Grace could. She was thirteen, and so very lovely.

Her mother had explained it to her, so she wouldn't be frightened. It was something she could do for them, like a gift, she could help her dad be happy, and help her mom, it would be as though she was even more a part of them, and her dad would love her more than he ever had before. At first, Grace didn't understand, and then she cried . . . what would her friends think if they ever knew? How could she do *that* with her father? But her mother kept telling her how she had to help them, how she owed it to them, how her mother would die if someone didn't help her, and maybe he would leave them, and then they'd be alone, with no one to take care of them. She painted a terrifying pic-

ture, and put the leaden mantle of responsibility on
Grace's shoulders. The girl sagged at the weight of it,
and the horror of what was expected of her. But they
didn't wait to hear her answer. That night, they came
into her room, and her mother helped him. She held
her down, and crooned to her, and told her what a
good girl she was, and how much they loved her. And
afterwards, when they went back to their room, John
held Ellen in his arms and thanked her.

It was a lonely life for Grace after that. He didn't
come to her every night, but almost. Sometimes she
thought she would die of shame, and sometimes he
really hurt her. She never told anyone, and eventually
her mother stopped coming into the room with him.
Grace knew what was expected of her, and that she had
no choice except to do it. And when she argued with
him, he'd hit her hard, and eventually she knew there
was no way out, no choice. She did it for her, not for
him. She submitted so he wouldn't beat her mother
anymore, or leave them. But anytime Grace didn't cooperate with him, or do everything he asked, he went
back to his own room and beat up her mother, no
matter how sick she was, or how much pain she was in.
It was a message that Grace always understood, and she
would run shrieking into their room, and swear that
she'd do anything he wanted. And over and over and
over again, he made her prove it. For over four years
now, he had done everything he could dream of with
her, she was his very own love slave, his daughter. And
the only thing her mother had done to protect Grace
from him was get birth control pills for her so she
wouldn't get pregnant.

She had no friends at all once he started sleeping
with her. She had had few enough before, because she

was always afraid that someone would find out he was beating her mother, and Grace knew she had to protect them. But once she started sleeping with him, it was impossible to talk to any of the kids in school, or even the teachers. She was always sure they'd know, that they'd see something on her face, or her body, like a sign, like a malignancy that, unlike her mother, she wore on the outside. The malignancy was his, but she never really understood that. Until now. Now she knew that with her mother gone, she didn't have to do this. It had to stop. She just couldn't now. Not even for her mother. It was too much . . . and especially in this room. He had always come to Grace's room, and forced her to let him in. He had never dared take her in his own room. But now it was as though he expected her to step right into her mother's shoes, and fill them in ways that even her mother never could. It was as though he expected her to be his bride now. Even the way he talked to her was different. It was all out in the open. He expected her to be his woman.

And as he looked at her body shimmering enticingly at him, her frantic pleas and arguments only served to arouse him further. He looked hard and ominous as he stood holding her in his powerful grip, and with a single gesture he threw her onto his bed, precisely where his invalid wife had lain until only two days before, and for all the empty years of their marriage.

But this time, Grace struggled with him, she had already decided that she wasn't going to submit again, and as she fought with him, she realized that she had been crazy to think she could stay under the same roof with him, and not have the same nightmare continue. She would have to run away, but first she had to resist, and survive what he was doing to her. She knew she

couldn't let him do it to her again . . . she couldn't.
Even if her mother had wanted her to be good to him,
she had been good enough. She couldn't do it anymore . . . never again . . . never . . . but as she
flailed her arms helplessly, he pinned her down with
his powerful arms, and the weight of his body. Her legs
were swiftly parted by his own, and the familiarity of
him forced his way through her with more pain than
she had ever known or imagined. For a moment, she
almost thought he might kill her. It had never been
this way before, he had never hurt her as much as he
did now. It was as though he were beating her with a
fist from inside this time, and wanted to prove to her
that he owned her and could do anything he wanted. It
was almost beyond bearing and for an instant she
thought she might faint, as the room swirled around
her, and he hammered at her again and again, tearing
at her breasts, chewing at her lips, forcing himself into
her again and again, until she seemed to drift in a half
state near death, wishing that finally, mercifully, he
would kill her.

But even as he ravished her, she knew she couldn't
do this again. He couldn't do it to her, she couldn't
survive it, for him, or anyone. She knew that she was
within an inch of falling off the edge of a dangerous
ledge, and suddenly as she fought and clawed at him,
she knew through the blur that she was fighting for her
survival. And then, without even knowing how she had
remembered it, she knew that they had rolled closer to
her mother's night table. For years now, there had
been neat rows of pills there and a glass and a pitcher
of water. She could have poured the water over him, or
hit him with the pitcher, but it was gone. There were
no more pills, no water, no glass, and no one to take

them. But without thinking, Grace groped her hand along the table, as he continued to pound at her, shouting and grunting. He had slapped her hard several times across the face, but now he was only interested in punishing her with his sexual force and not his hands. He was squeezing her breasts, and pressing her into the bed. He had almost knocked the wind out of her, and her vision was still blurred from when he had hit her, but she felt the drawer of the night table open as she pulled at it, and then she felt the sleek cool steel of the gun her mother had hidden there against intruders. Ellen would never have dared to use it on her husband, or even to threaten him. No matter what he had done to her, or Grace, Ellen had truly loved him.

Grace felt her fingers go around its smooth surfaces, and she got a grip on it, and brandished it above him, for an instant wanting to hit him with it, just to stop him. He was almost finished with her, but she couldn't let him do this to her again. She had to stop him, no matter what or how, she knew she had to stop him before it went any further. She couldn't survive this again. And tonight only told her that he intended this to be her fate for a lifetime. He wouldn't let her go anywhere, he would never let her leave or go to college, or do anything else. She would have no life except to service him, and she knew that whatever it took, she had to stop him. And as she held the gun in her shaking, flailing hand, he came with a huge shuddering shout that made her wince with pain and anguish and revulsion. Just hearing that again made her hate him. And as she pointed the gun at him, he looked up and saw it.

"You little bitch!" he shouted at her, still shaken by the strength of his orgasm. No one had ever aroused him as Grace did. He wanted to take her and turn her inside out, tear her limb from limb, and devour her. Nothing excited him more than his own flesh, it was deeply primeval. And he was outraged now that she was still going to fight him. He moved to grab the gun from her, and she could see what he was going to do to her. He was going to beat her again and beating her always aroused him further. She couldn't let him do it, couldn't let him take her ever again. She had to save herself from him. He was still inside her, as he reached over to grab the gun from her, and in panic she squeezed the trigger as he tried to take it. He looked stunned for just an instant as the gun went off with a sound that terrified her, his eyes bulged, and then he fell down on her with a crushing weight. She had shot him through the throat, and he was bleeding profusely, but he wasn't moving. She tried to fight her way out from under him, and free herself from him, but she couldn't do it. He was too heavy, and she couldn't breathe, and there was blood in her eyes and her mouth now. She was gasping for air, and then with all the strength she had, she forced him from her. He rolled over on his back on the bed, and made a terrifying gurgling sound as he looked at her, but nothing moved and his eyes were open.

"Oh my God . . . oh my God . . ." she said, still gasping for air, and clutching her own throat now as she stared at him. She could still taste his blood on her tongue, and she didn't want to touch him. There was blood all over her and the bed, and all she could think of were her mother's words . . . "Be good to Daddy, Grace . . . be good to him . . . take care of him . . . always take care of your father . . ." And she had. She had shot him. His eyes moved around the room, but he seemed to be paralyzed, nothing moved, as he stared at her in terror. She backed into the corner then, and looked at him, and as she did, her whole body shook violently and she threw up on the carpet. When she stopped, she forced herself to go to the phone, and dial the operator.

"I need . . . an ambulance . . . ambulance . . . my father's been shot . . . I shot my father. . . ." She was gasping for air, and she gave them the address, and then she stood staring at him. He hadn't moved since he'd fallen back on the bed, and his organ was limp now. The thing that had so terrified her, that had tortured her for so long, looked suddenly so small and harmless, as did he. He looked terrifying and pathetic, blood was bubbling from his throat, and he moaned from time to time. She knew she had done a terrible thing, but she couldn't help it. The gun was still in her hand, and she was cowering naked in the corner when the police came. And she was gasping from her asthma.

"My God . . ." the first officer into the room said softly, and then he saw her and took the gun from her as the others walked into the room behind him. The youngest of them thought to wrap her in a blanket, but he had seen the marks on her, the blood smeared everywhere, and the look in her eyes. She seemed crazy. She had been to hell and only halfway back.

Her father was still alive when the ambulance and the paramedics came, but barely. She had severed his spinal cord and the paramedics suspected that the bullet had gone into his lung after that. He was completely paralyzed, and couldn't speak to them. But he didn't even see Grace as he left. His eyes were closed, and they were giving him oxygen. He was barely breathing.

"Is he gonna make it?" the senior policeman asked the paramedics as they put him into the ambulance and turned the siren on in a hurry.

"Hard to say," they answered, and then in an undertone, "Not likely." They left the scene then, and the older officer shook his head. He had known John Adams since he was in high school. John had handled his divorce for him. Hell of a guy, and why in God's name had the kid shot him? He'd seen the scene when they'd arrived, and he'd noticed that neither of them was dressed, but that could mean anything. Obviously, it had happened after they went to bed in their own rooms, and John probably didn't sleep in pajamas. Why the girl was naked was another thing. She was obviously unbalanced, and maybe her mom's death had been too much for her. Maybe she blamed her father for the mother's death. Whatever it was, they'd find it out in the investigation.

"How is she?" he asked one of his junior officers. There were a dozen officers on the scene by then. It was the biggest thing that had happened in Watseka since the minister's son had taken LSD and committed suicide ten years before. That had been a tragedy, but this was going to be a scandal. For a man like John Adams to be shot by his own kid, that was a real crime, and a loss for the whole town. No one was going to believe it. "Is she on drugs?" he asked as a photographer took pictures of the bedroom. The gun was already in a plastic bag in the squad car.

"She doesn't look like it," the young cop said. "Not obviously, at least. She looks kind of out of it, and very scared. She has asthma, and she's having a hard time breathing."

"I'm sorry to hear it," the senior officer said sarcastically as he glanced around the neat living room. He had been there only hours before, after the funeral. It was hard to believe why he was back now. Maybe the kid was just plain crazy. "Her father's got a lot worse than asthma."

"What did they say?" The junior officer looked concerned. "Is he gonna make it?"

"It doesn't look great. Seems like our little shooter here did quite a job on her old man. Spinal cord, maybe a lung, God only knows what else, or why."

"Think he was doing her?" the younger man asked, intrigued by the situation, but the older man looked outraged.

"John Adams? Are you nuts? Do you know who he is? He's the best lawyer in town. And the most decent guy you'd ever want to meet. You think a guy like him would do his own kid? You're as crazy as she is and not much of a cop if you can come to a conclusion like that."

"I don't know . . . it kind of looked like it, they were both naked . . . and she looks so scared . . . there's a bruise coming up on her arm . . . and . . ." He hesitated, given the senior man's reaction, but he couldn't conceal evidence, no matter who the guy was. Evidence was evidence. "There was come on the sheets, it looked like . . ." There had been a lot of blood, but there were other spots too. And the young cop had seen them.

"I don't give a damn what it looked like, O'Byrne. There's more than one way for come to get on a man's sheets. The guy's wife just died, maybe he was lonely, maybe he was playing with himself when she came in with the gun, maybe she didn't know what he was doing and it scared her. But there's no way in hell you're gonna come in here and tell me that John Adams was doing it to his kid. Forget it."

"Sorry, sir." The other officers were already rolling up the sheets as evidence anyway and putting them in plastic bags too, and another officer was talking to Grace in her bedroom. She was sitting on the bed, still wearing the blanket they had given her when they got there. She had found her inhaler and she was breathing more easily now, but she looked deathly pale, and the officer questioning her wondered how clear she was on what had happened. She seemed so dazed that he almost wondered if she understood him. She said she didn't remember finding the gun, it was suddenly just in her hand, and it went off. She remembered the noise, and then her father bleeding all over her. And that was all she remembered.

"How was he bleeding on you? Where were you?" He had the same impression of the scene as O'Byrne, though it seemed hard to believe of John Adams.

"I don't remember," she said blankly. She sounded like an automaton, her breath was still coming in little short gasps, and she seemed a little shaky from the medication.

"You don't remember where you were when you shot your father?"

"I don't know." She looked at him as though she didn't see him sitting there on her bed with her. "In the doorway," she lied. She knew what she had to do. She owed it to her mother to protect him.

"You shot him from the doorway?" It was impossible, and they were getting nowhere. "Do you think someone else shot your father?" He wondered if that was where she was going with her story. An intruder.

But that was even less believable than the story about the doorway.

"No. I shot him. From the doorway."

The officer knew without a doubt that her father had been shot at close range, maybe no more than an inch or two, by a person right in front of him, obviously his daughter. But where were they?

"Were you in bed with him?" he asked her pointedly, and she didn't answer. She stared straight ahead, as though he weren't even there, and gave a little sigh. "Were you in bed with him?" he asked again, and she hesitated for a long time before she answered.

"I'm not sure. I don't think so."

"How's it going in here?" the senior officer inquired, as he poked his head in the door. It was three o'clock in the morning by then, and they had done everything they needed to do at the crime scene.

The officer questioning Grace gave a hopeless shrug. It was not going well. She was not making a lot of sense, she was shaking violently, and she was so dazed that at times he really wondered if she even knew what had happened. "We're going to take you in, Grace. You're going to be in custody for a few days. We need to talk to you some more about what happened." She nodded, and said nothing to him. She just sat there, with bloodstains all over her, in the blanket. "Maybe you'd like to clean up a little bit, and put your clothes on." He nodded at the officer who'd been talking to her, but Grace didn't move, she just sat there. "We're taking you in, Grace. For questioning," he explained again, wondering if she really was crazy. John had never mentioned it, but it wasn't the kind of thing one said to clients.

"We're going to hold you for seventy-two hours,

pending an investigation of the shooting." Had it been premeditated? Had she meant to shoot him? Had it been an accident? What was the deal here? He wondered too if she was on drugs, and he wanted her tested.

She didn't ask if they were arresting her. She didn't ask anything. And she didn't get dressed either. She seemed completely disoriented, which was what suggested to the officer in charge more and more clearly that she was crazy. In the end, they called for a female officer to come out and help them, and she dressed Grace like a small child, but not without noticing assorted marks and bruises on her body. She told her to wash the bloodstains off, and Grace was surprisingly obliging. She did whatever she was told, but she offered no information.

"Did you and your dad have a fight?" the woman officer inquired as Grace stepped into her old jeans and T-shirt. She was still shaking as though she were standing naked in the Arctic. But Grace never answered her question. "Were you mad at him?" Nothing. Silence. She wasn't hostile. She wasn't anything. She looked as though she were in a trance, as they walked her through the living room, and she never once asked about her father. She didn't want to know where he'd gone, where they'd taken him, or what had happened once he got there. She stopped only for an instant as they crossed the living room, and looked at a photograph of her mother. It was in a silver frame, and Grace was standing next to her in the picture. She had been two or three years old, and both of them were smiling. Grace looked at it for a long time, remembering what her mother had looked like, how pretty she had been, and how much she wanted of Grace. Too much. She wanted to tell her she was sorry now. She just couldn't do it. She had let her mother down. She hadn't taken care of him. She couldn't anymore. And now he was gone. She couldn't remember where he had gone. But he was gone. And she wasn't going to take care of him anymore.

"She's really out of it," the woman officer said right within earshot, as Grace stared at her mother's picture. She wanted to remember it. She had a feeling she might not be seeing it again, but she wasn't sure why. She only knew that they were leaving. "You going to call in a shrink?" the officer asked.

"Yeah, maybe," the senior officer said. More than ever, he was beginning to think she was retarded. Or maybe not. Maybe it was all an act. Maybe there was more to it than met the eye. It was hard to say. God only knew what she'd really been up to.

When Grace stepped outside in the night air, the front lawn was swarming with policemen. There were seven squad cars parked outside, most of them had come just to see what had happened, some were responsible for checking out the crime scene. There were lights flashing and men in uniform everywhere, and the young cop named O'Byrne helped her into the back of a squad car. The female officer got in beside her. She wasn't particularly sympathetic to her. She'd seen girls like her before, druggies, or fakes who pretended to be out of it so they wouldn't get blamed for what they'd done. She'd seen a fifteen-year-old who'd killed her entire family, and then claimed that voices on television had made her do it. For all she knew, Grace was a smart little bitch pretending she was crazy. But something about her told the officer that this one might be for real, maybe not crazy, but something was wrong with her. And she kept gulping air, as though she couldn't catch her breath. Something was definitely odd about the girl. But then again, she had shot and almost killed her old man, that was enough to push most people over the edge. Anyway, it wasn't their job to figure out if she was sane. The shrinks could work out that one.

The ride to Central Station downtown was a short one, particularly at that hour, but Grace looked worse than ever when she got there. The lights were fluorescent and bright, and she looked almost green as they put her in a holding cell where she waited until a burly male officer walked into the room and looked her over.

"Are you Grace Adams?" he asked curtly, and she only nodded. She felt as though she was going to faint or throw up again. Maybe she would die. That was all she had wanted anyway. Dying would be fine. Her life was a nightmare. "Yes or no?" he asked, shouting at her.

"Yes, I am."

"Your father just died at the hospital. We're arresting you for murder." He read her her rights, dropped some papers into the hands of a female officer who had walked in just behind him. And then, without another word, he left the room, with a heavy clang of the metal door that sealed them into the cell where she had been waiting. There was a moment's silence, and then the female officer told her to strip all her clothes off. To Grace, it was all like a very bad movie.

"Why?" Grace said hoarsely.

"Strip search," the officer explained, as Grace slowly began undressing, with shaking fingers. The entire process was utterly humiliating. And after that, they took fingerprints, and did mug shots.

"Heavy rap," another female officer said coldly as she handed Grace a paper towel to wipe the ink off her fingers. "How old are you?" she asked casually, as Grace looked at her. She was still trying to absorb what they had told her. She had killed him. He was dead. It was over.

"Seventeen."

"Bad luck for you. You can be tried as an adult for murder in Illinois if you're over thirteen. If they find you guilty, you pull down at least fourteen, fifteen years. Death penalty too. You're in the big leagues now, baby." Nothing seemed real to Grace as her hands were cuffed behind her back and she was led from the room. And five minutes later, she was in a cell with four other women, and an open toilet that reeked of urine and human waste. The place was noisy and filthy, and all of the women in her cell were lying on bare mattresses and covered with blankets. Two were awake, but no one was talking. No one said a word as she was uncuffed, handed a blanket, and went to sit on the only unoccupied bunk in the small cell.

She looked around her in disbelief. It had come to this. But there had been no other way out. She couldn't take it anymore. She'd had to do it . . . she hadn't meant to . . . hadn't planned it . . . but now that she had, she wasn't even sorry. It was her life or his. She would have just as soon died, but it hadn't happened that way. It had just happened, without intent or plan. She had had no choice. She had killed him.

Chapter 2

Grace lay on the thin mattress all night, barely feeling the sharp metal coils beneath her. She didn't feel anything. She wasn't shaking anymore. She just lay there. Thinking. She had no family anymore. No one. No parents. No friends. She wondered what would happen to her, would she be found guilty of murder? Would she get the death penalty? She couldn't forget what the booking officer had told her. She was being charged as an adult, and accused of murder. Maybe the death penalty was the price she had to pay. And if it was, she'd pay it. At least he could never touch her again, he couldn't hurt her anymore. Her four years of hell at his hands were over.

"Grace Adams?" a voice called out her name just after seven o'clock in the morning. She'd been there for three hours by then, and she hadn't slept all night, but she didn't feel as disembodied as she had the night before. She knew what was happening. She remembered shooting her father. And she knew he had died, and why. She knew that better than anything else. And she wasn't sorry.

She was escorted to a small dingy room with heavy locked doors at either end. They put her in it without explanation. There was a table, four chairs, and a

bright light overhead. She stood there, and five minutes later, the door at the other end of the room
opened. A tall blond woman walked in. She looked
cool as she glanced at Grace, and waited for a moment
as she watched her. She didn't smile, she didn't say
anything, she just observed Grace for a long moment.
And Grace said nothing to her, she stayed at the far
end of the room, looking like a young doe about to
bolt from the room, except she couldn't. She was in a
cage. She was quiet, but afraid. And even in her jeans
and T-shirt, there was a quiet dignity about her. There
was an unmistakable quality about her, as though she
had suffered and come far, paid a high price for her
freedom, and felt it was worth it. It wasn't anger one
sensed about her, it was a long-suffering kind of patience. She had seen too much in her short years, life
and death, and betrayal, and it showed in her eyes.
Molly York saw it the moment she looked at Grace, and
she was touched by the raw pain she saw there.

"I'm Molly York," she explained quietly. "I'm a
psychiatrist. Do you know why I'm here?"

Grace shook her head, and didn't move an inch
closer, as the two women stood at opposite sides of the
room.

"Do you remember what happened last night?"

Grace nodded slowly.

"Why don't you sit down?" She pointed to the
chairs, and they each took a seat on opposite sides of
the table. Grace wasn't sure if the woman was sympathetic to her or not, but she was clearly not her friend,
and she was obviously part of the police investigation,
which meant that she was potentially someone who
wanted to hurt her. But she wasn't going to lie to her.
She would tell her the truth in answer to anything she

asked, as long as she didn't ask too much about her
father. That was nobody's business. She owed it to him
not to expose him, and to her mother, not to embarrass them. What difference did it make now anyway?
He was gone. It never occurred to her for an instant to
ask for an attorney, or try to save herself. That just
didn't matter.

"What do you remember about last night?" the
psychiatrist asked carefully, watching her every move
and expression.

"I shot my father."

"Do you remember why?"

Grace hesitated before replying, and then said
nothing.

"Were you angry at him? Had you been thinking
about shooting him for a while?"

Grace shook her head very quickly. "I never
thought about shooting him. I just found the gun in
my hand. I don't even know how it got there. My mom
used to keep it in her night table. She was sick for a
long time, and she'd get scared sometimes if we were
out, so she liked to have it. But she never used it." She
seemed very young and innocent as she explained it to
the psychiatrist, but at first glance, she seemed neither
insane, nor retarded, as the arresting officers had suggested. Nor did she seem dangerous. She seemed very
polite and well brought up, and oddly self-possessed
for someone who'd been through a shocking experience, had had no sleep at all, and was in a great deal of
trouble.

"Was your father holding the gun? Did you fight
over it? Did you try and take it from him?"

"No. I was holding it on him. I remember feeling
it in my hand. And . . ." She didn't want to tell her

that he had hit her. "Then I shot him." She looked down at her hands then.

"Do you know why? Were you angry at him? Did he do something to you that made you angry? Did you have a fight?"

"No . . . well . . . sort of . . ." It was a fight . . . it was a fight for survival. . . . "I . . . it wasn't important."

"It must have been very important," the psychiatrist said pointedly. "Important enough to shoot him over it, Grace. Important enough to kill him. Let's be honest here. Had you ever shot a gun before?"

She shook her head, looking sad and tired. Maybe she should have done it years before, but then her mother would have been heartbroken. In her own sad way, she had loved him. "No. I never shot a gun before."

"Why was last night different?"

"My mom died two days ago . . . three days ago now, I guess. Her funeral was yesterday." She'd obviously been overwrought. But what were they fighting about? Molly York was intrigued by Grace as she watched her. She was hiding something, but she wasn't sure what. She wasn't sure if it was something damaging to herself, or her father. And it wasn't the psychiatrist's job to unearth the answers as to her innocence or guilt. But it was up to her to determine if the girl was sane or not, and knew what she was doing. But what *had* she been doing? And what was *he* doing that caused her to shoot him?

"Did you have a fight about your mom? Did she leave him some money, or something you wanted?"

Grace smiled at the question, looking too wise for her years, and not at all retarded. "I don't think she had anything to leave anyone. She never worked, and she didn't have anything. My dad made all the money. He's a lawyer . . . or . . . was . . ." she said calmly.

"Is he going to leave you something?"

"I don't know . . . maybe . . . I guess so . . ." She didn't know yet that if you commit murder, you cannot inherit from your victim. If she were to be found guilty, she would not inherit anything from her father. But that had never been her motive.

"So what did you two fight about?" Molly York was persistent, and Grace didn't trust her. She was much too pushy. There was a relentlessness about her questions, and a look of intelligence in her eyes that worried Grace. She would see too much, understand too much. And she had no right to know. It was no one's business what her father had done to her all these years, she didn't want anyone to know. Not even if saying it saved her. She didn't want the whole town to know what he had done to her. What would they think of them then, and of her, or her mother? It didn't bear thinking.

"We didn't fight."

"Yes, you did," Molly York said quietly. "You must have. You didn't just walk into the room and shoot him . . . or did you?" Grace shook her head in answer. "You shot him from less than two inches away. What were you thinking when you shot him?"

"I don't know. I wasn't thinking anything. I was just trying to . . . I . . . it doesn't matter."

"Yes, it does." Molly York leaned toward her seriously from across the table. "Grace, you're being charged with murder. If he did something to you, or hurt you in any way, it's self-defense, or manslaughter,

not murder. No matter how great a betrayal you think
it is, you have to tell me.''

"Why? Why do I have to tell anyone anything? Why
should I?'' She sounded like a child as she said it. But
she was a child who had killed her father.

"Because if you don't tell someone, Grace, you
could end up in prison for a lot of years, and that's
wrong if you were trying to defend yourself. What did
he do to you, Grace, to make you shoot him?''

"I don't know. Maybe I was just upset about my
mother.'' She was squirming in her seat, and looked
away as she said it.

"Did he rape you?'' Grace's eyes opened wide and
she looked at her at the question. And her breath
seemed short when she answered.

"No. Never.''

"Did he ever have intercourse with you? Have you
ever had intercourse with your father?'' Grace looked
horrified. She was coming too close, much too close.
She hated this woman. What was she trying to do?
Make everything worse? Make more trouble? Disgrace
all of them? It was nobody's business.

"No. Of course not!'' she almost shouted, but she
looked very nervous.

"Are you sure?'' The two women's eyes met for a
long time, and Grace finally shook her head.

"No. Never.''

"Were you having intercourse with him last night
when you shot him?'' She looked at Grace pointedly,
and Grace shook her head again, but she looked agi-
tated, and Molly saw it.

"Why are you asking me these questions?'' she
asked unhappily, and you could hear the wheeze of her
asthma as she said it.

"Because I want to know the truth. I want to know if he hurt you, if you had reason to shoot him." Grace only shook her head again. "Were you and your father lovers, Grace? Did you like sleeping with him?" But this time when she raised her eyes to Molly's again, her answer was totally honest.

"No." I hated it. But she couldn't say those words to Molly.

"Do you have a boyfriend?" Grace shook her head again. "Have you ever had intercourse with a boy?"

Grace sighed, knowing she never would. How could she? "No."

"You're a virgin?" There was silence. "I asked if you were a virgin." She was pressing her again, and Grace didn't like it.

"I don't know. I guess so."

"What does that mean? Have you fooled around, is that what you mean by you 'guess so'?"

"Maybe." She looked very young again, and Molly smiled. You couldn't lose your virginity from petting.

"Have you ever had a boyfriend? At seventeen you must have." She smiled again, but Grace shook her head in answer.

"Is there anything you want to say to me about last night, Grace? Do you remember how you felt before you shot him? What made you shoot him?" Grace shook her head dumbly.

"I don't know."

Molly York knew that Grace wasn't being honest with her. As shaken as she may have been at the time of the shooting, she wasn't dazed now. She was fully alert, and determined not to tell Molly what had happened. The tall attractive blonde looked at the girl for a long

time, and then slowly closed her notebook and un-
crossed her legs.

"I wish you'd be honest with me. I can help you,
Grace. Honest." If she felt that Grace had been defending herself, or that there had been extenuating
circumstances it would be a lot easier for her. But
Grace wasn't giving her anything to go on. And the
funny thing was that, in spite of her circumstances and
the fact that she wasn't cooperating at all, Molly York
liked her. Grace was a beautiful girl, and she had big,
honest, open eyes. Molly saw so much sorrow and pain
there, and yet she didn't know how to help her. It
would come. But for the moment, Grace was too busy
hiding from everyone to let anyone near her.

"I've told you everything I remember."

"No, you haven't," Molly said quietly. "But maybe
you will later." She handed the girl her card. "If you
want to see me, call me. And if you don't, I'll be back
to see you again anyway. You and I are going to have to
spend some time together so I can write a report."

"About what?" Grace looked worried. Dr. York
scared her. She was too smart, and she asked too many
questions.

"About your state of mind. About the circumstances of the shooting, such as I understand them.
You're not giving me much to work with for the moment."

"That's all there is. I found the gun in my hand,
and I shot him."

"Just like that." She didn't believe it for a moment.

"That's right." She looked like she was trying to
convince herself but she had not fooled Molly.

"I don't believe you, Grace." She looked her right in the eye as she said it.

"Well, that's what happened, whether you believe it or not."

"And what about now? How do you feel about losing your father?" Within three days she had lost both of her parents and become an orphan, that was a heavy blow for anyone, particularly if she had killed one of her parents.

". . . I'm sad about my dad . . . and my mom. But my mom was so sick and in so much pain, maybe now it's better for her."

But what about Grace? How much pain had she been in? That was the question that was gnawing at Molly. This was not some bad kid who had just blown away her old man. This was a bright girl, with a sharp mind, who was pretending that she had no idea why she had shot him. It was so aggravating to listen to her say it again that Molly would have liked to kick the table.

"What about your dad? Is it better like this for him?"

"My dad?" Grace looked surprised at the question. "No . . . he . . . he wasn't suffering . . . I guess this isn't better for him," Grace said without looking up at Molly. She was hiding something, and Molly knew it.

"What about you? Is it better for you like this? Would you rather be alone?"

"Maybe." She was honest again for a moment.

"Why? Why would you rather be alone?"

"It's just simpler." She looked and felt a thousand years old as she said it.

"I don't think so, Grace. It's a complicated world

out there. It's not easy for anyone to be alone. Especially not a seventeen-year-old girl. Home must have been a pretty difficult place if you'd rather be alone now. What was 'home' like? How was it?"

"It was fine." She was as closed as an oyster.

"Did your parents get along? Before your mom got sick I mean."

"They were fine."

Molly didn't believe her again but she didn't say it. "Were they happy?"

"Sure." As long as she took care of her father, the way her mother wanted.

"Were you?"

"Sure." But in spite of herself, tears glistened in her eyes as she said it. The wise psychiatrist was asking far too many painful questions. "I was very happy. I loved my parents."

"Enough to lie for them? To protect them? Enough not to tell us why you shot your father?"

"There's nothing to tell."

"Okay." Molly backed off from her, and stood up at her side of the table. "I'm going to send you to the hospital today, by the way."

"What for?" Grace looked instantly terrified, which interested Molly greatly. "Why are you doing that?"

"Just part of the routine. Make sure you're healthy. It's no big deal."

"I don't want to do that." Grace looked panicked and Molly watched her.

"Why not?"

"Why do I have to?"

"You don't have much choice right now, Grace.

You're in a pretty tight spot. And the authorities are in control. Have you called a lawyer yet?''

Grace looked blank at the question. Someone had told her she could, but she didn't have one to call, unless she called Frank Wills, her father's law partner, but she wasn't even sure she wanted to. What could she say to him? It was easier not to.

"I don't have a lawyer."

"Did your father have any associates?"

"Yes . . . but . . . it's kind of awkward to call them . . . or him, he had a partner.''

"I think you should, Grace," she said firmly. "You need an attorney. You can ask for a public defender. But you're better off with someone who knows you.'' It was good advice.

"I guess so." She nodded, looking overwhelmed. There was so much happening. It was all so complicated. Why didn't they just shoot her, or hang her, or do whatever they were going to, without drawing it out, or forcing her to go to the hospital. She was terrified of what they would find there.

"I'll see you later, or tomorrow," Molly said gently. She liked the girl, and she felt sorry for her. She had been through so much, and what she had done certainly wasn't right, but Molly was convinced that something terrible had caused her to do it. And she intended to do everything she could to find out what had really happened.

She left Grace in the holding cell, and went out to talk to Stan Dooley, the officer in charge of the investigation. He was a veteran detective, and very little surprised him anymore, though this had. He'd met John Adams a number of times over the years, and he couldn't imagine a nicer guy. Hearing he had been shot by his own kid had really stunned him.

"Is she nuts, or a druggie?" Detective Dooley asked Molly as she appeared at his desk at eight o'clock in the morning. She had spent an hour with Grace, and in her mind, had gotten nowhere. Grace was determined not to open up to her. But there were some things that she wanted to know, that they could find out whether or not Grace wanted.

"Neither one. She's scared and shaken up, but she's lucid. Very much so. I want her to go to the hospital today, for an exam, now in fact." She didn't want too many hours to elapse before they did it.

"What for? Drug screen?"

"If you like. I don't think that's the issue here. I want a pelvic."

"Why?" He looked surprised. "What are you after?" He knew Dr. York and she was usually pretty sensible, though every now and then she went off the deep end, when she got carried away over one of her patients.

"I've got a couple of theories here. I want to know if she was defending herself. Seventeen-year-old girls don't usually go around shooting their fathers. Not from homes like this one."

"That's bullshit, and you know it, York," he said cynically. "What about the fourteen-year-old shooter we had last year who took out her whole family, including grandma and four younger sisters? You gonna tell me that was self-defense too?"

"That was different, Stan. I read the reports. John Adams was naked and so was she, and there was come all over the sheets. You can't deny it was a possibility."

"Yes, I can, with this guy. I knew him. Straight-

arrow as they come, and the nicest guy you'll ever
meet. You'd have liked him." He gave her a look,
which she ignored. He loved to tease her. She was very
good-looking, and she came from a pretty fancy family
in Chicago. He loved to accuse her of "slumming."
But she never fooled around on the job, and he also
knew that she had a regular guy who was a doctor. But
it didn't hurt to razz her a little. She was always good-
humored and pleasant to work with. She was smart too,
and Dooley respected her for it. "Let me tell you something, Doctor, this guy would not have been fucking
his kid. He just wouldn't. Trust me. Maybe he was jacking off. What do I know?"

"That's not why she shot him," Molly York said
coolly.

"Maybe he told her she couldn't have the keys to
the car. My own kids get nuts when I tell them that.
Maybe he hated her boyfriend. Trust me, it's not what
you think here. This is not self-defense. She killed
him."

"We'll see, Stan. We'll see. Just do me a favor, get
her over to Mercy General in the next hour. I'm writing an order."

"You're terrific. And we'll get her there. Okay?
Happy?"

"Thrilled. You're a great guy." She smiled at him.

"Tell that to the chief," he grinned at her. He
liked her, but he didn't believe a word of her self-
defense theory. She was clutching at straws. John Adams just wasn't that kind of guy. No one in Watseka
would have believed it, no matter what Molly York
thought, or the hospital told her.

Two women officers came to pick Grace up in her
cell half an hour later, handcuffed her again, and

drove her to Mercy General in a small van with grilles on the windows. They didn't even talk to her. They just chatted to each other about the prisoners they'd transferred the day before, and the movie they were going to see that night, and the vacation one of them was saving up for in Colorado. And Grace was just as glad. She didn't have anything to say to them anyway. She was just wondering what they were going to do to her at the hospital. They had a locked ward they took her to in an elevator that went up directly from the garage, and when they got there, they uncuffed her and left her with a resident and an attendant. And they let Grace know in no uncertain terms that if she didn't behave herself they would handcuff her again and call a guard to control her.

"You got that?" the attendant asked her bluntly, and Grace nodded.

They didn't bother explaining anything to her. They just went down a list of tests that Dr. York had ordered. They took her temperature first, and her blood pressure, checked her eyes and ears and throat, and then listened to her heart.

They did a urine test, and an extensive blood test, checking for illnesses as well as drug screens, and then they told her to undress and stand naked in front of them, and they checked her over carefully for bruises. She had a number of them that caught their interest, there were two on her breasts, several on her arms, and one on her buttocks, and then in spite of her efforts to conceal them from them, they discovered a bad one on her inner thigh where her father had grabbed her and squeezed her. It was high up, and led to another that surprised them further. They took photographs of all of them, despite her protests, and wrote extensive notes about them. She was crying by then, and objecting to everything they were doing.

"Why are you doing this? You don't have to. I admitted I shot him, why do you have to take pictures?" They had taken several graphic ones of her crotch, but there were two bad bruises hidden there and some lesions, and they told her that if she didn't cooperate they would tie her down and take the pictures. It was humiliating beyond words, but there was nothing she could do to stop them.

And then, as they put the camera down, the resident told her to hop on the table. Until then, he had scarcely spoken to her. Most of the directions had been from the attendant, who was a very disagreeable woman. Both of them ignored Grace totally, and referred to various parts of her as though they were looking at them in a butcher shop, and she weren't even a human being.

The resident was putting on rubber gloves by then, and covering his fingers with sterile jelly. He pointed at the stirrups and offered Grace a paper drape to cover herself with. She grabbed it gratefully, but she didn't get on the table.

"What are you doing?" she asked in a terrified voice.

"Haven't you ever had a pelvic?" He looked surprised. She was seventeen after all, and a good-looking girl, it was hard to believe she was a virgin. But if she was, he'd know in a minute.

"No, I . . ." Her mother had gotten her birth control pills four years before, and she'd never been to a doctor for an examination. No one knew for certain that she wasn't a virgin, and she didn't see what difference it made now. Her father was dead, and she had admitted that she had shot him. So why put her through this? What right did they have to do this? She felt like an animal, and she started to cry again as she clutched the paper drape and stared at them, as the female attendant threatened to tie her down. There was no choice except to agree to do it. She got up on the table, with shaking legs, and she pressed her knees tightly together, as she lay back and put her feet in the stirrups. But given everything that had happened to her, it wasn't the worst thing that she'd ever been through.

He made a lot of notes, and put fingers into her at least four or five times, shining a light so close to her that she could feel it warm her bottom. Then he inserted an instrument into her, and did all the same things again. This time he took a smear and made a slide, which he set carefully on a tray on the table. But he said nothing to Grace about his findings.

"Okay," he said indifferently to her, "you can get dressed now."

"Thank you," she said hoarsely. She had no idea what they'd found, or what he'd written, but he had made no comment on whether or not she was a virgin, and she was still naive enough not to be entirely sure if he could really see the difference.

She was dressed and ready to go five minutes later, and this time two men ferried her back to her cell at Central Station, and she was left alone with the women in her cell until after dinner. Two of them had been released on bail, they had been there for drug sales and prostitution and their pimp had come to get them, and of the other two one was in for grand theft auto, and the other for possession of a large amount of cocaine. Grace was the only one being held for murder, and everyone seemed to leave her alone, as though they knew that she didn't want to be bothered.

She had just eaten a barely edible, very small, over-cooked hamburger, sitting on a sea of wet spinach, while trying not to notice that the cell reeked of urine, when a guard came to the cell, opened it and pointed at her, and led her back to the room where she had met with Molly York that morning.

The young doctor was back, still wearing jeans, af-ter a long day at the hospital where she worked, and then in her office. It was fully twelve hours later.

"Hello," Grace said cautiously. It was nice to see a familiar face, but she still felt as though the young psy-chiatrist represented danger.

"How was your day?" Grace shrugged with a small smile. How could it have been? "Did you call your fa-ther's partner?"

"Not yet," she said almost inaudibly. "I'm not sure what to say to him. He and my father were really good friends."

"Don't you think he'll want to help you?"

"I don't know." But she didn't think so.

Molly was looking at her pointedly as she asked the next question. "Do you have any friends at all, Grace? Anyone you could turn to?" She suspected long before Grace spoke that she didn't. If she had, maybe none of this would have happened. Molly knew without asking her that she was isolated. She had no one in her life except her parents. And they had done enough to ruin anyone's life, or at least her father had. At least that was what she suspected. "Did your parents have any friends you were close to?"

"No," Grace said thoughtfully. They really didn't have any close friends, they didn't want anyone to get too close to their dark secret. "My father knew everyone. And my mom was kind of shy . . ." And she had never wanted anyone to know that she was being beaten. "Everyone loved my dad, but he wasn't really close to anyone." That in itself made Molly wonder about him.

"And what about you? Any real close friends at school?" Grace only shook her head in answer. "Why not?"

"I don't know. No time, I guess. I had to go home and take care of my mom every day," Grace said, still not looking at her.

"Is that really why, Grace? Or did you have a secret?"

"Of course not."

But Molly wouldn't let go of her. Her voice reached out to Grace and pulled her toward her. "He raped you that night, didn't he?" Grace's eyes flew open wide, and she looked at Molly, and hoped the young doctor didn't see her tremble.

"No . . . of course not . . ." But her breath caught, and she found herself praying she wouldn't have an asthma attack. This woman already knew too much without that. "How can you say such a thing?" She tried to look shocked but she was only terrified. What if she knew? Then what? Everyone else would know their ugly secret. Even after their deaths, she still felt an obligation to hide it. It was her fault too. What would people think of her if they knew it?

"You have bruises and tears all through your vagina," Molly said quietly, "that doesn't happen with normal intercourse. The doctor who examined you said it looked like you had been raped by half a dozen men, or one very brutal man. He did an awful lot of

damage. That's why you shot him, isn't it?" She didn't
answer. "Was that the first time, after your mother's
funeral?" She looked pointedly at Grace as though she
expected an answer, and the teenager's eyes filled with
tears that spilled down her cheeks in spite of all of her
best efforts to stop them.

"I didn't . . . no . . . he wouldn't do a thing
like that . . . everyone loved my dad . . ."

She had killed him, and all she could do now was
defend his memory so no one would ever know what
he had really been like.

"Did your father love you, Grace? Or did he just
use you?"

"Of course he loved me," she said woodenly, furious at herself for crying.

"He raped you that night, didn't he?" But this
time, Grace didn't answer. She didn't even deny it.
"How often had he done that before? You have to tell
me." Her life depended on it now, but Molly didn't
want to say that.

"No, I don't. I'm not going to tell you anything,
and you can't prove it," Grace said angrily.

"Why are you defending him?" Molly asked in total frustration. "Don't you understand what's happening? You've been charged with murdering him, they
could even decide to charge you with murder in the
first degree, if they can get away with it, and they think
you have a motive. You have to do everything you can
to save yourself. I'm not telling you to lie, I'm telling
you to tell the truth, Grace. If he raped you, if he hurt
you, if you were abused, then there were extenuating
circumstances. It could reduce the charges to manslaughter or even self-defense, and it changes everything. Do you really want to go to prison for the next

twenty years in order to preserve the reputation of a man who did that to you? Grace, think about it, you have to listen to me . . . you have to hear me." But Grace knew that her mother would never have forgiven her for sullying her father's memory. It was her father whom Ellen had loved so blindly, and needed desperately. It was he she had always wanted to protect, even if it meant holding her thirteen-year-old daughter down for him. She wanted to make him love her at any price, even if the price was her own daughter.

"I can't tell you anything," Grace said woodenly.

"Why? He's dead. You can't hurt him by telling the truth. You can only hurt yourself by not telling it. I want you to think about that. You can't be loyal to a dead man, or to someone who hurt you very badly. Grace . . ." She reached out and touched her hand across the table from where she sat. She had to make her understand, she had to pull her out from the place where she was hiding. "I want you to think about this tonight. And I'm going to come back and see you tomorrow. Whatever you tell me, I'll promise not to tell anyone else. But I want you to be honest with me about what happened. Will you think about that?" Grace didn't move for a long time, and then she nodded. She'd think about it, but she wasn't going to tell her.

Molly left her that night with a heavy heart. She knew exactly what was going on, and she couldn't seem to bridge the gap with Grace. She had worked with abused children and wives for years, and all their loyalty was always to their abusers. It took everything she had to break that bond, but usually she was successful. But so far, Grace wasn't giving an inch. Molly was getting nowhere.

She stopped in the detective's office to look at the

hospital report and the Polaroids again, and it made
her feel sick when she saw them. Stan Dooley came in
while she was reading the report, and he was surprised
to see her still at work, fourteen hours after she had
started.

"Don't you have anything else to do at night?" he
said amiably. "A girl like you ought to be out with
some guy, or hanging out in bars, looking for her future."

"Yeah," she laughed at him, her long blond hair
hanging invitingly over her shoulder. "Just like you,
huh, Stan? You were here the same time I was this
morning."

"I have to. You don't. I want to retire in ten years.
You can be a shrink until you're a hundred."

"Thanks for the vote of confidence." She closed
the file and put it on his desk with a sigh. She was
getting nowhere. "Did you see the hospital report on
the Adams girl?"

"Yeah. So?" He looked unmoved.

"Oh come on, don't tell me you can't figure it
out." She looked angry at the casual shrug of his
shoulders.

"What's to figure? So she got laid, nobody says she
got raped. And who says it was her father?"

"Bullshit. Who do you think laid her? Six gorillas
from the zoo? Did you see the bruises, and read what
he found internally?"

"So she likes it lively. Look, she's not complaining.
She isn't saying that she was raped. What do you want
from me?"

"Some sense for chrissake," she blazed at him.
"She's a seventeen-year-old kid, and he was her father.
She's protecting him, or some misguided illusion

about saving his reputation. But I can tell you one thing, that girl was defending herself, and you know it.''

'' 'Protecting him.' She blew the guy away. What kind of protection is that? I think your theory is real nice, Doctor, but it won't hold water. All we know is that she may have had a little rough sex. There is nothing to prove that she had it with her father, or that he was roughing her up. And even if, God help me, she did fuck her old man, that's still no reason to shoot him. That still doesn't make it self-defense, and you know that too. There's nothing to prove that her father hurt her. She's not even saying that. *You* are.''

"How the hell do you know what he did?'' she shouted at him, but he looked unmoved. He didn't believe a word of what she was saying. "Is this what she told you, or are you just guessing? I'm looking at the evidence, and a seventeen-year-old girl who is isolated and so removed she's practically on another planet.''

"Let me tell you a little secret, Dr. York. This is not a Martian. She's a shooter. Simple as that. And you want to know what I think, with all your exams, and fancy theories? I think probably she went out and got laid that night after her mother's funeral, and her old man thought it wasn't right. So she came home and he gave her hell, and she didn't like it, got pissed off, and killed him. And the fact that he was jacking off in bed is pure coincidence. You can't take a guy that the whole community knows as a good guy and convince anyone that he raped his daughter and she shot him in self-defense. As a matter of fact, I talked to his partner today, and he said pretty much the same thing I did. I didn't share the evidence with him, but I asked him what he thought must have happened. The idea that

John Adams would do anything to harm his child, and I didn't even say what you thought it might have been, horrified him. He said the guy adored his wife, and his kid. He said he lived for them, never cheated on his wife, spent every night with them, and was devoted to his wife till the day she died. He said that the kid was always a little strange, very unfriendly and withdrawn, didn't have many friends. And wasn't that keen on her father.''

"There goes your theory that she was out with her boyfriend.''

"She doesn't have to have a regular to go out and give it away for half an hour, does she?''

"You just don't see it, do you?'' Molly said angrily. How could he be so blind and stubborn? He was buying the guy's reputation, without even looking to see what was behind it.

"What am I supposed to see, Molly? We've got a seventeen-year-old girl who shot and killed her father. Maybe she was odd, maybe she was crazy. Maybe she was scared of him, what the hell do I know? But the fact is she shot him. *She* isn't saying he raped her, she isn't saying anything. *You* are.''

"She's too scared, she's too afraid that someone is going to find out their secret.'' She had seen it a hundred times. She just knew it.

"Did it ever occur to you that maybe she doesn't have a secret? Maybe this is all your invention because you feel sorry for her and want to get her off, what do I know?''

"Not much, from the sound of it,'' she answered him tartly. "I didn't invent that report, or the photographs of the bruises on her thighs and buttocks.''

"Maybe she fell down the stairs. All I know is that

you're the only one yelling rape, and that's not good enough, not with a guy like him. You're just not going to sell it.''

"What about her father's partner? Is he going to defend her?''

"I doubt it. He asked about bail, and I said it's not likely in a murder case, unless they reduce it to manslaughter, but I doubt that. He said it was probably just as well, because she had nowhere to go now anyway. She has no other relatives. And he doesn't want to take responsibility for her. He's a bachelor, and he's not prepared to take her in. He said he didn't feel right defending her. Said he just couldn't and we should get a public defender for her. I can't say that I blame him. He was obviously pretty upset about losing his partner.''

"Why can't he use the father's funds to pay for a private attorney?'' She didn't like the sound of it, but Grace had guessed that Frank Wills wouldn't help her. And she'd been right, much to Molly's disappointment. She wanted him to help her. Molly wanted Grace to get a top-notch attorney.

"He didn't volunteer to get an attorney for her,'' Stan Dooley explained. "He said that John Adams was his closest friend, but apparently he owed him a bunch of money. The wife's long illness pretty much wiped them out. All he has left is his share of the law practice and their house, and it's mortgaged to the hilt. Wills doesn't think there'll be much left of Adams's estate, and he certainly wasn't volunteering attorney fees out of his own pocket. I'll call the P.D. office tomorrow morning.''

Molly nodded, shocked again by how alone Grace was. It wasn't unusual among young people accused of crimes, but with a girl like her, it should have been different. She came from a nice middle-class family, her father was a respected citizen, they had a nice home, and they were well known in the community. It seemed extraordinary to the young doctor that Grace should find herself completely abandoned. And although it was unusual, she decided to call Frank Wills herself that night and jotted down his number.

"What's Dr. Kildare up to these days," Dooley teased her again as she started to leave, referring to her boyfriend.

"He's busy saving lives. He works even longer hours than I do." She smiled at Dooley in spite of herself. He drove her buggy sometimes, but most of the time he had a good heart and she liked him.

"Too bad, he'd keep you out of a lot of trouble if he'd take a little time off now and then."

"Yeah, I know." She smiled, and left him, tossing a tweed jacket over her shoulder. She was a pretty girl, but more importantly, she was good at what she did. Even the cops she knew admitted that she was smart, and a pretty good shrink, even if she did come up with some pretty wild theories.

Later, when Molly called Frank Wills from home that night, she was shocked by his callousness. As far as he was concerned, Grace Adams deserved to hang for killing her father.

"Nicest guy in the world," Wills said, sounding deeply moved, and Molly wasn't sure why, but she didn't believe him. "Ask anyone. There isn't a person in this town who didn't love him . . . except her . . . I still can't believe she shot him." He had spent the morning arranging a memorial for him. The whole town would be there undoubtedly, except Grace. But this time, there would be no gathering at the house, no family there for John. All he had was his wife and daughter. Wills's voice broke when he said as much to Molly.

"Do you think there's any reason why she would have shot him, Mr. Wills?" Molly asked politely when he'd regained his composure. She didn't want to get him more upset than he was, but maybe he would have some insight.

"Money, probably. She probably thought he was leaving everything to her, and even if he didn't have a will, it would all go to her as his only survivor. What she didn't figure, naturally, was that legally she couldn't inherit from him if she killed him. I guess she didn't know that."

"Was there much to leave?" Molly asked innocently, not referring to what she had heard from Detective Dooley. "I imagine his share of the law practice must be quite valuable. You're both such respected attorneys." She knew that he would like that, and he did, he warmed considerably to the subject after that, and told her more than he should have.

"There's enough. But he owes most of it to me anyway. He always told me he'd leave his share of the practice to me when he died, not that he planned to check out as early as this, poor devil."

"Did he leave that in writing?"

"I don't know. But it was an agreement between us, and I lent him some money from time to time, to help with expenses for Ellen."

"What about the house?"

"He's got a mortgage on it, it's a nice place. But not nice enough to get shot for."

"Do you really think a girl her age would shoot her

father for a house, Mr. Wills? That sounds a little far-fetched, doesn't it?''

"Maybe not. Maybe she figured it was enough to pay for some fancy eastern college.''

"Is that what she wanted to do?'' Molly sounded surprised. Somehow Grace didn't seem that ambitious, she seemed far more homebound, almost too much so.

"I don't know what she wanted to do, Doctor. I just know that she killed her father and she ought to pay for it. She sure as hell shouldn't profit from it, the law is right on that score. She won't get a dime of his money now, not the practice, not the house, nothing.'' Molly was startled by his venom, and she wondered if his motives were entirely pure, or if in fact he had his own reasons for being pleased that Grace was out of the way now.

"And who will get it, if she doesn't? Are there other relatives? Did he have other family somewhere?''

"No, just the girl. But he owed me a lot. I told you, I helped him out whenever I could, and we practiced together for twenty years. You can't just pass over that like it was nothing.''

"Of course not. I understand completely,'' she said soothingly. She understood a lot better than he thought, or wanted her to, and she didn't like it. She thanked him for his time after that, and spent a long time thinking about Grace that night, and when her boyfriend came in from work at the hospital she told him all about it. He was exhausted from a twenty-hour day in the emergency room, which had been an endless parade of gunshot wounds and car accidents, but he listened anyway. Molly was all wound up about the case.

She and Richard Haverson had lived together for

two years, and talked from time to time about getting married, but somehow they never did. But they got on well, and were familiar with each other's work. For both of them, it was the perfect arrangement. And he was as tall and lanky and blond and good-looking as she was.

"Sounds like the kid is screwed, if you ask me, there's no one to take her part in this, and it sounds like the father's partner wants her out of the way anyway, so he can get whatever money is left. Not a great situation from the sound of it. And if she won't admit that the old man was raping her, then what more can you say?" he said, looking tired, and she sipped coffee and stared at him in frustration.

"I'm not sure yet. But I'm trying to think of something. I wish I could get her to tell me what really happened. I mean, hell, she didn't just wake up in the middle of the night, find a gun in her hand and decide to shoot him. They found her nightgown torn in half on the floor, but she wouldn't explain that either. All the evidence is there, for God's sake. She just won't help us use it."

"You'll get to her eventually," he said confidently, but this time Molly looked worried. She had never had such a hard time reaching anyone. The girl was completely fossilized into a state of self-destruction. Her parents had all but destroyed her, and she still wouldn't give them up. It was amazing. "I've never seen you lose one yet." He smiled at her and touched the long blond hair as he went out to the kitchen for a beer. They both worked like demons, but it was a good relationship for both of them, and they were happy with each other.

And at six o'clock the next morning when they got

up, Grace was already on her mind again. On her way to work, Molly glanced at her watch and thought about going back to see her. But there was something else she wanted to do first. She went to her office and made some notes for the file, and then she went to the public defenders' office at eight-thirty.

"Is David Glass in yet?" she asked the receptionist. He was the junior attorney on the team, but Molly had worked on two cases with him recently, and she thought he was terrific. He was unorthodox and tough and smart. He was a street kid from New York who had clawed his way out of the ghettos of the South Bronx, and he wasn't going to give in to anyone. But at the same time, he had a heart of gold, and he fought like a lion for his clients. He was exactly what Grace Adams needed.

"I think he's in the back somewhere," the receptionist said. She recognized Molly from other cases she'd been on and she waved her back into the inner sanctum.

Molly wandered the hallways looking for him for a few minutes, and then she found him in the office library, sitting next to a stack of books, sipping a cup of coffee. He looked up as she walked next to him, and smiled when he saw her.

"Hi, Doc. How's biz?"

"The usual. How's by you?"

"I'm still working on getting the latest ax murderers off. You know, same ol' same ol'."

"Want a case?"

"Are you assigning them now?" He looked amused. He was shorter than she was, and he had dark brown eyes and curly black hair, and in his own way, he was nice-looking. What he had most of all was personality, which overcame any shortcomings he might have had in terms of looking like Clark Gable. He had sex appeal too. And from the way his eyes danced when he talked to her, it was obvious that he liked Molly. "When did they let you start dishing out cases?"

"Okay, okay. I just wanted to know if you were up for one. I'm working on it, and they're going to assign a P.D. today. I'd really like to work on it with you."

"I'm flattered. How bad is it?"

"Bad enough. Possibly murder one. Could even be the death penalty. A seventeen-year-old girl shot her father."

"Nice. I always love cases like that. What did she do? Take his head off with a shotgun, or have her boy-friend do it for her?" He had seen plenty of ugliness in New York, out here, though, things were a lot tamer.

"Nothing quite so picturesque." She looked at him with a worried frown, thinking of Grace. "It's complicated. Can we go talk somewhere?"

"Sure." He looked intrigued. "If you're willing to stand on my shoulders, we can go talk in my office." His cubicle was barely bigger than his desk, but at least it had a door and some privacy, and she followed him there, as he juggled his books and his coffee. "So what's the story?" he asked as she sat in the room's only extra chair and sighed. She really wanted him to take it. And for the moment, Grace was doing absolutely nothing to help herself. She really needed someone as good as David.

"She shot him at slightly less than two-inch range with a handgun that she says she 'found in her hand,' and then it went off, and she shot him. According to her, for no reason in the world. They were just one happy family, except for the fact that they'd buried her mother that day. Other than that, no problems."

"Is she sane?" He looked interested, but only mildly. Most of all, he loved a challenge. And he liked kids in particular. All of which was why Molly wanted him to take the case. He was the only chance Grace had. Without him, she was lost, if she even cared. But Molly cared, a lot, she wasn't sure why, but she did. Maybe because Grace seemed so beaten and so helpless. She had already given up everything, all hope, even her own life seemed unimportant to her. And Molly wanted to change that.

"She's sane," Molly confirmed to him, "deeply depressed and not without neurosis, but I think for good reason. I think he was abusing her, sexually and otherwise." She described the kind of internal damage and bruises they had found, and her state of mind when Molly saw her. "She swears he never touched her. I don't believe her. I think he raped her that night, and I think he'd done it before, maybe even for a long time, and maybe without her mother there, she'd lost her only protection and she panicked. He did it again, and this time she lost it and shot him. He had to be right on top of her for her to shoot him at that range. Think of it, if he'd been lying on top of her, raping her, and she had the gun, it would have been just that kind of range when she shot him."

"Has anyone else thought of that?" He was intrigued now. "What do the cops think?"

"That's the problem. They don't want to hear it. Her father was Mr. Perfect Community Loved by Everyone Attorney. No one wants to believe that the guy might have been sleeping with his own daughter, or worse, forcing her. Maybe he held the gun on her, for all we know, and she got it away from him. But something has gone on in that girl's life, and she just won't tell me. She has no friends, no life outside of school. No one seems to know much of anything about her. She went to school, and she went home, and took care of her dying mother. The mother died a few days ago, and now the father's gone, and that's it. No relatives, no friends, just an entire town who swears the guy is the most decent man they ever knew and couldn't possibly have hurt his daughter."

"And you don't believe them? Why not?" After working two cases with her, he had learned to trust her instincts.

"Because she won't tell me anything, and I know she's lying. She's terrified. And she's still defending him, as though he's going to come back from the dead and get her."

"She won't say *anything*?"

"Not really. She is frozen in pain, it's written all over her. Something terrible has happened to that girl, and she won't give it up."

"Not yet," he smiled at her, "but she will. I know you better than that. It's early days yet."

"Thanks for the vote of confidence, but we don't have much time. The arraignment is today, and they're going to assign a P.D. to her case this morning."

"No family attorney, or associate of her old man to take care of it for her? I would think someone would turn up." He looked surprised as the young doctor shook her head.

"His law partner claims that he was just too close to her father to want to defend her, since she's the

killer. He also says there's no money left, because of
the mother's illness. Just the house, and the law practice. And he might just inherit all of it, now that she
can't, and he claims her father owed him quite a bit of
money. He's not offering ten cents to help in her defense, which is why I came to see you. I don't like the
guy, and I don't trust him. He portrays the deceased as
a saint, and claims he will never forgive the daughter
for what she did. He thinks she ought to get the death
penalty for it.''

"At seventeen? Nice guy." He looked seriously intrigued now.

"And what does our girl say to all this? Does she
know this guy won't help her, and may even take everything her father had, against his supposed debts?"

"Not really. But she seems ready to go down in
flames for the cause, as long as she keeps her mouth
shut. I think she is deluding herself that she owes that
to her parents."

"Sounds like she needs a shrink as much as an
attorney." He smiled at Molly. He liked the idea of
working on another case with her. She was great to
work with, and now and then he cherished a small
hope that a romance would spring up between them,
but it never had, and a part of him knew it never
would. But it was fun to imagine sometimes. And his
hopes never got in the way of their work together.

"What do you think?" Molly asked him with a worried look.

"I think she's in big trouble. What are they actually
charging her with?"

"I'm not sure yet. They were talking about murder
one, but I think they're having a hard time proving it.
There's no real 'inheritance' there to provide her with

a motive for premeditation, just a house and a pretty good-sized mortgage on it, and the law practice which the partner claims was promised to him anyway.''

"Yeah, but she didn't necessarily know that. And she didn't necessarily know that she couldn't inherit from her father if she killed him. They could try for murder one, if they really want to.''

"If she denies any intent to kill him, they might give her a break, and charge her with second-degree,'' Molly said hopefully. "It would carry a sentence of fifteen years to life in prison. She could be forty or more by the time she was free again, if she was convicted. But at least it's not the death penalty. They've already said they're going to prosecute her as an adult, and there was some talk about the death penalty. If she'd just tell us what happened, you might even be able to reduce it to manslaughter.''

"Shit. You really did bring me a peach, didn't you?''

"Can you get assigned to it?''

"Maybe. They probably figure it's a loser anyway, with her father so prominent in the community she'll never get a fair trial here. You'd almost have to ask for a change of venue. Actually, I'd like to try it.''

"Do you want to meet her first?''

"Are you kidding?'' He laughed. "Have you seen what I defend here? I don't need an introduction. I'd just like to know I have a chance. It would be nice if she'd talk to us, and tell us what really happened. If she doesn't, she could be facing a life sentence, or worse. She's got to tell us what happened,'' he said earnestly, and Molly nodded.

"Maybe she will, if she trusts you,'' Molly said

hopefully. "I was going to go back and see her this afternoon. I still have to finish my evaluation for the department, as to whether or not she's competent to stand trial. But there's really no question of it. I was just dragging my feet a little bit because I wanted to keep seeing her. I think she needs some real live human contact." Molly looked genuinely worried about her.

"I'll go over there with you today, if they give me the case. Let me see what I can do first. Call me at lunchtime." He jotted down Grace's name and the case number, and Molly thanked him before she left. She was immensely relieved to think that he might be Grace's attorney. It was the best thing that could possibly happen to her. If there was any chance of saving her at all, David Glass would find a way to do it.

Molly didn't have time to call him back until after two o'clock and when she did, he was out of the office. And it was four before she had time to try again, but she was worried about what had happened. She had had a hellish day doing rounds, making evaluations for the courts, and working with a fifteen-year-old who had tried to commit suicide and failed, but left himself a quadriplegic. He had jumped off a bridge into concrete, and in this case the stamina of youth had betrayed him. Even she had to wonder if he wouldn't have been better off dead than spending the next sixty years able only to wiggle his nose and his ears. Even his speech had been affected. She called David again at the end of the day, and apologized for the delay.

"I just got back myself," David explained.

"What did they say?"

"Good luck. They claim it's open-and-shut. She

wanted his money, what little he had, according to them, but she didn't know how badly her mother's illness had eaten up their savings or that she'd never inherit if she killed him. They're holding to the theory that it was premeditated, or at the very least that they had a fight, she got mad, had a tantrum and killed him. According to them, it's all very simple. Murder one, at worst. Murder two, at best. Anywhere from twenty to life, or the death penalty if they get really crazy.''

"She's just a kid . . . she's a girl . . .'' Molly had tears in her eyes as she thought of it, and then reproached herself for getting too involved, but she just couldn't help it. There was something so wrong here. "What about the defense?''

"I just don't know. There's no evidence that he attacked her or endangered her life, unless your rape theories turn out to be correct. Give me a chance, kid. They only assigned me the case two hours ago, and I haven't even met her yet. They postponed the arraignment till I could see her at least. It's at nine o'clock tomorrow morning. I thought I'd go over there at five if I can get out of here by then. Want to come? It might speed things up and break the ice, since she knows you.''

"I'm not sure she likes me though. I keep pushing her about her father and she doesn't like it.''

"She's going to like the death penalty even less. I suggest you meet me there at five-thirty. Can you make it?''

"I'll be there. And David?''

"Yes?''

"Thanks for taking it.''

"We'll do our best. See you at five-thirty at Central."

And Molly knew as they hung up that they were not only going to have to do their best, but pray for a miracle, if they were going to help her.

Chapter 3

Molly York and David Glass met outside the jail promptly at five-thirty, and went upstairs to see Grace. David had gotten all the reports from the police by then, and Molly had brought her notes and the ones from the hospital to show him. He glanced at them as they rode upstairs, and raised an eyebrow when he saw the pictures.

"It looks like someone hit her with a baseball bat," he said as he looked at them, and glanced at Molly.

"She says nothing happened." Molly shook her head, and hoped that Grace was willing to open up to David. Her life literally depended on it, and she still wasn't sure that Grace understood that.

They were led into the attorneys' room, with the two separate doors, and the table and four chairs. It was where Molly had met Grace before and at least it would be familiar to her.

They sat down for a few minutes and waited for her. David lit a cigarette and offered one to Molly but she declined it. It was a full five minutes before the guard appeared at the window in the door to the jail, as the heavy door was unlocked, and Grace stood looking at them hesitantly. She was wearing the same jeans and T-shirt. There was no one to bring her clothes, and she had nothing else with her. All she had was what she had worn the night she had killed her father and been arrested.

He watched her carefully as she entered the room, she was tall and thin and graceful, and in some ways she looked young and shy, but when she turned to look at him, he saw that her eyes were a dozen years older. There was something so sad and defeated there, and she moved like a doe about to dash away into the forest. She stood staring at them, not sure what to make of their visit. She had spent four hours with the police that day, answering questions, and she was exhausted. They had advised her that she had the right to have an attorney present at the questioning but she had already admitted to shooting her father, and didn't think there was any harm in answering their questions.

She had gotten the message that David Glass was going to be her attorney, and he would be over to see her later. She had heard nothing from Frank Wills, and she still hadn't called him. There was no one to call, no one she could have turned to. She had read the papers that day, the front page and several articles were devoted to stories about the murder, about her father's admirable life, his law practice, and what he had meant to so many. It said relatively little about her, except that she was seventeen, went to Jefferson High, and had killed him. Several theories had been offered as to what must have occurred, but no one ever came close to what had really happened.

"Grace, this is David Glass." Molly broke the silence by introducing them. "He's from the public defenders' office, and he's going to represent you."

"Hello, Grace," he said quietly. He was watching

her face, he hadn't taken his eyes off hers since she'd entered the room, and it was easy to see that she was desperately frightened. But in spite of it, she was polite and gracious when she shook his hand. He could feel her hand shaking in his own as soon as he touched her fingers. And when she spoke, he could see that she was a little breathless, and he remembered Molly's comment about her asthma. "We've got some work to do here." She only nodded in answer. "I read your files this afternoon. It's not looking so good for the moment. And mostly what I'm going to need from you is information. What happened and why, whatever you can remember. Afterwards, we'll get an investigator to check things out. We'll do whatever we have to." He tried to sound encouraging, and hoped she wasn't too frightened to listen.

"There's nothing to check out," she said quietly, sitting very straight in one of the four chairs. "I killed my father." She looked him right in the eye as she said it.

"I know you did," he said, seeming unimpressed by the admission, and watching her intently. He knew what Molly had seen in her. She looked like a nice girl, and she looked as though someone had beaten the life out of her. She was so remote, one almost wondered if one could touch her. She was more like an apparition than a real person. There was nothing ordinary about her. Nothing to suggest that she was a seventeen-year-old girl, a teenager, none of the life or ebullience one would have expected. "Do you remember what happened?" he asked her quietly.

"Most of it," she admitted. There were parts of it that were still vague, like exactly when she had taken the gun out of her mother's night table. But she remembered feeling it in her hand, and then squeezing the trigger. "I shot him."

"Where did you get the gun?" His questions seemed very matter-of-fact, and oddly unthreatening as they sat there. He had an easy style, and Molly thanked her lucky stars again that he had gotten the case assigned to him. She just hoped he could help her.

"It was in my mother's nightstand."

"How did you get it? Did you just reach over and take it?"

"Sort of. I just kind of took it out."

"Was your father surprised when you did that?" He made it sound like the most mundane question, and she nodded.

"He didn't see it at first, but he was surprised when he did . . . and then he tried to grab it and it went off." Her eyes glazed as she remembered, and then she closed them.

"You must have been standing pretty close to him, huh? About like this?" He indicated the three feet between them. He knew she had been closer than that, but he wanted to hear her answer.

"No . . . uh . . . kind of . . . closer. . . ." He nodded, as though her answer were ordinary too, and Molly tried to feign disinterest, but she was fascinated by how quickly Grace had started talking to him, and how much she seemed to trust him. It was as though she knew that she could. She was much less defensive than she had been with Molly.

"How close do you think? Like a foot maybe? Maybe closer?"

"Pretty close . . . closer . . ." she said softly, and then looked away from him, knowing what he must be thinking. Molly must have told him her suspicions. "Very close."

"How come? What were you doing?"

"We were talking," she said hoarsely, sounding breathless again, and he knew she was lying.

"What were you talking about?"

His question and the ease of it caught her off guard and she stammered as she answered. "I . . . uh . . . I guess, my mother." He nodded as though that were the most natural thing, and then leaned back in his chair pensively and looked at the ceiling. He spoke to her then, without looking at her, and he could feel his heart pound in his ears as he addressed her.

"Did your mom know what he'd been doing to you, Grace?" He said it so gently, it brought tears to Molly's eyes, and then slowly he looked at Grace, and there were tears in her eyes too. "It's okay to tell me, Grace. No one's ever going to know, except us, but I have to know the truth if I'm going to help you. Did she know?"

Grace stared at him, wanting to deny it again, wanting to hide from them, but she couldn't anymore, she just couldn't. She nodded, and the tears spilled from her eyes, and ran slowly down her cheeks. As he watched her, he took her hand and squeezed it. "It's okay, Grace. It's okay. You couldn't do anything to stop it." And then she nodded again, and an anguished sob escaped her. She wanted to have the courage not to tell them anything, but they were all hounding her, the doctor, the police, now him, and they asked so many questions. And for some reason she herself didn't know, she trusted David. She liked Molly too, but it was David whom she wanted to turn to.

"She knew." They were the saddest words he had

ever heard, and without knowing John Adams, he wanted to kill him.

"Was she very angry at him? Was she angry at you?"

But Grace stunned both of them when she shook her head again. "She wanted me to . . . she said I had to . . ." she choked on the words and had to battle her asthma, ". . . had to take care of him, and be nice to him . . . and . . . she wanted me to," she said again, her eyes brimming with tears, and pleading with them to believe her. They both did, and their hearts went out to her as they watched her.

"How long did it go on?" he said softly.

"A long time." She looked drained as she glanced back at him. She looked so tired and frail, he almost wondered if she would survive it. "Four years . . . she made me do it the first time."

"What was different that night?"

"I don't know . . . I just couldn't anymore . . . she was gone. I didn't have to do it for her anymore . . . he wanted me to do it in her bed . . . I'd never done that before . . . and . . . he . . . he hit me . . . and did other things." She didn't want to tell them all that he'd done to her, but they knew it anyway from the exam and the photos. "I remembered the gun . . . I just wanted him to stop . . . to get off of me . . . I didn't really mean to shoot him . . . I don't know. I just wanted to stop him." And she had. Forever. "I didn't know I'd kill him." But she had told them what had happened at least. And in a way, she felt relieved. And exhausted. It was different from telling the police. She knew that Molly and David wouldn't tell anyone, and they believed her. She knew that the police never would. They thought her father was perfect. They all knew him professionally and some even played golf with him at his club. It seemed like everyone in town knew him and loved him.

"You're a brave girl," David said quietly, "and I'm glad you told me." It all added up exactly the way Molly had said, only it was even worse, the mother had made her do it. At thirteen, when it started. It made him feel sick to think of it. The guy was a real sick bastard. He deserved to be shot. But now the big question was if he could convince a jury that Grace had been defending herself after four years of hell at her father's hands. Molly hadn't been able to convince the police, they were too sold on John Adams's public image. He couldn't help wondering if a jury would suffer from the same delusions.

"Would you tell the police what you told me?" David asked her calmly, but she was quick to shake her head that she wouldn't.

"Why not?"

"They won't believe me anyway, and . . . I can't do that to my parents."

"Your parents are dead, Grace," he said firmly, and she would be too if she didn't help herself and tell the truth. Self-defense was her only chance. They had to prove now that she had felt her life was in danger. And even if they didn't believe that, the worst they could make of it was manslaughter, not murder. "We're going to have to talk about this. You're going to have to tell someone, other than me, or the doctor here, what really happened."

"I can't. What'll they think of me? It's so awful." She started to cry again, and Molly got up and put her arms around her.

"It makes them look awful, not you, Grace. It

shows you as you are, a victim. You can't pay for their sins by staying silent. You have to speak up, David's right.'' They talked about it for a long time, and she said she'd think about it, but she still didn't look convinced that telling the whole truth was the best solution. And when they finally left her at the jail, Molly was still amazed that David had gotten her to open up so quickly.

"Maybe we should switch jobs, except that I can't do what you do either," Molly had said glumly. She felt like a failure for not getting Grace to trust her.

"Don't be so hard on yourself. The only reason she talked to me is because you had softened her up first. She needed to get it off her chest. It's been festering for four years. It has to be a relief now." Molly nodded in agreement, and then David shook his head ruefully. "Of course, killing him had to be a relief too. Damn shame she didn't do it sooner. What a sick son-ofabitch he was, while the whole town thinks he's a saint, the perfect husband and father. Makes you retch, doesn't it? It's a wonder she's as sane as she is." She was damaged and scarred, but she was still there, and she hadn't lost her grip yet. He didn't want to think though of what it would be like for her for twenty years in prison. But the next morning, when David saw her before the arraignment, Grace still refused to tell the police what had happened. The best he could do was convince her to plead not guilty at the arraignment. The charges were murder, with intent to kill, which would carry the maximum sentence, possibly even the death penalty if the jury imposed it.

The judge refused to set bail, which was irrelevant anyway, because there would have been no one to pay it. And David became the attorney of record.

And for the next several days, David did everything he could to try to convince her to tell the police that her father had raped her, had been for years. But she just wouldn't. And after two incredibly frustrating weeks, he threatened to throw in the towel. Molly was still visiting her frequently, on her own time now. Her report for the court had already been completed. She had judged Grace to be sane, and fully competent to stand trial, in her opinion.

David took her through the preliminary hearing, and he had his one lone investigator talking to everyone in town, hoping that someone, anyone, had suspected what John Adams was doing to his daughter. People's reactions ranged from mild surprise to total outrage at the suggestion, and absolutely no one thought him capable of it, and they said so. Instead they thought it was a crazy theory invented by the defense to justify what many of them referred to as Grace's cold-blooded killing of her father.

David himself went to talk to teachers at her school, to see if they had suspected anything, but they had seen nothing either. They described Grace as awkward and shy, very withdrawn, even as a young child, to the point of being antisocial, and she had virtually had no friends at all. Ever since her father had started having sex with her, she had been afraid that everyone would know, so she shunned them all. It was obvious that teachers thought she was a little strange, but she was polite and a good student. Most of them had been aware of how ill her mother was and thought that had affected her too, which it had, but not as much as her father's sexual demands on her. Several of them had mentioned the severe asthma that had only begun to affect her at the onset of her mother's illness.

Oddly enough, it didn't surprise any of them that she had done something so outrageous. They thought she was strange, and she had obviously "snapped," as they put it, when her mom died.

It was easy to construct it that way, and to think what the police did, that she had been after an inheritance, or that she had some kind of a temper tantrum, or a fight with him. It was difficult for anyone to believe that John Adams had led a life of utter perversion for four years, at the expense of his wife and daughter. And even more impossible for anyone to believe that he had beaten his wife for years before that. But no matter how little corroborating evidence there was, David never doubted her for a moment. Her story had the ring of truth, and throughout the summer he worked with her, trying to find evidence, and build a case to defend her. She had finally agreed to tell her story to the police, but they had refused to believe her. They thought it was a clever defense fashioned by her attorney and attempts to plea bargain with the prosecution on her behalf had gotten him nowhere. Like the police, the prosecution wouldn't buy it. In a moment of desperation, David had gone to the D.A., fearing a life sentence or the death penalty for her, but the D.A. wouldn't budge. He didn't believe her story either. There was nothing left to do now except take the same story to the jury. The trial was set for the first week in September.

She turned eighteen in jail.

She was in a cell by herself by then, and the newspapers had been hounding her all summer. They would show up at the jail, and ask for interviews. And now and then the guards would let them in to take her picture. The reporters would slip them a crisp bill or

two and the next thing she knew they were outside her
cell, with their flashbulbs. Once they even got a picture
of her on the toilet. And the whole story she'd told the
police had long since come out in the papers. It was
everything she hadn't wanted. She felt she had betrayed herself, and her parents, but David had convinced her it was her only hope to stay out of prison or
worse, the death penalty. And even that hadn't worked.
She was resigning herself to a life in prison by then,
and she still wondered if she would get the death sentence in the end. It was possible, even David admitted,
though he didn't like to. It would be up to the jury. He
was still sure he could convince a jury that she killed
her father to stop him from raping her, or even killing
her. She was young, she was beautiful, she was vulnerable, and she was telling the truth, which had an undeniable ring to it. To David and Molly, there was
absolutely no doubt about her story.

But the first real blow came when they were denied
a change of venue. David had petitioned on the basis
that there was no way she could get a fair trial in Watseka, people were just too prejudiced in favor of her
father. The papers had been hanging her for months,
embellishing the story wherever possible, and enhanc-
ing each new twist they could invent. By September,
she sounded like a sex-crazed teenage monster who
had spent months plotting her father's death, so she
could get his money. The fact that there seemed to be
almost no money there seemed to have escaped everyone's notice. They also referred to her as promiscuous,
and implied that she had had sexual designs on her
father, and killed him in a jealous fit. The story had
been told a thousand ways, but none of them true, and
all of them damaging to Grace. David couldn't imagine

how they would ever get a fair shake from a jury, certainly in this town, or maybe in any other.

The selection of the jurors took a full week, and because of the seriousness of the case, and based on an impassioned petition from David, the judge agreed to sequester the jury. The judge himself was a crusty old man, who shouted at everyone from the bench, and had frequently played golf with her father. But he refused to disqualify himself on the grounds that they hadn't been close friends, and he felt he could be impartial. The only thing that encouraged David was that if they didn't get a fair trial, or a favorable verdict, he could try to get a mistrial. Or it might help them on appeal. He was already planning ahead, and he was seriously worried.

The prosecution presented their case, and it was powerfully damning. According to them, she had planned to kill her father the night of her mother's funeral, to inherit what little they had left before he could spend it, or remarry. She had had no idea that she could never inherit from him if she killed him. Photographs presented as evidence showed her father to be an attractive man, and the prosecution implied repeatedly that Grace was in love with him, her very own father. So much so that she had not only tried to seduce him that night, by tearing her nightgown in half and exposing herself to him, now that her mother was gone, but she had also gone so far as to accuse him of rape after she killed him. There was evidence that she had had intercourse that night, they explained, but nothing supported the theory that it had been with her father. And what they suspected was that she had snuck off to meet someone that night, and when her father scolded her, she had tried to seduce him, and when he turned her down, Grace then killed him.

The prosecution was asking for a verdict of murder with intent to kill, which required an indeterminate sentence in prison, or even the death penalty. Hers was a heinous crime, the prosecutor told the jury and the people in the courtroom, which included an army of reporters from all over the country, and she had to pay for it to the ultimate degree. There would be no mercy for a girl who would wantonly kill her own father, and afterwards besmirch his reputation in an attempt to save herself from prison.

It was agonizing listening to what they said about her, it was like listening to them talk about someone else, as scores of people paraded to the witness stand to praise her father. Most of them said she was either shy, or strange. And her father's law partner gave the worst testimony of all. He claimed that she had asked him repeatedly the day of the funeral about her father's financial state, and what was left, after her mother's long illness.

"I didn't want to frighten her by telling her how much he'd spent on medical bills, or how much he owed me. So I just told her he had plenty of money." He looked unhappily at the jury then. "I guess I never should have said that. Maybe if I hadn't, he'd be alive today," he said, looking at Grace with reproach that was palpable in the courtroom, as she stared at him in horrified amazement.

"I never said anything to him," she whispered to David, as they sat at the defendant's table. She couldn't believe Frank had said that. She had never asked him anything about her father or his money.

"I'm sure you didn't," David said unhappily. Molly

had been right. The guy was a snake, and he was trying to get rid of Grace. David knew by then that John Adams had left everything to Frank in the event of Grace's death, or should she become incapacitated in any way, the house, the practice, and any cash he had. There wasn't much, but David suspected that there was more than Frank wanted anyone to know. And all he wanted now was to ensure that Grace would never inherit. If she was acquitted, she might still be able to appeal and maybe inherit a portion of the estate. Frank Wills wanted to be certain that didn't happen. "I believe you," David reassured Grace again, but the problem was that no one else would. Why should they? She had killed her father, admittedly. And Frank Wills was a convincing witness.

The prosecution eventually rested their case, and then it was David's turn to bring witnesses forward to testify about her character and her behavior. But there were so few people who knew her, a few teachers, some old friends. Most people said she was shy and withdrawn, and David explained exactly why that was, she was hiding a dark secret at home, and living a life of terror. And then he put the resident who had examined her at Mercy General on the stand. He explained in graphic detail the extent of the damage when he'd seen her.

"Could you say for certain that Miss Adams had been raped?" the prosecutor asked on cross-examination.

"Not with absolute certainty, one never can. One has to rely to some extent on the reports of the victim. But one could definitely say that there had been abusive sex over a long period of time. There were old scars of tears and damage that had been caused, and of course extensive new ones.''

"Could that kind of 'abuse' occur in normal sex, or sex of an unduly energetic, or even somewhat degenerate nature? In other words, if Miss Adams was masochistic in any way, or liked to be 'punished' by any of her supposedly various boyfriends, would it lead to the same kind of results?'' he asked pointedly, with flagrant disregard for the fact that everyone who knew her said she had never gone out with anyone, or had a boyfriend.

"Yes, I guess if she liked it rough, you could say that the same damage might occur . . . it would have to be very rough though,'' the resident said thoughtfully, and the prosecutor smiled evilly at the jury.

"I guess that's how some people like it.''

David objected constantly, and he did a heroic job, but it was an uphill struggle to battle their claim of premeditation. He put Molly on the witness stand, and finally, Grace herself, and she was deeply moving. In any other town, she would have convinced anyone made of stone, but not in this one. The people of Watseka loved John Adams, and they didn't want to believe her. People were talking about it everywhere. In stores, in restaurants. It was constantly all over the papers. Even the local TV news carried daily reports of the trial, and flashed photographs of Grace on the screen at every opportunity. It was endless.

The jury deliberated for three days, and David and Grace and Molly sat waiting in the courtroom. And when they got tired of it, they walked the halls for hours, with a guard walking quietly behind them. Grace was so used to handcuffs now, she hardly noticed when they put them on, except when they put them on too tightly on purpose. That usually happened with deputies who had known and liked her father. And it was stranger than ever to realize that if the jury acquitted her, she would suddenly be free again. She would walk away from all of this, as though it had never happened. But as the days droned on, it seemed less than likely that she would win her freedom. David tormented himself over the obstacles he'd been unable to overcome. And Molly sat and held Grace's hand. The three of them had become very close in the past two months. They were the only friends Grace had ever had, and she had slowly come not only to trust them, but to love them.

The judge had instructed the jury that they had four choices for their verdict. Murder, with premeditated intent to kill, which could call for the death penalty, if they believed that she had plotted in advance to kill her father, and knew that her acts would result in his death. Voluntary manslaughter, if she had indeed wanted to kill him, but not planned it, but believed falsely that she was justified in killing him, because she felt he was harming her at the time. Voluntary manslaughter would require a sentence of up to twenty years. Involuntary manslaughter if he had been harming her, and she had intended to hurt or resist him or cause him great bodily harm, but not kill him, but her "reckless" behavior had caused his death. Involuntary manslaughter would put her in prison for anywhere from one to ten years. And justifiable force if they believed her story that he had raped her that night and over the previous four years, and she was defending herself against his potentially life-threatening attack on her person. David had addressed them powerfully, and demanded justice in the form of a verdict of "defense with the use of justifiable force" for this innocent young girl who had suffered so much and lived a life of torture at the hands of her parents. He had made her tell all of it to the jury. That was her only hope now.

It was a late September afternoon when the jury finally came in, and Grace almost fainted when she heard the verdict.

The foreman rose solemnly, and announced that they had reached a verdict. She had been found guilty of voluntary manslaughter. They believed that John Adams had done something to her, though they were not quite sure what, and they did not believe that he had raped her, then or ever. But he had hurt her possibly, and two of the women on the jury had been insistent that even good men sometimes had dark secrets. There had been enough doubt in their minds for them to shy away from murder one and the death penalty. But the next step down from there was voluntary manslaughter, and that was how they had charged her. They believed, as the judge had explained in his instructions to them, that Grace had believed *falsely,* and therein lay the key, that she was justified in killing her father. Because of his glowing reputation in the community, they had been unable to accept that her father had been truly harming her, but they did believe that Grace had believed that, though incorrectly. Voluntary manslaughter carried a sentence of up to twenty years, at the judge's discretion.

And in the end, because of her extreme youth, and the fact that Grace herself had believed it to be both a crime of passion and of justifiable defense, the judge gave her two years in prison, and two years probation. Considering the possibilities, it was something of a gift, but it sounded like a lifetime to Grace as she listened to the words, and tried to force herself to understand it. In some ways, she thought death might have been easier. The judge had agreed to seal her records too, because of her age, and in the hope of not damaging her life any further when she got out of prison.

But Grace couldn't help wondering what would happen to her now. What would they do to her in prison? In jail, she had had the occasional scare, of other women threatening her, or taking her magazines or her toothpaste. Molly had been bringing things like that to her, and Frank Wills had reluctantly agreed to give her a few hundred dollars of her father's money, when David asked him.

But in jail, the women came and went in a few days, and she never felt truly in danger. She was there the longest by far, and on the worst charges. But prison would be filled with women who really had committed murder. She looked up at the judge with dry eyes and a look of sorrow. She was a person whose life had long since been lost, and she knew it. She had never had a chance from the first. For Grace, it was already over. Molly saw that look too, and she squeezed her hand as she stood beside her. Grace left the courtroom in handcuffs and leg irons this time. She was no longer merely the accused, she was a convicted felon.

That night, Molly went to see her in jail, before they transferred her to Dwight Correctional Center the next morning. There was so little she could say to her, but she didn't want Grace to give up hope. One day, there would be a new life for her. If she could just hold on till she got there. David had been to see her too, and he was beside himself over the verdict. He blamed himself for failing her, but Grace didn't blame him. It was just the way her life worked. He promised her an appeal, and he had already called Frank Wills, and he had negotiated a very unusual arrangement. With a great deal of prodding from David, Wills had agreed to let her have fifty thousand dollars of her father's money, in exchange for which she would agree never to return to Watseka, or interfere with him in any way, or anything he had inherited from her father. He was already making plans to move into their home in the coming weeks, and he told David he didn't want her to know that. As far as he was concerned, it was none of her business. He wanted no trouble from her, and he was planning to keep all of their possessions, and all of the house's furniture and contents. He had already thrown most of Grace's things away, and all he was offering her was the fifty thousand in exchange for staying away forever. He didn't want any hassles or arguments with her later. David had agreed on her behalf, knowing that one day, when she was free again, she'd have good use for the money. It was all she had now.

Molly tried desperately to encourage her that night when she saw her. "You can't give up, Grace. You just can't. You've made it this far. Now you've got to go the rest of the way. Two years isn't forever. You'll be twenty years old when you come out. It'll be time enough to start a whole new life, and put all this behind you." David had told her the same thing. If she could just hang on, and stay as safe as possible in prison. But they all knew that wouldn't be easy.

She had to be strong. She had no choice now. But she had been strong for so long, and at times she wished she hadn't survived it. Being dead had to be easier than what she'd been through, and going to prison. She said as much that night to Molly, that she wished she had shot herself, instead of her father. It would have been so much simpler.

"What the hell does that mean?" The young psychiatrist looked outraged. She strode across the room nervously, with her eyes blazing. "Are you going to lie down and give up now? Okay, so you've got two years of this. But two years is not a lifetime. It could have been a lot worse. It's finite. You know exactly how long it will last, and when it will be over. You never knew that with your father."

"What's it going to be like?" Grace asked with a look of terror, as the tears filled her eyes and then ran down her cheeks in two lonely rivers. Molly would have given anything to change things for her, but there just wasn't any more she could do now. All she could do was offer her love and support and friendship. She and David had both grown extremely fond of Grace. They talked about her for hours sometimes, and the injustice of all she'd been through. And now there was going to be more. She was going to have to be very strong. Molly held her in her arms that night as she cried, and prayed that somewhere she would find the strength to survive whatever she had to. Just the thought of it made Molly tremble for her.

"Will you visit me?" Grace asked in a small voice, as Molly sat next to her with an arm around her shoulders. Lately, she had talked about her constantly. Even Richard was tired of hearing about Grace, and so were all of Molly's friends and fellow doctors. Like David, she was obsessed with her, and only he seemed to understand what she was feeling. But the injustices she'd suffered for so long, the pain, and now the danger she would be in night and day were a constant worry to both David and Molly. They felt like her parents.

Molly cried when she left her too, and promised to drive to Dwight the following weekend. David was already planning to take a day off to see her, to discuss her appeal, and make sure she was as comfortable as possible in her surroundings. It didn't sound like a pleasant place, from all he'd heard, and like Molly, he would have done anything he could to change it. But their efforts hadn't been enough for her, no matter how hard they had tried or how much they cared about her. No matter what they had done for her, and they had done all they could with whatever resources had been available to them, it hadn't been enough to save her, or win her an acquittal. In all fairness to David, the cards had been stacked against her.

"Thanks for everything," she said quietly to David the next morning when he came to say goodbye to her at seven in the morning. "You did everything you could. Thank you," she whispered, and kissed him on the cheek, as he hugged her, willing her to survive and remain as whole as possible during her two years in prison. He knew that, if she chose to, she could do it. There was a great deal of inner strength in her. It had kept her going, and sane, during the nightmarish years with her parents.

"I wish we could have done better," David said sadly. But at least it hadn't been murder one. He couldn't have stood it if she'd gotten the death penalty. And as he looked at her, he realized something he had never let himself think before, that if she'd been older than eighteen he'd have been in love with her. She was that kind of person, there was something beautiful and strong hidden deep inside her, and it drew him toward her like a magnet. But knowing all she'd been through, and how young she was, he couldn't allow his feelings to run wild, and he had to force himself to think of her as a little sister.

"Don't worry about it, David. I'll be fine," she said with a quiet smile, wanting to make him feel better. She knew that a part of her had long since died, and the rest of her would just have to hang on until a higher force decided that her life was over. Dying would have been so easy for her, because she had so little to lose, so little to live for. Except, somewhere, deep inside of her, she felt that she owed it to him to survive, and to Molly. They had done so much for her, they were the first people in her whole life who had really been there. She couldn't let them down now. She couldn't let go of life yet, if only for their sakes.

Just before they led her away, she gently touched his arm, and for an odd instant, as he looked at her, he thought there was something almost saintly about her. She had accepted her fate, and her destiny. And she looked dignified beyond her years, and strangely beautiful as they led her away in handcuffs. She turned once to wave to him, and he watched her with eyes blurred by tears that ran slowly down his cheeks as soon as she left him.

Chapter 4

At eight o'clock they put her on the bus to Dwight in leg irons and chains and handcuffs. It was just routine to transfer prisoners that way, and no particular reflection on her. And oddly, she found that once she was all trussed up in chains, the guards no longer spoke to her. To them, she had ceased to be a real person. There was no one to say goodbye to her, to wish her well. Molly had come the night before, and David that morning before she left, and the guards watched her leave without a word. She'd been no trouble for them, but she was just another convict to them, a face they would soon forget, in a daily lineup of felons.

The only thing memorable about her, as far as the guards were concerned, was that her case had been written about a lot in the papers. But essentially, it was nothing special to them. She'd killed her father, so had a lot of other convicts before her. And she hadn't gotten away with it. They thought she'd been lucky to get convicted of manslaughter instead of murder. But luck wasn't something Grace had seen a lot of.

The ride to Dwight took an hour and a half from Watseka, and the bus bounced along, as her chains rattled and her ankles and wrists ached. It was an uncomfortable trip to a fearsome destination. Grace sat alone for most of the trip, and then an hour before Dwight, they picked up four more women at a local jail, and one of them was chained to the seat beside her. She was a tough-looking girl about five years older than Grace, and she looked her over with interest.

"You ever been to Dwight before?" Grace shook her head, and was less than anxious to start a conversation. She had already figured out that the more she kept to herself, the better off she'd be once she got to prison. "What are you in for?" The girl got straight to the point, as she sized Grace up. She knew her for a fish the minute she saw her. It was obvious to her that Grace had never been to prison before, and it was unlikely that she'd survive it. "How old are you, kid?"

"Nineteen," Grace lied, adding on a year, hoping to convince her inquisitor that she was a grown-up. To her, nineteen sounded really old.

"Playing with the big girls, huh? What'd you do? Steal some candy?"

Grace just shrugged and for a short while they rode on in silence. But there was nothing to see or do. The windows of the bus were covered so they couldn't see out, and no one could look in, and it was stifling.

"You read about the big drug bust in Kankakee?" the girl asked Grace after a while, sizing her up. But there was no mystery to Grace. She was almost what she appeared to be, a very young girl who didn't belong here. What the other girl couldn't see was how much she had suffered to get there. But nothing showed on Grace's face as she looked at her, it was as though the last of her soul had been boarded up when she left David and Molly. And no one could see inside now.

She intended to keep it that way, and with luck, they would leave her alone once she got to prison.

She had heard hideous stories about rape and stabbings while she was in jail, but she forced herself not to think of that now. If she had lived through the last four years, she could make it through the next two. Somehow, some tiny shred of what Molly and David had said to her had given her hope, and in spite of all the miseries in her life, if only for their sakes, she was determined to make it. It was different now. Someone cared about her. She had two friends, the first she'd ever had. They were allies.

"No, I didn't read about the drug bust," Grace said quietly, and the other girl shrugged in annoyance. She had bleached blond hair that looked as though it had been sawed off at her shoulders with a butcher knife and hadn't seen a comb in decades. Her eyes were cold and hard, and Grace noticed when she glanced at her arms that she had powerful muscles.

"They tried to get me to turn state's evidence against all the big guys, but I'm no snitch. I got integrity, ya know? Besides, I ain't lookin' to have them come lookin' for me at Dwight and fry my ass. Know what I mean? You work out?" Her accent said she was from New York, and she was exactly who Grace expected to meet in prison. She looked angry and tough and as though she could take care of herself. She seemed anxious to talk, and she started to tell Grace about the gym she'd helped build and her job in the laundry the last time she'd been in prison. She told her about two escapes that had taken place while she was there, but they had caught all the women who'd gotten out within a day. "It ain't worth it, they stick on another five years every time you do it. How long you

got? I'm in for a dime this time, I should be out in a
nickel." Five years . . . ten . . . it seemed like a lifetime to Grace as she listened. "What about you?"

"Two years," Grace said, not volunteering anything more than that. It seemed long enough to her,
although it was certainly better than ten years, or what
she might have gotten with another verdict.

"That's nothin', kid, you'll do that in a minute.
So," she grinned, and Grace could see that all her
teeth along the sides were missing. "So, you're a virgin,
huh?" Grace glanced at her nervously at the question.
"I mean this is your first time, right?" She really was a
fish, and the idea amused the older girl. This was her
third time at Dwight, and she was twenty-three years
old. She'd been very busy.

"Yes," Grace answered softly.

"What'd you do? Burglary, grand theft auto,
dealin' drugs? That's me. I been doin' cocaine since I
was nine. I started dealin' in New York when I was
eleven. I spent some time in a youth facility there, what
a shit place that was. I been there four times. Then I
moved out here." She had spent a lifetime in institutions. "Dwight's not bad." She talked about it like a
hotel she was going back to. "They got some good girls
there, some gangs too, all that Aryan Sisterhood shit.
You gotta watch out for them, and some pissed-off
black girls who hate 'em. You stay out of their hair and
you won't have no problem."

"What about you?" Grace looked at her cautiously,
but with interest. She was a phenomenon that three
months ago Grace would never even have dreamed of.
"What do you do when you're there?" Five years was
an eternity to spend in prison. There had to be something to do there. Grace wanted to go to school. She'd

already heard that there were courses you could take, other than beauty school and learning to make brooms and license plates, which was somewhat less useful. If there was any chance at all, Grace wanted to take correspondence courses from a local college.

"I don't know what I'll do," the other girl said. "Just hang out, I guess. I ain't got nothin' to do. I got a girlfriend who's been there since June. We were pretty tight before I got busted."

"That's nice for you." It would be nice to have a friend there.

"Yeah, ain't it just." The other girl laughed, and finally introduced herself and said her name was Angela Fontino. Introductions were rare in prison. "It sure makes the time roll along when you got a cute little piece of ass in your cell, waiting for you to come home from your job in the laundry." Those were the stories that Grace had heard, and which she dreaded. She nodded at the other girl, and didn't pursue the conversation further, but Angela was clearly amused by Grace's shyness. She loved teasing the little baby fishes. She'd been in and out of enough correctional facilities over the years that she had become very versatile about her sex life. There were even times when she actually preferred it this way.

"Sounds pretty raw to you, hey kid?" Angela grinned, showing her missing teeth in all their glory. "You get used to anything. Wait a while, by the end of two years you may even figure you like girls better." There was nothing Grace could say to her, she didn't want to encourage her, or insult her. And then Angela laughed out loud, as she tried to rub her wrists where they were deeply chafed by her handcuffs. "Oh my God, maybe you really are a virgin, huh, baby? You ever even had a guy? If not, you may never even have to shake your little ass at one, maybe you just stick to this for good. It ain't bad at all," she smiled, and Grace felt her stomach turn over. It reminded her of the afternoons when she'd come home and knew what was in store for her that night. She would have done anything not to come home, but she knew she had to take care of her mother, and then she knew what would happen. It was as inevitable as the setting sun. There had been no escaping it. She felt the same way now. Would she be raped by them? Or just used, as she had been by her father? And how would she ever fight them? If there were ten or twelve of them, or even two, what chance would she have? Her heart quailed as she thought of it, and the promises she had made to Molly and David that she would be strong and survive it. She'd do everything she could, but what if it was just too unbearable . . . what if . . . she stared hopelessly at the floor as they left the highway and drove up to the gates of Dwight Correctional Center. The other inmates were hooting and jeering and stamping their feet, and Grace just sat there, staring straight ahead, trying not to think of what Angela had told her.

"Okay, baby. We're home." Angela grinned at her. "I don't know where they're gonna put you, but I'll catch up with you after a while. I'll introduce you to some of the girls. They're gonna love you." She winked at Grace, and Grace could feel her skin crawl.

But two minutes later, they were all being shepherded from the bus, and Grace could hardly walk when she stood up, her legs were so stiff from sitting there and being shackled.

What she saw in front of her, as they got out of the bus, was a dismal-looking building, a watchtower, and a seemingly endless barbed-wire fence, behind which was a sea of faceless women in what looked like blue cotton pajamas. It was some kind of a uniform, Grace knew, but she didn't have time to look any further, they were immediately shoved inside, down a long hallway, and through endless gates and heavy doors, clanking their chains, and hobbling in their leg irons, their wrists still burning from the handcuffs.

"Welcome back to Paradise," one of the women said sarcastically as three huge black female guards growled at them, as they shoved them toward the next gate without further greeting. "Thank you, I'm thrilled to be back, nice to see you . . ." she went on, and a few of the women laughed.

"It's always like this when you get here," a black woman said to Grace under her breath, "they treat you like shit for the first couple of days, but then they leave you alone most of the time. They just want you to know who's boss."

"Yeah. Me," a huge black girl said, "they touch my big black ass, and I'm callin' the NAACP, the National Guard, and the President. I know my rights. I don't give a shit if I'm no convict or not, they ain't layin' a hand on me." She was over six feet, and probably close to two hundred pounds, and Grace couldn't imagine anyone pushing her around, but she smiled anyway at the look on the girl's face as she said it.

"Don't pay no attention to her, girl," the other black girl said. It surprised Grace that many of them seemed so friendly. Yet there was still an aura of menace. The guards were armed, there were signs everywhere warning of danger or penalties or punishments, for escaping, or assaulting a guard, or breaking the rules. And the prisoners coming in with her looked

like a rough group, particularly in what was left of their
street clothes. Grace was wearing a clean pair of jeans
and a pale blue sweater Molly had bought her as a gift.
She just hoped the authorities would let her keep it.

"Okay, girls." A shrill whistle blew, and six female
guards in uniform, wearing guns, lined up at the front
of the room, looking like coaches on a ladies' wrestling
team. "Strip. Everything you have on in a pile on the
floor at your feet. Down to bare-ass nothing, please."
The whistle blew again to stop them from talking, and
the woman with the whistle introduced herself as Sergeant Freeman. Half of the guards were black, the others white, which was fairly representative of the mix of
the prison population.

Grace carefully took her sweater off, and folded it
on the floor at her feet. One of the officers had uncuffed them, and now she was going around removing
the circlet of steel around their waists that the chains
were attached to, and the leg irons so they could re-
move their jeans. It was a great relief to have the leg
irons off, and Grace slipped out of her shoes. She was
surprised when the whistle blew again, and they told
them all to take everything out of their hair, any rubber bands or bobby pins. They were to let their hair
loose, and as she slipped the rubber band off her long
ponytail, her dark auburn hair fell in a silken sheet
well past her shoulders.

"Nice hair," a woman behind her murmured, and
Grace did not turn around to see her. It made her
uncomfortable knowing the woman was watching her
as she took the rest of her clothes off. And in a few
minutes, all their clothes were in little piles on the
floor, along with their jewelry, their glasses, their hair
accessories. They were stripped entirely naked, as six

guards walked among them, examining them, telling them to stand with their legs apart, their arms high, and their mouths open. Hands riffled through her hair to see if there was anything hidden there, and their hands were rough as they tugged at the long hair and moved her head from side to side. They shoved a stick in her mouth and moved it around, gagging her, and they had her cough and jump up and down, to see if anything fell out of anywhere. And then one by one, they had them stand in line, and get on a table with stirrups. Sterile instruments were used, and a huge flashlight to see if anything had been concealed in their vaginas. And as Grace stood in line, she couldn't believe that she had to do that. But there was no arguing with them, no discussion about what they would or wouldn't do. One scared girl tried to refuse and they told her that if she didn't cooperate, they'd tie her down, it was all the same to them, and then they'd throw her in the hole for thirty days, in the dark, buck naked.

"Welcome to Fairyland," one of the familiars said. "Nice here, huh?"

"Ah, stop bitching, Valentine, you'll get your turn."

"Shove it, Hartman." The two were old friends.

"I'd love to. Wanna look when it's my turn?"

Grace's heart was pounding as she got on the table, but the exam was medical, and no worse than most of what she'd been through, it was just humiliating going through it with an audience, and half a dozen of the other women seemed to be eyeing her with interest.

"Pretty cute . . . here, little fishie, swim to Mama . . . let's play doctor . . . can I take a look too?" She

seemed not to hear them at all as she followed the rest
of the line to the other side of the room and stood
waiting for further instruction.

They led them to a shower room then, and literally
hosed them down with near boiling water. They used
insecticides on any area with hair, and sprayed lice
shampoo on them, and then hosed them down again.
At the end of it, they reeked of chemicals and Grace
felt as though she'd been boiled in disinfectants.

Their belongings were placed in plastic bags with
their names, anything forbidden had to be sent back at
their own expense, or disposed of on the spot, like
Grace's jeans, but she was pleased that she was allowed
to keep her sweater. They were issued uniforms then, a
set of rough sheets, many of which had blood and
urine stains on them, and given a slip of paper with
their B numbers and their cells, and then they were led
away for a brief orientation as to the rules, and they
were told that they would each be given job assign-
ments the following morning. Depending on their
jobs, they would be paid between two and four dollars
a month for working, failure to show up for work
would result in an immediate trip to the hole for a
week. Failure to appear a second time would result in a
month in the hole. Failure to cooperate generally
would wind them up in solitary for six months with
nothing to do and no one to talk to.

''Make it easy on yourselves, girls,'' the guard in
charge of orienting them said in no uncertain terms,
''play it our way. It's the only way to go at Dwight.''

''Yeah, bullshit,'' a voice whispered to Grace's
right, but it was impossible to tell who it was. It had
been a disembodied whisper.

In a way, they made it sound easy. All you had to

do was play their game, go to work, go to chow, stay out
of trouble, go back to your cell on time, and you'd do
easy time and get out right on schedule. Fight with
anyone, join a gang, threaten a guard, break the rules,
and you'd be there forever. Try to escape and you were
"dead meat hanging on the fence," or so they said.
They certainly made themselves clear, but there was
more to it than just pleasing them, you had to live with
the other inmates too, and they looked as tough as the
guards, or worse, and they had a whole other agenda.

"What about school?" a girl in the back asked, and
everyone jeered.

"How old are you?" the inmate standing next to
her asked derisively.

"Fifteen." She was another minor, like Grace, who
had been tried as an adult, but they were rare here.
Dwight was almost entirely for grown-ups. And surely
for grown-up crimes. Like Grace, the other girl had
been accused of murder, she had plea-bargained it
down to manslaughter and saved herself from the
death penalty. She had killed her brother, after he'd
raped her. But now she wanted to go to school and get
out of the ghetto.

"You've had enough school," the woman standing
next to her said. "What do you need school for?"

"You can apply after you've been here ninety
days," the guard said, and then moved on to explain
what would happen to them if they ever had the bad
judgment to participate in a riot. Just the thought of it
made Grace's blood run cold, as the guard explained
that in the last riot, they had killed forty-two inmates.
But what if she got caught in the middle? What if she
was taken hostage? What if she was killed by an inmate

or a guard while she was just minding her own business? How was she ever going to survive this?

Her head was reeling as they finally walked her to her cell. They went in a single line, watched by half a dozen guards and hooted and jeered at by most of the inmates, standing on the tiers, looking down at them and squealing and laughing. "Hey, look at the little fishies . . . yum yum!" They blew kisses, they shrieked, the girl in front of Grace in the line was even hit with a flying Tampax, and Grace almost retched when she saw it. It was a place like nothing Grace had ever dreamed. It was your worst nightmare come to life. A trip to hell from which Grace could no longer imagine returning. She could still smell the insecticide on her face and hair, and as they stopped at the cell she'd been assigned to, she could feel her asthma starting to choke her.

"Adams, Grace. B-214." The guard unlocked the door, signaled for her to step in, and the moment Grace had, she heard the door clang shut, and the key turn. She was standing in a space roughly eight feet square, there was a double bunk, and the walls were covered with pictures of naked women. There were cutouts from *Playboy* and *Hustler* and magazines Grace couldn't imagine that women would read, but they did here. Or at least, her roommate did. The lower bunk was neatly made, and with shaking hands, she set about making the top bunk, and put her toothbrush on a little ledge with a paper cup they'd given her. She'd been told that she had to buy her own cigarettes and toothpaste. But she didn't smoke anyway, she couldn't with her asthma.

When the bed was made, she climbed up and sat on it, and she just sat there, staring at the door, wondering what would happen next, or how bad it would be when she met her roommate. It was obvious what her preferences were from the photographs on the walls, and Grace was braced for the worst, but she was surprised when a sour-looking woman in her late forties was let into the cell two hours later. She glanced up at Grace, and said not a word. She paused for one long instant, looking at her, and there was no denying that Grace was beautiful, but her cellmate didn't look impressed, and it was fully half an hour later before she said hello and that her name was Sally.

"I don't want no shit in here," she said tersely to Grace, "no funny stuff, no visitors from the gangs, no porno, no drugs. I been here seven years. I got my friends and I keep my nose clean. You do the same and we'll be fine, you give me a pain and I'll kick your ass from here to D Block. Got that nice and clear?"

"Yes," Grace nodded breathlessly. Her chest had been getting tighter and tighter since that morning, and by dinnertime, she could hardly breathe. She was wheezing badly and they had taken her inhaler away from her when she arrived.

"You need help, you call a guard," she'd been told, but she didn't want to do that unless she really had to. She would die first before calling attention to herself, but as they blew the whistle for chow, and she got off her bunk, Sally saw that Grace was in trouble.

"Oh Christ . . . looks like I got me a baby. Look, I hate kids. I never had any. I never wanted any. And I don't now. You gotta take care of yourself here." Grace noticed as she looked down at her as Sally put on a clean shirt that her back, chest, and arms were covered with tattoos, but in some ways she was a relief to Grace. She was fully prepared to mind her own business.

"I'm fine . . . really . . ." she wheezed, but she could barely breathe by then, and Sally watched her as she fought for air. She needed her inhaler desperately, and she didn't have it.

"Sure you are. Just sit down. I'll take care of it . . . this time . . ." She looked vastly annoyed as she buttoned her shirt and kept her eye on Grace, who was deathly pale as the guard unlocked the door for dinner. Sally signaled to him before he could move on, and waved vaguely at Grace, standing in the corner. "My fish is having a little problem," she said quietly, "looks like asthma or something, can I run her to sick bay?"

"Sure, if you want, Sally. You think she's fakin' it?" But when they looked at her again, Grace looked more gray than pale by then, and it was obvious that her distress was real. Even her lips were faintly blue. "Nice of you to play nursemaid, Sal," the guard teased. Sally was known to be one of the hardest women in the prison. She didn't take shit from anyone, and she was in for two counts of murder. She had murdered her girlfriend on the outside, and the woman she'd been cheating with. "It lets people know how I think," she always explained to the women she was involved with. But she had had the same lover in C Block for the past three years. Everyone in the place knew they were as good as married, and no one ever crossed Sally.

"Come on," she said to Grace over her shoulder, and then shoved her out of the cell with a look of annoyance. "I'll take you to the nurse, but don't pull this shit on me again. You got a problem, you handle it. I ain't gonna wipe your ass for you, kid, just because you're my cellmate."

"I'm sorry," Grace said, her eyes brimming with

tears. It was not a great beginning, and the woman was clearly pissed at her. At least that was what Grace thought. She didn't know that the older woman felt sorry for her. It was obvious even to her that Grace didn't belong there.

Five minutes later, she left Grace with the nurse, as she continued to gasp for air. The nurse gave her oxygen, and finally relented and decided to let her have, and keep, her inhaler. She wasn't going to be worth the trouble she caused if they didn't. But this time, they had to give her some other medication as well, because the attack had gotten too far out of hand in the past half hour. Grace knew only too well that without her medicine, she could die from suffocation. But at this point, she wasn't totally convinced that that wouldn't be a blessing.

She arrived at dinner half an hour later, shaken and pale, and most of the edible food was gone, the rest was all grit and grease and bone, and the stuff no one had wanted. She wasn't hungry anyway, the asthma attack had made her feel sick, and the medicine always made her feel shaky. She was too upset to eat anyway. She wanted to thank Sally for taking her to the nurse, but she didn't dare speak to her when she saw her with a group of tough older women, covered with tattoos, and Sally gave no sign of recognition.

"What'll it be? Filet mignon, or roast duck?" a pretty black girl asked from behind the counter, and then she smiled at Grace. "Actually, I've got a couple of slices of pizza left in the back. Any interest?"

"Yeah, thanks," Grace smiled, looking exhausted. "Thanks a lot." The young black girl produced them for her, and watched as Grace made her way to a table.

She sat down at an empty place at a table with

three other girls, no one said hello or seemed to notice
her. And across the room, she could see Angela, from
the bus, with a group of women, engaged in lively conversation. But this group seemed to want nothing to do
with her, and she was grateful to keep to herself, and
eat her slice of pizza. She was still having trouble
breathing.

"My, my, what a pretty little fish you have at your
table today, girls," a voice said from behind her as she
sipped her coffee. Grace didn't move when she heard
the words, but she felt herself jostled by someone
standing directly behind her. She tried to pretend she
didn't know what was happening, and she stared
straight ahead, but she could see that the other young
women at her table were looking nervous. "Doesn't
anyone talk around here? Christ, what a bunch of rude
bitches."

"Sorry," one of them muttered, and then hurried
away, and Grace suddenly felt a warm body pressed
against the back of her head. There was no avoiding it
now, she leaned forward and then turned around, and
found herself looking up at an enormously tall blonde
with a spectacular figure. She looked like a Hollywood
version of a bad girl. She was wearing plenty of
makeup, and a tight men's T-shirt that you could see
through. She looked like one of Sally's pinups. She was
almost a caricature of a sexy inmate.

"What a pretty girl," the tall blonde said, looking
down at her. "You lonely, baby?" her voice was a sensual purr, as she seemed to press her pelvis toward
Grace as she stood there, and Grace could see now that
her T-shirt was damp, which allowed everyone a clear
view of her breasts and nipples. It was as though she
were wearing nothing. "Why don't you come and see

me sometime? My name's Brenda. Everyone knows where I live," she said, grinning.

"Thanks." Grace still sounded breathy from her asthma attack, and the big blonde smiled at her.

"What's your name? Marilyn Monroe?" She made fun of the way Grace had sounded.

"Sorry . . . asthma . . ."

"Oh poor baby . . . you take anything for it?" She sounded concerned and Grace didn't want to be rude and get her angry. The big blonde was tough and sure of herself, and she looked to be about thirty.

"Yeah . . . I've got an inhaler." She pulled it out of her pocket and showed her.

"Take good care of it." She laughed then, and tweaked the tip of Grace's breast before sauntering off to her buddies.

Grace was shaking as the other girl walked away, and she stared down into her coffee, thinking about all of them. It was truly a jungle.

"Watch out for her," one of the girls at her table whispered, and then walked away. Brenda was a tough one.

Grace went straight back to her cell after that. They were showing a movie that night, but she had no interest in going. She just wanted to go back to her cell, and stay there until morning. She lay on her bunk, and heaved a sigh of relief. She had to use her inhaler two more times that night before she relaxed and felt like she could breathe again. And she was still awake at ten o'clock when Sally got back from the movies.

Sally didn't say a word to her, but Grace turned on her bunk and thanked her for taking her to the nurse for her asthma.

"She gave me my inhaler back."

"Don't show it to anyone," Sally said wisely. "They play with people here for things like that. Just keep it to yourself, and use it in private." That wasn't always possible, but Grace sensed that it was good advice, and nodded. And then, as they turned off the lights, and Sally got into her lower bunk, she spoke to Grace again in the darkness. "I saw Brenda Evans talking to you at chow. Watch out for her. She's dangerous. You're going to have to learn to swim here real quick, little fish. And watch your back till you do. This place ain't no playground."

"Thank you," Grace whispered in the dark, and she lay there for a long time, as silent tears slid down her cheeks onto the mattress. She lay there for what seemed like hours, listening to the clattering and banging outside, the shouts, and occasional screams, and through it all she listened to the comfortable purr of Sally's snoring.

Chapter 5

After two weeks, Grace knew her way around Dwight, and she had a job in the supply room, handing out towels and combs, and counting out toothbrushes for the new arrivals. Sally got her the job, although she pretended not to have any interest in helping Grace. But she seemed to keep an eye on her from a distance.

Molly had been to see her once by then, and she was devastated by what she heard and saw there. But Grace insisted that she was all right. And much to her own surprise, no one had really bothered her. They called her a fish whenever they got the chance, and Brenda had stopped to talk to her again once or twice at chow, but it never went beyond that. She hadn't even tweaked Grace's breast again. So far, she felt pretty lucky. She was safe, she had a decent job. Her roommate was taciturn, but basically kind. No one had threatened her, or invited her to join a gang. It looked like what they called "easy time." At this rate, she would survive the two years. And she was in pretty good spirits when David saw her, which reassured him. He hated her being there, and he felt more than ever that she didn't belong there, but at least nothing untoward had happened to her, and she insisted that she wasn't in any danger. It was something to be cheered about at least. And they spent their time together talking about her future.

She had already made up her mind that after she did her time at Dwight, she was going to Chicago. She had to stay in the state for two years of probation, but Chicago would suit her perfectly. And the fifty thousand dollars of her father's that Frank Wills had given her would give her a nest egg. She wanted to get a job when she got out, but before that, she wanted to learn to type, and take her college courses, as soon as she could start them.

David told her about the appeal, and he was encouraging, but it was hard to say what would happen.

"Don't worry about it. I'm okay here," she said gently, and as he watched her leave the visiting room that afternoon, he marveled at the quiet dignity of her carriage. She held herself straight, and she was thinner than she had ever been. She looked beautiful and neat and clean, and it was hard to believe, looking at her, that she was an inmate in a prison. She looked like a college girl, or a cheerleader. She looked like someone's really good-looking wholesome little sister. It was impossible to see her history as one looked at her, except if you saw her eyes. The pain one saw there told a different story. And all that he knew of her made him ache for her. It was never easy for him to forget her.

He waved sadly as he drove away, and she stood outside watching his car disappear in the distance. It was even harder for her than it was for him. For her it was like being deserted in the jungle.

"Who's that?" a voice behind her asked, and when Grace turned to look at her, she saw Brenda. "Your boyfriend?"

"No," Grace said, with quiet dignity, "my attorney."

Brenda laughed openly at her. "Don't waste your time. They're all pricks. They tell you what they're gonna do, and how they're gonna save your ass, and they don't do shit except fuck you, literally if you let them, and every other way too. I never met one worth a damn. Actually," she laughed again, "I never met a guy worth a damn either. What about you?" She looked pointedly at Grace. She was wearing one of her wet T-shirts again, and Grace noticed that she had a tattoo on one arm, of a large red rose with a snake under it, and next to her eyes she had tattoos of tiny teardrops. "You got a boyfriend?" Grace knew that here it was a dangerous question, whatever you said, you were in a precarious position. She just shrugged noncommittally. She was learning. And she started to walk slowly back inside after her visit. "You in a hurry to go somewhere?"

"No, I . . . I thought I'd write some letters."

"Oh how cute," Brenda laughed. "Just like camp. You got a mommy and daddy at home to write to? You still didn't answer me about the boyfriend."

"Just a friend." She had wanted to write to Molly, about David's visit.

"Hang around. It can be a lot of fun around here. If you want it to be. Or it can be a real drag. It's up to you, babe."

"I'm okay," she said, looking for a way to exit without enraging Brenda. But Brenda wasn't making it easy.

"Your cellie's a real creep, and so's her girlfriend. You met her yet?" Grace shook her head. Sally was very discreet about her private life. She had never said anything to Grace, nor did she seek her out when they were out of their cell. She minded her own business. "Big black bitch. They're a real drag. What about you? You like to party? Little magic dust, little weed?" Brenda's eyes sparkled at the thought of it, and Grace tried to look vague and then shook her head.

"Not really. I've got pretty bad asthma." And no interest in drugs. But she didn't say that. The last thing she wanted was to offend Brenda. She had already gathered from others that Brenda was considered bad news. She was involved with one of the gangs, and the rumor was that she not only did drugs, but sold them, and one of these days, she was going to get in a whole lot of trouble.

"What's asthma got to do with it? I had a room-mate in Chicago who only had one lung, and she used to freebase."

"I don't know . . ." Grace said vaguely, "I'm not into that."

"I'll bet there's a lot of things you haven't tried yet, baby girl." Brenda laughed again, and Grace walked away with a friendly wave, and then she hurried back to her cell, feeling breathless. She touched the inhaler in her pocket and was reassured to know it was close at hand. Sometimes just knowing that it was there made her breathing easier.

There were movies again that night, and Sally went out again. Her one weakness in life, other than pinups, seemed to be movies. The more violent the better. But Grace hadn't been to one yet, and she was grateful for time alone in her cell after dinner. The room was so small and claustrophobic, but there were times when she was so relieved to be there, and away from every-one, that it actually seemed cozy.

After dinner, their cells were left unlocked unless one requested they be locked up. It allowed for some visiting time for inmates to stop by and see each other, or play games. They played a lot of cards, and a few of them played chess, or Scrabble. It was just understood that from six to nine the cells would be open, and inmates could come and go to various approved locations.

Grace was lying on her bed writing to Molly after dinner that night, and she heard the door open, but didn't bother to look up. She assumed it was Sally, back from the movie, and the other woman didn't say anything when she came in. She rarely did, so Grace thought nothing of the silence, until she sensed a presence next to her, and looked up to find herself staring into Brenda's face. She had uncovered one breast and it was resting on Grace's bunk, and just behind her was another woman.

"Hi, babycakes," she purred with a smile, caressing her nipple casually, as Grace sat up. The other girl was not quite as tall, but she looked a lot tougher than Brenda. "This is Jane. She wanted to come by and meet you." But Jane said nothing. She just stared at Grace, as Brenda reached out and stroked Grace's breast this time. Grace tried to move away, and Brenda grabbed her arm and held her firm. It reminded her, for just an instant, of her father, and she could feel her chest tighten. "Want to come out and play?" It was not an invitation, but a command, and she looked like an Amazon as she stood there in all her blond splendor.

"Not really, I . . . I'm kind of tired." Grace didn't know what to say to her, and she wasn't old enough or tough enough or savvy enough to prison ways, to know how to ward off Brenda.

"Why don't you come rest at my place for a while? We got another hour till lockdown."

"I don't think so," Grace said nervously, feeling her chest get even tighter. "I'd rather not."

"How polite." Brenda laughed out loud, and squeezed Grace's breast hard, and then pinched her nipple. "Want to know something, sweetheart? I don't give a shit what you want. You're coming with us."

"I . . . I don't think so . . . I . . . please . . ." She didn't want to whine, but it sounded that way even to her own ears, and as she looked at Brenda she suddenly heard a grating sound, and Jane moved closer to them. Grace saw instantly that she had a switchblade concealed in the palm of her hand, and she flashed it at Grace with a menacing expression.

"Ain't that nice?" Brenda smiled. "An engraved invitation from Jane. In fact, she's done a lot of that kind of work. She does some real nice engraving." This time they both laughed, and Brenda pulled open Grace's shirt and licked her nipple. "Nice, huh? You know, I'd hate to have Jane get excited and want to start doing some engraving right there . . . you know . . . sometimes she makes little mistakes, and it could get kind of messy. Okay? So why not hop down off your bunk and come with us? I really think you're gonna like it." This was what she had feared. This was it. A gang rape using God knows what, and maybe carving her face off with a knife. Nothing in her life had prepared her for this, not even her father.

She was breathless as she hopped off her bunk, still clutching her pen and her letter in her hand. And then, with a smooth gesture, she turned, as though to set it down, and as she did, and left the paper on Sally's bunk, she wrote one small word. *Brenda.* Maybe it would be too late. And maybe Sally couldn't help her, or wouldn't even want to. But it was all she could do, as she left the cell between Brenda and Jane. She was about as tall as they were, but she looked like a child next to them, and in many ways she was. She knew nothing of women like them.

She was surprised when they didn't take her to their cell, but walked past the gym instead, and then outdoors, as though they wanted to get some air. The guards were watching them, but the guards saw nothing untoward about three women going for a walk outside before lockdown. A lot of the women did that to get some air, or have a smoke, or just relax before they went to bed. And Brenda joked with the guards as they walked by them. Jane stayed close to Grace. The knife in her hand out of sight, but held close to Grace's neck, as she draped an arm casually over her shoulder. They looked like they were friends, and no one seemed to notice Grace's terror.

And once outside, Brenda wandered over to a small shed that Grace had never even noticed. The guards in the tower weren't watching them. There was no danger there, it was just an old shed with no windows they used to store maintenance equipment. Brenda had a key to it, and the moment she opened the door, the threesome disappeared inside. There were four more women in there, leaning against the machinery that was stored, smoking cigarettes, and holding a single flashlight. It was the perfect place for anything they wanted to do to her, even kill her.

"Welcome to our little clubhouse," Brenda said, laughing at her. "She really wanted to come and play," Brenda said to the others. "Didn't you, Gracie . . . oh pretty girl . . . pretty, pretty girl . . ." she purred,

carefully unbuttoning Grace's shirt, as Grace tried to
stop her. If at all possible, they didn't want to leave any
signs of damage, like torn clothing, unless of course
they really had to. If she forced them to, they could do
a lot of damage, and if she was smart, she'd be too
afraid to tell anyone who had done it.

Grace felt Jane's knife pressed against her flesh,
and her shirt stayed unbuttoned, as Brenda pulled her
bra down. "Nice fresh meat, huh, girls?" Everyone
laughed and one of the others who'd been waiting
there said to hurry the hell up. Lockdown was in less
than an hour. They didn't have all night for chrissake.

"God, I hate to rush when I eat," Brenda said, and
everyone in the shed laughed. And then Grace saw two
of them come forward with lengths of rope, and a rag.
They were going to tie her down and gag her. "Come
on, kid. Let's get this show on the road," one of the
older women said. She grabbed an arm, and another
woman grabbed another, and Grace was dragged backwards and thrown to the ground so hard it left her
breathless. They moved as a single team then. Two
women tied her arms to the heavy machines, then they
yanked off her pants and her underwear and threw
them aside as two more tied her legs, as the last two sat
on them, and Jane managed to sit on one leg to keep
her knife pressed into Grace's stomach. There was no
point in fighting or screaming, and she knew it. They
would have killed her. But she could hardly breathe,
and as she glanced anxiously toward the inhaler in the
pocket of her discarded shirt, Brenda remembered it
too. She reached for it, found it, and held it out to
Grace tauntingly, but Grace's hands were tied, and
Brenda dropped it on the ground next to her, as one

of Jane's big boots came forward and stomped it into splinters.

"Sorry, kid." Brenda smiled mockingly. "Okay? You know the rules of this game?" Brenda asked, tossing her blond hair back over her shoulder, and then standing up to slip off her own pants. "First we do you, and then you do us . . . one by one . . . we'll tell you how . . . and when and where, and just how we like it. And after this," Brenda growled at her, and bit hard on her nipple, as she rubbed her crotch, "you belong to us. You understand? You come out here whenever we want, as often as we want, with whoever we want, and you do exactly what we tell you to do. You got that? And if you squeal, you little bitch, we cut out your tongue and cut your tits off. You get it? You know, kind of like a mastectomy." Everyone laughed at her wit, except Grace, who was shaking and wheezing, lying on the cold floor, terrified of what they were going to do to her.

"Why? Why do you have to do this? . . . you don't need me . . . please . . ." She was begging, and they thought it was funny. She was so new, so fresh, so young, and they knew that if they didn't get her, someone else would. It was first come, first served in prison.

"You're gonna be our sweetie, aren't you, Grace?" Brenda said, leaning down slowly to the place where Grace's legs met, as she knelt on the ground in front of her. Grace was naked by then, and Brenda slowly began to lick her. She loved that part, breaking them in, having someone no one else had ever had, turning them on, scaring them, using them, showing them how helpless they were, making them do anything she wanted. She stopped for a minute, and pulled a tiny tube out of the pocket of her jacket. She opened it, and quickly inhaled the white powder, and then ran a tiny bit of it around her gums, and with a single finger she put a little bit on Grace, and licked it off with vigor. "Nice . . ." Brenda moaned, loving it, feeling Grace with her fingers as the others told her to hurry up. She was shoving her whole hand in then and Grace winced in pain. But the others were complaining. They wanted a turn too. They didn't have all night. This wasn't Brenda's honeymoon. "Maybe it is, you cunt," she said to one of the girls grumbling at her, "maybe I'll keep her for myself if she's any good." But Grace was squirming and trying to move away from her, and the relentless prodding of her fist, although she couldn't go far with her legs tied. She wanted to scream, but didn't dare, for fear of Jane's knife. But they hadn't gagged her. They needed her mouth to please them, when they were through with her.

Grace closed her eyes then, trying to pretend she wasn't there, that it wasn't happening, and then suddenly she heard a noise and a bang, like a door slamming. She heard Brenda gasp and felt her pull her hand out and jump aside, and when Grace opened her eyes, she saw a tall, graceful black girl standing in the doorway. She didn't know if the girl was one of them or not, but the others didn't seem happy to see her.

"Okay, you fools, untie her." The black girl was very tall and very cool, and strangely good-looking. And the whites of her eyes looked enormous in the light of the flashlight. "You've got five seconds to get her out of here, or Sally's going to the Man. If I'm not outta here in three minutes, she's gone. And I guess maybe you babes are in the hole until Christmas."

"Bullshit, Luana. Get your black ass outta here before we kill you." Jane was addressing her and flashing the switchblade at her and Brenda looked furious, but she seemed somewhat distracted. The cocaine had taken hold and she wanted to proceed with Grace, without their damn interruptions.

"Why don't you cunts go fight someplace else?" Brenda said with a small groan as she moved away from Grace for a moment.

"You got two minutes left," Luana said icily. "I said untie her." Luana looked terrifying as she stood staring at them in the light of the flashlight. She had muscles almost like a man's and the long sinewy legs of an Olympic runner. She was the prison's female karate and boxing champ, and she was someone that no one wanted to mess with. Jane always swore she wasn't afraid of her, and she'd said more than once that she would have liked to carve her face off. But the rest of them knew it was more talk than action. Luana had powerful connections.

There was a long moment of hesitation, and then one of the other women untied Grace's hands and arms, and another began to untie her legs, as Brenda whined in unfulfilled passion.

"You bitch. You want her for yourself, don't you?"

"I've got what I want. Since when do you have to fuck with babies?" But Luana knew as well as they did that Grace was a beauty. Lying there, all sprawled out, she had almost made them drool with anticipation.

"She's old enough," Brenda spat at the black girl in frustrated fury. "What are you now, the Lone Ranger? Go fuck yourself, Luana."

"Thanks."

Grace was on her feet, and struggling into her clothes, and trying to button her shirt with trembling hands again a moment later. She didn't even dare look at them, for fear that they would kill her.

"Party's over, girls," Luana announced with a smile. "You touch her again, and I'll kill you."

"What the fuck does that mean?" Brenda said with a tone of complete annoyance.

"She's mine. You heard me?"

"Yours?" For once, Brenda looked stunned. No one had told her that. That might have made things a little different.

"What about Sally?" Brenda asked suspiciously.

"We don't owe you any explanations," Luana said coldly, as she shoved Grace toward the door. She was wheezing and shaking, and Luana pushed her so hard she almost fell. This was not a woman to mess with. None of them was. Grace was way out of her league, and she realized now that she'd been crazy to think she could be safe here. All the stories were true. They had just been waiting.

"Christ, you guys are into threesomes now?" Brenda whined at her.

"You heard me. She's mine. Stay away from her. Or there's gonna be trouble. You got that?" No one answered her, but the message was clear, and Luana was too important in the political scheme of things to be worth annoying. With a single word from her, a riot could come down. Two of her brothers were the most powerful Black Muslims in the state, and the two others had staged the biggest riots in the history of Attica, and San Quentin.

Having warned them to stay away from Grace, Luana quickly opened the door, and shoved Grace outside. She grabbed her arm, and growled at her to stroll along, chatting with her as though nothing had happened. Five minutes later, they were in the gym, and Grace was deathly pale and wheezing, and she no longer had her inhaler. Sally was waiting for them there, with a look of concern. And when she saw Grace, she looked really angry.

"What the hell were you doing with Brenda?" she asked in an irate undertone, as Luana watched them.

"She came into our cell. I thought it was you at first, I didn't even look up until she was nose to nose with me, and Jane was flashing a knife right behind her."

"You've got a lot to learn." But she'd been impressed that she'd been smart enough to leave a message on her bunk, with the single scrawled word *Brenda*. "Are you okay?" She wondered how far it had gone, and she glanced at Luana for an answer.

"She's okay. Stupid, but okay. They didn't get too far. Brenda was too busy getting coked up to do a whole lot of damage." Over the years they had all seen girls raped and ruined for life by baseball bats and broomsticks. But Luana was still annoyed that this kid had almost dragged Sally into it. It was Luana who had insisted on going herself, and leaving Sally to tell the guards, if she had to. Luana took good care of her. They had been together for years and no one dared to bother either of them, because of Luana's brothers who came to see her when they could. Two lived in Illinois, one in New York, and the other in California. All four were on parole, but everyone knew who they were, and what they could do, if they ever got angry. Even Brenda and her friends wouldn't dare mess with them, or with Luana or Sally. Now Grace was going to be under their protection.

"What did you tell them?" Sally asked Luana conversationally as they walked back to the cell she shared with Grace.

"That she was ours now," Luana said quietly, looking at Grace with annoyance. She had told Sally to watch out for her. The kid was so green she was liable to bring the house down. And Luana didn't pull any punches with her when they got back to the cell and Grace started crying. She also knew she didn't dare ask for another inhaler till the next day, and she was wheezing badly.

"I don't give a shit how scared and sick you are," Luana said, looking murderous. "If you ever put Sally's ass on the line again, I'll kill you. You don't leave her any notes, don't tell her who kidnapped you. Don't go whining to her about your medicine or who pinched your ass on the chow line. You got a problem, you come to me. I don't know what the hell you did to get sent here, and I don't want to know. But I can tell you one thing, you weren't sent here for having brains, and if you don't get them quick, you're gonna die, simple as that. So get smart real fast. Ya hear? And in the meantime, you do every goddamn thing Sally tells you. She tells you to lick the floor, or clean her latrine with your eyebrows, you do it. You got that, kid?"

"Yes, yes, I do . . . and thank you . . ." She knew that she was safe with them. Sally had already proven that to her. And from now on, if she was faithful to them, they would protect her. They wanted nothing from her, not sex, not money, they felt sorry for her, and they both knew she didn't belong there.

But from that day on, things changed. People stayed away from Grace, and treated her with respect. No one hassled her, no one whistled or jeered. It was as though she didn't exist. She led a sort of charmed life, going her own way in the jungle, amidst the lions and the snakes and the alligators. And her only friends were Sally and Luana.

She had gotten religious while she was there. And her asthma was troubling her less than it had in years. She had started her correspondence course from the local junior college. She could finish in two years, and go to school at night to get her B.A. once she got out. She was taking secretarial classes too, to help her find a job when she got out and went to Chicago.

Even David saw a change in her in time. When he visited her, he saw that there was a quiet confidence, and an odd peace about her. It allowed her to accept the news philosophically when he told her that they had lost the appeal, and she would have to serve her full two-year sentence. It had been exactly a year since her conviction, and David could barely bring himself to believe that they had lost again, but she took it very calmly. It was Grace who consoled him, when he told her how badly he felt to have failed her yet again, but she reminded him that it wasn't his fault. He had done his best. And all she had to do now was survive another year there. It wasn't easy, but all she could do now was look forward. It touched him more than ever as he listened to her, but it pained him too. He found that he came to see her less often because seeing her always reminded him of all that he hadn't been able to accomplish for her. He still had an odd kind of obsession with her. She was so beautiful, so young, so pure, and she had had such rotten luck in her short life, and yet, despite all he felt for her, he had been able to do nothing to change it. It made him feel helpless and angry and inadequate. Sometimes, he wondered if he had won the appeal for her, would things have been differ-

ent? If, maybe then, he would have had the guts to tell
her he loved her. But as things stood, he had never
said it, and Grace never suspected his feelings for her.

Molly had been aware of his feelings for Grace for
a while, but she had never said anything to him about
it. But the young lawyer David had been taking out
recently had said plenty. She had sensed long since
how obsessed he was with Grace. He talked about her
constantly. His new friend had called him on it more
than once, and told him it wasn't healthy. She told him
he had a "hero complex" and was trying to save her.
She told him a lot of things, some of which were truly
painful. But the simple fact was, in his own mind, he
had failed Grace. Knowing that made him feel worse
each time he saw her. And in her second year at
Dwight, he came to see Grace less and less often. He
had less reason to now. There was no appeal. There
was nothing he could do for her anymore, except be
her friend. And his girlfriend kept telling him he had
to get on with his own life.

Grace missed seeing him, but she also understood
that there was nothing he could do. And she knew that
he was seeing someone who meant a lot to him. He
had said something to Grace about it the last few times
he'd seen her, and Grace had sensed that somehow he
felt guilty now when he came to see her. She wondered
if maybe his girlfriend was jealous.

Molly still came, not as often as she would have
liked, but as often as her busy life allowed, and it always
cheered Grace when she saw her. And other than that,
Grace was comfortable with her only other two friends,
Luana and Sally. She spent her second Christmas at
Dwight with them, in their cell, sharing the chocolates
and cookies that Molly had sent her.

"You ever been to France?" Luana asked as Grace shook her head and smiled. They asked her funny things sometimes, as though she came from another planet. And in some ways she did. Luana was from the ghettos of Detroit, and Sally was from Arkansas. Luana loved teasing her and calling her "the Okie."

"Nope, I've never been to France," Grace smiled at them. They were an odd trio, but they were good friends. In a strange way, they were like the parents she had never had. They protected her, they watched over her, they scolded her, and taught her the things she needed to know to survive there. And in a funny way, they loved her. She was just a kid to them, but there was hope for her. She could have a life someday. They were proud of her when she got good grades. And Luana told her all the time that one day she'd be someone important.

"I don't think so," Grace laughed at them.

"What are you gonna do when you get outta here?" Luana always asked her, and she always said the same thing.

"Go to Chicago, and look for a job."

"Doin' what?" Luana loved hearing about it, she was in for life, and Sally had three more years to do. Grace would be out in a year, and then she had a life ahead of her, a future. "You should be one of those models, like on TV. Or maybe on a game show?" Grace always laughed at their ideas, but there were things she wanted to do. She loved psychology, and sometimes she thought about helping girls who'd been through what she had, or women like her mother. It was hard to know. She was only nineteen, and she had another year to do in prison.

Then right after the first of the year, David Glass

came to see her. He hadn't been to see her in three months, and he apologized for not sending her anything for Christmas. He seemed to feel uncomfortable with her, and it was one of those visits that felt awkward right from the beginning. At first, she wondered if something was wrong, if something had changed for the worse about her release date. But when she asked, he was quick to reassure her.

"That's not going to change," he said gently, "unless you start a riot, or hit a guard. And that's not likely. No, it's nothing like that." But he knew he had to tell her. He hesitated for a long moment, fantasizing again, and then, as he looked at her, he knew that his fiancée was right. His obsession with Grace was crazy. She was just a kid, she had been his client, and she was in prison. "I'm getting married," he said, almost as though he owed her an apology, and then he felt foolish for his unspoken feelings.

Grace looked pleased for him. She had suspected, from little things he'd said, that he was pretty serious about his current girlfriend. "When?"

"Not till June." But there was more, and as she looked at him, she knew it. "Her father has asked us both to join his law firm in California. I'm going to be leaving next month. I want to get settled in L.A. I have to pass the California bar, we want to buy a house, and I have a lot to do before we get married."

"Oh." It was a small sound, as she realized that she probably wouldn't see him again, or at least not for a very long time. Even after her two years of probation when she could leave the state, she couldn't imagine going to California. "I guess it'll be nice for you out there." She looked suddenly wistful at the thought of losing a good friend. She had so few, and he had been so important to her.

As he looked at her, he took one of her hands in his own. "I'll always be there if you need me, Grace. I'll give you my number before I go. You'll be fine." She nodded, but they sat there in silence for a long time, holding hands, thinking of her past and his future, and suddenly for that brief moment in time, the girl from California seemed a lot less important to David.

"I'm going to miss you," she said so openly that it tore at his heart. He wanted to tell her that he would always remember her, just the way she was now, so young and beautiful, her eyes were huge and her skin was so perfect it was almost transparent.

"I'm going to miss you too. I can't even imagine what life is going to be like in California. Tracy seems to think I'll love it." But he sounded a little less sure now.

"She must be pretty terrific to make you want to move." Grace's eyes met his, and he had to steel himself against her.

He laughed then, thinking that leaving Illinois was not exactly a heartbreak, but leaving Grace was. As little as he saw her now, he liked knowing that he was still near enough to help her if she needed him. "You call me in L.A. if you need anything. And Molly will still be coming to see you." He had spoken to her only that morning.

"I know. She thinks she might be getting married too." He had heard that too. It was time for all of them to settle down. And in another eight months it would be time for Grace to start her life. They were already on their way. They had careers, they had histories, they had mates. For Grace, it would all be a fresh beginning when she got out of prison.

He stayed with her longer than usual that afternoon, and he promised he'd come back again before he left town, but when he said goodbye to her, Grace somehow knew that he wouldn't. She heard from him again a couple of times, and then he was gone, apologizing profusely in a letter from L.A. that he hadn't had time to visit her again before he left. But they both knew that he hadn't had the courage. It would have just been too painful, and it was time to leave her. His fiancée wanted it that way too. She had been very definite with him about it. But Grace couldn't know that. She wrote him a few letters that spring, and then she stopped. She knew instinctively that her relationship with David Glass was behind her.

She talked to Molly about it once or twice, about how sad she felt sometimes when she thought of him. She had so few friends that it really hurt to lose one. And he had been so important to her too. But it seemed as though he had another life now.

"Sometimes you have to let people move on," Molly said quietly. "I know how much he cared about you, Grace, and I think he felt pretty bad about not being able to get you off, or win the appeal for you."

"He did a good job," Grace said loyally. Unlike most of the inmates at Dwight, she didn't blame her lawyer for her winding up in prison. "I just miss him, that's all. Did you ever meet his girlfriend?"

"Once or twice." Molly smiled. She knew that Grace still had no idea of the feelings David had had for her after the trial. In some ways, she had been like a little sister to him, in others like a dream he knew he could never have, but still wanted. But his fiancée had been smart. She had sensed it too, and Molly didn't think it was a complete accident that she had asked him to move to California. "She's a very bright young woman," the young doctor said diplomatically. She didn't want to tell Grace that she hadn't really liked her. But she was probably good for him. She was smart and tough and ambitious, and according to people who knew her, a damn good lawyer.

"What about you? When are you and Richard getting married?" Grace teased her.

"Soon." And then finally in April, she and Richard set the date. They were getting married on July first, and going to Hawaii for their honeymoon. She and Richard had spent six months trying to coordinate their vacations. And two and a half months after that, Grace would be free. It was hard to believe almost two years had passed. In some ways, it seemed like moments, in others an entire lifetime.

The day before her wedding, Molly went to visit Grace, and she had asked her to come and stay with them for a few days when she got out of prison, and before she went to Chicago. Grace had already promised to spend Thanksgiving with them, and maybe even Christmas. And on their wedding day, Grace sat in her cell most of the day, thinking about them, wishing them well, and knowing all their plans, all the details. She had seen photographs of the dress, she knew who would be there. She even knew the time of their flight to Hawaii. They were leaving at four o'clock, and flying from Chicago to Honolulu, arriving at ten o'clock, local time. And they were staying at the Outrigger Waikiki. Grace could envision all of it, and she felt as though she had actually been to the wedding herself, by the time she sat down and watched the news with the other inmates at nine o'clock, just before lockdown.

She was talking to Luana about working out with her the next afternoon, when she saw something about a plane crash out of the corner of her eye. They were talking about a TWA plane that had exploded and blown up an hour before, over the Rockies. The details were still unknown, but the airline feared a bomb, and there had been no survivors.

"What was that?" Grace asked, turning to the woman next to her. "Where were they?"

"It was over Denver, I think. They think it was terrorists blew it up. It was a flight from Chicago to Honolulu, via San Francisco." Grace felt her skin grow cold and her heart ache. But it couldn't be. That wasn't it. It didn't work like that . . . not after all these years. Not both of them . . . on their honeymoon . . . her only friend . . . the only person she could rely on and go home to. She was looking deathly pale and she started to wheeze, and Sally saw it as she took out her inhaler. And she understood immediately what Grace was afraid of.

"It's probably not them, you know. There are a dozen flights a day to Honolulu." Sally knew about Molly's honeymoon. She had been bored to death hearing about the wedding for weeks, but now she was worried for them, and wanted to reassure Grace. It really was unlikely that that was their plane. But a week later, after seven sleepless nights, and endless days, she knew it. She had written to the hospital, inquiring if Molly was okay, and had received a sad letter explaining to her that Dr. York and Dr. Haverson had died in the crash she'd heard about, on their honeymoon. The letter said that the whole hospital was in mourning.

Grace went to bed that day, and three days later she hadn't gotten up yet. Sally had covered for her as best she could, and so had Lu. They claimed it was her asthma again, and that she'd had a terrible time getting any relief, even from her pills and her inhaler. Her inhaler was familiar to everyone by now, and she no longer worried about using it. With Lu watching over her, no one was liable to take it from her, or steal it. But the nurse knew this time when she came to their cell that it wasn't asthma that was bothering her. Grace wouldn't even answer her. She just lay there, staring at the wall, and refusing to get up, or even answer.

Molly had been her only friend, and with David so far away, now she really had no one to turn to. Grace was alone again, except for her two friends in prison.

The nurse had told her she had to go back to work the next day, and she was lucky they hadn't already sent her to the hole for not showing up at work for two days. But she was pushing her luck now. And the next day, she made no effort to get up, in spite of all of Sally and Luana's threats and pleas. She just lay there, wishing herself dead, like Molly.

They took her to the hole that day, and left her there in the dark, with no clothes, and only one meal a day. And when she came back, she looked rail thin and very pale, but Sally could see from her eyes that she was alive again, deeply hurt, but she had turned the corner.

She never mentioned Molly again after that day. She never spoke of anyone in the past, not David, or Molly, or her parents. She lived only in the here and now, and now and then she would talk about moving to Chicago.

The day finally came, and she wasn't sure she was

ready for it. She had no plans, no clothes, no friends, and a little money to last her for a lifetime. She had the AA degree she'd gotten from her correspondence course, and she had grown wise and patient and strong in prison. She was tall and thin and beautiful and stronger than she'd ever been. Luana had made her lift small weights and run, and she had really toned her figure. She was very beautiful, with her dark auburn hair pulled back in a ponytail, and she was wearing a white shirt and jeans when they released her. She looked like any other college girl, so fresh and young, just twenty, but there was a lifetime of experience there, lodged in her soul, a handful of people in her heart she would never forget, like Molly, and Luana and Sally.

"Take care," she said hoarsely when she left. She had hugged each of them, and held them tight. And Luana had kissed her on the cheek like a little girl they were sending out to play.

"Be careful, Grace. Be smart. Look around, trust your gut . . . go someplace, girl. Be someone. You can do it."

"I love you," she whispered to her. "I love you both so much. I couldn't have made it without you." And she meant it. They had saved her.

She kissed Sally on the cheek too, and Sally was embarrassed by it. "Just don't do anything stupid."

"I'll write to you," she promised, but Sally shook her head. She knew better. She had seen a lot of friends come and go. When you left, it was over, until next time.

"Don't," Luana said brutally. "We don't want to hear from you. And you don't want to know us. Forget us. Go have a life. Grace, put all this behind you. Start fresh and new . . . go out there and don't ever look back. You don't have to take any of this with you.''

"You're my friends,'' she said, with tears in her eyes, but Luana shook her head again.

"No, we're not, girl. We're ghosts. All we are is memories. Take us out once in a while, and then be glad you're not here. And don't you come back again, ya hear!'' She wagged a finger at her, and Grace laughed through her tears. Some of what Luana had said was good advice, but she couldn't just leave them there, and forget them. Or was that what you had to do? Did she have to leave them all behind in order to move forward? She wished she could have asked Molly. "Now get lost!'' Luana had given her a little shove forward, and a few minutes later she was going through the gate in a van on the way to the bus station in town. They were standing at the fence waving at her, and she turned and waved from the window until she couldn't see them any longer.

Chapter 6

The bus trip from Dwight to Chicago took just under two hours. They had given her a hundred dollars cash when she left the correctional center. And David had set up a small checking account for her before he moved west. It had five thousand dollars in it, and the rest was in a savings account she had vowed not to touch.

In Chicago, she had no idea where to stay, or where to go. She had to tell the authorities where she was going and they had given her the name of a parole officer in Chicago. She had to check in with him within two days. She had his name and address and phone number. Louis Marquez. And one of the girls at Dwight had told her where to go for a cheap hotel.

The bus station in Chicago was on Randolph and Dearborn. The hotels they'd told her about were only a few blocks away from it. But when she saw the kinds of people on the street by the hotels, she hated to go inside them. There were prostitutes hanging around, people renting rooms by the hour, and there were even two cockroaches on the desk in one hotel when she rang the bell for the desk clerk.

"Day, night, or hour?" he asked, shooing the cockroaches aside. Even Dwight hadn't been as bad as that. It was a lot cleaner.

"Do you have prices by the week?"

"Sure. Sixty-five bucks a week," he said without batting an eye, and it sounded expensive to her, but she didn't know where else to try. She took a single room with private bath on the fourth floor for seven days, and then she went out to find a restaurant to get something to eat. Two bums stopped her and asked her for change, and a hooker on the corner looked her over, wondering what a kid like her was doing in this neighborhood. Little did they know that a "kid like her" had just been at Dwight. And no matter how seedy the neighborhood was, she was glad to be free. It meant everything to walk the streets again, to look up at the sky, to walk into a restaurant, a store, to buy a newspaper, a magazine, to ride a bus. She even took a tour of Chicago that night, and was stunned by how beautiful it was. And feeling extravagant, she took a cab back to her hotel.

The prostitutes were still there, and the johns, but she paid no attention to them. She just took her key, and went upstairs. She locked her door, and read the papers she'd bought, looking for employment agencies. And the next day, with the newspaper in hand, she hit the streets and started looking.

She went to three agencies, and they wanted to know how much experience she had, where she'd worked before, where she'd been. She told them she was from Watseka, had graduated from junior college there, and had taken secretarial courses in shorthand and typing. She admitted that she had no experience at all, hence no references, and they told her that they couldn't help her find work as a secretary without them. Maybe as a receptionist, or as a waitress, or sales-girl. At twenty with no experience and no references, she didn't have much to offer and they weren't embarrassed to say so.

"Have you thought of modeling?" they asked her in the second agency. And just to be nice, the woman jotted down two names. "They're modeling agencies. Maybe you should talk to them. You've got the look they want." She smiled at Grace, and promised to call her at the hotel if any jobs opened up that didn't require experience, but she didn't hold out much hope to her.

Grace went to see her probation officer after that, and just seeing him was like a trip back to Dwight, or worse. It was incredibly depressing, and this time she didn't have Luana and Sally to protect her.

Louis Marquez was a small, greasy man, with beady little eyes, a severely receding hairline, and a mustache. And when he saw Grace walk in, he stopped what he was doing and looked at her in amazement. He had never seen anyone who looked like that in his office. Most of his time was spent with drug addicts, and prostitutes, and the occasional dealer. It was rare for him to handle juveniles, and rarer still to see someone with charges as major as hers, who looked like Grace, and seemed as young and wholesome.

She had bought herself a couple of skirts by then, a dark blue dress to go job-hunting in, and a black suit with a pink satin collar.

She was wearing the dark blue dress when she visited him, because she'd been out looking for work all day, and her feet were killing her from the high heels she was wearing.

"Can I help you?" he asked, looking puzzled, but

intrigued. He was sure that she had come to the wrong office. But he was glad she had. He was happy for the distraction.

"Mr. Marquez?"

"Yes?" He gazed hungrily at her, unable to believe his good fortune. And his eyes grew wide, as she reached into her handbag and pulled out the familiar forms for probation. He glanced at them summarily, and then stared at her, unable to believe what he was reading. "You were at Dwight?" She nodded, looking calm. "That's a pretty heavy place," he looked really startled. "How did you manage that for two years?"

"Very quietly." She smiled at him. She looked very wise for her years. In fact, looking at her now in the dark blue dress, it was hard to believe she was only twenty. She looked more like twenty-five. And then he looked even more surprised when he read the file notes on her conviction.

"Voluntary manslaughter, eh? You have a fight with your boyfriend?"

She didn't like the way he asked her that, but she answered him very coolly. "No. My father."

"I see." He was enjoying this. "You must be no one to mess with." She didn't answer him, and he was taking her measure with his beady little eyes. He was wondering just exactly how much he could get away with. "You have a boyfriend now?"

She wasn't sure what to say, or why he was asking. "I have friends." She was thinking of Luana and Sally. They were her only friends in the world now. And of course David, far away in California. She still felt Molly's loss terribly. They were all her only friends. And she didn't want him to think she had no one.

"You have family here?"

But this time she shook her head. "No, I don't."

"Where are you living?" He had the right to ask her those questions, and she knew that. She told him the name of the hotel, and he nodded and jotted it down. "Not much of a neighborhood for a girl like you. Plenty of hookers. Maybe you noticed." And then with an evil glint in his eye, "If you get busted, you're back to Dwight for another two years. I wouldn't get any ideas about picking up some extra money." She wanted to slap him, but prison had taught her not to react, and to be patient. She said nothing. "Are you looking for work?"

"I've been to three agencies, and I'm checking the papers. I have some more ideas. I'm going to check them out tomorrow, but I wanted to come here first." She didn't want to be late reporting in, or he could make trouble for her. And she had no intention of going back to Dwight. Not for two years, or two minutes.

"I could give you some work here," he said thoughtfully. He'd love having someone like her around, and he was in an ideal situation. She'd be scared to death of him, and she'd have to do anything he wanted. The more he thought about it, the more he liked it. But Grace was too smart for that now. She wasn't falling for the Louis Marquezes of the world. Those days were over.

"Thank you, Mr. Marquez," she said quietly. "If some of my opportunities don't pan out, I'll call you."

"If you don't find work, I could send you back," he said nastily, and she forced herself not to answer. "I can violate you anytime I want, and don't you forget it. Failure to find work, failure to support yourself, failure to stay clean, failure to follow conditions of parole.

There are plenty of grounds to ship you back there.''
Someone was always threatening her, trying to spoil
things for her, wanting to blackmail her into doing
what they wanted. And as she stared at him unhappily,
thinking of what a pig he was, he reached into a drawer
in his desk, and handed her a plastic cup with a lid.
''Give me a specimen. There's a ladies' room across
the hall from my office.''

''Now?''

''Sure. Why not? You been getting loaded?'' He
looked evil and hopeful.

''No,'' she said angrily. ''But why the specimen?
I've never been in trouble for drugs.''

''You been in trouble for murder. You been in the
joint. And you're on probation. I got a right to ask you
for anything I think is called for. I'm calling for a
urinalysis. Okay with you, or you gonna refuse? I can
send you back to the joint for that too, you know.''

''All right, all right.'' She stood up, holding the
cup, and headed for the door to the hallway, thinking
what a bastard he was.

''Normally, my secretary would have to watch, but
she left early today. Next time, I'll have it observed. But
I'll give you a break this time.''

''Thanks.'' She looked at him with barely hidden
fury. But he had her by the throat, just the way everyone had for years, her parents, Frank Wills, the police
in Watseka, the guards at Dwight, even bitches like
Brenda and her friends, until Luana and Sally had res-
cued her. But there would be no rescuers now. She had
to rescue herself, and hold her own against vermin like
Louis Marquez.

She came back five minutes later with a full cup,
and balanced it precariously on his desk, with the lid

barely closed. She was hoping he would spill it all over his papers.

"Come back in a week," he said casually, eyeing her again with obvious interest. "And let me know if you move, or find a job. Don't leave the state. Don't go anywhere unless you tell me."

"Fine. Thanks." She stood up to leave, and with a leer, he watched her slim hips and long legs disappear out of his office. And a minute later, he stood up and poured her urine out in his sink. He wasn't interested in doing a drug test. All he wanted to do was humiliate her and let her know that he could make her do anything he wanted.

Grace was steaming when she took the bus back to her hotel. Louis Marquez represented everything she had been fighting all her life, and she wasn't going to give in to it now. She wasn't going to let him send her anywhere. She would die first.

She checked the Yellow Pages that night for all the modeling agencies in town. She had liked the woman's suggestion to try them, but not for modeling. She thought maybe she could work as a receptionist, or someone in the office. She had a long list of places to try, and wished that she knew which one was the best one. But she had no way of knowing. All she could do was try them.

She got up at seven the next day, and she was still in her nightgown and brushing her teeth when she heard someone pounding on her door, and wondered who it could be. It had to be a hooker, or a john, maybe someone who had the wrong room. She put a towel around her nightgown and opened the door, with her toothbrush still in her hand, and her dark coppery hair cascading past her shoulders. It was Louis Marquez.

"Yes?" For an instant, she almost didn't recognize him, and then she remembered.

"I came to see where you live. A probation officer is supposed to do that."

"How nice. I see you got an early start too," she said, looking angry. What did he think he was pulling? It was her father all over again, and just thinking about that made her tremble.

"You don't mind my coming by, do you?" he said smoothly. "I wanted to be sure you really lived here."

"I do," she said coldly, holding the door wide. She was not going to invite him in, or close the door behind him. "And whether or not I mind depends on what you have in mind to do here." She looked at him without flinching for an instant.

"What do you mean?"

"You know what I mean. Why did you come here? To see where I live? Fine. You've seen it. Now what? I'm not planning to serve breakfast."

"Don't get smart with me, you little bitch. I can do anything I want with you. And don't you forget it."

But the way he said it made something snap deep inside her, and she took a step closer to him, and put her face close to his with a look of fury. "I shot the last man who said that to me, and tried to act on it. And don't *you* forget that, *Mr.* Marquez. Are we clear now?" He was fuming, but he was also out of line, and he knew it. He had come here to see just how much he could get away with, and how scared she was of him. But Luana had taught her well, and she wasn't buying.

"You'd better watch what you say to me," he said in a malevolent tone as he hesitated in the doorway.

"I'm not going to take any shit from some little punk
kid who shot her old man. You may think you're tough,
but you won't know what tough is till I send your
skinny little ass back to Dwight for another two years,
and don't think I won't do it."

"You'd better have a reason before you try, Marquez, or I'm not going anywhere, just because you
show up at my hotel at seven o'clock in the morning."
She knew exactly why he was there, and so did he. And
she had just called his bluff, and he knew it. Actually,
she had surprised him. He had thought she would
scare more easily, and he was more than a little disappointed. But it had been worth a try, and if she ever
looked like she was weakening, he was going to pounce
on her just like a little cockroach. "Anything else I can
do for you? Want me to pee in a glass for you? Happy
to oblige." She looked at him pointedly, and without
saying another word, he turned and hurried down the
stairs of her hotel. It wasn't over yet. She was stuck with
him for two years, and he had plenty of time to torment her.

After he left, she put on the black suit with the
pink collar and she was particularly careful when she
did her hair and dressed. She wanted to look just right
for the modeling agencies. She wanted to look cool
and sure and well dressed, but not so flashy she com-
peted with the models.

The first two agencies told her they had no open-
ings, and they hardly seemed to notice her at all, and
her third stop was Swanson's on Lake Shore Drive.
They had a luxurious-looking waiting room and big
blown-up photographs of their models everywhere.
The place had been designed by an important decora-
tor, and Grace was more than a little nervous when

they called her in to one of the offices for Cheryl Swanson to meet her. She met all their potential employees personally, and so did her husband, Bob. There was a definite look to the Swanson employee. Their models were the best in town, for runway and photography, as well as commercial. And everything about the agency suggested success and high style and beauty. Looking around the office where she waited for Cheryl, Grace was particularly glad she had worn the little Chanel knockoff.

And a moment later, a tall, dark-haired woman walked into the room with a long stride, and a neat bun at the back of her neck. She wore huge glasses and a sleek black dress. She wasn't pretty, but she was very striking.

"Miss Adams?" She smiled at Grace, and sized her up immediately. She was young, and scared, but she looked bright, and she had a good look to her. "I'm Cheryl Swanson."

"Hello. Thank you for seeing me." Grace shook her hand across the desk, and sat down again, feeling her asthma start to fill her chest, and she prayed she wouldn't have an attack now. It was so terrifying walking in cold, asking for interviews, and then trying to talk them into hiring her. She'd been at it for almost a week, and so far there was no hope yet. And she knew that if she didn't get a job by the following week, her probation officer really would give her trouble.

"I hear you're interested in a job as a receptionist," Cheryl said, glancing at a note her secretary had given her. "That's an important job here. You're the first face they see, the first voice. Their very first contact with Swanson's. It's important that everything you do represents who and what we are, and what we stand for. Do you know the agency?'' Cheryl Swanson asked, taking off her glasses and scrutinizing Grace more closely. She had good skin, great eyes, beautiful hair. It made her wonder as she looked at her. Maybe she was just trying to get in the back door. Maybe she didn't even have to. "Are you interested in modeling, Miss Adams?'' Maybe that's what this was all about, and it was all a ploy, but Grace was quick to shake her head in answer to the question. That was the last thing she wanted, guys pawing all over her, thinking she was easy because she was a model, or photographers chasing her around in a bathing suit, or less. No, thank you.

"No, I'm not. Not at all. I want a job in the office."

"Maybe you should look beyond that," she glanced at her note again, "Grace . . . maybe you should think about modeling. Stand up." Grace did, reluctantly, and Cheryl was very pleased to see how tall she was. But Grace looked like she was about to cry, or run screaming from the office.

"I don't want to model, Mrs. Swanson. I just want to answer the phone, or type, or run errands for you, or do whatever I can . . . anything but model."

"Why? Most girls are dying for a modeling career." But Grace wasn't. She wanted a real life, a real job, a real family. She didn't want to start her new life chasing rainbows.

"It's not what I want. I want something . . . more . . . more . . ." she groped for the right word and then found it, ". . . solid."

"Well," Cheryl said regretfully, "we do have a job open here, but I think it's a terrible waste. How old are you, by the way?"

Grace thought about lying to her, and then decided not to. "Twenty. I have an AA degree, I can type, but not very fast. And I'll be good, and work hard, I swear it." She was begging for the job, and Cheryl couldn't help smiling at her. She was a sensational girl, it was just such a waste to have her answering phones behind a desk. But on the other hand, she certainly set the right tone for what Swanson had to offer. She looked like one of their models.

"When can you start?" Cheryl looked at her with a motherly smile. She liked her.

"Today. Now. Whenever you like. I just came to Chicago."

"From where?" she asked with interest, but Grace didn't want to tell her that she was from Watseka in case she had heard of her father's murder two years before, nor did she want to say she'd just come from Dwight, in case she knew about the prison.

"From Taylorville," she lied. It was a small town two hundred miles from Chicago.

"Are your parents there?"

"My parents both died when I was in high school." It was close enough to the truth, and vague enough not to get her in any trouble.

"Do you have any family here at all?" Cheryl Swanson asked, looking worried about her. But Grace only shook her head.

"No one."

"Normally, I'd ask you for references, but with no prior experience, there really isn't much point, is there? All I'd get is a nice letter from your high school gym teacher and I can see what you're made of. Welcome to the family, Grace."

Her new boss stood up and patted her arm in warm welcome.

"I hope you'll be happy here for a long, long time,

at least until you decide to start modeling," she laughed. They had offered her the receptionist's job at a hundred a week, which was all she wanted.

Cheryl took her out into the hall, and introduced her to everyone. There were six agents, and three secretaries, two bookkeepers, and a couple of people Grace wasn't quite sure who they were, and at the end of the hall, Cheryl walked into a sumptuous office done in gray leather and suede, and introduced her to her husband. They both looked as though they were in their mid-forties, and Cheryl had already explained that they had been married for twenty years, but had no children. The models are our kids, she had said. They're our babies.

Bob Swanson sized Grace up from behind his desk, and looked at her with a warm smile that really did make her feel part of the family, and then he got up and walked around his desk to shake her hand. He was about six feet four, very rugged-looking with dark hair and blue eyes and movie star handsome. He had been a child actor in Hollywood as a kid, and a model, of course, as Cheryl had been, in New York. And eventually, they had moved to Chicago, and opened the business.

"Did you say 'receptionist,' " he asked his wife, "or new model?" He beamed down at her, and Grace felt as though she was home at last. They were really nice people.

"That's what I said." Cheryl smiled at him, and it was obvious immediately that they liked each other, and worked well together. "But she's a stubborn one. She says she wants a desk job."

"What makes you so smart?" he laughed as he looked at Grace. She was really a pretty girl, and his

wife was right. She could have done well as a model.
"It took us years to figure that out. We learned the
hard way."

"I just know I'd never be good at it. I'm happy
behind the scenes, making things work." Just like
she'd run her mother's house, and made the supply
room hum at Dwight. She had a knack for organizing
things, and she was willing to work long hours and do
anything she had to, to get the job done.

"Well, welcome aboard, Grace. Get to work." He
sat back down at his desk again, waved at them both as
they left, and sat staring at them going down the hall
for a few minutes. There was something interesting
about the girl, he decided as he looked at her, but he
wasn't sure what it was yet. He prided himself on having a sixth sense about people.

Cheryl asked two of the secretaries to take Grace
under their wings, and show her how the phone system
worked, and the office machines. And by noon, it
seemed as though she had always been there. Their last
receptionist had quit the week before, and they'd been
making do with temps in the meantime. It was a relief
for everyone to have someone efficient on hand, to
take calls, make appointments, and register their bookings. It was a complicated job, and required a lot of
juggling at times, but by the end of the first week, she
knew she loved it. The job was perfect.

When Grace reported to Louis Marquez at the end
of the week there was nothing for him to complain
about. She had a good job, a decent salary. She was
leading a respectable life, and she was planning to
move as soon as she could find a small apartment. She
would have loved to live closer to work, but the apartments around Lake Shore Drive were unbelievably ex-

pensive. She was scouring the paper, looking for one, when four of the models were hanging around one afternoon, waiting to hear about a go-see. Grace was always overwhelmed by how beautiful they were, and how exquisitely put together. They had fabulous hair, perfect nails, their makeup always looked like it had been done by professionals, and their clothes made her stare at them with envy. But she still had no desire to do the kind of work they did. She didn't want to trade on her looks, or her sex appeal, or draw that kind of attention to herself. It was too much for her, emotionally. She couldn't handle it, and she knew it. After everything she'd been through in her life, her survival had depended on her ability not to attract attention. And even at twenty, it was too late for her to change that now. She liked nothing better than not being the center of attention. But the models always included her in their conversations. This time they were talking about renting a town house they'd seen. It sounded fabulous to her, but also way out of reach, they were talking about a thousand dollars. It had five bedrooms, though, and they only needed four. Maybe even fewer since one of them was thinking about getting married.

"We need someone else to come in with us," a girl called Divina said, sounding disappointed. She was spectacular-looking, and she was Brazilian. "Any interest?" she asked Grace casually, but she couldn't imagine living with them, or being able to afford sharing a rent they could manage.

"I'm looking for a place," she said honestly, "but I don't think I can afford the kind of rents you'd want to pay," she said glumly.

"If we cut this one five ways, it's only two hundred apiece," the twenty-two-year-old German model, Brigitte, said matter-of-factly. "Could you afford that, Graze?" Grace loved her accent.

"Yeah, if I stop eating." It meant giving up half her salary, which wouldn't leave her much for food or fun, or any other needs she might have. And she hated to dip into her savings, but she knew she could if she had to. And maybe living in a nice place, in a good neighborhood, with decent people, would be worth it. "Let me think about it."

One of the two American girls laughed and looked at her watch. "Great. You have till four o'clock to make up your mind. We have to go look at it again, and tell them by four-thirty. Want to come?"

"I'd love to, if I can leave by then. I have to ask Cheryl." But when Grace asked, Cheryl was thrilled. She'd been horrified to hear that Grace was living in a fleabag hotel while looking for an apartment. She had even invited her to stay in her apartment, with her and Bob, on Lake Shore Drive, until she found something, but Grace hadn't accepted.

"Thank *God*!" Cheryl exclaimed, and practically shoved Grace out the door with the others. They were nice girls, and she also thought that maybe if Grace lived with them, she might decide to become a model. Cheryl hadn't given up on that yet, but on the other hand, she had discovered that Grace's unfailing sense of organization was a godsend.

The town house turned out to be spectacular. It had five good-sized bedrooms, and three baths, a decent-sized kitchen, a patio, and a sunken living room with a view of the lake. It had everything that each of them wanted, and they signed the lease that afternoon. For a long time, Grace stood there and stared at it, unable to believe that this was her home now. It was partially furnished with a couch and some chairs, and a dining room set, and the other girls all claimed that they had enough stuff to fill it. All Grace had to do was buy a bed, and some furniture for her own bedroom. It was incredible. She had a job, she had a home, she had friends. As she stood and looked at the lake, tears filled her eyes, and she turned away and pretended to check out the patio so they wouldn't see them.

Marjorie, one of her new roommates, had followed her outside. She had seen the emotional look on Grace's face, and she was worried. Marjorie was the mother hen of the group, and the others always teased her that she fussed over them too much. She was only twenty-one, but she was the oldest of seven children. "You okay?" she asked. Grace turned to look at her as Marjorie walked up to her with a look of concern, and Grace sighed and smiled through her tears. It was impossible to conceal them.

"I just . . . it's like a dream . . . this is everything I ever wanted. And a lot more." She only wished she could have shown it to Molly. She would never have believed it. The poor, beaten, miserable creature she had been had flowered, even in the dismal barrenness of Dwight Correctional Center over the past two years. And now she had a new life, a new world, it was like a dream. David and Molly had been right. If she hung on long enough, the ugliness of the past would be behind her forever. And now, finally, she was past it.

She had sent Luana and Sally postcards only a few days before, telling them that she was okay and Chicago was great. But she knew them both well, and she suspected they'd never write her. But she still wanted to let them know that she was safe and well, and had reached a safe harbor. And that they weren't forgotten.

"You looked so upset a few minutes ago," Marjorie pursued it, but Grace was smiling now.

"I'm just happy. This is like a dream come true for me." Marjorie would never know how much so. The one thing she didn't want anyone to know here was that she had killed her father and served time in prison. She wanted to leave that behind her.

"It's like a dream for me, too," Marjorie confessed. "My parents were so poor I had to share my only good pair of shoes with two of my sisters. And they had feet two sizes smaller, and Mom always bought them in their size. I never lived in a place like this, till I came here. And now I can afford it, thanks to the Swansons." It was thanks to her own good looks, and she knew that. She was planning to move on to New York when her contract was up, and do some modeling there, or even Paris. "It's fun, isn't it?"

"It's terrific."

The two girls chatted for a while, and eventually Grace went back to her hotel and packed. She didn't care if she had to sleep on the floor until her furniture arrived. But she was not going to spend one more night in that cheap hotel, killing cockroaches, and listening to old men spit and flush toilets. She moved out the next day, and dropped her bags off on her way to work. And at lunchtime, she went to buy a bed and some furniture at John M. Smythe on Michigan Avenue. She even bought herself two little paintings. They promised to deliver it all on Saturday, and in the meantime, Grace had every intention of sleeping on the carpet.

She had never been happier in her life, and the job was going splendidly. But on Friday, when she reported to Marquez, she found she was in trouble, and he loved it.

"You moved," he accused her, pointing a finger at her, almost as soon as she walked into his office. He'd been waiting for her for days. And the only reason he knew was that he dropped by at the hotel again, and they told him she'd checked out for good on Tuesday.

"Yeah? So? What's the problem?"

"You didn't notify me."

"The probation papers say I don't have to notify you for five days. I moved three days ago, and I'm notifying you right now. Does this take care of it, Mr. Marquez?" He was out to get her, and she knew it. But there was nothing he could say to her, she was right. She had five days to notify him that she had moved, and she had only moved on Tuesday.

"So what's the address?" he snarled at her, prepared to write it down, but as she looked at him, she realized what was going to happen.

"Does this mean you'll be dropping by on me from time to time?" she asked, looking worried, and he loved it. He liked making her uncomfortable, catching her off guard, frightening her, if possible. She brought out all his basest sexual instincts.

"It might. I have a right to drop by, you know. Do you have something to hide?"

"Yes. You." She looked right at him and he flushed all the way to his receding hairline.

"What's that supposed to mean?" He dropped his pen and stared at her in irritation.

"It means that I have four roommates who don't need to know where I've been for the past two years. That's what."

"You mean incarcerated for murder?" He glowed.

Now he had a wedge he could use on her. He could threaten to expose her to her roommates.

"I guess that's what I mean. You make it sound so charming."

"It is pretty charming, I'm sure they'd be fascinated to know your history. And by the way, what do you mean *four* roommates. Sounds like a bunch of call girls."

"You wish." She wasn't afraid of him, but he worried her a little bit, and she disliked him intensely. "They're models."

"That's what they all say."

"They're registered at the agency where I work."

"Too bad. I need the address anyway . . . unless you want me to violate you, of course." He looked ever hopeful.

"Oh for chrissake, Marquez." She told him the address then, and he raised one nasty little eyebrow.

"Lake Shore Drive? How are you going to pay for that?"

"Split five ways it's costing me exactly two hundred dollars." She had no intention of telling him about the money she'd gotten in her settlement with Frank Wills. Louis Marquez had absolutely no reason to know that. And the truth was, with the salary she earned, if she was willing to economize a little bit, she could afford the new town house.

"I'm going to have to look at this place," Marquez growled at her, and she shrugged.

"I figured you'd say that. Want to make an appointment?" she asked hopefully. But he wasn't inclined to be that accommodating.

"I'll just drop by."

"Great. Just do me a favor," she looked at him unhappily, "don't tell them who you are."

"What am I supposed to say?"

"I don't care. Tell them you're selling me a car. Tell them anything. But don't tell them I'm on probation."

"You'd better behave yourself, Grace," he looked pointedly at her, and his meaning was not lost on her, "or I might have to." And as she looked at him, for reasons she couldn't quite sort out, the ugly little man reminded her of Brenda in prison. He had her legs tied. And this time there was no Luana to save her.

Chapter 7

The group at the apartment got along splendidly. They never fought over bills, everyone paid their share of the rent, they were each nice to the other girls. They bought each other small gifts, and were generous with groceries. It was really the perfect arrangement. And Grace had never been happier in her life. Every day she wondered if it was real, or if she was dreaming.

The girls even tried to fix her up with their friends, but she drew the line at that. Groceries were one thing, but gifts of men were of no interest. She had no desire to go out with anyone, or complicate her life. At twenty, she was perfectly content to stay home and read a book, or watch TV at night. Every little freedom she had was a gift to her, and she wanted nothing more from life. Certainly not romance. Just the thought of it terrified her. She had no desire to go out with anyone, possibly ever.

Her roommates teased her about it at first, and then eventually, they decided she had a secret life. Two of them were sure she was seeing a married man, particularly when she started going out regularly, three times a week, on Monday and Thursday nights, and all day Sunday. During the week she would leave directly from work, and change there, and more often than not, she was home after midnight.

She had thought of telling them the truth, but eventually the fantasy that she was seeing someone worked a lot better for her. It made them leave her alone and stop trying to fix her up with their friends. In fact, in terms of how she wanted to live, it was perfect.

And the truth was that her three-times-a-week trysts were the heart and soul of her existence. Once she'd gotten settled in the town house with the girls, she had started looking for a place to work three times a week. Not for pay, but to give back some of what she had gotten out of life. She felt too fortunate not to do something to help others. It was something she had always promised herself, as she lay on her bunk at night, chatting with Sally, or while she worked out with Luana.

It had taken her a month to find the right place to volunteer. There had been no one she could ask, but she had read a number of articles, and there had been a special on TV about St. Mary's. It was a crisis center for women and children in an old brownstone, and when she'd first gone there, she was shocked at the condition it was in. Paint was chipping off the walls, there were bare bulbs hanging from sockets. There were kids shouting and running around everywhere, and dozens of women. Most of them looked poor, some were pregnant, all were desperate. And the one thing they had in common was that they had all been abused, some to within an inch of their lives. Many of them were scarred, some no longer functioned normally, or had been in institutions.

The place was run by Dr. Paul Weinberg, a young

psychologist who reminded her of David Glass, and after the first time she'd been there, Grace found herself aching for Molly. She would have loved to talk to her, and tell her all about it. It had been a deeply moving experience just being there. The place was mostly staffed by volunteers, and there was only a handful of paid employees, most of them doing internships for psych degrees, some of them registered nurses. The women and children living in the crisis center needed medical care, psychological help, they needed a place to live, they needed clothes, they needed tender loving care, they needed a hand to get out of the abyss they were in. Even for Grace, going to St. Mary's every week was like a light shining in the darkness. It was a place where souls were restored, and people were made whole again, as whole as they ever would be.

Just helping them helped her. It made her whole life worth something just to go there. She had volunteered for three shifts a week of seven hours each, which was a tremendous commitment. But it was a place where Grace felt at peace herself, and where she could bring peace to others. The women there had experienced many of the same things she had, and so had the children. There were pregnant fourteen-year-olds who had been raped by their fathers or brothers or uncles, seven-year-olds with glazed eyes, and women who didn't believe they would ever be free again. They were the victims of violence, and most of the time of abusive husbands. Many of them had been abused as children, too, and they were continuing to perpetuate the cycle for their own children, but they had no idea how to break it. That was what the loving staff at St. Mary's tried to teach them.

Grace was tireless when she was at St. Mary's. She

worked with the women sometimes, and most of all, she loved the children. She'd gather them close to her, hold them on her lap, and tell them stories she made up, or read to them by the hour. She took them to clinics at night, to see the doctor for injuries they'd had, or just to get exams or shots. It gave her life so much more meaning. And at times it hurt too. It hurt terribly, because it was all so familiar.

"It breaks your heart, doesn't it?" one of the nurses commented a week before Christmas. Grace had been putting a two-year-old to bed. She had been brain-damaged by her father, who was in jail now. It was odd to think that he was in jail, and her father, who had done things that were almost as bad, had died a hero.

"Yes, it does. They all do. But they're lucky." Grace smiled at her. She knew this story well. Too well. "They're here. They could still be out there getting battered. At least, for now, it's over." The real heart-break was that some of them went back. Some of the women just couldn't stay away from the men who beat them, and when they went back, they took the children with them. Some were hurt, some were killed, some never recovered in ways that couldn't be seen. But some got it, some learned, some moved on to new lives and came to understand how to be healthy. Grace spent hours talking to them, about the options they had, the freedom that was theirs, just for the taking. They were all so frightened, so blinded by their own pain, so disoriented by everything they'd been through. It made her think of the condition she had been in herself nearly three years before, when she'd been in jail and Molly tried to reach her. In a way,

Grace was doing this for her, to give back some of the love that Molly had shared with her.

"How's it going?" Paul Weinberg, their chief psychologist, and the head of the program, stopped to chat with her late one night. He had been working shoulder to shoulder with the volunteers and employees, doing intakes. Most of them came in at night. They came in hurt, they came in frightened, they came in injured in body and mind, and they needed everything the team had to give them.

"Not bad." Grace smiled at him. She didn't know him well, but she liked what she'd seen. And she respected the fact that he worked hard. They had sent two women to the hospital that night, and he had driven them there himself, while she cared for the children. Each of them had had four kids, and they were all in bed now. "It's a busy night."

"It always is right before Christmas. Everyone goes nuts over the holidays. If they're going to beat their kids and wives, this is the time to do it."

"What do they do? Run ads? 'Beat your wife now, only six more days to do it before Christmas.' " She was tired but still in good humor. She liked what she was doing.

"Something like that." He smiled at her, and poured her a cup of coffee. "Ever think of doing this for real? I mean, on a paid basis?"

"Not really," she said honestly, but she was flattered by the question, as she sipped the steaming coffee. Paul had the same woolly hair as David Glass, and the same kind eyes, but he was taller, and better-looking. "I used to think about getting a psych degree. I'm not sure I'm that good at this. But I like what I do here. I love the people, and the idea that we might make a difference. I think doing it as a volunteer is good enough for now. I don't need to get paid for it. I love it." She smiled again, and he seemed to be studying her carefully. She intrigued him.

"You're good at what you do, Grace. That's why I asked. You should think about that psych degree some more, when you have time." He was impressed by her, and he liked her.

She had worked until two o'clock that night. Half a dozen new women had come in, and there was just too much going on for her to leave them. When everyone was settled, Paul Weinberg had offered to drive her home, and she was grateful for the ride, she was exhausted.

"You were great tonight," he praised her warmly, and she thanked him. And he was surprised to see where she lived. Most people on Lake Shore didn't bother to volunteer three days a week at St. Mary's. "What's the deal?" he asked her, as they pulled up outside her house. "This is a pretty fancy place, Grace. Are you an heiress?" She laughed at the question, and she knew he was teasing her, but he was curious too. She was a very interesting young woman.

"I share a town house with four other girls." She would have invited him in but it was late. It was after two-thirty. "You'll have to come by sometime, if you can get away from St. Mary's." She was friendly, but he sensed that she wasn't flirting with him. She treated him like a brother, but his interest in her was definitely not platonic.

"I get away once in a while," he smiled. "What about you? What do you do when you're not helping women and kids in crisis?" He wanted to know more about her, even though it was late, and they were both tired.

"I work at a modeling agency," she said quietly. She liked her job, and she was proud of it, and he raised an eyebrow.

"You're a model?" He wasn't surprised, but he thought it was unusual that someone who'd have to spend so much time on themselves would give so much to others. Because she did give a lot, to the women, and the kids. He had watched her.

"I work in the office," she smiled at him, "but my roommates are all models, all four of them. You're welcome to come back and meet them." She was trying to tell him she had no interest in him. Not as a man, at least. It made him wonder if she had a boyfriend, but he didn't want to ask her.

"I'd like to come back and see you," he said pointedly. But he didn't have to do that. She was at St. Mary's three times a week, and he was always there when she was.

She volunteered for extra duty on Christmas Eve and couldn't believe how many women came in that night. She worked tirelessly, and she didn't get home till four a.m. And she managed to go to the Swansons' the next day for their annual Christmas party for all their photographers and models. It was fun, and much to her own surprise, Grace actually enjoyed it, when she went with the others. The only thing that bothered her was that Bob had danced with her several times, and she thought he held her a little too close, and once she couldn't have sworn to it, but she felt him brush her breast with his fingers as he reached for an hors d'oeuvre. She was sure it had been an accident and he hadn't even noticed. But one of her roommates made a comment later that night which made her worry. It was Marjorie who had noticed it, mother hen that she was. She was always checking on all of them, and she knew his tricks from her own experiences with him.

"Was Uncle Bobby warming up tonight?" she asked Grace, who looked startled.

"What's that supposed to mean? He was just being friendly. It's Christmas."

"Oh God, sweet innocence," she groaned, "tell me you don't believe what you're saying."

"Don't be a jerk." Grace was defending him. She didn't want to believe that Bob cheated on Cheryl. But he was certainly surrounded constantly by temptation.

"Don't be naive. You don't think he's faithful to her, do you?" Divina added to their conversation. "Last year he chased me around his office for an hour. I almost broke my knee on that damn coffee table of his, getting away from him. Oh yes, Uncle Bob is a busy boy, and it looks like you're his next target."

"Oh shit." Grace looked at them with dismay. "I thought maybe something was going on, and then I figured I'd imagined it. Maybe I did."

"In that case, so did I." Marjorie laughed at her. "I thought he was going to tear your clothes off."

"Does Cheryl know he does that stuff?" Grace asked unhappily. The last thing she wanted was to get caught in the middle, and she had no intention of inviting his advances, or of having an affair with Bob Swanson. She didn't want to have an affair with anyone. Not now anyway, and maybe never. It just wasn't what she wanted.

Paul Weinberg had called her several times to invite her to dinner, but she had declined. But on New

Year's Eve, when she was working at St. Mary's again, he insisted that she at least sit down with him for ten minutes, and share a turkey sandwich.

"Why are you avoiding me?" he accused her as she sat there with her mouth full of turkey. It took her a minute before she could answer.

"I'm not avoiding you," she said honestly. She just wasn't returning his phone calls. But she was perfectly happy eating a sandwich with him at St. Mary's.

"Sure you are," he objected. "Are you involved?"

"Yup," she said happily, and his face fell, "with St. Mary's, and my job, and my roommates. That's about it, but it's enough. More than enough. I hardly get time to read a newspaper or a book, or go to a movie. But I like it."

"Maybe you need to take some time off from here." He smiled at her, relieved that she hadn't mentioned a boyfriend. She was a great girl, and he really wanted to know her better. He was thirty-two years old, and he had never met anyone like her. She was bright, she was fun, she was deeply caring, and yet she was so shy and so distant. In some ways, she seemed very old-fashioned and he liked that. "You ought to at least get to a movie." But he hadn't been to one in months either. He had dated one of the nurses for a while, but it hadn't worked out. And he had had an eye on Grace since she'd started coming to St. Mary's.

"I don't want to take time off. I love it." She smiled at him, as she finished her sandwich.

"What are you doing here on New Year's Eve?" he questioned her, and she smiled at him again.

"I could ask you the same question, couldn't I?"

"I work here," he said smugly.

"So do I. You just don't pay me."

"I still think you should think about becoming a professional," but before he could say any more to her, they were both called away in separate directions. It was another late night for her, and she didn't see him until the following Thursday. And that night he offered to drive her home again, but she took a cab. She didn't want to encourage him. But he finally cornered her on Sunday at St. Mary's.

"Will you have lunch with me?"

"Now?" she looked startled. They had four new families to talk to.

"Not now. Next week. Whenever you want. I'd like to see you." He looked boyish and embarrassed when he asked her.

"Why?" The word just slipped out, and he laughed at the question.

"Are you kidding? Have you looked in the mirror this week? Besides which, you're intelligent and you're fun, and I'd like to get to know you."

"There's not much to know. I'm actually pretty dull," she said, and he laughed again.

"Are you brushing me off?"

"Maybe," she said honestly. "Actually, I don't date."

"You just work?" He looked amused, and she nodded in answer to his question. "Perfect. We ought to get along fine. All I do is work too, but I figure one of us has to break the cycle."

"Why? It suits us." She suddenly seemed very distant and a little frightened, which made him wonder about her.

"Will you just have lunch with me once for heaven's sake? Just try it. You have to eat. I'll come uptown if you want, during the week. Whatever you like." But she didn't like. She liked him, but she didn't want to date any man, and she didn't know how to tell him.

Eventually, she agreed to have lunch with him the following Saturday. It was a freezing cold day and they went to La Scala for pasta.

"All right, now tell the truth. What brought you to St. Mary's?"

"The bus." She grinned at him, and she looked very young and playful.

"Very cute," and then suddenly he wondered. "How old are you anyway?" He figured her for twenty-five or -six, because she was so mature in handling the battered women and children.

"I'm twenty," she said proudly, as though it was a major accomplishment, and he almost groaned as she said it. That explained a lot of things, or at least he thought so. "I'll be twenty-one next summer."

"Great. You make me feel like I'm robbing the cradle. I'll be thirty-three in August."

"You remind me a lot of someone I once knew, a friend of mine. He's an attorney in California."

"And you're in love with him?" Paul Weinberg asked unhappily. He knew that somewhere in her life there was an explanation for why she remained so distant. Her extreme youth was possibly part of it, but he knew there had to be more to it.

But she was laughing at him, explaining about David Glass. "No, he's married, and he's having a baby."

"So who's the lucky guy?"

"What guy?" she looked puzzled. "I told you, there's no one."

"Do you like guys?" It was an odd question, he knew, but these days, it was worth asking.

"I don't know," she said honestly, looking up at him, and for an instant his heart fell, and then he saw something else as he watched her. "I've never dated."

"Not at all?" He didn't believe her.

"Nope. Not at all."

"That's quite a record at twenty." It was also quite a challenge. "Any particular reason why not?" They had ordered pasta and were enjoying lunch by then as he asked her questions.

"Oh, a few reasons, I guess. I guess mostly I don't want to."

"Grace, that's crazy."

"Is it?" she said cautiously. "Maybe not. Maybe it's how I need to live my life. No one else can judge what's right for me." And then as he watched her, he knew it, and he realized what a fool he'd been. That was why she'd come to St. Mary's. To help others like her.

"Did you have a bad experience?" he asked gently, and she trusted him, but only to a point. She wasn't going to tell him all her secrets.

"You could say that. Pretty bad. But no worse than what you see every day at St. Mary's. It takes a toll, I guess."

"It doesn't have to. You can get over it. Are you seeing anyone? Professionally, I mean."

"I was. We were good friends. She died in an accident last summer." He was sorry for her, as she said it, she looked so lonely.

"What about your family? Have they been any help?"

She smiled, she knew he wanted to help her, but only time could do that. And she knew she had to help herself now. "I don't have any family. But it's not as bad as it sounds. I have friends, and a great job. And all the nice people at St. Mary's."

"I'd like to help, if you think I can." But the kind of therapy he had in mind frightened her too much. Although she knew that he would have seen her as a therapist too, if she'd wanted. But what he really wanted was to date her. And she knew she wasn't ready, and maybe never would be.

"I'll call if I need help." She smiled at him, and they both ordered coffee. They spent a lovely afternoon, walking around the lake, and talking about many things. But he knew now that he couldn't pursue her. It was too dangerous for her. Just knowing how he felt had already made her step back and put some distance between them.

"Grace," he said when he dropped her off at her place again, "I don't ever want to hurt you. I just want to be there, if you want a friend," and then he smiled boyishly, and he looked almost handsome. "I wouldn't mind more than that too, but I don't want to push you." And she was so young. That was part of it. He didn't dare press her if she wasn't ready.

"Thanks. I had a great time." She had, and they had lunch a few more times after that. He wasn't ready to give up completely, and she enjoyed his company, but it never grew to be more than a warm friendship. In some ways he had taken David's place in her life, if not Molly's.

Between work, her roommates, and her volunteer work, things rolled along smoothly until the spring. And then Lou Marquez started giving Grace trouble again. She didn't know it, but he had just broken up with his girlfriend and he was looking for trouble. He started showing up at Grace's apartment. The others always teased her about him. He never explained who he was, nor did Grace, she just said he was a friend of her father's. But whenever he came around, he asked all the girls a lot of questions. Did they do drugs? Did they like modeling? Did they meet a lot of guys that way? He even asked Brigitte for a date once, and Grace had raised hell with him when she reported to him at his office.

"You have no right to do that to me. You have no right to show up and harass my friends."

"I can harass anyone I want. And besides, she'd been giving me the eye for half an hour. I know what girls like that want. Don't kid yourself, sweetheart. She ain't no virgin."

"No, but she's not blind either," Grace flung at him, and he was madder than ever. She was getting braver with him mostly because he was so outrageous.

"Just be grateful I haven't told them that I'm your probation officer, and about your time in prison."

"You do that, and I'll report you. I'll sue you for embarrassing me and causing me to lose face in my own home, and with business associates."

"Bullshit. You're not gonna sue anyone."

She knew she wouldn't, but she had to stand up to him. Like most bullies, she knew, he'd back off if she really pressed him. He stopped coming around as often after that, and she continued to report to him weekly in his office.

When Brigitte took a three month modeling job in Tokyo in May, they found another girl to take her place. This time it was Mireille, a French girl. She was from the South of France, from Nice, and she was nineteen. And everyone really liked her. She had a passion for all things American, particularly popcorn and hot dogs. And she loved American boys, but not as much as they loved her. She was out every night from the moment she got there. Which left Divina, Marjorie, Allyson, and Grace to hang out with each other whenever they weren't busy.

The Swansons gave a party on the Fourth of July at their country house in Barrington Hills, and all the models drove out there for the day and evening. Grace invited Paul, and he had a field day ogling the models. Her roommates thought he was very nice, and wanted to know if he was the guy she spent all her time with.

"More or less," she said coyly. And they loved it.

And the girls gave her a birthday party after that. It was a big surprise, and they invited everyone from the agency, and Paul of course. It was Grace's twenty-first birthday. And afterwards, they and Paul sat in the patio, and she couldn't help thinking how far her life had come in the past year. He didn't know it, of course, but she had spent her last two birthdays in prison. And now she was here, with him, living with a bunch of beautiful girls, and working for a modeling agency. It was staggering when she thought about it sometimes. It made her think of Luana and Sally, and Molly and David. And it made her sad when she realized that she was doing just what Luana had said she should. She was taking them out, like memories, touching them with her heart from time to time, but only for a fleeting moment. And then she'd go back to her own life, and remember them briefly. But they were gone, all of them. Forever. She hadn't heard from David since his son was born in March, and she had finally stopped writing to Luana and Sally. They'd never answered her letters.

She looked up and saw a falling star, and without waiting, she closed her eyes, and thought about them, and then she made a wish that one day, it really all would be behind her. For the moment, Lou Marquez was still there, threatening to reveal her secrets to her friends. There was still someone with a leash on her. And she just hoped that one day she'd be free at last, for the first time in her life, with no one to be afraid of.

"What did you wish for just then?" Paul asked, watching her. He had never forced her to move ahead to a relationship she didn't want. But he still hoped that one day she'd be ready for him. He knew what he would have wished on a falling star. He would have wished for her to want him.

"I was just thinking about some old friends," she smiled sadly at him, "and hoping that one day all the bad times will be a distant memory." His heart went out to her as she said it.

"Aren't they by now?" He didn't know how far behind her the bad times were, or how close. She had never told him, and he hadn't pressed her. "Aren't they gone?" he asked gently.

"Almost," she smiled at him, glad that he was her friend, ". . . almost . . . Maybe next year."

Chapter 8

The Swansons continued to try to talk Grace into modeling for them, but instead she got a fat raise and became Cheryl's secretary, and both Swansons claimed that it was really Grace who ran the agency for them. She was efficient, she was fast, she was organized, and bright and quiet. She knew all of the girls who worked for them, and most of the men, and everyone liked her. Things were lively at the apartment too. Brigitte was back from Tokyo by then, but she had moved in with a photographer, instead of the girls at the town house. Allyson had gone to L.A. for a part in a movie. And Divina was modeling in Paris. Only Marjorie and Grace were left, and Mireille, who was threatening to move in with her latest boyfriend. Two new girls moved in as fast as the first two left. And at Christmas, Marjorie announced her engagement. But it was never a problem for Grace to find new roommates. Girls arrived in Chicago constantly, to find modeling work, and they always needed an apartment.

Louis Marquez, her probation officer, came to check her out regularly. And at least once a month, he forced Grace to take a drug test. But she was always clean, which was a disappointment to him. Out of sheer meanness, he would have liked to bust her.

"What a little shit he is," Marjorie said, when he
showed up again after Christmas, to check out their
new roommates. "Your father sure had some sleazy
friends," she said, annoyed that he had put a hand on
her behind again, while pretending to reach for an
ashtray. He reeked of cigarettes and sweat, and every
single piece of clothing he had was polyester. "Why
don't you just tell him to get lost?" she said, shuddering, after he left. He made you want to take a bath
every time you saw him. Grace would have liked nothing better than to tell him not to come to the house
anymore. But she had no choice. She had another nine
months of probation, and then the nightmare would
be over.

In March, the Swansons invited her to go to New
York with them, and she had to tell them that she
couldn't. She asked her probation officer for permis-
sion to go with them, and he absolutely refused to let
her do it. And she had to tell them that she had another commitment. She was disappointed not to go,
but she managed to keep busy anyway. She still spent
two nights a week and Sundays at St. Mary's. She saw
Paul Weinberg whenever she went, and she was very
fond of him, but she also knew that he had given up
waiting for her and was seriously involved with one of
the nurses.

Cheryl Swanson tried to fix her up with dates from
time to time, but Grace continued to have no interest
in that direction. She was too afraid, and too deeply
scarred by everything that had happened. Going out
with anyone always reminded her of the horrors she
had experienced with her father.

Until June. When Marcus Anders walked into the
agency to see Cheryl. He was one of the best-looking

men Grace had ever seen, with thick blond hair and a boyish smile, and freckles. He looked half man, half boy, and at first Grace thought he was one of their models.

He had just arrived from Detroit, and his portfolio was very impressive. He had done a lot of commercial work, and he was heading for the big time. He had thought about going to L.A. or New York, but he wanted to make it to the top in stages, which was smart of him. He was very cool, and very sure of himself, and he had a great sense of humor. He teased Grace a little bit, after his interview, and chatted with her about where to look for an apartment. She recommended some rental agencies, and introduced him to some of the models as they came in. But he didn't seem particularly interested in them. He saw models constantly. It was Grace who really caught his eye, and before he left, he asked about photographing her, just for fun, but she laughed and shook her head. She had had similar offers before, and she had no interest in them.

"No, thanks. I keep well away from cameras."

"What's that all about? Wanted by the cops? Hiding something?"

"Absolutely. I'm wanted by the FBI," she grinned easily. He was fun to talk to, but she didn't want to be snowed by him, or anyone. A lot of the photographers used their cameras to lure women. "I'm just not hung up on having my picture taken."

"Smart girl." He admired her, and he sat across her desk from her, looking breathtakingly young and healthy and handsome. "But you'd photograph incredibly. You have fabulous bones, and wonderful eyes," and as he looked at her, he could see there was more there than he had first suspected. There was sorrow in her eyes, an old deep pain that she hid from the world, but not from him. Marcus could see it plainly, and she turned away with a laugh and a shrug, sensing that he was coming too close to her, and she didn't want that. "Why don't we just play sometime, and see what we come up with? You might put the rest of these girls out of business." It was the only thing he understood, the only thing he truly loved. He had had a lifelong love affair with his camera.

"I wouldn't want to frighten them," Grace teased, turning to look at him again. She was wearing a tight black skirt and a black sweater. She had learned to dress with a certain amount of big city sophistication, after nearly two years of being with the Swansons.

"Give it a thought." Marcus smiled at her, and unreeled his long legs from the black leather chair in her office. "I'll be back on Monday."

But he called her again the next day, just to chat and tell her about the studios he'd looked at. According to him, they were all terrible, and he was really lonely. Grace laughed at him, and pretended to be sympathetic, and then he asked her out to dinner.

"Sorry. Can't," she said curtly, she was used to fending off men. It was never a problem. "I'm busy tonight." She always made it sound as though there were men in her life, but of course all there were were battered women and children.

"Tomorrow then."

"I've got to work late. We're shooting a big commercial with nine girls, and Cheryl wants me to be there."

"No prob. I'll come too. Come on." He sounded like a kid again, and it touched her a little bit, in spite of her resolve not to let it. "I'm a new boy in town, I don't know anyone. I'm lonely."

"Oh come on . . . Marcus . . . don't be a spoiled brat."

"But I am," he said proudly, and they both laughed. In the end, in spite of herself, she let him go to the commercial with them, and he was very helpful. There were so many people there that no one even noticed an extra body on the set. All the models seemed to like him a lot. He was bright, he was fun, and he wasn't as arrogant as a lot of the photographers were. He seemed like a terrific guy, and after he had shown up at the agency every day for a week, Grace finally relented and let him take her out to dinner. It was the first date she had had since Paul Weinberg.

Marcus couldn't believe she was only twenty-one when she told him, she was so mature for her age, and she had a sophisticated look to her that made her seem older. She still wore her thick auburn hair pulled straight back, but she often wore it in a chignon now, and she wore the kind of clothes she saw the models wear, whenever she could afford them. But Marcus was used to young girls who looked older than they were. Once or twice, he'd even been foolish enough to go out with fifteen-year-old models, thinking they were older.

"So what do you do yourself when you're not working?" he asked with interest over dinner at Gordon. He had just found a studio, it was a sensational loft, he'd explained, with living quarters and everything he needed.

"I keep busy enough." She had started bicycling, and one of her new roommates was teaching her to play tennis. They were pastimes she'd never had time for before. The only sports she'd ever done were a little weight lifting and some jogging in prison, but she wasn't about to tell him about her two years at Dwight. She never intended to tell anyone that, for the rest of her life. She had taken Luana's advice to heart, and left it firmly behind her.

"Do you have a lot of friends?" he asked, intrigued by her, she was very closed and very private, and yet he sensed that there was a wealth of woman within her.

"Enough," she smiled, but the truth was, she didn't, and he had already heard that. He had asked a lot of people about her. He already knew that she never went out with men, that she kept to herself, that she was very shy, and she did some kind of volunteer work. He asked her about it over coffee, and she told him a little about St. Mary's.

"Why that? What's so intriguing to you about battered women?"

"They need help desperately," she said in a serious tone, "women in that situation think they have no way out, no options. They stand on the edge of a burning building and you have to pull them out of it, they won't just jump to freedom." She knew better than anyone. She had never thought there was any way to get free of her own situation. She had had to kill to save herself, and then at what cost. She wanted others to have to go to less extreme measures than she did.

"What makes you care about them so much, Grace?" He was so curious about her, and she gave away so little. He had been conscious all through dinner how cautious she was, how outwardly friendly, but inwardly guarded.

"It's just something I want to do. It means a lot to me, especially working with the kids. They're so helpless, and so damaged by everything they've been through," just as she was, and she knew it. She knew fully how scarred she was, and she didn't want them to be too. It was her gift to them, and it made her life worth living, knowing that her pain would serve someone else, and keep them from traveling the same agonizing road she had. "I don't know, I guess I have a knack for it. I think about going back to school, and getting a psych degree sometimes, but I never seem to have time, with work and everything . . . maybe someday."

"You don't need a psych degree," he grinned, and she felt something for him she'd never felt before, and it frightened her more than a little. He was very appealing. "You need a man," he concluded.

"What makes you so sure?" She smiled at him. He was like a big beautiful kid, as he reached out and took her hand in his own.

"Because you're lonely as hell, in spite of everything you say, and all the bravado about how great your life is. My guess is you've never had a real man at all, in fact," he narrowed his eyes and looked at her appraisingly, as she laughed, "I'd bet my last ten cents you're a virgin." She made no comment and took her hand away gently. "I'm right, aren't I, Grace?" There was so much he didn't know, and she shrugged noncommittally. "I am," he said, with confidence, sure of exactly what she needed. Tutored by the right man, he sensed that she could be an extraordinary woman.

"Standard solutions are not the answer for everyone, Marcus," she said, sounding a lot older than twenty-one again. "Some people are a little more complicated than that." But Marcus thought he knew her and she was just scared, and shy, and very young, and she probably came from a very straitlaced background.

"Tell me about your family. What are your parents like?"

"Dead," she said coolly. "They died when I was in high school." That explained some of it to him, she had had a major loss, and had been alone for several years. That was some of the loneliness, he suspected.

"Any brothers or sisters?"

"Nope. Just me. No relatives at all, in fact." No wonder she seemed so grown up, she had obviously been on her own for years, he surmised. He had painted a portrait of her, entirely of his own invention.

"I'm surprised you didn't run out and marry your high school sweetheart," he said with new respect in his voice. "Most people would do something like that, if they found themselves all alone at your age." She was a strong girl, in fact she wasn't a girl at all, she was a woman. And he liked that.

"I didn't have a high school sweetheart to marry me," she said matter-of-factly.

"What did you do? Live with friends?"

"More or less. I lived with a bunch of people." In prison and jail . . . she wondered what he would say if she told him the truth. She couldn't even begin to imagine his reaction. He would surely be horrified if she told him she'd killed her father. And somehow the irony of it made her laugh. He really had no idea who she was, or what she was about. No one did. The people who knew her were all gone now, like Molly, or David, and Luana and Sally. She had stopped sending postcards to them and she didn't hear from David anymore. There was no point writing to him anyway. Her life was her own now. All she could do for the people she had cared for, and all the others, was the kind of work she was doing at St. Mary's. It was her way of paying back all the people who'd been kind to her over the years. There were so few, but in their memory, she wanted to help others.

"It must be rough for you on holidays," he said sympathetically. "Like Christmas."

"Not anymore," she smiled. Not after Dwight. Christmas could never be as bad as that again, no matter where she was. "You get used to it."

"You're a brave girl, Grace." Braver than he knew. Much, much braver.

They went out for drinks after dinner that night, to a place he'd discovered that had an old jukebox and fifties music. And on Sunday they went bicycling around the lake. It was a beautiful warm June afternoon and everything was blossoming. And in spite of all her warnings to herself, she loved being with him. He was very patient with her, and didn't try to rush anything. He seemed to understand that she needed time, and a lot of tender loving care before moving forward. But he was willing to spend the time with her, and he didn't do anything more than kiss her. He was the first man she had ever even been kissed by, other than her father. And even that was frightening at first, but she had to admit, she liked it.

But as usual, Marjorie was full of warnings when Grace came home after spending a Saturday afternoon with him three weeks after he'd come to town. They had been out buying secondhand equipment for his studio. The agency had already started assigning work to Marcus, and the Swansons were very pleased. He had a lot of talent. "Enjoy him while you can," Cheryl had said with a smile, "he won't be here long. I'll bet

he's in New York within a year, or Paris. He's too good
to last here."

But Marjorie had other things to say about him.
She had a network of friends all over the world, who
were all models. And a friend of hers in Detroit had
had some ominous things to report about Marcus.

"She told me he raped some girl a few years ago,
Grace. Watch it. I don't trust him."

"That's nonsense. He told me all about that. She
was sixteen and she looked twenty-five. And according
to Marcus, she practically raped him." Marcus had told
her she had practically torn his clothes off. It had been
four years earlier and he had been naive and foolish.
And he had seemed genuinely embarrassed when he
told her.

"She was thirteen, and her father tried to have
him put in jail," Marjorie said sternly. She didn't like
stories like that. There were lots of stories of abuse of
young models. "Supposedly, Marcus bought his way
out of it. And there was some other story like that,
maybe that was your sixteen-year-old. And Eloise said
he did a lot of porno work to pay the rent. He doesn't
sound like such a nice guy to me."

"That's bullshit," Grace said, defending him tartly.
He wasn't that kind of guy. She could tell. If there was
one thing she had learned from her experiences, and
working at the agency, it was people. "People always
say stuff like that when they're jealous. She probably
had the hots for him, and he didn't go for her so she's
pissed off," Grace said matter-of-factly, annoyed that
Marjorie was being so unfair to him. He didn't deserve
that. She was so hard on people sometimes, and so
uptight. She was like a real house mother. But Grace
knew she didn't need one.

"Eloise isn't like that," Marjorie said, defending her friend in Detroit. "And you'd better watch yourself. You're not as smart as you think you are. You don't go out with enough guys to be able to smell out the bad ones."

"You don't know what you're talking about." It was the first time she had gotten really furious at Marjorie, and her eyes were blazing. "He's a really decent guy, and he's never done more than kiss me."

"Great. I'm glad for you. I'm just telling you, the guy has a lousy reputation. Listen to that, Grace. Don't be stupid."

"Thank you for the warning," she said, with a tone of irritation. And five minutes later she went to her room and slammed the door behind her. What rotten things to say about poor Marcus. But their business was like that sometimes. People who didn't get jobs blamed photographers, and photographers who wanted to score and didn't said terrible things about models, claiming that they were drug addicts, or had come on to them. Models claimed they'd been raped. There were a lot of stories like that in the business, and Grace knew it. But so did Marjorie. She knew better than to listen to that kind of gossip. And shooting porno was really a lot of nonsense. He had told Grace that he had even waited on tables at times in order to pay the rent on his studio in Detroit. He had never said a word about porno, and even as unattractive as that was, Grace knew instinctively that he would have. He was a very open, straightforward person, and he was very honest about confessing his faults and past sins to her. She had never trusted anyone in recent years as much as she trusted Marcus.

They went to the Swansons' Fourth of July party

together in Barrington Hills, and Cheryl begged him
openly to get Grace to let him take some shots of her.
She was growing prettier by the day, and she thought
that Marcus was just the right man to break the ice and
get Grace to do it. But Grace laughed at them both,
and shook her head, as she always did. She had absolutely no interest in being a model.

Marcus talked to a lot of the models at the party
that afternoon, and he seemed to get along with everyone, and that night Marjorie told her pointedly that he
had made dates with two of them, and she thought
Grace should know it.

"He's not married to me," she said, defending
him again. They weren't sleeping with each other after
all. He had asked her to, and she had said she wasn't
ready to make that kind of commitment. But she was
close to it. She just needed more time with him, although she trusted him already. She thought she
might be falling in love with him. In a way, Marjorie's
telling her about the other girls pushed her a little
further in that direction. But she didn't dare ask him
about it when she saw him the next day, and he asked
about taking her pictures.

"Come on, Grace . . . it's not going to hurt anything . . . just for us . . . for me . . . you're so
beautiful . . . let me take some shots of you. I won't
show them to anyone if you don't like them. I promise.
Cheryl is right. You'd be fabulous as a model."

"But I don't want to be a model," she said, and
really meant it.

"Why not, for heaven's sake? You've got everything
it takes. Height, looks, style, you're thin enough, young
enough . . . most girls would give anything to have
what you've got, and have a chance. Grace, be sensible

. . . or at least just try it. What could be easier than to do it with me? Besides, I want to have some pictures of you. I've been seeing you for a month, and I miss you when you're not around.'' He teased, and nuzzled her neck, and much to her own amazement, by the end of the afternoon, she relented, just for him. And she made him promise not to show anyone the pictures. They made a date for a shoot the following Saturday, and he warned her that she'd better not cancel.

''I don't know what you're so shy about.'' He laughed as they made spaghetti in his kitchen in the loft. And that night they came closer to making love than ever before, but in the end, she said she needed to wait. It was the wrong time of the month for her, and that wasn't the way she wanted to start their relationship. Besides, she wanted to buy a little more time, and a week wouldn't hurt anything. The way she felt about him, it would only make it better.

She worried about their photo session all week, she hated the idea of being the center of attention like that, and of being a sex object. She hated everything it stood for. She liked working with the models at the agency, but she had never wanted to be one of them. It was really only for Marcus that she was doing it, and for fun. He made everything fun to do, as long as she did it with him. And the next Saturday she turned up promptly at ten o'clock, at the studio, as she'd promised. She'd been at St. Mary's the night before, she'd worked late, and she was tired.

He made her some coffee when she arrived, and he had already set up. There was a huge white leather chair, and a white fox throw covering part of it, and all he wanted was for her to sprawl on it in her jeans, and a white T-shirt. He made her untie her hair, and it fell over her shoulders lavishly, and then he exchanged the T-shirt for his own starched white shirt, and little by little he got her to unbutton it, but the shots were all very chaste and modest. And she was surprised by how much fun it was. He took her in a thousand poses, he had great music on, and each shot was almost like a caress as he danced around her.

They were still taking photographs at noon, and he handed her a glass of wine, and promised her a huge lunch of homemade pasta when she was finished.

"You know the way to a girl's heart at least," she laughed, and he stopped inches from her and peered around the camera sadly.

"I wish I did . . . I've been working awfully hard at it," he confessed, and she blushed and looked demure as he took a shot of her that he was thrilled with. Cheryl was going to love these. "Am I getting any closer, Grace? . . . to your heart, I mean," he whispered sensually, and she felt a hot flush shoot through her. The wine had made her feel woozy, and she remembered that she hadn't bothered to eat breakfast. It had been stupid to drink wine on an empty stomach, and he'd already poured her a second one, and she was halfway through it. She didn't usually drink wine in the daytime, and she was surprised at how strong this was, when he asked her shyly to take off her jeans, pointing out that the shirt was long enough to cover her completely. In fact it was halfway to her knees, but she balked at taking her jeans off. But finally, when he promised her again that he wouldn't even show Cheryl the shots, she slipped them off, and lay back against the fur again with bare legs and feet and only his shirt covering her, unbuttoned to the waist, but not revealing anything. Her breasts were covered. She felt herself drift off to sleep slowly then, as she lay on the chair, and when she woke up he was kissing her, and she felt his hands caressing her all over. She felt his lips and hands, and she kept hearing clicks, and seeing flashes, but she couldn't tell what was happening, everything was swirling around her, and she kept drifting off and waking up. She felt sick, but she couldn't move, or stop, or get up, or open her eyes and he kept kissing her, and then she felt him touching her, and for a minute she thought she felt an old familiar feeling of terror, but when she opened her eyes again, she knew she had been dreaming. Marcus was standing there, looking down at her, and smiling at her. Her mouth felt dry, and she felt strangely nauseous.

"What's happening?" She felt frightened and sick, and there were spots in front of her eyes now, and he was just standing there, laughing.

"I think the wine got the best of you."

"I'm really sorry." She was mortified, but then he knelt down next to her and kissed her so hard it made her dizzy again. But she liked it. There was a heady feeling to what was happening, she wanted it to stop, and yet she didn't.

"I'm not sorry at all," he whispered from between her breasts. "You're gorgeous when you're drunk." She lay back and closed her eyes then, and his tongue trailed tantalizingly down her stomach to her underwear, and then forced its way inside it, licking lower and lower, until suddenly her eyes flew open, and she jumped. She couldn't. "Come on, baby . . . please . . ." How long did she expect him to wait? "Please . . . Grace . . . I need you . . ."

"I can't," she whispered hoarsely, wanting him, but too afraid to let him take her. All she could think

of now was the night her father had died, as the room
spun around, and she felt sick again. The wine had
really done her in, and suddenly she felt like throwing
up and she was afraid to say it. Marcus was touching
her then, and feeling places where no one had been in
years, no one had ever been except her father. "I
can't . . ." she said again. But she couldn't muster the
strength to stop him.

"Oh for chrissake, why not?" For the first time
since he'd known her, Marcus lost his temper, but as
he did, she felt the wine take over again, and with no
warning, she swooned and fainted. And when she woke
up, he was lying beside her on the huge white leather
chair covered in the white fur, and he had all his
clothes off. She was still wearing his shirt and her underwear, and he was smiling at her. And all she could
feel was a sudden wave of terror. She couldn't remember anything except passing out. She didn't know how
long she'd been out, or what they'd done, but it was
obvious that something had happened.

"Marcus, what happened?" she asked him in a terrified voice, feeling very sick now, as she pulled his
shirt tight around her.

"Wouldn't you like to know." He looked amused,
he was laughing at her. She had been completely unconscious. "You were great, babe. Unforgettable." He
sounded cold and hard and angry.

"How can you say that?" She started to cry. "How
could you do that with me passed out?" She felt her
stomach rise to her throat again, and her chest tight-
ened with asthma, but she felt too sick to look for her
inhaler. She couldn't even sit up and look around her.

"How do you know what I did?" he said evilly, as
he walked across the room, his splendid body exposed

for her to see it. "Maybe I always work like this. It's so much cooler." He turned to face her then, so she could see all of him, and she looked away, trying not to see it. This was not how she had wanted their first time to be, and she didn't know if she was more hurt than angry. It was what it had always been for her. Rape. It was what he had wanted. "Actually," he went on, as he strolled slowly back toward her, "nothing happened, Grace. I'm not a necrophiliac. I don't go around fucking corpses. And that's what you are, isn't it? You're dead. You go around pretending you're alive, and teasing men, but when it gets down to the big time, you just roll over and play dead, and dish out a lot of excuses."

"They're not excuses," she said, sitting up awkwardly. She had found her jeans on the floor, and she pulled them on and then stood up unsteadily. She felt awful. And she turned away a moment later to take his shirt off and put her own on. She didn't even waste time putting her bra on. She felt too sick to worry about it. Her head was both pounding and reeling. "I can't explain it, that's all," she said in answer to his accusations. She was too sick to discuss it, and she kept having the feeling that something terrible had happened. She remembered kissing him, and his saying things to her, and for some reason she remembered lying there with him, but she couldn't remember anything else. She kept hoping it was all a nightmare induced by too much wine on an empty stomach. She kept having flashes of him tantalizing her with his body. But she had no memory of his raping her. And she was almost certain that he hadn't.

"Even virgins fuck eventually. What makes you think you're so special?" Marcus was still furious at her.

She was a tease and he was bored with it. There were
plenty of other girls he could have had, and he had
every intention of having all of them. He had had it
with Grace Adams.

"I'm just scared, that's all. It's hard to explain."
Why was he so angry at her? And why did she keep
remembering him naked above her?

"You're not scared," he said, picking up his camera and making no effort whatsoever to put his clothes
on. "You're psychotic. You looked like you were going
to kill someone when I put a hand on you. What is it
with you anyway? Are you gay?"

"No, I'm not." But he wasn't far from the truth
about her killing someone, and she knew it. Maybe she
would always be that way. Maybe she would never be
able to have sex with anyone. But she wanted to know
more than anything now, for sure, if anything had happened while she was unconscious. She wasn't sure at all
what he had done while she was passed out. And she
didn't like the feeling of the flashes she was having.

"Tell me the truth. What did you do to me? Did
you make love to me?" she said with tears in her eyes.

"What difference does it make? I told you I didn't
do anything. Don't you trust me?" After what had just
happened, not really. He had taken advantage of her
while she was out cold. He had gotten her to undress,
almost nude, but not entirely, and had taken his own
clothes off. It certainly didn't look like a wholesome
scene when she woke up, but nor did she feel as
though she'd been raped. She knew that would have
been a familiar feeling. Remembering that comforted
her. Maybe he had done nothing more than she remembered. A lot of fondling and kissing and touching.
And she had liked most of it, but she knew that it had

scared her. She had the feeling that he'd been close to making love to her, but then he hadn't. Maybe that was why he was so angry. It was plain old frustration.

"How can I trust you after what you just did?" she said softly, fighting a fresh wave of nausea.

"What did I do? Try to make love to you? It's not against the law, you know. People do it every day . . . some people even want to . . . And you're twenty-one, aren't you? So what are you going to do? Call the cops because I kissed you and took my pants off?" But she felt raped anyway. He had taken photographs she hadn't wanted him to take, and seduced her into exposing more of herself than she wanted, and he had tried to take advantage of her sexually when she was drunk. The odd thing was that she had never gotten drunk on a glass and a half of wine before. And even now, she felt ghastly. "I'm sick of playing games with you, Grace. I've invested a lot of time, and patience, and Saturday afternoons and pasta dinners. We should have been in bed two weeks ago. I'm not fourteen. I don't do shit like this. There are lots of other girls out there who are normal." It was a mean thing to say to her, but as she watched him now, in his natural habitat, so full of himself, as he finally put his pants on, she realized that he wasn't the man she'd thought he was. He had a real mean streak, and it was obvious he didn't love her. He had only been nice to her in order to get what he wanted.

"I'm sorry I wasted so much of your time," she said coldly.

"So am I," he said nonchalantly. "I'll send the contact sheets to the agency. You can pick the shots you like."

"I don't want to see them. You can burn them when you get them."

"Believe me, I will," he said acidly. "And you're right, by the way. You'd make a lousy model."

"Thanks," she said unhappily, as she put on her sweater. In a single instant, he had become a stranger. And then, she picked up her bag and walked to the door, and looked back over her shoulder at him. He was standing at a table taking film out of his camera, and she wondered how she could have been so wrong. But then, standing there, looking at him, the room spun around again and she almost fainted. She wondered if she was coming down with the flu, or just upset over everything that had happened. "I'm sorry, Marcus," she said sadly. He just shrugged, and turned away from her, acting as though he were the injured party. He had had fun with her for a while, but it was time to move on. Pretty girls, in his life, were a dime a dozen.

He never said a word to her as she left, and she practically crawled downstairs from his loft, hailed a cab, and gave the driver the address of the town house. And when they got there, the driver had to shake her to wake her up and tell her what the fare was.

"I'm sorry," she said thickly, feeling sick again. She was feeling really awful.

"You okay, miss?" He looked concerned as she handed him the fare and a good tip, and he watched her go inside. She was weaving.

And as she closed the door behind her, once she got in, Marjorie looked up from the couch. She'd been doing her nails, and she was horrified when she saw Grace. She was so pale she was green, and she looked as though she was going to pass out before she got to her bedroom.

"Hey! . . . are you okay?" Marjorie asked, jumping up and going to her, as Grace started to collapse in her arms. Marjorie helped her to her bed, and Grace lay there, feeling like she was dying.

"I think I have the flu," she said, slurring her words again. "Maybe I've been poisoned."

"I thought you were with Marcus," she said with a frown. "Weren't you going to shoot with him today?" Marjorie vaguely remembered.

Grace only nodded. She felt too sick to tell her the details, and she wasn't sure she wanted to anyway. But as she lay on her bed, she started to drift off again, just the way she had in the white chair, and then when she'd woken up and found him naked beside her. Maybe when she opened her eyes again, Marjorie would be naked, too. She laughed out loud, with her eyes closed, and Marjorie stared at her and went to get a flashlight and a damp cloth. She was back two minutes later, and put the cold cloth on Grace's forehead. Grace opened an eye but only briefly.

"What happened?" Marjorie asked firmly.

"I'm not sure," Grace said honestly with closed eyes, and then she started to cry softly. "It was awful."

"I'll bet it was," Marjorie said angrily. She could figure it out for herself, even if Grace couldn't. She turned the flashlight on, and told Grace to open her eyes.

"I can't," she said miserably. "My head hurts too much. I'm dying."

"Open them anyway. I want to see something."

"Nothing's wrong with my eyes . . . 's my stomach . . . head . . ."

"Come on, open them . . . just for a second."

Grace fought to open her eyes, and Marjorie shone the flashlight in them, which felt like daggers in her head to Grace, but Marjorie had seen what she wanted.

"Where were you today?"

"I told you . . . with Marcus . . ." Her eyes were closed again, and the room was spinning.

"Did you eat or drink anything?" There was silence. "Grace, tell me the truth, did you do any drugs?"

"Of course not!" She opened her eyes long enough to look insulted, and then fought to prop herself up on her elbows. "I've never done drugs in my life."

"You have now," Marjorie said angrily. "You're loaded to the gills."

"With what?" Grace looked frightened.

"I don't know . . . coke . . . Spanish fly . . . downers . . . LSD . . . some weird mixture. God only knows . . . what did he give you?"

"All I had was two glasses of wine . . . I didn't even finish the second one." She laid her head back on the pillow again. It made her feel too sick to sit up. She felt even worse than she had at the loft. It was as though the effect of whatever he had given her had heightened.

"He must have spiked it. Did you feel weird while you were there?"

"Oh did I . . ." Grace moaned. "It was so strange." She looked up at her friend and started to cry. "I couldn't tell what was a dream . . . and what was real . . . he was kissing me and doing things . . . and then I was asleep, and when I woke up he was naked . . . but he said nothing happened."

"Sonofabitch, he raped you!" Marjorie wanted to kill him, on behalf of Grace, and their entire sex. She had never liked him. She hated bastards like that, particularly the ones who took advantage of kids or greenhorns. It was such easy sport, and so damn vicious. But Grace just looked confused as she went on.

"I don't even know if he did . . . I don't think so . . . I don't remember."

"Why did he have his clothes off then?" Marjorie said suspiciously. "Did you have sex with him before you passed out?"

"No. I just kissed him . . . I didn't want to . . . I was scared . . . I did want to . . . but then I tried to stop him. And he was really mad at me. He said I was psychotic, and a tease . . . he said he wouldn't make love to me because it would be like . . . like doing it to a dead body . . ."

"But he let you think he did, is that it? What a nice guy." Marjorie was dripping venom for Marcus. "Did he take pictures of you with your clothes off?"

"I was wearing underpants and his shirt when I passed out," or at least that was what she remembered and she'd been wearing the same when she woke up. She couldn't remember her clothes ever coming off, even when he'd touched her.

"You'd better ask him to give you the negatives. Tell him you'll call the cops if he doesn't. If you want, I'll call and tell him."

"No, I'll call." She was too mortified to have anyone else involved. It was bad enough telling Marjorie what had happened. But it was comforting too to have her there. She brought Grace another damp cloth and a cup of hot tea, and half an hour later, she felt a little better, as Marjorie sat on the floor next to her bed and watched her.

"I had a guy do that to me once, when I first started working. He slipped me a Mickey in a drink, and the next thing I knew, he wanted me to do porno shots with some other girl who was as drugged out as I was."

"What did you do?"

"My father called the cops on him, and threatened to beat the crap out of him. We never posed for the shots anyway, but plenty of girls do. Some of them don't even have to be drugged. They're too scared not to. The guys tell them they'll never work again, or God knows what, and they do it."

Listening to her made Grace's blood run cold. She'd been falling in love with him. She'd trusted him. And what if he had taken photographs of her with her clothes off while she was passed out?

"Do you think he did something like that?" she asked in a terrified voice, remembering what Marjorie's friend from Detroit had said, and she hadn't believed, that Marcus had shot porno.

"Was there anyone else in the studio with you?" Marjorie asked worriedly.

"No, just the two of us. I'm sure of it. I think I was only out for a few minutes."

"Long enough for him to get his pants off anyway," Marjorie said, angry all over again. "No, I don't suppose he did. At worst, he got a couple of nude shots. And there's not much he can do with them without a release from you, if you're recognizable. He can't show your face in shots like that, without having you sign a release. The only use they'd be to him would be to blackmail you, and that's not worth much. What's he going to get out of you?'' She smiled at her friend. ''Two hundred dollars? Besides, it takes time and some cooperation to set up those pornos. They usually use a couple of girls, some guys, or at least one guy. Even if they drug you out, you've got to be alive enough to play the game. Sounds like you weren't a lot of fun after he hit you with his magic potion,'' Marjorie laughed, and Grace smiled for the first time in hours, ''sounds like he overestimated his victim, you must have gone over like a tree in the forest.''

They both laughed out loud, and it was a relief to laugh about it. It had been such an awful scene, and a brutal disappointment, but she couldn't help wondering if he hadn't drugged her or tried to force it, would she have been able to do it? Maybe she never would. But she certainly had no desire to try again, and certainly not with Marcus.

''I don't drink very much, and I've never done drugs. It just made me feel really sick.''

''So I noticed,'' Marjorie smiled sympathetically, ''you were the color of St. Patrick's Day when you got in.'' And then she decided to make a suggestion. ''I think the photographs are pretty much under control, or they will be when you ask him for the negatives. But maybe you'd like to check out something else. You want to make a quick trip to my doctor? She's real nice, and I'll take you, Grace. I think you ought to know if he did anything. They can tell. It's kind of embarrassing, but you ought to know. Maybe he just played around a little bit, or he could have done a lot worse while you were out cold. At least you should know it.''

''I think I'd remember . . . I remember being scared and telling him not to.''

''So does every rape victim in the world. It doesn't

stop anyone if they don't want to stop. Wouldn't you feel better knowing for sure? And if he did rape you, you could press charges." And then what? Start the nightmare all over again? She dreaded that, dreaded the attention, the stories in the news. Secretary accuses fashion photographer of rape . . . he says she wanted it, posed for nude photographs . . . the very thought of it made her skin crawl. But Marjorie was right. It would be better to know at least . . . and what if she got pregnant . . . it wasn't impossible, and the thought terrified her. She resisted at first and then finally she let Marjorie call the doctor for her, and at five o'clock they went to her office. Grace was a little more clearheaded by then, and the doctor confirmed that she'd been drugged with something.

"Nice guy," she commented, and Grace flinched at the exam. It reminded her of the police exams after she killed her father. But the doctor looked surprised at what she saw. There was no evidence of recent intercourse, but there was a lot of old scarring. She suspected what it meant, and she was very gentle when she asked Grace some questions. She reassured her that however great a cad the guy had been in drugging her, there was no sign of penetration or ejaculation.

"That's something at least." So all she had to worry about was the pictures. And what Marjorie had said was reassuring. Even if he had taken pictures of her that were compromising, if she was recognizable, he couldn't use them without a release, and if she wasn't, who cared. And with any luck at all, he'd give back the pictures. It was still disgusting to think he'd taken them if he had, but she was beginning to think he had just staged the whole thing to punish her for balking at sleeping with him. But the drugs hadn't helped, they had only made her more frightened.

"Grace, have you ever been raped?" the doctor asked, but she already knew the answer when Grace nodded. "How old were you?"

"Thirteen . . . fourteen . . . fifteen . . . sixteen . . . seventeen . . ." The doctor wasn't sure what she meant at first.

"You were raped four times?" That was certainly unusual. Maybe she'd had psychological problems that had led her to put herself at risk repeatedly, but Grace shook her head with a woeful expression.

"No. I was raped pretty much every day for four years . . . by my father . . ."

There was a long moment of silence as the doctor absorbed it. "I'm sorry," she said quietly. She saw cases like that sometimes and they broke her heart, particularly with young girls like Grace had been. "Did he get help? Did someone intervene?" Yes, she said to herself, I did. She had intervened. She had saved herself. No one else would have helped her.

"He died. That stopped it." The doctor nodded.

"Have you ever had intercourse . . . uh . . . normally . . . with a man, since then?" Grace shook her head in answer.

"I think that's what happened today. I think maybe he got overanxious, and wanted to make sure I'd play, so he put something in my drink . . . we'd been going out for a month, and nothing had happened . . . I was . . . I wanted to be sure . . . I was scared . . . he said I . . . he said I got really scared when he tried . . ."

"I'm sure you did. Drugging you is not the answer.

You need time, and therapy, and the right man. This one certainly doesn't sound like he is," she said calmly.

"I figured that out," Grace sighed, but she was relieved to know that he hadn't raped her. That would have been adding insult to injury.

The doctor offered her the name of a therapist, and Grace took it from her, but she didn't intend to call him. She didn't want to talk about her past anymore, her father, her four years of hell, and two years at Dwight. She had talked to Molly about all of it, and then Molly had died. She didn't want to open it up to anyone again. All she wanted was what she had. A few friends like Marjorie, and her roommates, her job, and the women and kids at St. Mary's to give her heart to. It was enough for her, even if no one else understood it.

She thanked the doctor and went home with Marjorie, and slept off the drugs. She went to bed at eight o'clock and woke up at two the next afternoon, much to Marjorie's amazement.

"What did he give you? An elephant tranquilizer?"

"Maybe." Grace grinned. She felt better. It had been a horrible experience, but she'd been through worse. And fortunately, she was resilient. She went to work at St. Mary's that afternoon, and that night, she called Marcus. She half expected to get his machine, but she was relieved when he picked up the phone himself. He sounded surprised to hear her.

"Feeling better?" he asked sarcastically.

"That was a lousy thing to do," she said simply. "I got really sick from whatever you gave me."

"Sorry. All it was was a few Valiums and some magic dust for chrissake. I figured you needed some help loosening up."

She wanted to ask him just how loose she'd gotten, but instead she said, "You didn't need to do that."

"So I noticed. It was a wasted effort. Thanks a lot for stringing me along for the past five weeks. I really enjoyed it."

"I wasn't stringing you along." She sounded hurt. "It's hard for me. It's difficult to explain, but . . ."

"Don't bother, Grace. I get it. I don't know what your story is, but it obviously doesn't include guys, or at least not guys like me. I get it."

"No, you don't," she said, getting angry. How the hell could he know?

"Well, maybe I don't want to. Nobody needs this shit. I thought you'd knock my head off when I laid a hand on you." She didn't remember that at all, but it was certainly possible. Obviously, she'd panicked. "What you need is a good shrink, not a boyfriend."

"Thanks for the advice. And the other thing I need are the negatives of the pictures you took. I want them back on Monday."

"Really now? And who says I took any pictures?"

"Let's not play that game," she said quietly. "You took plenty of pictures while I was awake, and I heard the camera clicking and flashing while I was woozy. I want the negatives, Marcus."

"I'll have to see if I can find them," he said coolly, "I have an awful lot of stuff here."

"Listen, I can call the police and say you raped me."

"The hell I did. I don't think anyone's been in that concrete box of yours in years, if ever, so you're going to have a hell of a time selling that one. I didn't do shit to you except kiss you a few times and take my own clothes off. Big fucking deal, Miss Virginal-don't-lay-a-hand-on-me. You can't go to jail for taking your clothes off in your own apartment. You never even had your pants off.'' She wasn't sure why, but she believed him, and she was relieved to hear it.

"And what about the pictures?"

"What about them? All they are is a bunch of pictures of you in a man's shirt with your eyes closed. Big fucking deal. You weren't naked for chrissake. You never even opened the shirt. And half the time you were snoring."

"I have asthma,'' she said primly. "And I don't give a damn how chaste the pictures are. I want them. You can't do anything with them without a release anyway, so they're no good to you.'' She was grateful for Marjorie's advice as she attacked him.

"What makes you think you didn't sign one?" he teased her as her heart sank. "Besides, maybe I want them for my scrapbook."

"You have no right to them. And are you telling me I signed a release while I was drugged?'' She was beginning to panic.

"I'm not telling you a damn thing. And for all the hoops you put me through, I have a right to anything I want. You're nothing but a prick tease, you little bitch. And you keep your hands off my fucking pictures. I don't owe you anything. Get lost, you got that?'' He already had a date that night with one of the other girls from the agency, and Grace heard all about it on Monday morning.

Cheryl asked her how the shoot with Marcus had gone on Saturday, and Grace was vague and said she'd had the flu and couldn't do it.

But on her birthday a few weeks after that, when she turned twenty-two, Bob Swanson took her to lunch to celebrate. Cheryl was in New York on business for the agency, and Bob had taken her to Nick's Fishmarket. He had just poured her a glass of champagne, when he turned to her with a smile and an appreciative look. Grace had always appealed to him, and he agreed with his wife, she was a godsend.

"I saw Marcus Anders the other day, by the way." She tried to look unconcerned and sip her champagne while he chatted. It was Dom Pérignon and the first alcohol she had touched since Marcus had drugged her. And even now, the excellent French champagne made her feel faintly queasy.

Bob lowered his voice and looked at her, as he slipped a hand over hers and squeezed it. "He showed me some pretty sensational pictures of you, Grace. You've been hiding from us . . . I think you've got a real future. They were the hottest shots I've seen in years . . . there aren't a lot of models who can heat it up like that. You're going to have guys panting." She felt sick as she looked at him, and tried to pretend she didn't know what he meant. But it was useless. What a bastard Marcus was to have shown him. He had never sent her either the photographs or the negatives, and he wouldn't return her calls now. He had never really answered her either about the release, but she was sure she had never signed one. She had been in no state to sign anything, and she didn't remember anything like that. He was just trying to scare her.

"I don't know what you mean, Bob," she said icily, sipping her champagne, and trying not to look embarrassed or worried. "We only took a few, and then I got sick. I had the flu that day."

"If that's how you look with the flu, you should get sick more often."

And then she couldn't stand it any longer, and looked her boss squarely in the eye. It was like facing a hungry lion. He was a big man, and he had a big appetite, she knew from a number of the models.

"What exactly did he show you?"

"I'm sure you remember the shots he took. Looked like you were wearing a man's shirt, it was open all the way down, and your head was thrown back . . . looked pretty passionate to me, like you'd just had sex with him, or were about to."

"I was dressed, wasn't I?"

"Yeah, pretty much. You had the shirt on anyway, for what that was worth. You couldn't see anything you shouldn't have, but that look on your face told the whole story." At least Marcus hadn't taken her shirt off. She was grateful for small favors.

"I was probably asleep. He drugged me."

"You didn't look drugged to me. You looked sensual as hell. Grace, I mean it. You really should be modeling, or in movies."

"Pornos maybe?" she said angrily.

"Sure," he said happily, "if that turns you on. You like pornos?" he said with interest. "You know, Gracie, I have an idea." In fact, he had had the idea well before lunch. He had called to rent a suite upstairs in the hotel before they arrived, and it was waiting for them with more champagne at that very moment. Marcus had pretty much let him know that she looked prim, but she was easy. Bob lowered his voice when he talked to her, and squeezed her hand again. "I've got a suite waiting for us upstairs, the biggest one in the place. I even requested satin sheets . . . and they've got a video channel that offers every porno movie you could ever want to see. Maybe you should see a few before you go into the business." She wanted to throw up listening to him, and she felt tears rise in her throat as she restrained a desire to slap him.

"I'm not going upstairs with you, Bob. Now or ever. And if that means you're going to fire me, then I quit. But I'm not a hooker, or a porno queen, or a piece of ass on the menu for you to grab like an hors d'oeuvre any time you want to."

"What's that supposed to mean?" He looked annoyed. "Marcus said you were the hottest babe in town, and I thought maybe you'd like to have some fun . . . I saw those pictures," he looked at her angrily. "You looked like you were about to come all over his lens, so what's the Virgin Mary routine? You afraid of Cheryl? She'll never know. She never does." No, but everyone else in town did. She wanted to scream looking at him, and what a rotten thing for Marcus to tell him.

"I like Cheryl. I like you. I'm not going to sleep with you, and I never slept with Marcus. I don't know why he told you that, except maybe to get even with me. And I told you, he drugged me. I was asleep when he took most of those pictures."

"In his bed apparently," Bob said with a look of vast annoyance. He hadn't thought she'd be so difficult with him, after what Marcus had said about her. He'd always thought she was pretty straight, and he had left her alone, but Marcus had told him she did a lot of drugs and loved kinky sex, and Bob had believed him.

"I was in a chair in his studio."

"With your legs three feet apart, I'd say." He got excited again thinking about it.

"With my clothes off?" She looked horrified at what he'd just said, and he laughed.

"I couldn't tell, the shirttails were hanging between your legs, but the message was pretty clear. So what about it? How about a little birthday present upstairs between you and Uncle Bob? Just our little secret.''

''I'm sorry.'' The tears welled up in her eyes, and spilled over. At twenty-two, she still felt like a child sometimes, and why did this keep happening to her? Why did men hate her so much that all they wanted to do was use her? ''I just can't, Bob,'' she said, crying at the table, which seemed to annoy him more because it attracted attention.

''Stop that,'' he said brusquely, and then narrowed his eyes as he leaned closer to her. ''Let me put it to you this way, Grace. We go upstairs for an hour or two, and celebrate your birthday, or you're out of a job as of this minute. Now is it 'Happy Birthday,' or 'Happy Trails to You,' which is it?'' If it hadn't been so awful, she would have laughed, but Grace wasn't laughing, she just cried harder, as she looked him in the eye and told him.

''I guess I'm out of a job then. I'll pick my paycheck up tomorrow.'' She left the table without saying another word and went back to her apartment in tears. And the next day she went back to the agency to pick up her things, and her last paycheck.

Cheryl returned from New York the next day, and she smiled broadly when she saw Grace come in that morning. Grace couldn't help wondering what Bob had told her. But it didn't matter anymore. She had made her mind up. She only had a little over two months left until her probation ended anyway, and then she could do anything she wanted.

''Feeling better?'' Cheryl asked sunnily. She'd had

a ball in New York. She always did. Sometimes she was sorry they didn't live there.

"Yeah, I'm fine," Grace said quietly. After twenty-one months of working for them, she was actually sorry to leave them, but she knew she had no choice now.

"Bob said you got a terrible case of food poisoning yesterday at lunch, and had to go home. Poor baby." Cheryl patted her arm, and hurried back to her office. She seemed to have no idea that Grace had been fired, or was quitting. And at that moment, Bob came out, and looked at her blankly.

"Feeling better, Grace?" he asked as though nothing had happened between them. And she spoke quietly, so no one else could hear her.

"I came to pick up my check, and pack my things."

"You don't need to do that," he said with no expression whatsoever. "I think we can both forget it, can't we?" He looked at her pointedly, and she hesitated for a long moment, and then nodded. There was no point creating a scandal over it, it had happened, and now she knew what she had to do. It was time.

She waited another six weeks till Labor Day, and then gave them a month's notice. Cheryl was heartbroken, and Bob pretended to be too, and Marjorie cried when Grace told her. But in another three weeks she'd be free from probation, and she knew it was time to leave Chicago. She was pretty sure by then that the photographs Marcus had taken were not obscene, even Bob Swanson had said she was completely covered by the man's shirt and nothing was exposed, but they were unpleasant anyway, and he had it in for her. And so did Bob. Marcus was prepared to lie and tell people she was a cheap trick. And God only knew what Bob would say to protect himself, maybe that she'd put the make on him, if it ever served his purpose. She was tired of people like them, photographers who thought they owned the world, and models who were all too willing to be exploited. And she felt as though she had done all she could at St. Mary's. It was time for her to move on. And she knew it.

They gave her a farewell party at the agency, and lots of photographers and models came. One of the girls had already agreed to take her place at the town house. The day after her last day of work, Grace went to see Louis Marquez. She was two days late checking out with him, because she'd been too busy packing up, and finishing at the agency, and legally, she was already out of his jurisdiction when she went to see him.

"So where are you going now?" he asked conversationally. He was really going to miss her, and his occasional drop-in visits to her apartment.

"New York."

He raised an eyebrow. "Got a job yet?" She laughed at the question. She no longer owed him any explanations. She owed nothing to anyone. She had fulfilled all her obligations, and Cheryl had given her a fantastic reference, which Bob had co-signed.

"Not yet, Mr. Marquez. I'll get one after I get there. I don't think it'll be too hard." Now she had references and experience. She had everything she needed.

"You shouldda stayed here and been a model. You're as good-looking as the rest of those girls, and a whole lot smarter." He actually said it almost kindly.

"Thanks," she would have liked to feel at least civil to him, but she didn't. He had been rotten to her for the entire two years, and she never wanted to see him again. She signed all the necessary papers, and as she handed him his pen, he grabbed her hand, and she looked up at him in surprise, and then pulled her hand back.

"You wouldn't wanna . . . you know . . . knock off a quick one for old times' sake, huh, Grace?" He was sweating noticeably, and his hand had been wet and slimy.

"No, I wouldn't," she said calmly. He didn't frighten her anymore. He couldn't do anything to her. She had done everything she was supposed to. And he had just signed off on her papers, and she had them firmly clutched in her hand. She was just an ordinary citizen now. Her past was finally behind her. And this little bastard wasn't going to revive it.

"Come on, Grace, be a sport." He came around the desk at her, and before she could move away, he grabbed her and tried to kiss her, and she pushed him back so hard, that he hit his leg on the corner of the desk and shouted at her. "Still scared of guys, huh, Grace? What are you going to do? Kill the next one who tries to fuck you? Kill 'em all?"

But as he said that to her, she moved toward him instead of away and grabbed him by his collar. He was probably stronger than she was, but she was a lot taller, and he was surprised when she grabbed him.

"Listen, you little shit, if you ever lay a hand on me again, I'm going to call the cops on you, and let them kill you. I wouldn't bother. You touch me, and you'll be doing time for rape, and don't think I wouldn't do it. Now don't ever come near me again." She flung him away from her, and he watched without a word, as she grabbed her bag and strode out of his office, banging the door hard behind her. It was over. It was all history. The moment Molly had promised her years ago had come. Her life was her own now.

Chapter 9

Leaving Marjorie was hard for Grace, she was the only friend Grace really had. And leaving the people at St. Mary's was sad too. Paul Weinberg wished her luck, and told her that he was getting married over Christmas. She was happy for him. But for a lot of reasons, she was glad to leave Chicago. She was glad to leave Illinois, and the nightmarish memories she had there. There had always been the fear that someone from Watseka would turn up and recognize her.

In New York, she knew that would never happen.

She took a plane to New York this time, not like when she had come into Chicago by bus from Dwight. And most of her savings were still intact. She had never spent much money, and she'd been paid well by the Swansons. She'd even managed to save a little extra money, and her nest egg was back up to slightly over fifty thousand. She had already wired it ahead to a bank in New York. And she already knew where she wanted to stay, and she had a reservation. One of the models had told her about it, and thought it was a dumb place, because they didn't let you bring in guys, but it was exactly what Grace wanted.

She took a cab from the airport directly to the Bar-

bizon for Women on Lexington and Sixty-third, and
she loved the neighborhood the moment she saw it.
There were shops and apartment houses, it was busy
and alive and residential. It was only three blocks from
Bloomingdale's, which she had heard about for years,
some of the girls had modeled for them, and it was a
block from Park Avenue, and three from Central Park.
She loved it.

She spent Sunday wandering lazily up Madison,
and looking at the shops, and then she went to the zoo
and bought a balloon. It was a beautiful October day,
and in a funny way, she felt like she'd come home
finally. She'd never been happier in her life, and on
Monday she went to three employment agencies to
look for work. The next morning they called her with
half a dozen interviews. Two at modeling agencies,
which she declined. She'd had enough of that life, and
the people who were in it. And the agencies were disappointed, since her reference from the Swansons was
so good, and she knew the business. The third interview was at a plastics firm, which seemed boring and
which she turned down, and the last one was at a very
important law firm, Mackenzie, Broad, and Steinway.
She'd never heard of them before, but apparently everyone in business in New York had.

She wore a plain black dress that she'd bought the
year before at Carson Pirie Scott in Chicago, and a red
coat she'd bought at Lord and Taylor that morning.
And she looked terrific. She was interviewed by personnel, and then sent upstairs to see the office manager,
and the senior secretary, and meet two of the junior
partners. Her office skills had improved over the years,
but she still didn't take proper dictation, but they
seemed willing to accommodate her, as long as she was

able to take fast notes and type. She liked everyone she met, including both of the junior partners she would work for, Tom Short and Bill Martin. They were both very serious and dry, one had gone to Princeton undergraduate and then Harvard Law, the other had gone all the way through Harvard. Everything looked predictable and respectable, and even their location suited her perfectly. They were at Fifty-sixth and Park, only eight blocks from her hotel, although now she knew she'd have to find an apartment.

The law firm took up ten floors, and there were over six hundred employees. All she wanted was to be a face in the crowd, and that's all she was. It was the most impersonal place she'd ever seen, and it suited her to perfection. She wore her hair tied back, very little makeup, and the same clothes she'd worn at Swanson's in Chicago. She had a little more style than necessary, but the office manager figured she'd tone it down. She was a bright girl, and he really liked her.

She had been hired as the assistant joint secretary for two of the junior partners. They shared two women, and Grace's counterpart was three times her age and twice her weight, and seemed relieved to have all the help she could get. She told Grace on her first day of work that Tom and Bill were nice guys and very reasonable to work for. Both were married, and had blond wives, one lived in Stamford, the other in Darien, and each had three children. In some ways, they seemed like twins to Grace, but so did most of the men there. There seemed to be a sea of young men working there who basically looked the same to her. And all they ever talked about was their cases. Everyone commuted to Connecticut or Long Island, most of them played squash, some belonged to clubs, and all of the secretar-

ies seemed equally faceless. It was precisely the anony-
mous world that Grace had wanted. No one seemed to
notice her at all as she started work. She fit in instantly,
did her work, and no one asked her a single question
about who she was, where she had worked, or where
she'd come from. No one cared. This was New York.
And she loved it.

And that weekend, she found an apartment. It was
at Eighty-fourth and First. She could take the subway to
work, or the bus, and she could afford the rent comfortably on her salary. She'd sold her bed and furniture to the girl who took her place in Chicago, and she
went to Macy's and bought a few things, but was worried to find them so expensive. One of the girls at work
told her about a discount furniture place in Brooklyn,
and she went there one night on the subway after work,
and smiled to herself as she rode alone. She had never
felt so grown up and so free, so much the mistress of
her own fate. For the first time in her life, no one was
controlling her, or threatening her, or trying to hurt
her. No one wanted anything from her at all. She could
do anything she wanted.

She did a little shopping on Saturday afternoons,
bought her groceries at the A&P nearby, and went to
galleries on Madison Avenue and the West Side, and
even made a few forays into SoHo. She loved New York,
and everything about it. She ate dim sum on Mott
Street, checked out the Italian neighborhood. And she
was fascinated going to a couple of auctions. And a
month after she'd arrived she had a job, a life, and an
apartment. She'd bought most of her furniture by
then, and it wasn't exciting or elegant, but it was comfortable. Her building was old, but it was clean. They
had given her curtains and the place had beige wall-to-

wall that went with everything she'd bought. The apartment had a living room, a tiny kitchen and dining nook, and a small bedroom and bath. It was everything she'd ever wanted, and it was her own. No one could take it away, or spoil it.

"How's New York treating you?" the personnel manager asked her when she saw him again one day at lunch in the firm's cafeteria. She only ate there in bad weather or when she was broke just before her next paycheck. Otherwise, she liked wandering around Midtown at lunchtime.

"I love it." She smiled at him. He was little and old and bald, and he had told her he had five children.

"I'm glad." He smiled. "I hear good reports about you, Grace."

"Thank you." The best thing about him, as far as she was concerned, was that he loved his wife, and had absolutely no interest in Grace. None of them did. She had never felt as comfortable in her life. People went about their business, and sex seemed to be the last thing on their minds. No one seemed to notice her at all, especially not Tom and Bill, the two young partners that she worked for. She could have been five times her age, and she suspected they would never have noticed. They were nice to her, but they were all work. They worked as late as eight and nine o'clock sometimes, and she wondered if they ever saw their children. They even came in on weekends when they had briefs to write for the senior partners.

"Do you have any plans for Thanksgiving?" the secretary who worked with her asked in mid-November. She was a nice older woman with a thick waist and heavy legs, but a kindly face framed by gray hair, and

she had never been married. Her name was Winifred
Apgard and everyone called her Winnie.

"No, but I'll be fine," Grace said comfortably. Holidays had never been her forte.

"You're not going home?" Grace shook her head
and didn't mention that she didn't have one. Her
apartment was home, and she was very self-sufficient.

"I'm going to Philadelphia to see my mother, or
I'd have you over," Winnie said apologetically. She
looked like someone's maiden aunt, and she seemed
to love her work, and the men she worked for. She
clucked over them like a mother hen, and they teased
her all the time. She told them to wear their galoshes
when it snowed, and warned them of impending
storms if they were driving home late.

It was a very different relationship from the one
Tom and Bill had with Grace. It was almost as though
they pretended not to see her. She wondered sometimes if her youth was threatening to them, or if their
wives would have been annoyed, or if Winnie was less
of a threat to them, and more comfortable. But it
didn't seem to matter. They never said anything of a
personal nature to Grace, and while they made jokes
with Winnie sometimes, they were always poker-faced
with Grace, as though they were being particularly
careful not to get to know her. It was a far cry from
Bob Swanson, but she liked that a lot about her job.

The week before Thanksgiving, she spent some
time on her lunch hour making a few personal phone
calls. She had meant to do it for a while, but she'd
been busy settling into her apartment. But now it was
time to start giving back again. It was something she
intended to do for the rest of her life, something she
felt she owed the people who had helped her. It was a

debt she would never stop paying back. And it was time to begin again now.

She finally found what she was looking for.

The place was called St. Andrew's Shelter, and it was on the Lower East Side, on Delancey. There was a young priest in charge, and he had invited her to come down and meet them the following Sunday morning.

She took the subway down Lexington, changed trains, and got off at Delancey, and walked the rest of the way. It was a rough walk, she realized once she got there. There were bums wandering the streets aimlessly, drunks hunched over in doorways, dozing, or lying openly on the sidewalks. There were warehouses and tenements, and battered-looking stores with heavy gates. There were abandoned cars here and there, and some tough-looking kids cruising for trouble. They glanced at Grace as she walked along, but no one bothered her. And finally, she got to St. Andrew's. It was an old brownstone that looked like it was in pretty bad shape, with paint peeling off the doors, and a sign that was barely hanging by a thread, but there were people coming in and out, mostly women with kids, and a few young girls. One of them looked about fourteen, and Grace could see that she was hugely pregnant.

There were three young girls manning a reception desk when she got inside. They were talking and chattering, and one of them was doing her nails. And there was more noise than Grace thought she'd heard anywhere. The building sounded like it was teeming with voices and kids, there was an argument going on somewhere, there were blacks and whites, Chinese and Puerto Ricans. It looked like a microcosm of New York, or as though someone had hijacked a subway.

She asked for the young priest by name, and she

waited a long time for him, watching the action, and when he appeared he was wearing jeans and an old battered oatmeal-colored sweater.

"Father Finnegan?" she asked curiously. He had a real twinkle about him, and he didn't look like a priest. He had bright red hair, and he looked like a kid. But crow's-feet near his eyes, in a sea of freckles on his fair skin, said he was somewhat older than the kid he looked like.

"Father Tim," he corrected her with a grin. "Miss Adams?"

"Grace." She smiled at him. You couldn't help but smile at him. He had a real look of joy about him.

"Let's go talk somewhere," he said calmly, weaving in and out of half a dozen children chasing each other around the main lobby. The building looked as though it might have been a tenement, and had been opened up to provide a home to those who needed it. He had told her on the phone that they had only been in existence for five years and needed a lot of help, especially from volunteers. He had been thrilled to hear from her. She was one of the many miracles he said they needed.

He led her to a kitchen with three old dishwashers that had been donated to them and a big old-fashioned sink. There were posters on the walls, a big round table and some chairs, and two huge pots of coffee. He poured a cup for each of them, and led her to a small room with a desk and three chairs. It looked as though it had been a utility room and was now his office. The place was badly in need of paint and some decent furniture, but sitting there, talking to him, it was easy to forget anything but him. He had that kind of presence about him, and he was completely unaware of it, which was why everyone loved him.

"So what brings you here, Grace? Other than a good heart and a foolish nature?" He grinned at her again, and took a sip of steaming coffee, as his eyes danced with glee.

"I've done this kind of volunteer work before, in Chicago. At a place called St. Mary's." She gave Paul Weinberg's name as a reference.

"I know it well. I'm from Chicago myself. Been here for twenty years now. And I know St. Mary's. In some ways, we've modeled ourselves on them. They run a very good operation."

She told him the number of people they serviced at St. Mary's each year, and that there were as many as a dozen families in residence at any given time. Not to mention the people who came and went constantly in a day's time, and returned frequently to avail themselves of the comfort offered at St. Mary's.

"We offer the same thing here," he said thought-fully, looking at her. He wondered why someone like her wanted to do this kind of work. But he had learned long since not to question God's gifts to him, but to use them well. He had every intention of putting Grace to work at St. Andrew's. "We see more people here. Maybe close to eighty or a hundred a day, give or take a dozen, mostly give." He grinned again. "We've had over a hundred women staying here at one time, some-times twice as many children. Generally, we keep it to a dull roar, and we have about sixty women and a hun-dred and fifty kids here most of the time. We don't turn anyone away at St. Andrew's. That's the only rule here. They come to our door, they stay, if that's what they want. Most of them don't stay long. They either go

back, or they move on, and start new lives. I'd say the
average stay is anywhere from a week to two months,
maximum. Most of them are out in two weeks." It had
been pretty much the same at St. Mary's.

"Can you house that many people here?" She was
surprised. The building didn't look that big, and it
wasn't.

"This used to be twenty apartments. We stack 'em
as high as we have to, Grace. Our doors are open to
everyone, not just to Catholics," he explained, "we
don't even ask that question."

"Actually . . ." She smiled at him, there was a
warmth that came from him that touched her very
soul. There was an innocence and purity about Father
Tim that made him seem particularly holy, in a real
sense. He was truly a man of God, and Grace felt instantly at ease with him and blessed to be near him.
"The doctor who ran St. Mary's was Jewish," she said
conversationally, and he laughed.

"I haven't gone that far yet, but you never know."

"Is there a doctor in charge here?"

"Me, I guess. I'm a Jesuit, and I have a doctorate in
psychology. But Dr. Tim sounds a little strange, doesn't
it? Father Tim suits me better." They both laughed this
time and he went to pour them both another cup of
coffee from one of the two huge pots.

"We have half a dozen nuns, not in habit, of
course, who work here, and about forty volunteers at
various times. We need every one of them to keep the
place running. We've got some psychiatric nurses who
give us time, from NYU, and we get a lot of kids doing
psych internships, mostly from Columbia. It's a good
group, and they work like demons . . . sorry, angels."
She really loved him, with his freckles and his laughing

eyes. "And what about you, Grace? What brings you to us?"

"I like this kind of work. It means a lot to me."

"Do you know much about it? I suppose you do after two years at St. Mary's."

"Enough, I guess, to be useful." It was all too familiar to her, but she wasn't quite sure whether or not to say it to him. She almost wanted to. She trusted him more than she had anyone in a long time.

"How many times a week or month did you volunteer at St. Mary's?"

"Two nights a week, and every Sunday . . . most holidays."

"Wow." He looked impressed, and surprised. Priest or no, he could see easily that she was young and beautiful, too young to be giving up so much of her life to a home like this one. And then he looked at her carefully. "Is this a special mission for you, Grace?" It was as though he knew. He sensed it. And she nodded.

"I think so. I . . . understand about these things." She wasn't sure what else to say to him, but he nodded, and touched her hand gently.

"It's all right. Healing comes in many ways. Blessing others is the best one." She nodded, and her eyes were blurred with tears. He knew. He understood. She felt as though she had come home, just being here, and being near him. "We need you, Grace. There's a place for you here. You can bring joy, and healing, to a lot of people, as well as yourself."

"Thank you, Father," she whispered as she wiped her eyes and he smiled at her. He didn't pry any further. He knew all he needed to know. No one knew better what these women were going through than one who'd been through it, battered and abused by husbands and fathers, or mothers or boyfriends.

"Now, let's get down to business." His eyes were laughing again. "How soon can you start? We're not going to let you get away from here that easily. You might come to your senses."

"Right now?" She had come prepared to work, if he wanted her, and he did. He led her back into the kitchen, where they left their empty mugs in one of the dishwashers, and then he walked her out to the hallway and started introducing her to people. The three girls at the desk had been replaced by a boy in his early twenties, who was a medical student at Columbia, and there were two women talking to a gaggle of little girls, whom Father Tim introduced as Sister Theresa, and Sister Eugene, but neither of them looked like nuns to Grace. They were friendly-looking women in their early thirties. One was wearing a sweat suit, and the other jeans and a threadbare sweater. And Sister Eugene volunteered to take Grace upstairs to show her around the rooms where the women stayed, and the nursery where they sometimes kept the children, if the women were too battered to deal with them for the time being themselves.

There was an infirmary staffed by a nurse who was a nun, and she was wearing a clean white smock over blue jeans. The lights were kept dim, and Sister Eugene walked Grace in on soundless feet, as she signaled to the nurse on duty. And as Grace looked around her at the women in the beds, her heart twisted as she recognized the signs she had lived her entire life with. Merciless beatings and heartrending bruises. Two women had arms in casts, one had cigarette burns all over her face, and another was moaning as the nurse tried to bandage her broken ribs again, and put ice packs on her swollen eyes. Her husband was in jail now.

"We send the worst cases to the hospital," Sister Eugene explained quietly as they left the room again. Without thinking, Grace had stopped to touch a hand, and the woman had looked at her in suspicion. That was another thing Grace was familiar with too. These women were sometimes so far gone and so badly treated that they didn't trust anyone anymore not to hurt them. "But we keep whoever we can here, it's less upsetting for them. And sometimes it's only bruises. The really ugly stuff goes to the emergency room." Like the woman who'd come in two nights before whose husband had put a hot iron to her face, after hitting her with a tire iron on the back of her head. He had almost killed her, but she was so terrified of him, she had refused to bring charges. The authorities had taken their children away from them, and they were in foster homes now. But the woman had to be willing to save herself, and many of them didn't have the courage to do it. Being battered was the most isolating thing in the world. It made you hide from everyone, Grace knew only too well, even those who could help you.

Sister Eugene took her to see the children then, and in minutes Grace had her arms full of little girls and boys, she was telling them stories, and tying bows on braids, and shoelaces, as children told her who they were, and some of them talked about what had happened and why they had come there. Some couldn't. Some of their siblings had been killed by their parents. Some of their mothers were upstairs, too battered to move, too ashamed even to see them. It was a disease that destroyed families, and the people who lived through it. And Grace knew with a sinking heart how few of them would ever grow up to be whole people or be able to trust anyone again.

It was after eight o'clock before she left them that night. As she did, Father Tim was standing at the door, talking to a policeman. He had just brought a little girl in, she was two years old, and she had been raped by her father. Grace hated cases like that . . . at least she had been thirteen . . . but she had seen babies at St. Mary's who had been raped and sodomized by their fathers.

"Rough day?" Father Tim asked sympathetically, as the policeman left.

"Good day." She smiled at him. She had spent most of it with kids, and then the last few hours, talking to some of the women, just being there, listening, trying to give them the courage to do what they had to. No one could do it for them. The police could help. But it was up to them to save themselves. And maybe, if she talked to enough of them, she told herself, they wouldn't have to go to the same lengths she had. They wouldn't have to wind up in prison to be free. It was her way of repaying the debt, of atoning for a sin she knew her mother would never have forgiven her for. But she had had no choice, and she didn't regret it. She just didn't want anyone else to have to pay the same price she had.

"You run a great place here," she complimented him. She liked it even better than St. Mary's. It was livelier, and in some ways warmer.

"It's only as great as the people who work here. Can I interest you in coming back? Sister Eugene says you're terrific."

"So is she." The nun had been tireless working

there all day, as was everyone Grace had seen. She liked everyone she had met there. "I don't think you'll be able to keep me away." She had already signed up for two nights that week and the following Sunday. "I can come in on Thanksgiving too," she said easily.

"You're not going home?" He looked surprised. She was awfully young to be so unencumbered.

"No home to go to," she said without hesitation. "It's not a big deal. I'm used to it." He watched her eyes, and nodded. There was a lot there that she wasn't saying.

"We'd love to have you." The holidays were always rough for people with bad home situations, and the number of people they saw come in often doubled. "It's always a zoo here."

"That's just what I want. See you next week, Father," she said, as she signed out on the logbook. She was going to be reporting to Sister Eugene, and she was thrilled that she'd come here. It was exactly what she wanted.

"God bless you, Grace," Father Tim said as she left.

"You too, Father," she called, and closed the door behind her.

It was a long, cold, somewhat scary walk back to the subway again, threading her way through the bums and the drunks, and young hoods looking for fun. But no one bothered her, and half an hour later, she was home, walking down First Avenue to her apartment. She was tired from her long day, but she felt renewed again, and as though at least for some, the horrors in her life had been useful. For Grace, knowing that always made the pain she carried seem worthwhile. At least it wasn't wasted.

Chapter 10

Grace spent Thanksgiving at St. Andrew's Shelter, as she'd promised them. She even helped to cook the turkey. And after that, she fell into a familiar routine, of going down there on Tuesday and Friday nights, and all day Sunday. Fridays were always busy for them, because it was the beginning of the weekend, and paychecks had come in. Husbands who were prone to violence went out and got drunk and then came home and beat their women. She found that she never left the shelter before two a.m., and sometimes later. And on Sundays, they were trying to deal with all the women and kids who had come in over the weekend. It seemed like it was only on Tuesday nights that she and Sister Eugene had a chance to chat. The two women had become good friends by Christmas. Sister Eugene had even asked her if she'd ever thought of herself as having a vocation.

"Oh my God, no! I can't even imagine it." Grace looked stunned at the idea.

"It's not very different from what you're doing now, you know." Sister Eugene smiled at her. "You give an awful lot of yourself to others . . . and to God . . . no matter how you view it."

"I don't think it's quite as saintly as all that,"

Grace smiled, embarrassed at what the nun was saying. "I'm just repaying some old debts. People were good to me at one point, as much as I let them. I'd like to think that I can pass it on to others now." Not very many people had been good to her. But a few had. And she wanted to be one of the few people in these people's anguished lives who made a difference. And she did. But not enough so to want to give her life to God, only to battered women and children.

"Do you have a boyfriend?" Sister Eugene had asked her once, giggling like a girl, and Grace had laughed at the question. Sister Eugene was curious about her life and Grace seldom offered any information. She was very closed about herself, but she felt safer that way.

"I'm not much good with men," Grace said honestly. "It's not my forte. I'd rather come here and do something useful."

And she did. She spent Christmas and New Year's with them, and sometimes she had a kind of peaceful glow on her face after she'd been there. Winnie noticed it sometimes at work and always thought it was a man in her life. She seemed so happy and so at ease with herself. But it came from giving to others, and sitting up all night with a battered child in her arms, crooning to it, and holding it, as no one had ever done for her. She wanted more than anything to' make a difference in these children's lives, and she did.

Finally, after they'd worked together for nearly five months, Winnie asked her to lunch on a Sunday, and Grace was really touched but she explained to her that she had a standing obligation on Sundays. She would never have canceled. They met on a Saturday instead.

They met at Schrafft's on Madison Avenue and then walked over to watch the skaters at Rockefeller Center.

"What do you do on Sundays?" Winnie asked her curiously, still convinced that Grace probably had a boyfriend. She was a pretty girl, and she was so young. There had to be someone.

"I work on Delancey Street, at a home for battered women and kids," she explained, as they watched women in short skirts swirl on the ice, and children fall and laugh as they chased their parents and friends. They looked like such happy children.

"You do?" Winnie looked surprised by Grace's admission. "Why?" She couldn't imagine a girl as young and beautiful as Grace doing something so difficult and so dismal.

"I do it because I think it's important. I work there three times a week. It's a great place. I love it," Grace said, smiling at Winnie.

"Have you always done that?" Winnie asked her in amazement, and Grace nodded, still smiling.

"For a long time anyway. I did it in Chicago too, but actually I like the place here better. It's called St. Andrew's." And then she laughed and told her about Sister Eugene suggesting she become a nun.

"Oh my Lord," Winnie looked horrified, "you're not going to do that, are you?"

"No. But they seem pretty happy. It's not for me though. I'm happy doing what I can like this."

"Three days a week is an awful lot. You must not have a lot of time to do anything else."

"I don't. I don't want to. I enjoy my work, I enjoy working at St. Andrew's. I've got Saturdays if I need time to myself, and a couple of nights a week. I don't need more than that."

"That's not healthy," Winnie scolded her. "A girl of your age ought to be out having fun. You know, with boys," she scolded Grace in a motherly way, and Grace laughed at her. She liked her. She liked working with her. She was responsible and efficient and she really cared about "her" partners, and Grace. She acted almost like a mother to her.

"I'm all right. Honest. I'll have plenty of time for boys when I grow up," Grace teased, but Winnie shook her head at her, and wagged a finger.

"That comes a lot faster than you think. I took care of my parents all my life, and now my mother's in a home in Philadelphia, so she can be with my aunt, and I'm all alone here. My father's gone, and I never got married. By the time he died and Mama went to Philadelphia to be with Aunt Tina, I was too old." She sounded so sad about it that Grace felt sorry for her. Grace suspected that she was very lonely, which was why she'd met her for lunch. "You'll regret it one day, Grace, if you don't get married, and have a life of your own before that."

"I'm not sure I will." She had come to think recently that she really didn't want to get married. She'd been burned enough, and even her brief encounters with men like Marcus, and Bob Swanson, and even her probation officer, had taught her something. She really didn't want any of it. And the nice ones like David and Paul still didn't make her feel any different. They were both good men, but she really didn't want one. She was satisfied to be alone. She didn't make any effort to meet men, or to have any life other than her volunteer work at St. Andrew's.

Which was why she was utterly amazed when one of the other junior partners, who worked in an office near hers, asked her out to dinner one day. She knew he was a friend of the tax men she worked for, and he was recently divorced and very good-looking. But she had no interest at all in going out with him, or anyone else at work.

He had stopped at her desk at lunch hour one day, and in an embarrassed undervoice had asked her if she would like to have dinner with him the following Friday. She explained that she did volunteer work on Friday nights, and couldn't but she didn't look particularly pleased that he had asked her, and he retreated, looking awkward and feeling somewhat embarrassed.

She was even more surprised when one of her bosses asked her the next afternoon why she had turned Hallam Ball down when he asked her out to dinner. "Hal's a really nice guy," he explained, "and he likes you," as though that were all he needed to qualify for a date. None of them could understand her refusal.

"I . . . uh . . . that's very nice of him, and I'm sure he is." She was stammering. It was embarrassing having to explain why she had refused him. "I don't go out with people at work. It's never a good idea," she said firmly, and the young partner nodded.

"That's what I told him. I figured it was something like that. That's smart, actually, it's just too bad, because I think you'd like him, and he's been really down since the divorce last summer."

"I'm sorry to hear it," she said coolly. And then Winnie scolded her and said that Hallam Ball was one of the most eligible men in the law firm, and she was a very foolish girl. She warned her that she'd be an old maid if she didn't watch it.

"Good." Grace smiled at her. "I can hardly wait.

Then no one will ask me out anymore, and I won't
have to think up excuses."

"You're crazy!" Winnie scolded. "Silly fool," she
clucked at her, and grumbled, and when a legal assistant asked her out the following month and Grace
turned him down too, and gave the same reason, Winnie went absolutely crazy. "You are the most foolish
girl I've ever known!" the older woman railed at her.
"I'm absolutely not going to let you do this! He's an
adorable boy, and he's even as tall as you are!" Grace
only laughed at her reasoning and refused to recon-
sider, and in a very short period of time, it became well
known that Grace Adams did not date men from the
office. Most of them figured that she had a boyfriend
or was engaged, and a few decided to meet the challenge. But she never changed her mind, and she never
gave anyone a different answer. No matter how attractive they were, or how seemingly interested, she never
accepted their invitations. In fact, she seemed totally
indifferent to all men. And a number of people wondered about her.

"And just how do you plan to get married?" Winnie almost shouted at her one afternoon as they were
about to leave work.

"I don't plan to get married, Win. Simple as that."
Grace looked touched but unmoved by the older
woman's concern for her. Winnie was livid.

"Then you *should* become a nun!" Winnie yelled
at her. "You practically are one."

"Yes, ma'am," Grace said with a good-natured
smile, and Bill, one of "their" partners, raised an eyebrow as he left his office and overheard them. He
agreed with Winnie and felt that Grace was missing
opportunities. Youth and beauty couldn't last forever.

"Fighting in the aisles, ladies?" he teased, putting on his coat and grabbing his umbrella. It was March and it hadn't stopped raining in weeks. But at least it wasn't snowing.

"She's a damn fool!" Winnie exclaimed, huffing into her own overcoat and getting all tangled up in it as Grace helped her and the partner laughed at them.

"Grace? My goodness, Grace, what did you do to Winnie?"

"She won't go out with anyone, that's what!" She yanked her coat away from Grace, and buttoned it incorrectly, as the two watching her tried to keep straight faces. "She'll wind up an old maid like me, and she's much too young and pretty for that." But Grace saw then that she was almost crying, and she leaned over and kissed her cheek in genuine affection. She was almost like a mother to her at times, and a dear friend at others.

"She probably has a boyfriend, you know," he said soothingly to the older of his two secretaries. In fact, recently, he had started wondering if Grace was involved with someone married. Her constant refusals of all the young men in the office sort of fit the pattern. "She's probably keeping it a secret." He no longer believed that her reticence was entirely caused by virtue and clear thinking, there had to be more to it than that, and several of the other junior partners agreed with him.

Winnie looked up at her and Grace smiled and said nothing, which immediately convinced Winnie that he was right, and that maybe there was a married man in her life after all.

The two women left each other in the lobby and

said good night, and Grace went downtown to Delancey Street and spent the night caring for the needy.

And the next morning, she looked tired when she came to work, which convinced Winnie that their boss was right, and she had been up to some mischief the night before. Grace actually thought she was coming down with the flu. After her long walk down Delancey Street in the pouring rain, to get to St. Andrew's, she got soaking wet. And she was in no mood for the favor the personnel director asked her for at lunchtime. She got a call at eleven o'clock and was asked to come to his office. She was concerned, and Winnie was clearly worried. She couldn't imagine what he might be complaining about, unless one of the men she'd turned down had decided to make trouble for her. She had lived through that before, and it certainly wouldn't have surprised her.

"Now don't tell him anything you don't have to," Winnie warned her as she went upstairs. But he wasn't calling to complain, but to praise her.

He told her she was doing a marvelous job, and everyone in her department liked her, as did the two partners she worked for.

"In fact," he said hesitantly, "I have a little favor to ask of you, Grace. I know how disruptive it can be to have to leave one's work for a little while, and I know Tom and Bill won't be pleased. But Miss Waterman had an accident last night, on the subway. She slipped on the stairs, and broke her hip. She's going to be out for two months, maybe even three. It sounds like it was pretty nasty. She's at Lenox Hill, and her sister called us. You do know her, don't you?" Grace was racking her memory and couldn't think of who she was. Obviously, one of the secretaries in the law firm. She wondered if it would be a step up or down, and whom she worked for. She only hoped that it wasn't one of the men who had asked her out to dinner. That certainly would have been awkward.

"I don't think I do know her," Grace looked at him blankly.

"She works for Mr. Mackenzie," the personnel director said solemnly, as though that said it all. And Grace looked confused as she faced him.

"Which Mr. Mackenzie?" she asked, continuing not to understand him.

"Mr. Charles Mackenzie," he said, as though she were very stupid. Charles Mackenzie was one of the three senior partners of the law firm.

"Are you kidding?" She almost shouted at him. "Why *me*? I can't even take dictation." Her voice was suddenly squeaky. She was comfortable where she was, and she didn't want to be under that kind of pressure.

"You take fast notes, and the partners you work for said your skills are excellent. And Mr. Mackenzie is very definite about what he wants." He looked uncomfortable because he wasn't supposed to admit it to anyone, but Charles Mackenzie hated grumpy old secretaries who complained about working late, and his constant demands. The job needed someone young to keep up with him, but the personnel man couldn't say that to her. As a rule, Mackenzie preferred his secretaries under thirty. And even Grace had heard that. "He wants someone fast, who's doing an excellent job and won't get in his way, while Miss Waterman is gone. And of course as soon as she returns, you can go back where you are, Grace. It's just for a couple of months." He probably wanted to get laid, she thought miserably. She knew his kind. And she didn't want to play. She loved her job, and working with Winnie. And the two partners she worked for were no trouble at all. They scarcely paid any attention to her, which was why she liked them.

"Do I have a choice?" she asked with an unhappy frown.

"Not really," he said honestly. "We presented three résumés to him this morning, and he chose yours. It would be very difficult to explain to him that you didn't want it." He looked at her mournfully. He hadn't expected her to resist him. It would look bad for him if she refused, and Charles Mackenzie was not used to being told he couldn't have what he wanted.

"Great." She leaned back in the chair unhappily.

"I'm sure we could arrange for a raise, commensurate with the position you're filling." But that didn't really sweeten it for her. More than anything she didn't want to work for some old guy who wanted to chase a twenty-two-year-old secretary around his desk. She really did not want to do that. And if he did, she would quit immediately. She'd have to start looking for another job. She'd try it for a few days, and if the guy was a jerk, she was going, but she didn't say that to the head of personnel. She just made up her own mind in silence.

"Fine," she said icily. "When do I start?"

"After lunch. Mr. Mackenzie had a very difficult morning with no one to help him."

"How old is Miss Waterman, by the way?" She had understood the message.

"Twenty-five, I think. Maybe twenty-six. I'm not sure. She's excellent. She's been with him for three years now." Maybe they were having an affair, Grace decided, and they'd had a fight, and now she was out looking for another job. Anything was possible. She'd see for herself in an hour. He told her to report to Mr. Mackenzie's office at one o'clock. And when she went back to pick up her things, she told Winnie.

"How wonderful!" Winnie exclaimed generously. "I'll miss you, but what a great break for you!" Grace didn't see it that way, and she almost cried when a girl from the typing pool came to replace her. She said goodbye to the two partners she'd worked for for almost six months, and took a bag of her things up to the twenty-ninth floor to Mr. Mackenzie's office. Winnie had promised to call her that afternoon to see how it was going.

"He sounds like a jerk," Grace had said to her under her breath, but Winnie was quick to reassure her.

"He's not. Everyone who works for him loves him."

"I'll bet," she said tartly, and kissed Winnie on the cheek before she left. It was like leaving home, and she was in a rotten mood when she got upstairs. She was annoyed over the high-handedness of it. And she hadn't had time for lunch, and had a terrible headache. Besides which, she really did feel like she was getting the flu from her long walk in the rain the night before. And even being shown to her new office, with a spectacular view up Park Avenue, didn't cheer her. They treated her like royalty, and three of the secretaries who worked nearby made a point of coming out to meet her. It was like a little club up there, and had she been in a better mood, she would have admitted that everyone was very pleasant.

She looked through some papers that the personnel director had left for her, and a list of instructions from her new boss, about some things he needed done that afternoon. They were mostly research calls, and some personal calls too, an appointment with his tailor, and another one for a haircut, and a reservation at '21' the following night, for two people. How sexy, she complained to herself as she read the list. And then started making the phone calls.

When he came back from lunch at two-fifteen, she had made all his calls for him, finished half the research, and taken several messages. In each case, she had handled what the caller wanted from him, and he had no need to return the calls, just to know about their resolution. He was immensely surprised by her efficiency, but not nearly as much as she was when she saw him. The "old guy" she'd expected him to be was forty-two years old, tall, had broad shoulders, deep green eyes, and jet black hair with salt and pepper at the temples. He had a rugged jaw that made him look like a movie star, and he was totally without pretension. It was as though he had absolutely no idea he was even handsome. He walked in very quietly, he had had a working lunch downstairs with some of the other partners. And he was casual and friendly when he greeted her, and praised her for the work she'd done for him so quickly.

"You're as good as they said you were, Grace." He smiled warmly at her, and she vowed instantly to resist him. She was not going to fall for his looks, or for who he was, no matter what Miss Waterman had done for him. As far as Grace was concerned, she wasn't part of the service. She was extremely formal with him, and not particularly friendly.

For the next two weeks, she made every appointment for him, both business and personal, handled all his calls, attended meetings with him and took accurate notes, and proved herself to be very near perfect.

"She's good, isn't she?" Tom Short asked possessively when he saw Mackenzie alone for a few minutes before a meeting.

"Yes," the senior partner said cautiously, but without much zeal, and Tom noticed.

"Don't you like her?" Tom immediately sensed a hesitation.

"Honestly? No. She's disagreeable as hell, and she walks around with a broomstick up her ass all day long. She's the most uptight human being I've ever met. She makes me want to throw a bucket of water on her."

"Grace?" Her old boss looked stunned. "She's so nice, and so easygoing."

"Maybe she just doesn't like me. Christ, I can't wait to get Waterman back." But four weeks later, Elizabeth Waterman delivered news that upset them both deeply. She had thought about it a great deal, but after her accident and the way people had treated her as she lay in the subway with a broken hip and leg, she had decided to leave New York for good when she recuperated, and go back to Florida where she came from.

"I suspect this isn't good news for either of us," Charles Mackenzie said to Grace honestly after he heard. For six weeks, Grace had done an impeccable job for him, and she'd barely said a civil word to him. He had been nothing but friendly with her, and accommodating, but each time she saw him, and noticed again how good-looking he was, and how at ease he was with her and everyone, she hated him all the more. She had convinced herself that she knew his type, he was just waiting for an opportunity to pounce on her and harass her sexually, just like Bob Swanson had done, and she wasn't going to take it. Never again. And certainly not from him. Week after week she saw the women come into St. Andrew's and it reminded her again and again of how rotten men were, how dangerous, and how much damage it could do if you let yourself trust them.

"You're not happy here, are you, Grace?" Charles Mackenzie asked her in a kind tone finally, and she sat noticing how green his eyes were again, reminding herself of how many women he had probably had fall all over him in his life, including Elizabeth Waterman, and God alone knew how many others.

"I'm probably not the right secretary for you," she said quietly. "I don't have the experience you need. I've never worked in a law firm like this before, or for anyone as important." He smiled at what she said, but she looked as tense as ever.

"What did you do before this?" He had forgotten.

"I worked in a modeling agency for two years," she said, wondering what he was after. Maybe he was going to strike now. He would eventually. They all did.

"As a model?" he asked, not surprised, but she shook her head in answer.

"No, as a secretary."

"It must have been a lot more interesting than a law firm. My job isn't exactly exciting." He smiled and looked surprisingly young. She knew he'd been married to a well-known actress and they'd never had children. He had been divorced for two years, and according to most reports, he dated a lot of women. She had certainly made plenty of dinner reservations for him, but not all were with women. Some were with his partners and clients.

"Most jobs aren't very interesting," Grace said sensibly, surprised that he was willing to spend so much time talking to her. "Mine at the agency wasn't either. Actually," she said, thinking about it, "I like this better. The people here are a lot nicer."

"It's just me, then," he said almost sadly, as though she had hurt his feelings.

"What do you mean?" She didn't understand him.

"Well, it's obvious you're not enjoying your work, and if you like the law firm, then it must be me. I get the feeling you hate working for me, to be honest with you, Grace. I feel like I make you miserable every time I walk into the office." She flushed in embarrassment as he said it.

"No . . . I . . . I'm really sorry . . . I didn't mean to give you that impression . . ."

"Then what is it?" He wanted to work it out with her. She was the best secretary he'd ever had. "Is there something I can do to smooth things out between us? With Elizabeth leaving permanently, we either have to make it work or give it up, don't we?" Grace nodded, embarrassed now that her dislike for him had been so blatant. It wasn't really anything he had done personally. It was just what she thought he represented. The truth was that he was a lot less of a womanizer than she thought. Only his highly publicized marriage to his famous actress ex-wife had won him that reputation.

"I'm really sorry, Mr. Mackenzie. I'll try and make things a little easier for you from now on."

"So will I," he said kindly, and she felt somewhat guilty toward him as she left her office. And even more so when Elizabeth Waterman came to say goodbye to him on her crutches. She said it was like leaving home again for her, and that he was the kindest person she had ever known. She cried when she said goodbye to him and everyone in the office. Grace didn't get the feeling that she was ending a love affair, but felt that she was genuinely heartbroken to leave a much-loved employer.

"How's it going up there?" Winnie asked her one afternoon.

"Okay." Grace was embarrassed to admit to her how unpleasant she'd been, but she hadn't made any friends on the twenty-ninth floor so far, and her old bosses had been told by several people how disagreeable she was. She knew the reputation she was getting, and that she deserved it. And it embarrassed her even more when Winnie said she'd heard from a number of people that Grace was being very hard on Mr. Mackenzie.

After he talked to her, she made an effort to be pleasant to him a little bit, at least, and she actually started to enjoy the job. She had resigned herself by then to the fact that she was probably not going back to work with Winnie, and her two junior partners. She was no longer fighting it and she had to admit that the job with him was more interesting, when suddenly, in May, Charles Mackenzie told her he had to fly to Los Angeles and he needed her to go with him. She almost had apoplexy over it, and she was shaking when she told Winnie that she was going to refuse to go with him.

"Why, for heaven's sake? Grace, what an opportunity!" For what? To get laid by her boss? No! She wasn't going to do it. In her mind, it was all a setup, and she would be walking into a trap. But when she went in to tell him the next day that she wouldn't go, he thanked her so nicely for being willing to give up her own time and come with him, that she felt awkward refusing to go with him. She even thought about quitting over it, and much to her own surprise, she found herself talking to Father Tim about it at St. Andrew's.

"What are you afraid of, Grace?" he asked gently. She had fear stamped all over her, and she knew it.

"I'm afraid . . . oh I don't know," she was embarrassed to tell him but she knew she had to, for her own sake, "that he'll be like everyone else in my life and take advantage of me, or worse. I finally got away from all that when I came here, and now it's starting all over again with this stupid trip to California."

"Has he ever shown signs of wanting to take advantage of you?" Father Tim asked quietly, "or of sexual interest in you?" He knew exactly what they were talking about and what she was afraid of.

"Not really," she conceded, still looking miserable.

"Even a little bit? Be honest with yourself. You know the truth here."

"All right, no, not even a little bit."

"Then what makes you think that's going to change now?"

"I don't know. People don't take their secretaries on trips unless they want to . . . you know." He smiled at her discretion in talking to him. He had heard a lot worse in his life, and a lot more shocking stories. Even her own story wouldn't have shocked him.

"Some people do take their secretaries on trips without 'you know.' Maybe he really does need help. And if he misbehaves, you're a big girl, get on a plane and come home. End of story."

"I guess I could do that." She thought about it and nodded.

"You're in control, you know. That's what we teach people here. You know that better than anyone. You can walk away anytime you want to."

"Okay. Maybe I'll go with him." She sighed and looked at him gratefully, still not totally convinced though.

"Do whatever you think is right, Grace. But don't make decisions out of fear. They never get you anywhere you want to go. Just do what's right for you."

"Thank you, Father." The next morning she told Charles Mackenzie that she was definitely able to go to California with him. She still had misgivings about the trip, but she had told herself repeatedly that if he misbehaved, all she had to do was buy herself a ticket and come home. Simple as that, and she had a credit card with which to do it.

He picked her up in a limousine on the way to the airport, and she came out carrying a small bag and looking very nervous. He had a briefcase with him, and he made calls from the car, and jotted down some notes for her. And then he chatted with her for a few minutes and read the paper. He didn't seem particularly interested in her, and she could tell that one of his phone calls had been to a woman. She knew that there was a well-known socialite who called him frequently at the office, and he sounded as though he liked her. But Grace didn't get the feeling that he was madly in love with anyone at the moment.

They flew to Los Angeles in first class, and he worked most of the way there, while Grace watched the movie. He was going out to help put together the financial end of a big movie deal for one of his clients. The client had an entertainment lawyer on the West Coast, but Mackenzie represented the big money in the deal, and it was interesting watching him put it together.

It was even more interesting once they got to L.A. They arrived at noon, local time, and went straight to the offices of the entertainment lawyer, and Grace was fascinated by the meetings that took place all day. They were there till six o'clock, which was nine o'clock for her and Charles Mackenzie. He had a dinner date after that, and he dropped her off at the hotel, and told her to charge anything she wanted to the room. They were staying at the Beverly Hills Hotel, and she had to admit she was excited by four movie stars she saw just passing through the lobby.

She tried to get David Glass's number that night, but he wasn't listed in Beverly Hills or L.A. And she was disappointed. She hadn't heard from him in years, but she would have loved to try to see him. She had a feeling, though, that his wife had wanted him to break the connection with her. She'd divined that just from little things he'd said in his letters. And now she hadn't heard from him at all since the birth of their first baby. It would have been nice to tell him that she was doing well, had a good job, and was happy with her new life. She hoped that all was well with him and was sorry that she couldn't reach him. She still thought of him sometimes, and now and then she missed him.

She ordered room service and watched TV, and ordered a movie she had wanted to see for years but never had time to. It was a comedy, and she laughed out loud alone in her room, and then locked all the windows and doors and even put the chain on the door. She half expected him to pound on her door when he got back, and try to get in, but she slept soundly until seven the next morning.

He called and asked her to meet him in the dining room, and at breakfast he explained the meetings that would take place that day, and what he expected her to do. Like her, he was extremely organized, and he enjoyed his work, and always made hers easier by telling her exactly what was expected.

"You did a great job yesterday," he praised her, looking very proper in a gray suit and a starched white shirt. He looked more like New York than L.A. She had worn a pink silk dress and she had a matching sweater over her shoulders. It was a dress she had bought two years before in Chicago, and it was a little softer-looking than most of the clothes she wore to work at the law firm.

"You look very pretty today," he said casually, and she stiffened imperceptibly, but he didn't see it. "Did you see any movie stars in the lobby last night?" And then, forgetting his remark about how she looked, she told him excitedly about the four she'd seen, and the movie that had made her laugh so hard when she watched it. For a brief instant, they were almost friends, and he sensed it. She had relaxed a little bit, which made things easier for him. It was so difficult being with her when she was so uptight, he wondered why she was like that sometimes, but he would never have dared to ask her.

"I love that movie," he laughed, thinking about it. "I saw it three times when it first came out. I hate depressing movies."

"So do I," she admitted as their breakfast came. He was eating scrambled eggs and bacon, and she had oatmeal.

"You don't eat enough," he said sounding fatherly, watching her.

"You should watch your cholesterol," she chided, although he was very thin, but eggs and bacon were out of favor.

"Oh God, spare me. My wife was a vegetarian, and a Buddhist. All of Hollywood is. It was worth getting divorced just so I could eat cheeseburgers in peace again." He smiled at Grace and she laughed in spite of herself.

"Were you married for a long time?"

"Long enough," he grinned. "Seven years." He had been divorced for two. It had cost him nearly a million dollars to get out of it, but at the time it had seemed worth it, in spite of the economic stress it had caused him. No one had snagged his heart seriously since, and the only thing he really regretted was never having children. "I was thirty-three when I married her, and at the time, I was sure that being married to Michelle Andrews was the answer to all my prayers. It turned out that being married to America's hottest movie star wasn't as easy as I thought. Those people pay a high price for celebrity. Higher than the rest of us know. The press is never kind to them, the public wants to own their souls . . . there's no way to survive it, except religion or drugs, and either way is not an ideal solution, as far as I'm concerned. Every time we turned around there was another headline, another scandal. It was tough to live with, and eventually it takes a toll. We're good friends now, but three years ago we weren't." Grace knew from *People* magazine that she had been married twice since, to a younger rock star, and her agent. "Besides, I was too square for her. Too stiff. Too boring." Grace suspected that he had offered his former wife the only stability she'd ever had, or would have. "What about you? Married? Engaged? Divorced seven times? How old are you anyway, I forget. Twenty-three?''

"Almost," she blushed, "in July. And no, not married or engaged. I'm too smart for either one, thanks very much.''

"Oh sure, Grandma, give me a lecture." He laughed and she tried not to think about how attractive he was when he did. She didn't really want to get to know him. "At twenty-two, you're too young to even go out. I hope you don't." He was teasing but she wasn't, and he sensed that.

"I don't.''

"You don't? You're not serious?''

"Maybe.''

"Are you planning to become a nun when you grow up, after your career in a law firm?" He was amused by her now that she was opening up a little bit. She was an intriguing girl. Smart and bright, and funny when she let it show, which wasn't often.

"I have a friend who's trying to talk me into it actually.''

"Who is that? I'll have to have a talk with this friend. Nuns are completely out of style these days. Don't you know that?''

"I guess not," Grace laughed again, "she is one. Sister Eugene. She's terrific.''

"Oh God, you're a religious fanatic. I knew it. Why am I cursed with people like you . . . my wife wanted me to bring the Dalai Lama over from Tibet to stay with us . . . you're all crazy!" He pretended to brush her away, as a waiter poured their coffee and Grace laughed at him.

"I'm not a religious fanatic, I swear. Sometimes it's appealing though. Their life is so simple.''

"And so unreal. You can help the world without giving it up," he said solemnly. It was something he felt strongly about. He liked helping people without taking extreme positions. "Where do you know this nun from?" He was still curious and they didn't have to leave the hotel for another ten minutes.

"We work together at a place where I do volunteer work."

"And where's that?" She saw as he talked to her that he was perfectly shaved, and everything about him was immaculate, and she tried not to notice. This was business.

"It's called St. Andrew's, on the Lower East Side. It's a home for abused women and children."

"You work there?" He seemed surprised, there was more to her than he had suspected, even though she was young, and sometimes very crabby. He was starting to like her better.

"I do. I work there three times a week. It's an amazing place. They take in hundreds of people."

"I never figured you for doing something like that," he said honestly.

"Why not?" she was surprised.

"Because that's a big commitment, a lot of work. Most girls your age would rather go to the discos."

"I've never been to one in my life."

"I'd take you, but I'm too old, and your mother probably wouldn't want you to go with me," he said, implying no threat at all, and for once even Grace didn't react. But she also didn't tell him she had no mother.

The limousine picked them up for their meetings a few minutes after ten. And the next day they concluded the deal, in time to fly back to New York on the

nine p.m. flight, which got them back to New York at
six the following morning. As they were landing he
told her to take the day off. It had been a long two
days, and they hadn't slept on the plane. He had
worked, and she had helped him.

"Are you taking the day off?" she asked.

"I can't. I've got a meeting at ten with Arco, and
I've got a lot to do. Besides, I have a partners' lunch
and there's some complaining I want to do."

"Then I'm going to work too."

"Don't be silly. I'll make do with Mrs. Macpherson
or someone from the typing pool."

"If you're working, so am I. I don't need a day off.
I can sleep tonight." She was very definite about it.

"The joys of youth. Are you sure?" He eyed her
thoughtfully. She was becoming just what the others
had said she was, loyal, hardworking, and nice to be
around. It had been a long time coming.

He dropped her off at her apartment on the way
home, and told her to take her time coming in, and if
she changed her mind, he'd understand. But she was
there before he was. She had all his notes from the
plane typed up, his memos for his ten o'clock meeting
on his desk, and a series of files she knew he'd want
laid out. And his coffee exactly the way he liked it.

"Wow!" He smiled at her. "What did I do to deserve all this?"

"You put up with me for the past three months. I
was pretty awful, and I'm sorry." He had been a perfect gentleman in California, and she was prepared to
be his friend now.

"No, you weren't. I guess I had to prove myself. We
both did." He seemed to understand it perfectly, and

he was really grateful for the caliber of her work, and the minute attention she paid to detail.

At three-thirty that afternoon, he forced her to go home, and said he'd fire her if she didn't. But something had changed between them, and they both knew it. They were allies now, not enemies, and she was there to help him.

Chapter 11

June was incredible in New York that year. It was warm and lush, with hot, breezy days, and balmy nights. The kind of nights where people used to sit on their stoops and hang out the windows. The kind of weather that made people fall in love or wish they had someone to fall in love with.

There were two new women in Charles Mackenzie's life that month, and Grace was aware of both of them, though she wasn't sure she liked either one of them.

One was someone he said he had grown up with, she was divorced and had two kids in college. The other was the producer of a hit Broadway show. He seemed to have a definite attraction to the theater. He had even given two tickets to the play to Grace, and she had taken Winnie and they'd loved it.

"What's he really like?" Winnie asked her afterwards when they went to Sardi's for cheesecake.

"Nice . . . very, very nice . . ." Grace admitted. "It took me a long time to say that. I kept thinking he was going to try and tear my clothes off, and I hated him for it before he even tried."

"Well, did he?" Winnie asked hopefully. She was desperate for Grace to fall in love with someone.

"Of course not. He's a perfect gentleman." She told her about California.

"That's too bad." Winnie sounded disappointed. Grace was her vicarious thrill in life, her only contact with youth, and the daughter she'd never had. She wanted great things for her. And especially a handsome husband.

"He's got a bunch of women running after him. But I don't think he's really crazy about anyone. I think his ex-wife really burned him. He doesn't say much, and he's pretty decent about her, but I get the impression she took a chunk of him." Not only financially, but a piece of his heart that had never recovered.

"One of the girls on fourteen said it cost him close to a million dollars," Winnie said in a whisper.

"I meant emotionally," Grace said primly. "Anyway, he's a nice man. And he works like a dog. He stays there till all hours." He always called a cab for her, or a limousine when she worked late for him, and he was always careful to let her go on time the nights she worked at St. Andrew's. "He's very considerate." And he had been complaining ever since she'd told him about St. Andrew's. He thought the neighborhood was just too dangerous for her to be going there by subway at night. He didn't even like it on Sundays.

"At least take a cab," he growled. But it would have cost her a fortune. And she had been doing it for months now with no problem.

Winnie told her then that Tom's wife was having another baby. And they both laughed wondering how long it would take for Bill's wife to start another baby too. The two men were like clones of each other.

After they left the restaurant, they hailed a taxi and

Grace dropped Winnie off and went home herself, thinking how much she liked her job now.

Charles went to California again in June, but he didn't take her this time. He only stayed for a day, and he said it wasn't worth it. And the weekend he came back, she worked with him on Saturday in the office. They worked till six o'clock, and he apologized for not taking her to dinner afterwards. He had a date, but he felt terrible working her all day and then not doing anything to reward her.

"Next week you should take a friend to '21' and charge it to me," he suggested, looking pleased at the idea, "or tonight, if you like." Grace knew immediately that she'd take Winnie, and the older woman would be ecstatic about it.

"You don't have to do that for me," Grace said shyly.

"I want to. You have to get something out of this, you know. There are supposed to be perks for working for the boss. I'm not sure what they're supposed to be, but dinner at '21' should definitely be one of them, so make yourself a reservation." He never tried to take her out and she loved that about him. She was completely relaxed with him now. And she thanked him again before they both left. She thought he had a date with someone new, and she somehow had the impression that she was a lawyer in a rival law firm. There had been a lot of messages lately from Spielberg and Stein.

She stayed home and watched television that night, but she called Winnie and told her about their dinner at '21,' and Winnie was so excited, she said she wouldn't sleep in the meantime.

And the next day, Grace went down to St. Andrew's as usual. The weather was still warm, and there were lots of people in the streets now, which, in some ways, made it safer for her.

She had a long, hard day, working with the new intakes. The warm weather was bringing them in in droves. Somehow, there always seemed to be new excuses for their beatings.

She had dinner in the kitchen with Sister Eugene and Father Tim and she was telling them about the movie stars she'd seen in the lobby of the hotel when she went to California.

"All was well?" he asked. They hadn't had time to talk about it in the month since she'd been there and back, but he assumed so, or she would have told him.

"It was great." She beamed.

It was eleven o'clock when she left, which was later than she usually left on a Sunday. She thought about taking a cab, but the weather was so warm, she decided to take the subway after all. She hadn't even gotten a block away when someone grabbed her arm and yanked her hard into a doorway. She saw instantly that he was a tall, thin black man, and she suspected that he was a drug addict or just a petty thief. Something in her gut went tight, and she watched him as he shook her hard and then slammed her against the door where they were standing.

"You think you're a smart bitch, don't you? You think you know it all . . ." He put his hands around her throat, and her eyes never left his. He didn't seem to want her money. All he wanted was to abuse her.

"I don't know anything," she said calmly, not wanting to frighten him, as he almost strangled her in a fury. "Let go, man . . . you don't want to do this."

"Oh yes, I do," and then, in a single gesture, he flicked out a long, thin knife and pressed it to her throat with a single practiced gesture. Without moving an inch, she was instantly reminded of her time in prison. But there was no one to save her now . . . no Luana . . . no Sally . . .

"Don't do it . . . just take my bag. There's fifty dollars in it, it's all I've got . . . and my watch." She held her arm out. It was the farewell gift Cheryl had given her in Chicago. A small price to pay for her life now.

"I don't want your fucking watch, bitch . . . I want Isella."

"Isella?" She had no idea what he was talking about. He reeked of cheap Scotch and sweat as he held her against his chest with his switchblade at her throat.

"My wife . . . you took my wife . . . and now she won't come back . . . she says she's goin' back to Cleveland . . ."

It was about St. Andrew's, then, and one of the women she'd helped there.

"I didn't take her . . . I didn't do anything . . . maybe you should talk to her . . . maybe if you get help, she'll come back . . ."

"You took my kids . . ." He was crying then, and his whole body seemed to be twitching, as she frantically searched her memory for a woman named Isella, but she couldn't remember her. She saw so many women there. She wondered if she'd ever seen this one. Usually, she remembered who they were. But not Isella.

"No one can take your kids away from you . . . or your wife . . . you have to talk to them . . . you need help . . . what's your name?" Maybe if she called him by name he wouldn't kill her.

"Sam . . . why do you care?"

"I care." And then she thought of what might have been her only salvation. "I'm a nun . . . I gave my life to God for people like you, Sam . . . I've been in prisons . . . I've been in a lot of places . . . it's not going to do anyone any good if you hurt me."

"You a nun?" he practically shrieked at her. "Shit . . . nobody told me that . . . shit . . ." He kicked the door behind her hard, but no one came. No one saw. No one cared on Delancey. "Why you messin' with my bizness? Why you tell her to go home?"

"So you can't hurt her anymore. You don't want to hurt her, Sam . . . you don't want to hurt anyone . . ."

"Shit." He started to cry in earnest. "Fucking nun," he spat at her, "think you can do anything you want, for God. Fuck God . . . and fuck you . . . fuck all of you, bitch . . ." He grabbed her by the throat then, and banged her head hard into the door, it felt like it was full of sand and everything went gray and blurry for an instant, and then as she started to fall, she felt him kick her hard in the stomach, and then again, and someone was pounding on her face and she couldn't stop him. She couldn't call out to him. She couldn't say his name. It was a hailstorm of fists pounding on her face, her head, her stomach, her back, and then it stopped. She heard him run, she heard him shouting at her again, and then he was gone, and she lay tasting her own blood in the doorway.

The police found her that night, on their late night rounds, slumped over in the doorway. They poked her with their nightsticks, like they did the drunks, and then one of them saw her blood on it, shining in the streetlights.

"Shit," he said, and called out to his partner, "get

an ambulance, quick!'' The officer knelt down next to
Grace and felt for a pulse. It was barely there, but she
still had one. And as he turned her over slowly on her
back, he could see how badly she'd been beaten. Her
face was covered with blood, and her hair was matted
to her head. He wasn't sure if there were any broken
bones or internal injuries, but she was gasping for air
even in her unconscious state, and his partner came up
to him a minute later.

"Whatcha got?"

"A bad one . . . she's not dressed for this neighborhood. God only knows where she came from." He
opened her handbag and looked in her wallet as they
waited for the ambulance to come from Bellevue. "She
lives on Eighty-fourth, she's a long way from home. She
should know better than to walk around down here."

"There's a crisis center down the street," the policeman who had called the ambulance said as the
other one checked her pulse again and put her handbag under her head as they laid her gently on the
street. "She might work there. I'll check it out after
you hop the ambulance, if you want." One of them
had to ride with her to make the report, if she lived
that long. She wasn't looking good to either of them,
her pulse was getting weaker, and so was her breathing.

The ambulance came less than five minutes later,
with shrieking sirens, and the paramedics were quick
to put her on a backboard and give her oxygen as they
slid the board into the ambulance.

"Any idea how bad it is?" one of the cops asked
the senior paramedic. Grace was completely unconscious and had never stirred since they found her. All
she'd done was gasp for air, and they were giving her
oxygen with a bag and mask.

"It doesn't look good," the paramedic said honestly. "She's got a head injury. That could mean anything." From death to retardation to a permanent coma. There was no way for them to tell there. She looked terrible in the light as they raced uptown to Bellevue.

Her face was battered almost beyond recognition, her eyes were swollen shut, there was a knife wound on her neck, and when they pulled open her shirt and unzipped her jeans, they saw how bad the bruises were there. Her attacker had very nearly killed her. "It looks pretty bad," the paramedic said to the cop in a whisper. "There's not much left of her. I wonder if the guy knew her. What's her name?"

The policeman opened her wallet again and read it aloud to one of the paramedics, as he nodded. They had work to do here. They had to try to keep her going till they got to Bellevue.

"Come on, Grace . . . open your eyes for us . . . you're okay . . . we're not going to hurt you . . . we're taking you to the hospital, Grace . . . Grace . . . Grace . . . shit. . ." They had an IV going and a blood pressure cuff on her and it was dropping sharply. "We're losing her," he said to his colleague. It was going down, down, down . . . and then it was gone, but the paramedics were quick to respond and one of them grabbed a defibrillator and literally yanked her bra off and put it on her.

"Stand back," he told the cop as they pulled into the driveway, "got 'er," her body received a huge shock, and her heart started again, just as the driver yanked open the doors and two attendants from the emergency room rushed forward.

"She was in cardiac arrest a second ago," the paramedic who had shocked her explained as he covered her bare chest with her jacket. "I think we're dealing with some internal bleeding . . . head injury . . ." He told them everything he knew and had seen as all five of them ran into the emergency room, running beside the gurney. Her blood pressure plummeted again as soon as they got inside, but this time her heart didn't stop. She already had an IV in her, and the chief resident came in with three nurses and started issuing orders, as the paramedics and the policeman disappeared, and went to the front desk to fill out papers.

"Christ, she's a mess," one of the paramedics who'd come in with her said to the policeman. "Do you know what happened to her?"

"Just your average New York mugging," the policeman said unhappily. He could see from her driver's license that she was twenty-two years old. It was too young to give your life to a mugger. Any age was, but especially a young kid like that. There was no way of telling if she'd been pretty, or ever would be, if she even lived, which seemed doubtful.

"Looks like more than a mugging," the paramedic said, "nobody can beat up someone like that unless they've got a beef with them. Maybe it was her boyfriend."

"In a doorway on Delancey? Not likely. She's wearing designer jeans, and she's got an Upper East Side address. She was mugged."

But when his partner went to St. Andrew's, Father Tim suspected that it was more than bad luck that had felled Grace Adams. He'd had a visit from the police only the day before to tell him that a woman called Isella Jones had been murdered by her husband that day, he had killed both of his kids as well, and then disappeared. And the policeman had suggested that Father Tim warn his nurses and social workers that the man was violent and on the run. It was possible that he would never come to St. Andrew's at all. Or he might, if he blamed them for encouraging Isella to leave him and try to get home to Cleveland. But it never dawned on him to say anything to Grace. She had been in California when Isella had shown up, beaten and terrified, with her children. Father Tim had warned the others and told them to spread the word and watch out for a man called Sam Jones. They had been going to put a bulletin on the board to alert everyone, but they had had so much to do for the past two days that they never did it.

When Father Tim heard what had happened to Grace, he was sure that the incident was related, and they put out an APB on Sam Jones, with a mug shot and his description. He'd been in plenty of trouble before and he had a record an arm long, and a history of violence. If they ever found him, the murder of his wife and kids would put him away forever, not to mention what he had done to Grace in the doorway on Delancey.

Father Tim looked sick when he asked him, "How bad is it?"

"It looked pretty bad when the ambulance left, Father. I'm sorry."

"So am I." There were tears in his eyes, as he pulled off a black T-shirt, and grabbed a black shirt with a Roman collar. "Can you give me a ride to the hospital?"

"Sure, Father." Father Tim quickly told Sister Eugene where he was going, and hurried out to the patrol car with the officer. Four minutes later they were at

Bellevue. Grace was still in the emergency room and a whole team of doctors and nurses was working on her. But so far, none of them was encouraged by the results. She was barely hanging on at that moment.

"How is she?" Father Tim asked the nurse at the desk.

"Critical. That's all I know." And then she looked at him, he was a priest after all, and she probably wasn't going to make it. That's what one of the interns had told her. She was so bashed up inside, it was almost hopeless. "Do you want to see her?" He nodded, feeling responsible for what happened. Sam Jones had gone after Grace, and nearly killed her.

Father Tim followed the nurse into the room and he was shocked at what he saw there. Three nurses were hovering over her, two interns, and the resident. She was almost naked, swathed in sheets, and her whole body was black it was so bruised and swollen. Her face looked like a deep purple melon. She was covered in ice packs, swathed in bandages, there were screens and scans and IVs and instruments everywhere. It was the worst thing he'd ever seen, and at a nod from the resident, he gave her last rites. He didn't even know what religion she was, but it didn't matter. She was a child of God, and He knew how much she had given Him. Father Tim was crying as he stood in the corner and prayed for her, and it was hours before they stopped working on her, and looked up. Her head was wrapped in bandages by then, they had stitched up her face and her throat. He had only used the knife on her neck, he had lacerated her face with his fist. One arm was broken, and five ribs. And they were going to operate as soon as she was stable. They knew by then from scans that she had a ruptured spleen, and he had damaged her kidneys, and her pelvis was broken too.

"Is there anything he didn't get?" Father Tim asked miserably.

"Not much." The resident was used to it, but this time it looked bad even to him. She had barely survived it. "Her feet look pretty good." The doctor smiled and the priest tried to.

She went to surgery at six o'clock and it was noon before they were through. Sister Eugene had joined him by then, and they were sitting together quietly, praying for her, when the chief resident came to find them.

"Are you her next of kin?" he asked, confused by the priest's collar. At first he'd just thought he was the hospital priest, but now he realized that he was there specifically for Grace, as was the woman with him.

"Yes, I am," Father Tim said without hesitation. "How is she?"

"She made it through the surgery. We took out her spleen, patched up her kidneys, put a pin in her pelvis. She's a lucky girl, we managed to get all the important stuff put back together. And the house plastic surgeon sewed up her face and swears it'll never show. The big question mark right now is the head injury. Everything looks okay on the EEG but you can't always tell. It could look fine and she might never wake up again, and just stay in a coma. We just don't know yet. We'll know a lot more in the next few days, Father. I'm sorry." He touched his arm, and nodded at the young nun before he walked away to get some rest. She had been a tough case, but at least she'd made it and they hadn't lost her. For a while there, it had been mighty close. Grace had been lucky.

Before the resident left, Father Tim had thanked him and asked when they could see her and he said that as soon as she was out of the recovery room in a few more hours, she would be taken to ICU upstairs. He and Sister Eugene went to the cafeteria for something to eat then, and she told Father Tim that he should go home and get some rest, but he didn't want to leave yet.

"I was thinking that maybe we should call her office. No one knows what's happened to her, except us. They must be wondering why she didn't come in," which was exactly the case. Charles Mackenzie had had one of the secretaries call her half a dozen times at home, but there was no answer. She could have overstayed on a weekend romance, but he kept insisting that it wasn't like her. He had no idea who else to call, but for all he knew, she could have slipped and hit her head in the bathtub. He had even thought of trying to locate her superintendent but decided to let it wait till after lunch. As soon as he got back, there was a call from Father Timothy Finnegan, and the secretary who answered said it was about Grace.

"I'll take it," he said, and picked up the phone with a sudden queasy feeling. "Hello?"

"Mr. Mackenzie?"

"Yes, Father, what can I do for you?"

"Not a great deal, I'm afraid. It's about Grace." Charles felt his blood run cold. Without hearing more, he knew something terrible had happened to her.

"Is she all right?"

There was an endless silence.

"I'm afraid not. She had a terrible accident last night. She was mugged and badly beaten after leaving St. Andrew's, the crisis center where she does volunteer

work. It was late, and . . . we don't know all the details yet, but we're afraid it may have been the crazed
husband of one of our clients. He killed his wife and
children on Saturday. We're not sure if it was he that
attacked Grace. But whoever did it, beat Grace within a
hair of killing her.''

"Where is she?'' Charles's hand shook as he
grabbed his pen and a notepad.

"She's at Bellevue. She's just come out of surgery.''

"How bad is it?'' It was so unfair, she was so young,
and so alive, and so pretty.

"Pretty bad. She lost her spleen, though the doctor says she can live without it. Her kidneys are damaged, she has a broken pelvis and half a dozen broken
ribs. Her face was pretty badly cut up, and he sliced her
throat but only superficially. The worst of it is that she
has a head injury. That's the main concern now. They
said we'll just have to wait and see. I'm sorry to call
with such bad news. I just thought you'd want to
know,'' and then, he didn't know why he told him, but
he felt he had to, "She thinks a lot of you, Mr. Mackenzie. She thinks you're a great person.''

"I think the world of her too. Is there anything we
can do for her at this point?''

"Pray.''

"I will, Father, I will. And thank you. Let me know
if there's any change, will you?''

"Of course.''

The moment he hung up, Charles Mackenzie
called the head of Bellevue, and a neurosurgeon he
knew well, and asked him to have a look at Grace immediately. The head of the hospital had promised to
put her in a private room, and see that she had private

nurses. But first she was going to intensive care, where they were experts at dealing with trauma.

Charles couldn't believe what they'd told him when he called the hospital. He remembered telling her how dangerous the neighborhood was, and that she should be taking cabs. And now look what had happened. He felt shaken for the rest of the afternoon, and he called at five and asked if there was any improvement. She was in intensive care by then, but they didn't have any news. She was listed as critical. And at six o'clock, he was still at the office when his neurosurgeon friend called him back.

"You wouldn't believe what that guy did to her, Charles. It's inhuman."

"Will she be all right?" Charles asked him sadly. He hated to see something like that happen to her, or anyone. And he was surprised to realize how fond of her he had grown. She was so young, she could have been his daughter, he realized, feeling startled.

"She could be all right," the doctor answered. "It's hard to say yet. The other injuries should heal pretty well. The head is another story. She could be fine, or she couldn't. It all depends if she comes out of it in the next few days. She didn't need brain surgery, which is fortunate, but there's going to be some swelling for a while. We just have to be patient. Is she a friend of yours?"

"My secretary."

"Damn shame. She's just a kid, from what I saw on the chart. And there's no family, is there?"

"I don't really know. She doesn't talk about it. She never told me." It made him wonder now what her situation was. She never talked about her personal life and family. He knew almost nothing about her.

"I spoke to a nun who was sitting with her. The priest who came in earlier had apparently gone home to rest. But the Sister says she has no one in the world. That's pretty rough for a young kid. The Sister says she's a nice-looking girl, though it's a little hard to tell at the moment. The plastic resident sewed her up so she should look okay. It's just the head we have to worry about now." Charles felt sick when he hung up. It was too much to bear. And how could she not have any family? How could she be alone at twenty-two? That didn't make sense to him. All she had was a nun and priest with her. It was hard to believe she had no one else, but maybe she didn't.

He sat at his desk for another hour, trying to work, and got nowhere, and finally he couldn't stand it any longer.

At seven o'clock he took a cab down to Bellevue, and went to the ICU. Sister Eugene had left by then too, though they were calling regularly from St. Andrew's for news, and Father Tim had said he'd be back later that night when things settled down at the shelter. But there were only nurses with her now, and for the moment nothing had changed since that morning.

Charles went and sat with her for a while, unable to believe what she looked like. She would have been completely unrecognizable, except for her long, graceful fingers. He held her hand in his own and gently stroked it.

"Hi Grace, I came down to see you." He spoke quietly, so he wouldn't disturb anyone, but he wanted to say something to her, on the off chance that she could hear him, although it certainly seemed unlikely in the state she was in. "You're going to be fine, you know . . . and don't forget that dinner at '21.' I'll take you there myself if you hurry up and get well . . . and you know, it would be nice if you would open your eyes for us . . . it's not too exciting like this . . . open your eyes . . . that's right, Grace . . . open your eyes . . ." He went on talking soothingly to her, and just as he was thinking about leaving her, he saw her eyelids flutter and signaled to the nurses at the desk. His heart was pounding at what he'd seen. Her survival was vital to him. He wanted her to live. He barely knew her, but he didn't want to lose her. "I think she moved her eyelids," he explained.

"It's probably just a reflex," the nurse said with a sympathetic smile. But then she did it again, and the nurse stood and watched her.

"Move your eyes again, Grace," he said quietly. "Come on, I know you can do it. Yes, you can." And she did. And then she opened them briefly, moaned, and closed them. He wanted to shout with excitement. "What does that mean?" he asked the nurse.

"That she's regaining consciousness." She smiled at him. "I'll call the doctor."

"That was great, Grace," he praised her, stroking her fingers again, willing her to live, just to prove she could do it, just so one more mugger wouldn't win a life he didn't deserve to take. "Come on, Grace . . . you can't just lie there, sleeping . . . we've got work to do . . . what about that letter you promised me you'd do . . ." He was saying anything he could think of and then he almost cried when he saw her frown, the eyes opened again and she stared at him blankly.

". . . What . . . letter? . . ." she croaked through bruised swollen lips as her eyes closed again, and this time he did cry. The tears rolled down his cheeks as he looked at her. She had heard him. And then the doctor came, and Charles explained what had happened. They did another EEG on her, and her brain waves were still normal, but now her reactions were slowly returning. She turned away when they tried to shine a light in her eyes, and she moaned and then cried when they touched her. She was in pain, which they thought was a great sign. Now she would have to move through various stages of misery in order to improve.

And at midnight, Charles was still there with her, he couldn't bring himself to leave her. But it appeared now that her brain was not damaged. They would have to do more tests, and they had to be sure that there was no further hidden trauma, but it looked as though she would in fact recover and be all right eventually.

Father Tim had come back by then, and he was in ICU too when the doctor told Charles that the prognosis looked pretty good. And then the two men went out into the hall to talk while one of the nurses attended to Grace and gave her a shot for the pain. She was in agony from all her bruises and the operation, and the damage to her head and face.

"My God, she's going to make it," Father Tim said with a look of joy and excitement. He had prayed for her all day, and had two masses said for her. And all the nuns were praying for her that night. "What a great girl she is." They had also caught Sam Jones earlier that night, and charged him with the murder of his wife and two children, and the attempted murder of Grace Adams. He had admitted mugging her, because she was the first one he saw come out of St. Andrew's, and he felt that that was where all his troubles began. "You don't know how much she's done for us, Mr.

Mackenzie. The girl is a saint," Father Tim said to Charles in the hallway.

"Why does she do it?" Charles looked puzzled, as the two men sat drinking coffee. They suddenly felt like brothers, and they were both relieved that Grace was going to recover.

"I think there's a lot about Grace that none of us know," Father Tim said quietly. "I don't think the life of battered women and children is new to her. I think she's a girl who's suffered a great deal and survived it, and now she wants to help others do the same. She'd make a great nun," he grinned, and Charles pointed a finger at him.

"Don't you dare! She should get married and have kids."

"I'm not sure she ever will," Father Tim said honestly. "I don't think that's what she wants, to be honest. Some of them heal, the way she has, but many of the children who suffer like the ones we see can never cross over into a life where they can trust enough to be whole people again. I think it's miraculous if they come as far as Grace has, and can give so much to others. Maybe wanting more than that is too much to ask."

"If she can give to so many, why not to a husband?"

"That's a lot harder." Father Tim smiled philosophically at him, and then decided to admit something to him. It might give him an insight. "She was desperately afraid to go to California with you. And eternally grateful when you didn't hurt her, or use her."

" 'Use' her? What do you mean?"

"I think she's seen a lot of pain. A lot of men do

unspeakable things. We see it every day. I think she fully expected you to do something unsuitable to her." Charles Mackenzie looked embarrassed at the mere idea of it, and he was horrified that she would think that of him, and even say it to another person.

"I guess that's why she was so upset when she first came to my office. She didn't trust me."

"Probably. She doesn't trust anyone a great deal. And I don't suppose this will help. But at least this wasn't personal. That's very different. It's when someone you love really hurts you that it destroys the soul . . . like a mother with a child, or a man and a woman." He was a wise man and Charles listened to him with interest, wondering how much of what he said applied to Grace. It sounded like he wasn't sure of her history either, and Charles wondered if he could be wrong about her. But he seemed to know Grace a lot better than Charles did. And the things he said about her tore at his heart. He wondered what terrible things had happened to her to leave her so badly scarred as a woman. He couldn't even begin to imagine what lay behind her cool facade and gentle manner.

"Do you know anything at all about her parents?" Charles was curious about her now.

"She never talks about them. I only know they're dead. She has no family at all. But I don't think that bothers her. She came here from Chicago. She never talks about relatives or friends. I think she's a very lonely girl, but she accepts it. Her only interest is working for you, and coming to St. Andrew's. She works twenty-five or thirty hours a week there."

"That doesn't leave much time for anything else except sleeping. She works forty-five or fifty for me."

"That's the whole of it, Mr. Mackenzie."

Charles was dying to talk to her now, to ask her questions about her life, to ask her why she really worked at St. Andrew's. Suddenly she wasn't just a girl he worked with every day, she was a great deal more interesting than that, and there were a thousand questions he wanted to ask her.

The nurse let them back in then. And Father Tim stood a little apart to let Charles talk to her about trivial things. He sensed that there was more interest there than the man knew, or than Grace suspected.

She was fuzzy again when Charles sat down at her bedside, the shot had made her woozy, but at least she wasn't in as much pain.

"Thank you . . . for coming . . ." She tried to smile but her lips were still too swollen.

"I'm so sorry this happened to you, Grace." He was going to have a talk with her about working at St. Andrew's, but that would come later, if she'd listen. "They caught the guy who did it."

"He was . . . angry . . . about his wife . . . Isella." She would remember the woman's name forever.

"I hope they hang him," Charles said angrily, and she opened her eyes and looked at him again. And this time she did manage a small smile, looking very dizzy. "Why don't you sleep . . . I'll come back tomorrow."

She nodded, and Father Tim spent a few minutes with her too, and then both men left to let her sleep. Charles dropped him off at the shelter in a cab, and then drove uptown, after promising to stay in touch with the young priest. He liked him. And Charles had also promised to come and visit the center. He was going to, too, he wanted to know more about Grace, and that was one way to do it.

Charles went back to visit Grace for the next three days, canceling his lunches to be there, even one with his producer friend, but he didn't want to let Grace down. When they moved her to a private room, Charles brought Winnie to the hospital with him. She cried when she saw Grace, and wrung her hands, and kissed her on the only tiny patch of her face with no bandages or bruises. She looked slightly better by then. A lot of the swelling had gone down, but everything hurt, and she found she could hardly move, between her ribs and her head, and her pelvis. Her kidneys were healing well, and the doctor said she wouldn't miss her spleen, but she was pretty miserable, every inch of her ached and felt as though it had been shattered.

On Saturday, almost a week after the accident, the nurse Charles had insisted on hiring for her coaxed her out of bed and made her walk to the bathroom. It hurt so much to do it that she almost fainted, but she celebrated her victory with a glass of fruit juice when she got back to bed. She was sheet white, but smiling, when Charles arrived with a huge bunch of spring flowers. He had been bringing flowers for her daily, and magazines, and candy, and books. He had wanted to cheer her up, and he wasn't sure how to do it.

"What are you doing here?" She looked embarrassed to see him, and it brought a little color back to her face when she blushed. "Today's Saturday, don't you have something better to do?" she scolded him, sounding more like herself than she had in days. She looked more like herself too. Her face looked like a rainbow of blues and greens and purples, but the swelling was almost all gone, and the stitches were healing so well you almost couldn't see them. The only thing Charles wondered about now was her spirit, after his conversation with Father Tim about what must have led her to St. Andrew's in the first place. But it was too soon to ask her how she felt about that.

"Aren't you supposed to be going away for the weekend?" She remembered making arrangements for him to attend a regatta on Long Island. She had rented him a small house in Quogue, and now it was wasted if he stayed in New York.

"I canceled." He was matter-of-fact, and watched her face carefully. "You're looking pretty good." He smiled and handed her some magazines he had brought her. All week he had sent her little trinkets, a bed jacket, some slippers, a pillow for her neck, some cologne. It was embarrassing, but she had to admit, she liked it. She had mentioned it to Winnie on the phone, and the older woman tittered like an old mother hen. Grace had laughed at her, and told her that she was outrageous, she never gave up on romance. "Of course not," Winnie confessed proudly. She had promised to come and visit Grace on Sunday.

"I want to go home," Grace said to Charles, looking mournful.

"I don't think that's in the cards for a while," Charles said with a smile. They had said three weeks the day before, which didn't appeal to Grace at all, and meant she'd still be in the hospital on her birthday.

"I want to go back to work." They had told her she'd be on crutches for a month or two, but she still wanted to go back to work as soon as she got out of the hospital. She had nothing else to do. And she also wanted to go back to St. Andrew's as soon as they'd let her.

"Don't push yourself, Grace. Why don't you take some time off when you get out, and go have some fun somewhere?"

But she only laughed at the idea. "Where? Like the Riviera?" She couldn't afford the time to go anywhere for very long. Maybe a weekend at Atlantic City. She didn't have any vacation coming. She hadn't worked at the firm long enough to qualify for a week off. She knew she had to work there a year before she could take two weeks off. It was already too much that he had told her the firm would pay for everything her insurance didn't. Her whole three weeks at Bellevue and everything they had to do for her would probably cost close to fifty thousand dollars.

"Sure, why not go to the Riviera? Charter yourself a yacht," Charles teased her. "Do something fun for a change." She laughed at him, and they sat talking for a while. She was surprised by how easy it was to talk to him, and he didn't seem to want to go anywhere at all. He was still there when her nurse went to lunch, and he even helped her hobble to the chair clutching his arm, and gently propped a pillow behind her when she got there, victorious but pale and exhausted.

"How come you never had any children?" she asked suddenly, as they sat and chatted, and he fussed over her and poured her a glass of ginger ale. He would have made a great father, she thought, but didn't say so.

"My wife hated kids," he smiled. "She wanted to be a child herself. Actresses are like that. And I indulged her," he said, sounding a little embarrassed.

"Are you sorry? That you didn't have kids, I

mean?" She made him sound very old, as though it was too late now, and he laughed as he gave it a moment's careful thought.

"Sometimes. I used to think I'd remarry and have children after Michelle left me. But maybe not. I think I'm too comfortable like this to do anything dramatic now." In the last couple of years, he had gotten lazy about finding a serious involvement. He liked his temporaries, and his freedom and independence. It was tempting to stay that way forever. But the question she had asked him opened a door for him as well. "What about you? Why don't you want a husband and children?" He knew a lot more about her now, but the question surprised her. It came out of nowhere.

"What makes you say that?" She looked away from him uncomfortably, afraid of his question. But when she looked back into his eyes, she saw someone she could trust there. "How did you know that's how I felt?"

"A girl your age doesn't spend all her time doing volunteer work, and with sixty-year-old spinsters like Winnie, unless she's got very little interest in finding a husband. I assume that I'm correct?" he questioned, looking at her pointedly with a smile.

"You are."

"Why?"

She waited a long time before she answered. She didn't want to lie to him, but she wasn't ready to tell him the truth either. "It's a long story."

"Does it have to do with your parents?" His eyes bore into hers, but not unkindly. He had already proven that she could trust him, and that he cared about her welfare.

"Yes."

"Was it very bad?" She nodded, and he felt a deep grief for her. It hurt him to think of anyone hurting her. "Did anyone help you?"

"Not for a long time, and it was too late by then. It was all over."

"It's never all over, and it's never too late. You don't have to live with that pain for the rest of your life, Grace. You have a right to be free of it, and have a future with a decent guy." He felt proprietary now and wanted her to have a good, solid future.

"I have a present, which means more to me. Used to be I didn't even have that. I don't ask too much of the future," Grace said quietly with a look of sorrow.

"But you should," he tried to urge her forward. "You're so young, you're practically half my age. Your life is just beginning."

But she shook her head, with a smile that was full of wisdom and sadness. "Believe me, Charles," he had insisted she call him that now that she was in the hospital, "my life is not beginning. It's half over."

"It just feels that way. It won't be over for a long time, which is why you need more in it than just working for me, and at St. Andrew's."

"You trying to fix me up with someone?" She laughed, stretching her long legs before her. He was a kind man, and she knew he meant well, but he didn't know what he was doing. She was not an ordinary twenty-two-year-old girl with a few rocky memories and a rosy future. She felt more like a survivor of a death camp, and in some ways she was. Charles Mackenzie had never encountered anything like that, and he wasn't sure what to do for her.

"I wish I knew someone worth fixing you up with," he answered her with a smile. All the men he knew were either too old, or too stupid. They didn't deserve her.

They talked of other things then, sailing, which he loved, and summers on Martha's Vineyard when he was a boy, and places he'd been. He still had a house in Martha's Vineyard, though he rarely ever went there anymore. They didn't talk about painful things again, and at the end of the afternoon, he left and told her to get some rest. He told her he was going to see friends in Connecticut the next day. She was touched that he spent so much time with her.

Winnie came Sunday afternoon, and Father Tim, and Grace was just settling down to watching television before she went to sleep that night, when Charles strode in, in khaki pants and a starched blue shirt, looking like an ad in *GQ*, and smelling like the country.

"I was on my way back into town, and I thought I'd stop by and see how you were," he said, looking happy to see her. And in spite of herself, she beamed at him. She had actually missed him that afternoon, and that had worried her a little. He was only her boss after all, not a lifelong friend, and she had no right to expect to see him. She didn't, but she enjoyed him, more than she would ever have expected.

"Did you have fun in the country?" she asked, feeling relieved that he was there.

"No," he said honestly, "I thought of you all afternoon. You're a lot more fun than they were."

"Now I know you're crazy." He came to sit on the foot of the bed and told her funny stories about the afternoon, and in spite of herself, she was disappointed when he left. It was ten o'clock by then, and he

thought she should get some sleep, although he didn't
want to leave either.

But that night, as she lay in bed and thought about
him, she started to panic. What was she doing with
him? What did she want from him? If she opened up to
him like this, he would only hurt her. She forced herself to remember the anguish and embarrassment of
Marcus, who had been so good to her at first, so patient, and then betrayed her. It terrified her just thinking about Charles. Maybe all she was to Charles
Mackenzie was a conquest. She could feel her chest
tighten as she thought about it, and as though he had
read her mind, the phone rang next to her bed. She
couldn't imagine who it was, but it was Charles, and he
sounded worried.

"I want to say something to you . . . and you may
think I'm crazy, but I'm going to say it to you anyway
. . . I want to be your friend, Grace. I won't hurt you,
but I just got worried, trying to imagine what you were
thinking. I don't know what's happening. I just know
that I think about you all the time, and I worry about
what's happened to you in the past, although I can't
even imagine it . . . but I don't want to lose you . . .
I don't want to scare you away, or frighten you, or
make you worry about your job. Let's just be two people for a little while, two people who care about each
other, if we do, and go very slowly from there." She
couldn't believe what she was hearing, but in a way, it
was a relief to have him say it.

"What are we doing, Charles?" she said nervously.
"What about my job? We can't pretend I don't work
for you. What happens when I come back?"

"You're not coming back for a while, Grace. We'll
know a lot more by then. I think we're both feeling

something we don't understand right now. Maybe we're just friends, maybe your accident scared us both. Maybe it's more than that. Maybe it never can be. But you need to know who I am, and I want to know who you are . . . I want to know your pain . . . I want to know what makes you laugh. I want to be there for you . . . I want to help you. . . ."

"And then what? You walk away from me? You find another secretary who amuses you for a few weeks and have her tell you all her secrets?" She was relieved that he called her but she was too afraid to let herself trust him.

Charles remembered Father Tim's words, that some of the survivors just can't let go. But he wanted her to be one who could, no matter what it took to get there.

"That's not fair," Charles chided her. "I've never been in a situation like this before. I've never gone out with anyone at the law firm, or anyone who worked for me." And then he smiled in spite of himself. "And you can hardly say I'm going out with you. You can't go anywhere except from the bed to the chair, and even I wouldn't have the bad taste to attack you."

She laughed at what he said, and her voice sounded deep and sexy as she lay in bed, and she wanted to let herself trust him, but she knew she couldn't . . . or could she?

"I just don't know," Grace said, still sounding nervous.

"You don't have to know anything right now . . . except if it's okay with you if I visit you. That's all you need to decide right now. I was just afraid you'd panic and start to go crazy once you were alone, and got to thinking."

"I was . . . tonight . . ." she said honestly with a little girl's smile. "I was starting to panic over what we're doing."

"We're not doing anything, so just shut up and get better. And one of these days," he said so gently, it was almost a caress, "when you feel strong enough, I want you to tell me what happened to you in the past. You can't expect me to really understand till you do that. Have you ever told anyone?" He worried about that. How could she live with all those dark secrets?

"Two people," she admitted to him. "A wonderful woman I knew, a therapist . . . she was killed in a plane crash on her honeymoon almost three years ago. And a man who was my lawyer, but I haven't talked to him in a long time either."

"You haven't had a lot of luck, have you, Grace?"

She shook her head sadly, and then shrugged. "I don't know . . . lately I have. I can't complain." She decided to take a huge leap then. "I was lucky when I met you." Saying those words to him almost choked her and he knew it.

"Not as lucky as I was. Now get some sleep, sweetheart . . ." he said softly into the phone, "I'll come by at lunch. And maybe I'll even come back for dinner. Maybe I can bring you something from '21.' "

"I was going to take Winnie there next week," she said guiltily.

"You'll have plenty of time for that when you're well. Now go to sleep," he whispered to her, wishing he could put his arms around her and protect her. She made him feel different than he had ever felt with any woman before. All he wanted to do was take care of her and keep her safe from harm. So many terrible things must have happened to her, even as recently as a week ago. But he wanted to change all that now.

They said good night and hung up, and she lay there thinking about him for a long time. He frightened her with the things he said to her, and his persistent attention, but oddly enough, as terrifying as it was, she liked it. And she felt a tingling sensation in her gut that she had never felt before for any man, until Charles Mackenzie.

Chapter 12

Charles came to see her twice the next day, and either once or twice a day for the next three weeks, until she was finally released from Bellevue. She could get around more easily on crutches by then, and take care of herself, but she still didn't have as much stamina as she would have liked. The doctor told her to wait another two weeks before she went back to work.

At the office, Charles was making do with temps, and Grace felt terribly guilty about it, but he was the first one to tell her not to rush back to work, not to come back in fact, until she was ready.

They spent hours together while she was in the hospital. She knew he'd had to cancel almost all his plans to be with her, but he pretended not to even notice. They laughed, and they talked, and played cards, and he joked with her. He didn't force any confidences from her, and he helped her walk down the hall, and promised her you couldn't see a single scar, and when she complained about how horrible the hospital gowns were, he brought her exquisite nightgowns from Pratesi. In a way, it was all embarrassing, and she was still terrified of where it would all lead, but she was no longer able to stop it. If he didn't come to lunch, she didn't eat, and if he had to miss an evening with her, she was so lonely she could barely stand it. Every time she saw his face appear in the doorway of her hospital room, she looked like a child who had found its only friend, or its teddy bear, or even its mother. He took care of everything for her, talked to the doctors, called in consultants, filed her insurance. No one at the office knew how involved he was with her, and even Winnie had no idea how much time he was spending with her. Grace had had a lifetime of practice at keeping secrets.

But once she went home, she was frightened again that everything would change. For about two hours, until he appeared at her apartment with champagne and balloons, and a picnic lunch. It was only two hours after he had brought her back from the hospital in a rented limo and left her briefly to do some errands.

"What are people going to think?" she said, as he drove her from the hospital, back to Eighty-fourth street. She imagined that everyone knew her boss was hanging out with her day and night, and they were going to put it up on billboards.

"I don't think anyone really cares, to tell you the truth. Except us. Everyone is busy screwing up their own lives. And frankly, I don't think we're screwing up ours. You're the best thing that ever happened to me." He repeated that to her when he arrived on her doorstep with a picnic. More importantly, he had a small blue box with him, and in it was a narrow gold bracelet.

"What's this for?" she said, awed by his generosity. It was from Tiffany, and it fit her perfectly, but she wasn't sure if she should accept it.

But he was laughing at her. "Do you know what day this is?" She shook her head. She had lost track of dates while she was in the hospital. She had spent the Fourth of July there, but she hadn't paid much attention after that. "It's your birthday, silly girl. That's why I had them let you out today instead of Monday. You can't stay in the hospital on your birthday!" Tears filled her eyes as she realized what he'd done, and he'd even brought a small birthday cake for her from Greenberg's. It was all chocolate, and very rich, and incredibly gooey and delicious.

"How can you do all this for me?" She felt shy with him suddenly, but so pleased. He had done nothing but spoil her since the mugging. Spoil her and be kind to her, and spend time with her. No one had ever been as kind to her as he was.

"Easy, I guess," he answered, "I don't have kids. Maybe I should adopt you. Now there's a thought. That certainly simplifies things for you, doesn't it?" She laughed at the suggestion. It would certainly have been easier than dealing with her feelings and fears of getting involved with him.

Their relationship changed subtly once she was back in her apartment. It was instantly more intimate, closer, and more difficult to pretend that they were just friends. They were suddenly all alone without nurses and attendants to chaperon and interrupt them. It made Grace feel shy with him at first, and he pretended not to notice. He had brought a funny nurse's hat with him with her birthday cake and gift and picnic lunch, and he put it on, and forced her to go to bed and rest. He watched TV with her, and made dinner for her in her tiny kitchen. She hobbled out to help, and he made her sit in a chair and watch, while she protested.

"I'm not helpless, you know," she objected vociferously.

"Yes, you are. Don't forget, I'm the boss here," he overruled her, and she laughed. It was so easy being with him, and so comfortable. They lay on her bed after dinner, and talked, and he held her hand, but he was desperately afraid to go any further, or of what would happen if he did. And finally, unable to stand it any longer, he turned and asked her one of the things he had wanted to know for weeks now.

"Are you afraid of me, Grace? I mean physically . . . I don't want to do anything that will frighten or hurt you." She was touched that he had asked her. He had been lying next to her on her bed for two hours, and holding her hand. They were like old friends, but there was also an undeniable electricity between them. And now it was Charles who was frightened. He didn't want to do anything that would jeopardize their relationship, or make him lose her.

"Sometimes, I'm afraid of men," she said honestly.

"Someone did some awful stuff to you, didn't they?" She nodded in answer. "A stranger?" She shook her head and there was a long pause.

"My father." But there were other things, and she knew she needed to explain those too. She sighed, and picked up his hand again and kissed his fingers. "All my life, people tried to hurt me, or take advantage of me. After . . . after he was gone . . . my first boss tried to seduce me. He was married, I don't know . . . it was just so sleazy. He just assumed that he had a right to use me. And another man I had business dealings with did the same thing." She was talking about Louis Marquez and didn't want to explain him to Charles just yet, although she knew that eventually, if this got serious, she'd have to. "This other man kept threatening, threatened that I'd lose my job if I didn't sleep with him. He used to show up at my apartment. It was disgusting . . . and then there was someone I went out with. He did pretty much the same thing, used me, made a fool of me, never gave a damn. He put something in my drink and I got horribly sick. But he didn't rape me at least. At first I was afraid that maybe he had after he'd drugged me, but he hadn't. He just made me look like a fool afterwards. He was a real bastard."

Charles looked horrified. He couldn't imagine people doing things like that. Especially to someone he knew. It was appalling. "How did you know he hadn't raped you?" he asked in an agonized voice, thinking of what she must have been through.

"My roommate took me to a doctor she knew. Nothing had happened. But he pretended that it had, and told everyone that. He told my boss, which was why he went after me, and I guess why he expected to sleep with me. That was why I quit my job and left Chicago."

"Good luck for me." He smiled, putting an arm around her shoulders and pulling her closer.

"Those were the only men I really had any dealings with. I only went out with that one guy in Chicago, and he made a real ass of me. I never went out with anyone in high school . . . because of my father . . ."

"Where did you go to college?" he asked, and she smiled at the memory.

"In Dwight, Illinois," she said honestly.

"And who did you go out with there?" This time she laughed, remembering what would have been her choices.

"Not a soul. It was an all-girls school, so to speak."
But she knew then that she'd have to tell him soon.
She just didn't want to tell him all of it on her birthday.
It was too hard to go through, and they'd had such a
nice time. It was the best birthday she'd ever had, even
with her broken bones and her stitches and her
crutches. He had made up for everything and a lot of
years with his dinner, and his present, and his kindness.

He didn't want to push her much further than he
already had, but he wanted to understand something
more clearly. "Am I correct in believing that you're
not a virgin?"

"That's right," she glanced up at him, looking
breathtakingly beautiful in a blue satin bathrobe he'd
bought her.

"I just wondered . . . but there hasn't been anyone in a long time, has there?"

She nodded. "I promise we'll talk about it sometime . . . just not tonight. . . ." He didn't want to
talk about it on her birthday either. He suspected cor-
rectly that it was going to be hard for her, and he
didn't want to spoil their evening.

"Whenever you're ready . . . I just wanted to
know . . . I don't ever want to do anything that scares
you." But as he said the words, and she had her face
turned up to his, listening to him, he found himself
melting toward her and he couldn't help it. He gently
took her face in his hands, and ever so carefully kissed
her. She seemed cautious at first, and then he felt her
responding to him. He lay down next to her, and held
her close to him, and kissed her again, wanting her
desperately, but he never allowed his hands to wander
toward her body.

"Thank you," she whispered, and kissed him this time. "For being so good to me, and so patient."

"Don't press your luck," he almost groaned after he'd kissed her again. This was not going to be easy. But he was determined to bring her back across the bridge eventually. He knew that whatever it took, and however long, he was going to save her.

He left her apartment late that night, after he'd tucked her into bed, and she was almost sleeping. He kissed her again, and let himself out. He had borrowed a key from her, so she didn't have to get up, and he could lock the door behind him. And the next morning, as she hobbled to the bathroom and brushed her hair, she looked startled as she heard him let himself into the apartment. He had brought orange juice and bagels with cream cheese, and the *New York Times,* and he made her scrambled eggs and bacon.

"High cholesterol, it's good for you, trust me." She laughed at him. And he told her to get dressed. He took her for a short walk down First Avenue, and then brought her back when she was tired. And he watched the baseball game while she slept in his arms that afternoon. She looked so beautiful and so peaceful. And when she woke up, she looked up at him, wondering how she'd been so lucky.

"What are you doing here, Mr. Mackenzie?" She smiled sleepily at him, and he leaned down to kiss her.

"I came over so you could work on your dictation."

"No kidding."

They ordered pizza that night, and he had brought some work with him, but he absolutely refused to let her help him. And after he'd finished, she looked at him, feeling guilty. It seemed late in the day to be keeping secrets from him, although she knew that he would never press her.

"I think I ought to tell you some things, Charles," she said quietly after a few minutes. "You have a right to know. And you may feel differently about me after you hear them." But it was time, before they went any further. Not everyone wanted a woman who had committed murder. In fact, she suspected that most wouldn't. And maybe Charles wouldn't either.

He took her hands in both of his, before she started and looked her in the eye squarely. "I want you to know that whatever happened, whatever they did to you, whatever you did, I love you. I want you to hear that now . . . and later." It was the first time he had told her that he loved her, and it made her cry before she'd even started. But now she wanted him to listen and see how he felt after she had told him all of it. Maybe everything would change then.

"I love you too, Charles," she said, holding him, with her eyes closed, and tears rolling down her cheeks. "But there's a lot you don't know about me." She took a deep breath, felt for the inhaler in her pocket, and started at the beginning. "When I was a little girl, my father beat my mother all the time . . . I mean *all* the time . . . every night . . . as hard as he could . . . I used to hear her screams, and the sound of his fists on her . . . and in the morning I'd see the bruises . . . she always lied and pretended it was nothing. But every night he'd come home, he'd yell and she'd cry and he'd beat her again. After a while, you stop having any kind of life when those things happen. You can't have friends, because they might find out. You can't tell anyone, because they might do something to your daddy," she said sadly. "My mother used to beg me not to tell, so you lie, and cover up, and pretend you don't know, and act like nothing's wrong, and little by little you become a zombie. That's all that I remember of my childhood." She sighed again. It was hard telling him, but she knew she had to. And he squeezed her hand more tightly.

"Then my mother got cancer," Grace continued. "I was thirteen. She had cancer of the uterus, and they had to do some kind of radiation, and . . ." She hesitated, looking for the right words, she didn't know him that well yet. "I guess that changed her . . . so . . ." Her eyes began to swim with tears, and she felt the asthma closing her throat, but she wouldn't let it. She knew she *had* to tell him. Her survival depended on it now just as it had on opening her eyes at Bellevue. "My mother came to me then, and told me I had to 'take care' of my father, to 'be good to him,' to be 'his special little girl,' and he would love me more than ever." Charles was looking seriously worried as she told the story. "I didn't understand what she meant at first, and then she and Daddy came into my room one night, and she held me down for him."

"Oh my God." Tears filled his eyes as he listened.

"She held me down every night, until I knew I had no choice. I had to do it. If I didn't, no matter how sick she was, he would beat her. I had no friends, I couldn't tell anyone. I hated myself, I hated my body. I wore baggy old clothes because I didn't want anyone to see me. I felt dirty and ashamed, and I knew that what I was doing was wrong, but if I didn't do it, he would beat her, and me. Sometimes he beat me anyway, and then raped me. It was always rape. He loved violence. He loved hurting me, and my mother. Once when I didn't do it, because . . ." she blushed, feeling fourteen again, "because I had . . . my period . . . he beat her so bad, she cried for a week. She already had bone cancer by then, and she almost died of the pain. I did it anytime he wanted after that, no matter how much he hurt me." She took a deep breath. It was almost over now. He'd heard the worst, or almost, and he couldn't stop crying. She gently wiped the tears from Charles's cheeks and kissed him.

"Oh Grace, I'm so sorry." He wanted to take the pain away from her, to erase her past, and change her future.

"It's all right . . . it's all right now . . ." And then she went on. "My mother died after four years. We went to the funeral, and lots of people came over afterwards. Hundreds of them. Everybody loved my father. He was a lawyer, and everyone's friend. He played golf with them, went to Rotary dinners with them, and Kiwanis. He was the nicest guy in town, people said. He was the man everyone loved and trusted. And no one knew what he really was. He was a sick, sick man, and a real bastard.

"The day of the funeral, everyone spent the afternoon eating and talking and drinking, and trying to make him feel better. But he didn't care. He still had me. I don't know why, but somehow in my mind, it was all tied up with my mother. I was doing it for her, so he wouldn't hurt her. But I figured when she was gone, he'd find someone else. But of course he didn't want that. He had me. Why did he need anyone else? Not right off anyway. So when everyone left, I cleaned up, washed the dishes, put everything away, and locked the door to my room. He came after me, he threatened to knock the door down, and he got a knife and sprung the lock. He dragged me into her room, and he'd

never done that before. He always came to my room.
But going to her room was like becoming her, it was
like knowing that it was forever and it would never
stop, never, until he died or I did. And suddenly, I just
couldn't do it." She was choking again, and Charles
had stopped crying, horrified by everything she'd told
him. "I don't know what happened after that. He
really hurt me that night, he pounded at me, he hit
me, he'd won, I was his to beat and rape and torture
forever. And then I remembered the gun my mother
kept in her nightstand. I don't know what I was going
to do with it, hit him, or scare him, or shoot him. I
don't really know anything except that he was hurting
me so much and I was so scared and half crazy with
misery and pain and fear. He saw the gun, and he tried
to grab it from me, and then the next thing I knew, it
went off, and he was bleeding all over me. I shot him
through the throat, and it severed his spinal cord and
punctured his lung. He fell on top of me and bled
horribly, and after that I don't remember anything until the police came. I'm not sure what I did. I called the
police, I guess, and the next thing I remember was
talking to them, wrapped in a blanket."

"Did you tell them what he'd done to you?"
Charles asked anxiously, wanting to change the course
of history, and agonized that he couldn't.

"Of course not. I couldn't do that to my mother.
Or to him. I thought I owed him total silence. In my
own way, I guess, I was as crazy as he was. But that's
what happens to children, and women too, in situations like that. They never tell. They'll die first. They
called in a psychiatrist to talk to me, when they took
me to jail that night, and she sent me to the hospital,

and they found out that he'd raped me, or 'someone had had intercourse' with me, according to the D.A.''

"Did you ever tell them the truth?"

"Not for a while. Molly, the psychiatrist, hounded me to tell her. She knew. But I lied to her. He was still my daddy. But finally, my lawyer wore me down, and I told them."

"And then what? I assume they let you off after that."

"Not exactly. The prosecution concocted a theory that I was after my father's money, that if I killed him, I'd get everything. Everything being one small but highly mortgaged house, and half of his law practice, which was a lot smaller than yours. I couldn't inherit any of it anyway, because I killed him. I had no friends. I had never told anyone. My teachers said that I was withdrawn and strange, kids said they never knew me. It was easy to believe I'd just flipped out and killed him. His law partner lied and claimed I'd asked about Dad's money after the funeral. I'd never said a word to him, but he claimed that Dad owed him a lot of money. And in the end, he grabbed everything, and gave me fifty thousand dollars to stay out of town and leave him to take it all. I did, and I still have the money by the way. Somehow, I can't bring myself to spend it.

"But the D.A. decided that I had killed my father for his money, and that I'd probably been out screwing around, and when I came home, Dad got mad and yelled at me, so I killed him." She smiled bitterly, remembering every detail. "They even said that I'd probably tried to seduce my father too. They'd found my nightgown on the floor where he threw it after he tore it in half, and they claimed I had probably exposed myself to him, and when he didn't want me, I shot him.

They charged me with murder one, which would have required the death penalty. I was seventeen, but they tried me as an adult. And aside from Molly, and David, my attorney, no one ever believed me. He was too good, too perfect, too loved by the community. Everyone hated me for killing him. Even telling the truth didn't save me. By then it was too late. Everybody loved him.

"They found me guilty of voluntary manslaughter, and I got two and two. Two years of prison, two years of probation. I served two years almost to the day in Dwight Correctional Center, where," she smiled sadly at him, "I did a correspondence course and got an AA degree from a junior college. Actually, it was quite an education. And if it weren't for two women there, Luana and Sally, who were lovers, I'd probably be dead now. I was kidnapped by a gang one night, and they were going to gang-bang me and use me as a slave, and Sally, who was my cellmate, and Luana, her friend, stopped them. They were the two toughest but kindest women you could ever meet, and they saved me. No one ever touched me after that, nor did they. I don't even know where they are now. Luana is probably still there, but Sally's time would be up, unless she did something dumb so she could stay with Luana. But when I left, they told me to forget them, and put it all behind me.

"I never went home again, and that was when I went to Chicago, where my probation officer kept threatening to send me back if I didn't sleep with him. But somehow I managed not to. And you pretty much know the rest. I told you that last night. I worked in Chicago for two years while I was on probation. No one ever knew where I'd been, or where I came from. They didn't know I'd been in prison, or had killed my father. They didn't know anything. You're the first person I've ever told since David and Molly." She felt drained but a thousand pounds lighter when she finished. It had been a relief to tell him.

"What about Father Tim? Does he know?"

"He's just guessed, but I've never said anything to him. I didn't think I had to. But I worked at St. Mary's in Chicago, and now St. Andrew's, because it's my way of paying back for what I did. And maybe I can stop some other poor kid from going through what I did."

"My God, my God . . . Grace . . . how did you survive it?" He held her close to him, cradling her head against his chest, unable to even begin to fathom the kind of pain and misery she'd been through. All he wanted to do now was hold her in his arms forever.

"I just survived, I guess," she answered him, "and in some ways, I didn't. I've only been out with one man. I've never had sex with anyone but my father. And I'm not sure I could. The man who drugged me said I almost killed him when he tried to lay a hand on me, and maybe I would have. I don't think that can ever be part of my life again." And yet . . . she had kissed him, and he hadn't frightened her at all. In some ways, she wondered if she could learn to trust him. If he even wanted her now, after all he'd heard. She searched his eyes looking for some sign of condemnation, but there was only sorrow and compassion.

"I wish I could have killed him for you. How could they send you to prison for that? How could they be so blind and so rotten?"

"It happens that way sometimes." She wasn't bitter. She had long since come to accept it. But she realized that if he betrayed her now, and told people about

her past, her life in New York would be ruined. She'd
have to move on again, and she didn't want to. Telling
him had required a great deal of trust from her, but it
was worth it.

"What makes you think that you could never deal
with intimacy again? Have you ever tried to?"

"No. But I just can't imagine doing that, without
reliving the nightmare."

"You've left the rest of it, and moved on. Why not
that too? You owe it to yourself, Grace, and to anyone
who loves you. In this case, me," he smiled, and then
he asked her another question.

"Would you go to a therapist if you needed to?" he
asked gently, but she wasn't sure. In a funny way, it
would seem like a betrayal of Molly.

"Maybe," she said uncertainly, maybe even therapy would be too hard to handle.

"I have a feeling you're sounder than you think. I
don't know why, but I don't think you could come
through all you did, if you weren't. I think you're just
scared, and who wouldn't be. And you're not exactly a
hundred years old, you know."

"I'm twenty-three," she said, as though it were a
major achievement, and he laughed at her and kissed
her.

"I'm not impressed, kiddo. I'm almost twenty years
older than you are." He would be forty-three in the
fall, and she knew that.

But she was looking at him very seriously then.
"Tell me honestly. Isn't that history more than you
want to deal with?"

"I don't see why. It's not your fault, any more than
being mugged on Delancey Street was your fault. You
were a victim, Grace, of two very sick people who used

you. You didn't do anything. Even when you had sex with him, you had no choice. Anyone would have done the same, any kid would have been terrorized into thinking they were helping their dying mother. How could you possibly resist them? You couldn't. You've been a victim all along. It sounds like you stayed a victim right up until you left Chicago and came to New York last October. Don't you think it's time you changed that? It's been ten years since the nightmare began. That's almost half your life. Don't you think you have a right to a good life now? I think you've earned it," he said, and then kissed her hard, and with everything he felt for her. There was no mistaking what he was feeling. He was deeply in love with her, and willing to accept her past, in exchange for her future. "I love you. I'm in love with you. I don't care what you did, or what happened to you, I'm just sorry as hell that you had to suffer so much pain, and so much misery. I wish I could wash it all away, and change your memory of it, but I can't. I accept you exactly as you are, I love you exactly as you are, and all I want is what we can give each other now. I want to thank my lucky stars for the day you walked into my office. I can't believe how blessed I was to have found you."

"I'm the lucky one," she said, in awe of his reaction. She could hardly believe what he was saying. "Why are you saying all this to me?" she asked, near tears again. It was impossible to fathom.

"I'm saying it because I mean it. Why don't you just relax and stop worrying for a while, and enjoy it? You've had a lot of worrying to do for a long time. Now it's my turn. I'll worry for both of us. Okay?" he asked, moving toward her again with a smile and wiping the tears from beneath her eyes. "Okay?"

"Okay, Charles . . . I love you."

"Not as much as I love you," he said, taking her in his arms again and holding her tight as he kissed her. And then after a while, he laughed softly.

"What's funny?" she whispered, touching his lips with her fingertips, which only aroused him further. He was dying for her, but he knew it would be a while before anything happened between them.

He smiled at her as he answered, "I was just thinking that, never mind your delicate psychology, I think the only thing that's saving you from being ravaged by me, is the pin they just put in your pelvis. Frankly, I think that's the only thing that stopped me."

"Shame on you," she teased, suddenly wondering if she wanted to be saved from him. It was an interesting question.

Charles took care of her for the next two weeks, coming to the apartment constantly, whenever he could, and sleeping next to her in the bed on weekends. It was a cozy feeling lying next to him, and waking up in his arms in the morning. He told her stories about his childhood, and his parents, who were no longer alive, but whom he had loved very much and had been very good to him. He was an only child, and he'd had a good life, and he knew it. And she told him funny things about Luana and Sally. It was an odd assortment of memories and exchanges. And after the first week, he hired a limousine and took her for a drive in Connecticut on the weekend. They stopped and had lunch at Cobbs Mill Inn in Weston, which was wonderful, and came back to New York relaxed and exhausted.

Her doctors said that she was doing well, and after another week they told her she could go back to work,

but Charles convinced her to take one more week off.
And she asked the doctors one other important question, and was satisfied with the answer. She went to visit
her friends at St. Andrew's too, arriving by cab, in the
daytime, and they were all thrilled to see her. She
promised them that she would come back to work
soon, but probably not until September, when she
would be off crutches.

And the following weekend Charles took her to the
Hamptons for the weekend. They stayed in a cozy little
inn, and the smell of the sea was delicious. They arrived late Friday night, and she made him take her for
a walk on the beach, even with her crutches. She lay
down on the sand, listening to the sound of the ocean,
and he sat down next to her.

"You don't know how great this is. You know, before I came to New York, I'd never seen the ocean."

"Wait till you see Martha's Vineyard." He promised to take her there over Labor Day, but she was still
worried about their future. And what were they going
to do in another week when she went back to the office? They'd have to keep their relationship a secret. It
was odd to think of it. It wasn't an affair yet, but it was
much, much more than a friendship.

"What were you thinking then?" he asked comfortably, as they sat on the beach in the dark.

"About you," she teased him a little bit, and he
loved it.

"What about me?"

"I was wondering when we were going to sleep
with each other," she said casually, and he stared at
her in confusion.

"What does that mean? Besides," he grinned, "I
thought we already had. You even snore sometimes."

"You know what I mean." She pushed him gently, and he laughed at her. She was so lovely.

"You mean . . ." He raised an eyebrow and pretended to look surprised. "Are you suggesting . . ."

"I think so." She blushed. "I saw the orthopedic surgeon yesterday and he says I'm okay . . . now all we have to worry about is my head and not my pelvis." As she said it, he laughed, and he was grateful they had had all these weeks to get to know each other without the complications of her history and their sex life. It had been well over a month now, and it was as though they had always been together. They were completely at ease with each other.

"Is this an invitation?" he said with a grin that would have melted any heart, hers had melted long since, but it dissolved yet again as she watched him. "Or are you just toying with me?"

"Possibly both." But she had been thinking about it for days now, and she wanted to try it. She had to know what would happen and if there was any chance at all for a future.

"Is this my cue to jump up off the warm sand and drag you back to our room by the hair, leaving your crutches behind us?"

"That sounds pretty good." She made him feel so young, and in spite of her serious history, she made him laugh all the time, and he loved it. It was so different from his time with his first wife. She'd been so intense, so self-involved, and so nervous. Life with Grace was completely different. She was relaxed, intelligent, giving, caring. She had been through so much, and yet she was still so kind and so gentle. And she still had a sense of humor.

"Come on, you, let's go back to the hotel." He

pulled her up off the sand, and they made their way slowly back, and then stopped for ice cream.

"Do you like banana splits?" she asked him casually, as she licked her ice-cream cone, and he smiled. She was like a kid sometimes, and a woman of the world at others. He loved the contrast and the combination. It was the advantage of her youth, and with it came endless possibilities, and a most appealing future. He wanted to have children with her, a life with her, make love with her . . . but first, she had to eat her ice cream.

"Yes, I like banana splits," he said, with a grin. "Why?"

"Me too. Let's have one tomorrow."

"Okay. Can we go back now?" It had taken them four hours to get to the Hamptons in the traffic from New York, and it was almost midnight.

"Yes, we can go back to the hotel now." She smiled at him, mysterious and womanly again. It was like watching different creatures appear from behind clouds. He loved her playfulness and the fact that she wasn't quite grown up yet.

Their room at the inn was done in rose-patterned chintzes and Victorian furniture. There was a sweet marble sink in the room, and the bed was canopied and very pretty. Charles had asked for champagne to be left cooling in the room, and there was a huge bouquet of lilac and roses, her favorites.

"You think of everything." She kissed him as they closed the door to their room.

"Yes," he said, proud of himself, "and I can't even ask my secretary to do it."

"You'd better not." She eyed him happily as he poured the champagne and handed her a glass, but she only took a small sip and then set it down. She was too excited to drink it. This was like a honeymoon, and the expectation was terrifying for them both, particularly since they didn't know what ghosts would join them.

"Scared?" he whispered as they slid into bed, he in his shorts, and she in a nightgown, and she nodded. "Me too," he confessed, and she nuzzled her face into his neck and held him. He had turned off the lights. And there was a single candle burning at the far end of the room. It was unforgettably romantic.

"What'll we do now?" she whispered in his ear after a minute.

"Let's go to sleep," he whispered back.

"You mean it?" she asked, looked startled, and he laughed.

"No . . . not really . . ." He kissed her then, almost wanting to get it over with, but not daring to yet, not sure which way to turn or what to do, and he didn't want to hurt her various injuries either. It was all a little more difficult than he'd expected. But as they kissed, he forgot about her broken bones, and the ugliness of her past slipped slowly from her. There was no memory, no time, no other person, there was only Charles and his incredible gentleness, his endless passion and love for her, as he moved ever so gently toward her, and they moved closer and closer, until suddenly they became one and she could feel herself melt into him and she could bear it no longer. It was all so exquisite, and then suddenly they both exploded in unison, and Grace lay in his arms in complete amazement. She had never known anything even remotely like that. There was no similarity at all with what had happened to her before, no memory, no pain, there was nothing but

Charles now and the love they shared, and a little while later, it was Grace who wanted him, who teased him and played with him, until he could bear it no longer.

"Oh God," he said afterwards, "you're too young for me, you're going to kill me . . . but what a way to die." And then suddenly he wondered if he had committed an awful faux pas, and looked at her in horror, but she only laughed. It was all all right now, much to their joint amazement.

She forced him to buy her a banana split the next day, and they had a lovely weekend. They spent much of it in their room, discovering each other, and the rest on the beach, in the sun, and when they got back to New York on Sunday night, they lay in her bed and made love again, just to make sure it had the same magic in her apartment. And Charles decided it was even better.

"By the way," he rolled over sleepily afterwards and whispered to her, "you're fired, Grace." He was half asleep but she sat bolt upright. What was he saying to her? What was this all about? She looked frightened.

"What?" She almost shouted the word in the darkness, and he opened an eye in surprise. "What do you mean?" She was staring at him.

"You heard me. You're fired." He smiled happily.

"Why?" She was near tears. She loved working for him, especially now, and she was due to go back that week. This wasn't fair. What was he doing?

"I don't sleep with my secretaries," he explained, and then he grinned as he lay there. "Don't look so worried. I have a new job in mind for you. It's a step up, or it could be, depending on how you see it. How would you like to be my wife?" He was wide-awake now, and she looked stunned. She was shaking when she answered.

"Are you serious?"

"No. I'm just kidding. What do you think? Of course I'm serious. Will you?"

"Really?" She still couldn't believe it as she sat looking at him in disbelief and he laughed at her.

"Of course really!"

"Wow!"

"Well?"

"I'd love to." And with that, she leaned down and kissed him, and he grabbed her.

Chapter 13

Grace never went back to work, and they were married six weeks later, in judge's chambers, in September. They flew to Saint Bart's for two weeks for a honeymoon, and she moved her few belongings to his apartment. He lived on East Sixty-ninth Street in a small, but extremely elegant little town house. They'd been home for exactly a week when they had their first real fight, and it was a lulu. She wanted to go back to do volunteer work at St. Andrew's, and she was horrified that he wanted to stop her.

"Are you crazy? Do you remember what happened the last time you went there? Absolutely not!" He was adamant. She could do anything she wanted, but not that. And he wasn't budging.

"That was a fluke," she kept insisting, but Charles was even more stubborn than she was.

"That was no fluke. Every one of those women has a dangerous husband. And you're down there advising them to bail out, and the guys are just as liable to come after you as Sam Jones was." He had plea-bargained himself into a lighter sentence with parole by then, for his attack on Grace, and the murders of his wife and children. And as far as they knew he was already in

Sing Sing. "You're not going. I'll talk to Father Tim if I have to, Grace, I forbid it."

"Well, what am I supposed to do with myself?" she said, near tears. She was twenty-three years old and she had absolutely nothing to do until he came home at six o'clock. He wouldn't let her work at the law firm either. She could have lunch with Winnie once in a while, but that was hardly enough to keep her busy. And Winnie was talking about moving to Philadelphia to be close to her mother.

"Go shopping. Go to school. Find a charity you like and sit on a committee. Go to the movies. Eat banana splits," Charles said firmly. He was trying to come home to her every day for lunch, but sometimes he couldn't and when Grace turned to Father Tim for support he turned her down too. In spite of himself, and how good she was at the work, Father Tim supported Charles in that decision. She had already paid too high a price for working there, and it was time for her to stop paying for other people's sins. She had her own life to live now.

"Enjoy your husband, be good to yourself, Grace. You've earned it," the priest said wisely, but Grace still fumed and was looking for a project. She was thinking of applying to school, but in November it became a moot point, six weeks to the day after they were married.

"What are you looking so smug about? You look like the cat that swallowed the canary." Charles had just dashed home to have lunch with her. He was becoming famous in the office for his long lunches, and his partners were teasing him about how much work it was to have a young wife. But he knew that they were all jealous, and would have given anything to be in his shoes . . . or his boxers. "What have you been up to?" he questioned, wondering if she had found something to do with herself. She'd been unhappy for weeks over his edict about St. Andrew's. "Where'd you go today?"

"The doctor." She grinned.

"How's the pelvis?"

"Fine. It's healed beautifully." She was grinning from ear to ear by then, and he was laughing at her. She looked so cute when she had a secret. "There's something else though."

Charles's face grew serious. "Something wrong?"

"No." She grinned and kissed him on the lips as she unzipped his trousers. Considering how cautiously they had begun, they had certainly made up for it since their engagement. "We're having a baby," she whispered as he grew passionate and was about to lay her down on their bed, and he looked at her with complete amazement.

"We are? *Now?*"

"Not now, silly. In June. I think I got pregnant in Saint Bart's."

"Wow!" He was going to be a father for the first time, at forty-three, and it completely bowled him over. He had never been as happy in his life, and he could hardly wait to tell the entire world. "Is it still all right if we make love?"

"Are you kidding?" she laughed at him. "We can make love till June."

"Are you sure we won't hurt anything?"

"Promise." They made love, as they always did, instead of lunch, and then he grabbed a hot dog from a stand on the street, and dashed back to his office. It was the best life had ever been for him, far better than being married to a movie star, far better than any romance he'd had as a kid. She was perfect for him, and he adored her.

They spent Christmas in St. Moritz, and at Easter he wanted to take her to Hawaii, but took her to Palm Beach instead because it was closer, and she was almost seven months pregnant.

She had an easy pregnancy, and everything had gone smoothly. The doctor was only mildly concerned about what would happen to her pelvis when she delivered. And if there was any sign of strain at all, he had warned her that he would do a cesarean section. But failing that, Charles had promised to be there, and in May they went to their Lamaze class at Lenox Hill. She had already decorated the nursery by then, and they went for long walks at night, up Madison Avenue, or down Park, and talked about their life, their good fortune, and their baby. It still startled them both, and they were both still amazed that, in bed at least, her past had never come back to haunt them.

He had asked her once how she would feel if the story ever came out, about her father, and going to prison, and she had said honestly that she would hate it.

"Why?" She wondered why he had even asked her.

"Because those things come out sometimes," he said philosophically. He had learned that with his last wife, and her constant exposure in the tabloids. Their divorce had made a huge stink and they had said everything from the rumor that she was on drugs, to the one that she was gay, to the one that he was. And finally, they had just left them alone, and they had gone their separate ways. But Grace's would undoubtedly be a much bigger story if it ever came out. But fortunately, for both of them, they were not in the public eye, and not important. He was just an ordinary citizen now, since he was no longer married to a star, and Grace was just his wife. It was perfect.

She went into labor one night as they walked home. They had been window shopping on Madison Avenue, and she scarcely noticed the first pains. It was only after a while that she realized what had happened. They called the doctor and he told them to take their time, first babies were usually in no hurry.

"Are you okay?" he asked her a thousand times, and she lay on their bed, watching TV, and eating Jell-O. "Are you sure that's what you're supposed to do?" he asked nervously. He felt a thousand years old as he watched her, fearing that she might have a hard time, or have the baby before they left the house. Lately, her belly had looked enormous. But she seemed unconcerned as she watched her favorite shows, drank ginger ale and ate ice cream. It was almost midnight when she finally started to look seriously uncomfortable and could no longer talk through the pains, which he knew was his sign to take her to the hospital and call the doctor.

He called him again, and the doctor told them to come in. And as Charles helped her down the stairs, she snapped at him several times, and he smiled at her. This was the real thing. Pretty soon, they'd have a baby. It was the most exciting thing that had ever happened to him, and to her. And by the time they settled her in a labor room, she had calmed down again, but Grace was surprised by how much the contractions hurt, and how strong they were. Finally, by two a.m. she was panting and said she couldn't stand them any longer.

Charles was doing everything he'd been taught to

do, but none of it was helping, and he was starting to
worry that they'd have to do a cesarean section. But as
the pains got worse, she started to scream, and clutch
at him, and he would have done anything to make it
end. He kept asking the nurses to give her some medication.

"Everything is fine, Mr. Mackenzie. Your wife is
doing beautifully." His wife looked like she was ready
to die as she screamed again, and then finally they took
her to the delivery room, and she started pushing.
Charles thought he had never seen anything so painful, and he was sorry they'd ever done it. All he wanted
to do was take her in his arms again, and make the
pain stop for her. But nothing helped her now, and the
doctor didn't want to give her medication. He said he
really preferred natural childbirth, for mother and
child. Charles wanted to kill him, as he watched what
Grace was going through.

She pushed for an hour, and it was five in the
morning by then, Grace was beside herself with pain,
and incoherent with the agony of each contraction.
And as he watched her, he vowed they'd never do this
again. He wanted to apologize to Grace for putting her
through it. And he swore to himself that if she and the
baby both came out of it alive, he'd never let this happen again. And just as he was about to promise never
to lay a hand on her again, there was a terrifying
scream from her, and a long, thin howl, and suddenly
he found himself looking into the face of the son they
had decided to call Andrew Charles Mackenzie. He
had huge blue eyes like Grace, and dark red hair, but
everything else about him was Charles, right down to
his tiny fingers. For his father, it was exactly like look-

ing into the mirror. He laughed and cried all at once as he looked at him.

"Oh my God . . . he's so beautiful," Charles said in awe of the baby, and bent to kiss his wife. She was lying flat now, after so much hard work, and looking suddenly ecstatic as she laughed and smiled at her husband.

"Is the baby all right?" she asked over and over again, and as soon as they had cleaned him off and checked his lungs again, they handed him to his mother, and he lay at her breast, and immediately nuzzled close to her, while Charles watched them.

"Grace . . . how can I ever thank you?" Charles said, wondering how he had managed to live so long without this baby. And how brave she was to go through all that for him. He had never been as touched or as much in love with anyone as he was with Grace at that moment.

They went back to her room after that, and little Andrew lay by her side, and much to Charles's astonishment, they all went home the next morning. She was healthy and young, the baby was fine, and weighed just under nine pounds. They had had natural childbirth. There was no reason for them not to go home, her obstetrician explained. And Charles realized that he had a whole new world to discover. It was terrifying taking a baby home so soon, but Grace acted as though it was completely natural, and seemed totally at ease with her son from the very first moment he was born. It took Charles a few days, but within a week, he seemed like a practiced hand, and he bragged to everyone constantly about the baby. The only thing his friends didn't envy him was the sleepless nights he was having to live with. He left for the office every day feeling as though he'd been running on the wheel of a hamster cage all night. Master Andrew was waking up every two hours to be nursed, and it took him roughly an hour to go back to sleep again, and Charles only slightly longer. He figured out that he was sleeping in fifteen-minute increments, and getting approximately two and a half hours sleep a night, which was roughly five and a half less than he needed. But it was fun anyway, and he was crazy about his wife and the baby.

They rented a house in East Hampton for the month of July, and spent Grace's birthday there. Charles commuted two or three times a week, and she came back and forth with the baby to be with him. And in August he took two weeks off and they went to Martha's Vineyard to his old house. Grace thought she'd never been happier, and in October she found out she was pregnant again, and Charles was as delighted as she was.

"Why don't we just have twins this time, and get it over with?" he said good-naturedly. He was really enjoying their son. And he was only getting four or five hours sleep a night which seemed like a lot now. It amused him that life could change so quickly.

Their second baby took longer to come, and once again Charles found himself ready to promise to the gods that he would never touch his wife again, but this time the doctor finally gave in, and gave her some medication. It didn't help much, but it was something. And nineteen hours after labor began, Abigail Mackenzie pushed her way into the world and looked up at her father with an expression of amazement. He melted on the spot when he saw her. She was a miniature version of her mother, only with her father's dark hair. She was a real beauty. And she managed to make a complete spectacle of herself by arriving on her mother's twenty-fifth birthday. Charles was almost forty-five, and those were the happy years.

Grace was constantly busy with her children. She went to playgrounds and play groups and kindergyms, and music classes for toddlers. She was totally involved in doing everything with them. She worried a lot about being boring to Charles, but he seemed to love their life. It was all so new to him, and he was the envy of all who knew him, with a young, beautiful wife and a young family, he seemed to have the world by the tail.

Grace had never gotten back to her charity work again, although she still talked about it. But just after Andrew was born, she gave a gift, in his name, to St. Andrew's Shelter. She gave them every penny she had left from Frank Wills. It seemed the best use for it she could think of. In some ways, it was blood money to her, and a relic of a life that had brought her nothing but grief. She was sure that Father Tim would find a happier use for it. And they gave another, smaller gift, when Abigail was born. But she hadn't been there to visit for a long time. She was too involved with her husband and children.

For three years after Abigail was born, Grace spent every daytime moment with them, and her evenings with Charles, going to partners' dinners and dinner parties. They went to the theater, and he introduced her to the opera, and she found that she liked it. Her entire life was opening up, and at times she felt guilty, knowing that in other places, other lives, people were less fortunate, and were suffering as she once had. She was so lucky and so free now.

She wondered what had happened to Luana and Sally sometimes, and the women she had tried to help at St. Andrew's. But there didn't seem to be time for things like that anymore. She thought about David in California sometimes too, and wondered where he was now. Her life seemed so far removed from those troubled years. Sometimes even she had a hard time remembering that she had had any other life before marrying Charles. It was as though she had been born again the day she met him.

She wanted to have another baby once Abigail started nursery school, but this time it didn't seem to happen. She was only twenty-eight by then, and her doctor said it was hard to know why sometimes it was easier to get pregnant than others. But she also knew that with all she'd been through before, she'd been lucky to get pregnant at all, and she was grateful to have the two children she had. She would stand there and just smile at them sometimes, watching them. And then she and Andrew would go to the kitchen and make cupcakes, or she and Abigail would cut out paper dolls, or string beads, or make pictures with spaghetti. She loved being with them, and she never got bored, or tired of them.

And then one morning, as she was waiting to pick them up from nursery school, she sat in her kitchen reading the paper and having a cup of coffee. And as she read the headline of the *New York Times,* she felt her stomach turn over. A New York psychiatrist had killed his adopted child, a six-year-old girl, and his battered, hysterical wife had stood by helplessly and watched him do it. It brought tears to her eyes as she read about it. It was inconceivable, he was an educated man, with an important practice, and a teaching position with a major medical school. And still he had killed their little girl. They had had her since birth, and their natural child had died in an accident two years before, which was now considered suspect. Grace started to cry as she read about it, wanting to comfort the little girl, imagining her cries as her father beat her. It was so vivid that even after she left for school, she was still crying. And she was quiet as she and the children walked home for lunch. Andrew asked his mother what was the matter.

"Nothing," she started to say, and then thought better of it. She wanted to be honest with him. "I'm sad."

"Why, Mommy?" He was four years old and the cutest little boy she'd ever seen. He looked just like Charles except for his dark red hair and blue eyes, but all his features and expressions were his father's. It always made her smile just looking at him, but today, even seeing her own children made her grieve for the little girl who had been killed. "Why are you sad?" Andrew persisted, and her eyes filled with tears as she tried to answer.

"Somebody hurt a little girl, and it made me sad when I heard about it."

"Did she go to the hospital?" he asked solemnly. He loved ambulances and police cars and sirens, even though they scared him a little too. But mostly they fascinated him. He was a lively child.

Grace wasn't sure what to say to him then, whether or not to tell him that she was dead. But that was just too much to tell a four-year-old child. "I think so, Andrew. I think she's very sick."

"Let's make her a picture." Grace nodded, and turned her head away so he wouldn't see her cry. There would be no more pictures for that little girl . . . no loving hands . . . no one to save her.

There was a huge outcry in New York over the next few days. People were shocked and outraged. Teachers at the private school where she had been in first grade defended themselves, claiming that they had suspected nothing. She had been a frail child and bruised easily, and she had never said anything about what was happening at home. But hearing that infuriated Grace. Children never told of abuse at home, they always defended their abusers. And teachers knew that, and had to be especially alert these days.

For days people left flowers and bouquets outside the Park Avenue building where she'd lived, and when Grace and Charles drove by it the next day, on their way to dinner with friends, Grace felt a sob catch in her throat as she caught sight of a big pink heart, made of tiny roses, with the little girl's name written on a pink ribbon across it.

"I can't bear it," she cried into a handkerchief he handed her. "I know what it's like," she whispered . . . why don't people understand? Why don't they see? Why can't they stop it? Why did no one suspect what went on behind closed doors when atrocities were happening there? The real tragedy was that sometimes people did know and did nothing about it. It was that indifference that she wanted to stop. She wanted to shake people to wake them.

Charles put an arm around her shoulders then. It hurt him to think of what she must have gone through, it made him want to be good to her every day, to make up for all of it, and he had been.

"I want to go back to work," she said as they drove along in the cab, and he looked at her, startled.

"In an office?" He couldn't imagine why she

would want to do that again. She was so happy at home with their children.

But she smiled at him as she shook her head and blew her nose again. "Of course not . . . unless you need a new secretary," she teased, and he grinned.

"Not that I know of. So what did you have in mind?"

"I was thinking of that little girl . . . I'd like to go back to working with battered women and kids again." Her death had reminded Grace again of her debt, to help those who were living the same hell that she had. She had escaped, and she had come to a better place in her life, but she could not forget them. She knew that, in some way, she would always have a need to reach a hand back to them, to offer to help them.

"Not at St. Andrew's," he said firmly. He had never let her go back there to work again, only to visit, once they were married. And Father Tim had been transferred to Boston the year before, to start a similar shelter there. They had had a Christmas card from him. But Grace had something else in mind. Something more complicated, and far-reaching.

"What about starting some kind of organization," she had been thinking about it for two days, trying to figure out how she could help, and really make a difference, "that would reach out to people, not only in ghettos but middle-class neighborhoods, where the abuse is more of a surprise and better hidden. What about reaching out toward education, to teach educators and parents and clergymen and day-care workers, and everyone who works with kids, what to look for and how to deal with it when they see it . . . and reaching out to the public, people like you and me,

and our neighbors and all the people who see abused
kids every day and don't know it.''

"That sounds like a big bite," he said gently, "but
it's a great idea. Isn't there some existing program you
could latch on to?''

"There might be." But five years ago there hadn't
been, there was only the occasional shelter like St. Andrew's. And the various committees set up to help victims of abuse she heard of seemed to be badly run and
ineffective. "I don't really know where to start. Maybe I
need to do some research.''

"Maybe you need to stop worrying so much," he
said, smiling at her in the cab, as he leaned over and
kissed her. "The last time you let your big heart run
away with you, you got pretty badly beaten up. Maybe
it's time for you to let other people take care of it. I
don't want you getting hurt again.''

"If I hadn't, you'd never have married me," she
said smugly, and he laughed.

"Don't be so sure. I'd had my eye on you for a
while. I just couldn't figure out why you hated me so
much.''

"I didn't hate you. I was scared of you. That's different." They both smiled, remembering the days
when they had met and fallen in love. Things hadn't
changed at all since, they were more in love than ever.

And when they came back from dinner that night,
Grace started talking about her idea again. She talked
about it for weeks, and finally Charles couldn't stand it.

"Okay, okay . . . I understand. You want to help.
Now where do we start? Let's do something about it.''

In the end, he talked to a few friends, and some of
his partners at the law firm, some of their wives were
interested, and others had useful references and sug-

gestions. At the end of two months, Grace had a wealth of research and material, and she knew exactly what she wanted to do. She had talked to a psychologist she had met, and the head of the children's school, and she decided that she had what she needed. She even tracked down Sister Eugene from St. Andrew's, and she gave her some names of people who would be willing to work hands-on and wouldn't expect a lot of money for it. She needed volunteers, psychologists, teachers, some businessmen, women, and even victims. She was going to put together a team of people who were willing to go out into the community and tell people what they needed to know about abuse of all kinds against children.

She set up an organization and gave it a simple name. "Help Kids!" was what she called it, and at first she ran it out of her home, and after six months she rented an office on Lexington Avenue two blocks from their house. By then, she had a team of twenty-one people who were talking to schools, parents' groups, teachers' associations, people who ran extracurricular activities like ballet and baseball. She was amazed at how many bookings they got. And she shook like a leaf the first time she gave a talk herself. She told a group of people she had never met how she had been abused as a child, how no one had seen it, and no one had wanted to, and how everyone had thought her father was the greatest guy in town. "Maybe he was," she said, her voice shaking as she fought back tears, "but not to me, or my mother." She didn't tell them that she had killed him to save herself. But what she did tell them moved them deeply. All of their speakers had stories like that, some of them firsthand, and some of them about students or patients. But the people she organized to speak were all powerful in their message. It was a message that came straight from the heart. Help kids! And they meant it.

The next thing she did was set up a hot line for people who knew about abusive friends or neighbors, or parents who wanted help, or kids in bad situations. She did everything she could to raise funds to place ads and buy billboards with the hot line number on it, and she managed to keep it manned twenty-four hours a day, which was no small feat. It was almost a relief when a year and a half later Abigail went to kindergarten, because it gave her more time for "Help Kids!" although she missed having her at home at eleven-thirty. She managed to keep all her work down to a dull roar so that she could spend her afternoons with her children. But "Help Kids!" had grown to a full-scale office by then, and it was funded by five foundations. And they were currently in the process of raising money and free creative help for commercials. She wanted to organize a TV campaign to reach even deeper into the community. Again and again she tried to touch the kids who were being abused, and the people who knew it. She was less interested in reaching the abusive parents. Most of them were too sick even to want help, and it was rare that they themselves would step forward and ask for it. It was easier to get the point across to observers.

It was hard to judge what kind of results they were getting, except that their hot line was jammed night and day with desperate callers. They were usually neighbors, friends, teachers who weren't sure whether or not to come forward, and more and more lately they had been getting calls from kids telling horrifying stories. Grace and Charles answered phones themselves for two long shifts a week, and more often than not, Charles came home and ached over the things he heard. It was impossible not to care about those children. The only people who didn't were their parents.

Grace was so busy she hardly noticed the days fly by anymore, and she was happier than ever. She was particularly surprised when she got a letter, praising what she'd done, from the First Lady. She said that people like Grace made a real difference in the world, like Mother Teresa.

"Is she kidding?" Grace laughed in embarrassment as she showed the letter to Charles when it arrived. It was embarrassing, but exciting. What meant more than anything to her was helping those kids, but it was nice to be recognized for it too. And Charles was generous with his praise. He was pleased for her, and genuinely excited when they got invited to the White House for dinner. It had been declared the Year of the Child, and they wanted to give Grace an award for her contribution with "Help Kids!"

"I can't accept that," she said uncomfortably, "think of all the people it took to put 'Help Kids!' together, think of all the people who work with us now in one capacity or another." Almost none of them was paid, and all of them gave of their hearts and souls, some gave generously from their pockets. "Why should I get all the recognition?" It didn't seem right to her, and she didn't want to go to the dinner. She thought the award should be given to "Help Kids!" as an organization, not to her as an individual person.

"Think of who started it," Charles said, smiling at her. She had no idea what a difference she was making in the world, and he loved that about her. She had turned a lifetime of pain into a blessing for so many.

And every moment of happiness he could give her was a joy to him. Charles had never been happier, and he loved her deeply. She was a good wife, a good woman, and someone he respected deeply. "I think we should go to Washington. I, for one, would certainly enjoy it. Tell you what, I'll collect the award and tell them it was all my idea to start 'Help Kids!' " He was teasing her and she laughed about it. She argued with him for two weeks, but he had already accepted the invitation on her behalf, and finally, grumbling, they hired a sitter they knew to help their housekeeper, and flew to Washington on a snowy afternoon in December. She swore it was an omen of doom, but as soon as they reached Pennsylvania Avenue, she knew that she had been foolish. The White House Christmas tree sparkled cheerily in front of them and the entire scene looked like a Norman Rockwell painting.

They were led inside by Marines, and Grace almost felt her knees shake as she shook hands with the President and then the First Lady. There were several people at the reception Charles knew, and he kept Grace's hand tucked into his arm to give her courage, and introduced her to a number of attorneys and some congressmen who were old friends. An old friend from New York teased Charles about when he was going to get brave and get into the political waters himself. He had once been a partner in Charles's law firm.

"I don't think that's for me. I'm too busy taking kids to school and answering phones for Grace," Charles said with a smile, but he had a good time, and even chatted for a few moments with the President, who said he was familiar with Charles's law firm, and complimented him on his handling of a difficult matter the year before that involved some government contracts.

After dinner, they danced, and there was a wonderful children's chorus to sing carols. They were the cutest kids Grace had ever seen, and for a minute they made her homesick for their children.

The congressman sought Charles out again before they left and told him to think about it again. "The political arena needs you, Charles. I'd be happy to talk to you about it anytime you like." But Charles was insistent that he was happy at his law firm. "It's a big world out there, a lot bigger than Park Avenue and Wall Street. One forgets that in one's ivory tower at times. You could do a lot of good, there are some important issues at hand. I'll call you," he said, and moved on, and Charles and Grace went back to the Willard at midnight. It had been a wonderful evening, and she'd been given a handsome plaque to commend her for her unselfish gifts to children.

"I'll have to show this to the kids the next time they tell me how mean I am," she smiled, and set it down on a table in their hotel suite. She was glad they had come after all. She had really enjoyed it, and then as they lay in bed, talking about the people they'd met, and how impressive it was to be in the company of the President and the First Lady, she asked Charles about his congressman friend.

"Roger?" he asked casually. "He used to be a partner in the firm. He's a good man, I always liked him."

"What about what he said?" She was curious about Charles's reaction.

"About going into politics?" He looked amused. "I don't think so."

"Why not? You'd be great at it."

"Maybe I'll run for president one day. You'd make a beautiful first lady," he teased, and then he turned to her with love on his mind, and kissed her hungrily, and as always she was quick to return his passion.

They were back in New York by two o'clock the next afternoon. Charles was in a festive mood, and decided not to go back to his office. He went home with Grace instead, and the children were delighted to see them. They jumped all over them and wanted to know what their parents had brought them from the trip.

"Absolutely nothing," Charles lied with a blank stare, and they squealed in disbelief. Their children knew them better. They had bought some toys and souvenirs for them at the airport. Whenever Charles went away on business, which was rare, he never came back empty-handed. And Grace told them what the White House had been like, and about the children who sang there, and the Christmas tree all lit up on the White House lawn.

"What did they sing?" Andrew wanted to know, but like the little lady she was, Abigail wanted to know what they were wearing. The children were five and six then.

Christmas was the following week, and that weekend they put up the tree, and it looked beautiful when they finished it. She and Charles put the ornaments up high, and the children decorated everything within reach below that, and strung popcorn and cranberries, which was a tradition they loved.

Grace took them ice-skating at Rockefeller Plaza, and to see Santa Claus at Saks, and all the beautifully decorated windows on Fifth Avenue once school was out, and they even dropped in on Daddy at work, and took him out to lunch. They went to Serendipity on

Sixtieth Street between Second and Third Avenues, and had huge hot dogs and giant ice-cream sodas. Grace ordered a banana split and Charles laughed, remembering the banana split he'd bought her the first time they went away for the weekend. This time she finished all of it, and he complimented her for being a member of the clean plate club.

"Are you making fun of me?" she grinned at him, with a spot of whipped cream on her nose. Abigail chuckled looking at her, and even Andrew loved it.

"Certainly not. I think it's wonderful that you didn't waste a bit of it." Charles smiled, feeling happy and young.

"Be nice, or I'll order another one." But she was as thin as she'd ever been, until after the New Year, when she explained that she couldn't get into any of her clothes. She had been answering the hot line several times a week over the holidays, she knew what an important time it was for troubled families and helpless kids, and she wanted to do it herself as much as she could. And as they all did, while she was answering phones at all hours, she sat around and ate cookies and popcorn, particularly at Christmas.

"I feel huge," she said miserably, zipping up her jeans to go for a walk in the park with him at the end of a lazy weekend.

"Most women would love to be as 'huge' as you are." In spite of two children, and the fact that she had turned thirty that year, she still looked like a model. And he had just turned fifty and was as handsome as ever.

They were a good-looking couple as they strolled along. She was wearing a big cozy fox hat, and a fox jacket he had given her for Christmas. It was perfect for the frigid New York winter.

There was snow on the ground in the park, and they had left the kids at home with a sitter for a few hours because the housekeeper was away. They liked to go for long walks sometimes on Sundays, or take a cab down to SoHo and go to a coffeehouse, or have lunch and browse through galleries looking at paintings or sculpture.

But this afternoon, they were content to stroll, and eventually wound up at the Plaza Hotel. They decided to go in and have some hot chocolate in the Palm Court. And they walked into the elegant old hotel hand in hand, talking softly.

"The kids will never forgive us if they find out," Grace said guiltily. They loved the Palm Court. But it was romantic being alone with him. She was talking about some plans she had for "Help Kids!" for the next year, to expand it further. She was always trying to broaden their outreach. And as she chatted with him, she devoured an entire plate of cookies and two hot chocolates with whipped cream. And as soon as she finished them, she felt sick, and was sorry she'd eaten.

"You're as bad as Andrew," Charles laughed. He loved being with her, she was like a girl to him, and at the same time very much a woman.

When they left the Plaza, he hailed a hansom cab, and had it drive them home, as they snuggled in the back, kissing and whispering and giggling under heavy blankets, just like teenagers, or honeymooners. And when they got to the house, he ran in to get the kids, and let them pet the horse. And then the driver agreed to take them around the block for an additional fee, and the four of them rode around the block to the house again. And then they went inside, and the sitter left, and Grace made pasta for dinner.

She was busy for the next few weeks, with new plans, and keeping up with the children. But she was surprised to find that she was exhausted all the time, so much so that she even skipped two shifts on the hot line, which was rare for her. And when Charles noticed it, he was worried, and asked about it.

"Are you all right?" He worried sometimes that her past life, and the beating outside St. Andrew's, would take a toll on her one day, and whenever she was sick, it really scared him.

"Of course I am," she said, but the circles under her eyes, and her pallor, didn't convince him. She hardly ever suffered from asthma anymore, but she was starting to look the way she had when he first met her. A little too drawn and a little too serious, and not entirely healthy.

"I want you to go to the doctor," he insisted.

"I'm fine," she said stubbornly.

"I mean it," he said sternly.

"Okay. Okay." But she didn't do anything about it, and insisted that she was busy. Finally, he made an appointment himself and told her he'd take her there if she didn't go the following morning. It was a month after Christmas by then, and she was in the midst of a big fund drive for "Help Kids!" She had a thousand calls to make, and a million people to visit. "For heaven's sake," she said irritably when he reminded her again the next morning. "I'm just tired, that's all. It's no big deal. What are you so upset about?" she snapped at him, but he took her by the shoulders and turned her to face him.

"Do you have any idea how important you are to

me, and this family? I love you, Grace. Don't screw around with your health. I need you."

"Okay," she said quietly. "I'll go." But she always hated going to the doctor. Doctors still reminded her of bad experiences, of being raped, and her mother dying, and the night she killed her father, and even when she'd been in Bellevue after the attack at St. Andrew's. To Grace, except for the babies she'd had, doctors never meant anything pleasant.

"Any idea what might be wrong? How do you feel?" their family doctor asked her pleasantly. He was a middle-aged man with an intelligent face and an easy disposition. He knew nothing of Grace's past, or her dislike for doctors.

"I feel fine. I'm just tired, and Charles is hysterical." She smiled.

"He's right to be concerned. Anything else except fatigue?" She thought about it and shrugged.

"Nothing much. A little dizziness, some headaches." She made light of it, but the truth was she had been very dizzy more than once lately, and several times she had been sick to her stomach. She thought it was nervous tension over their fund drive. "I've been pretty busy."

"Maybe you need some time off." He smiled. He gave her some vitamins, checked her blood count and it was fine. He didn't want to run any serious tests. She was obviously young and healthy, and her blood pressure was low, which accounted for the dizziness and headaches. "Eat lots of red meat," he advised, "and eat your spinach." He said to say hello to Charles, and she called from the phone outside to tell Charles she was fine. And then feeling better than she had in a while, she walked home in the brisk January air. It was cold and crisp and sunny, and she felt wonderful and strong as she walked along, feeling stupid for even having gone to see the doctor. She smiled thinking of what good care Charles took of her and how lucky she was, as she turned the corner and walked toward their town house. She felt a little light-headed as she did, but it was no worse than it had been before, until she reached their front door, and she suddenly found she was so dizzy, she could hardly stand. She reached out to steady herself, and found herself clutching an elderly man who stared at her strangely. She looked at him as though she didn't see him at all, and then she took two steps toward her house, said something unintelligible, and collapsed, unconscious, to the sidewalk.

Chapter 14

When Grace came to on the street outside their house, there were three people standing over her, and two policemen. The old man she had almost pulled down with her had gone to a phone booth and dialed 911, but she was conscious again by the time they came, and she was sitting on the sidewalk. She was embarrassed more than hurt, and still too dizzy to get up.

"What happened here?" the first policeman asked amiably. He was a big friendly man, and he had keen eyes as he took in the situation. She wasn't drunk or on drugs, from what he could see, and she was very pretty and well dressed. "Would you like us to call an ambulance for you? Or your doctor?"

"No, really, I'm fine," she said, getting up. "I don't know what happened. I just got light-headed." She had skipped breakfast that day, but she'd been feeling fine.

"You really should go to a doctor, ma'am. We'll be happy to take you to New York Hospital. It's straight down the street here," he said kindly.

"Really. I'm fine. I live right here." She pointed at the town house only a few feet away from them. She had almost made it. And she thanked the old man and apologized for almost knocking him down. He patted her hand and told her to have a nap and eat a good lunch, and then the policemen escorted her into her house, and looked around at the attractive surroundings.

"Do you want us to call anyone? Your husband? A friend? A neighbor?"

"No . . . I . . ." The phone interrupted them, and she picked it up as they stood in the hallway. It was Charles.

"What did he say?"

"I'm fine," she said sheepishly, except for the fact that she had just keeled over on the sidewalk.

"Do you want us to stay for a few minutes?" the policeman in charge asked and she shook her head.

"Who was that? Is someone there?" She was afraid to tell him what had happened.

"It's nothing, I just . . . the doctor said I'm in great shape. And . . ."

"Who was that talking to you?" He had a sixth sense about her, and he knew something was wrong as he listened.

"It's a policeman, Charles," she sighed, feeling foolish, but also feeling sick again, and the policeman watched her turn green and then swoon again as he caught her with one arm. She had no idea what was happening, but she felt awful. She actually felt too sick to talk to him, as she set down the phone, and sat down on the floor and put her head down between her knees. One of the policemen went to get a glass of water for her, and the other picked up the phone where she'd left it on the floor beside her.

"Hello? Hello? What's going on there?" Charles was frantic.

"This is Officer Mason. Who is this?" he said calmly, as Grace looked up at him in helpless mortification.

"My name is Charles Mackenzie and that's my wife there with you. What's wrong?"

"She's fine, sir. She had a little problem . . . she passed out just outside your house. We brought her inside, and I think she's feeling a little woozy again. Probably stomach flu, there's a lot of it going around."

"Is she all right?" Charles looked ghastly, as he stood up and grabbed his coat while he was still talking to the officer at his house.

"I think she's fine. She didn't want to go to the hospital. We asked her."

"Never mind that. Can you take her to Lenox Hill?"

"We'd be glad to."

"I'll meet you there in ten minutes."

The policeman looked down at her with a smile after he hung up. "Your husband wants us to take you to Lenox Hill, Mrs. Mackenzie."

"I don't want to go." She sounded like a child and he smiled at her.

"He was pretty definite about it. He's going to meet you there."

"I'm okay. Really."

"I'm sure you are. But it doesn't hurt to get it checked out. There's a lot of nasty bugs around. A woman passed out at Bloomingdale's yesterday with that Hong Kong flu. You been sick long?" he asked while he helped her toward the door as they chatted, and his partner joined them.

"Really, I'm fine," she said, as the police locked her door and put her in the squad car. And then suddenly she realized what it must have looked like, as though she were being arrested. It would have seemed funny to her except that suddenly it reminded her of the night she had killed her father, and by the time they got to Lenox Hill, she was having an asthma attack, the first she'd had in two years. And she wasn't even carrying her inhaler. She had gotten so confident, she left it home most of the time now.

They took her inside, and she explained to the nurse in the emergency room about her asthma, and they were quick to bring her an inhaler. But by the time Charles arrived, she was still deathly pale from the asthma and the medication, and her hands were shaking.

"What happened?" He looked horrified, and she spoke in an undertone.

"The police car made me nervous."

"That's why you fainted?" He looked confused by what was happening, and she shook her head.

"That's why I have asthma."

"But why did you faint?"

"I don't know that."

The policemen left them then, and it was another hour before they could be seen by one of the emergency room doctors. And she was much better by then, her breathing was almost normal, and she was no longer dizzy. He had brought her some chicken soup from a machine, and some candy and a sandwich. Her appetite was good, she explained to the doctor who examined her.

"Excellent," Charles confirmed.

The doctor checked her over carefully, and then asked a pointed question. He said it was probably the flu, but he had one other idea. "Could you be pregnant?"

"I don't think so." She hadn't used birth control since Abby was born, and she was going to be six in July. And Grace had never gotten pregnant again. "I doubt it."

"Are you on the pill?" She shook her head. "Then why not? Any reason?" He glanced at Charles.

"I just don't think so," Grace said firmly. She would have loved another child, but she just didn't think she could get pregnant. After six years, why would she?

"I think you are," Charles smiled slowly at her. He'd never even thought of it, but she had all the symptoms. "Could you check?" he asked the resident.

"You can buy a kit at the drugstore on the corner. My bet is you're right, and she isn't." He smiled at Grace. "I think maybe you have denial. You've got pretty much all the symptoms. Nausea, dizziness, increased appetite, fatigue, sleepiness, you feel bloated, and you missed your last period, which you think was from nerves. Professionally speaking, I don't. My guess is you're having a baby. I can call our o.b./gyn to check it out if you want, but it's just as easy to buy the kit and call your own doctor."

"Thank you," she said, looking stunned. She hadn't even thought of it. She had hoped for another baby for so long, and then finally given it up, and convinced herself it would never happen.

They went to the corner and bought the kit, and took a cab home, and Charles held her close to him, grateful that nothing terrible had happened. When the policeman had answered his phone, he had panicked, and feared the worst.

She did all the steps in the kit, and they waited precisely five minutes, using Charles's stopwatch, and she was smiling as they waited for it. They were both convinced now that she was pregnant, and she was.

"When do you suppose it happened?" she asked, looking stunned. She still couldn't believe it.

"I'll bet right after we had dinner at the White House," Charles laughed, and kissed her.

And he was right. She went to her obstetrician the next day, and the baby was due in late September. Charles made a few noises about being an old man when it was born. He would be fifty-one, but Grace wouldn't listen to his complaints about being "old."

"You're just a kid," she grinned. They were both excited and happy. And when the baby came, he was a beautiful little boy who looked like both of them, except he had pale blond hair, which they insisted was nowhere in their families. He was an exquisite child, and he looked almost Swedish. They named him Matthew, and the children fell in love with him the moment they saw him. Abby walked around holding him all the time and called him "her baby."

But with three children, their town house on Sixty-ninth began to burst at the seams, and that winter they sold it and bought a house in Greenwich. It was a pretty white house with a picket fence, and a huge backyard. And Charles bought a big chocolate Labrador for the children. It was the perfect life.

"Help Kids!" continued to thrive, and Grace went into town twice a week to check on things, but she had hired someone else to run the office, and she opened a smaller office in Connecticut, where she spent her mornings. Most of the time she took the baby with her in his stroller.

It was a comfortable life for them in Connecticut. The kids loved their new school. Abigail and Andrew were in first and second grades. And it was the following summer when Charles heard from Roger Marshall, his old partner who was now in Congress.

Roger wanted Charles to think about getting into politics, there was a very interesting seat in Connecticut coming up the following year, when a senior congressman finally retired. Charles couldn't imagine pursuing it, he was so busy at the firm, and he enjoyed his work. Running for Congress, if he won, would mean moving to Washington, at least some of the time, and that would be hard on Grace and the children. And political campaigns were costly and exhausting. They had lunch and talked about it, and Charles turned him down. But when the junior congressman from his district had a heart attack and died later that year, Roger called again, and this time Grace surprised Charles by pressing him to think about it.

"You're not serious," Charles looked at her cautiously, "you don't want that life, do you?" He had been in the public eye once, when he was married to his first wife, and he didn't really enjoy it. But he had to admit that government had always been something that intrigued him, particularly Washington.

In the end, he told Roger he'd think about it. And he did. He decided against it finally, but Grace argued with him about what a difference he could make, and how much he might enjoy it. She thought it would mean a great deal to him and, more than once recently, he had admitted to her that he wasn't feeling as challenged at the law firm. He was feeling old in the face of his fifty-third birthday. The only things that really mattered to him anymore were the children and her.

"You need something new in your life, Charles," she said quietly. "Something that excites you."

"I have you," he smiled, "that's exciting enough for any man. A young wife and three children ought to keep me busy for the next fifty years. Besides, you don't really want all that craziness in our life, do you? It'll be hard on you and the children. It's like living in a fishbowl."

"If it's what you want, we'll manage it. Washington's not on the moon. It's not that far. We can keep this house, and spend time here. You can even commute part of the week when Congress is in session."

He laughed at all the plans she was making. "I'm not sure we'll need to worry about it. There's a good possibility I won't win. I'm a dark horse, and no one knows me."

"You're a respected man in this community, with good ideas, a lot of integrity, and a real interest in your country."

"Do I get your vote?" he asked as he kissed her.

"Always."

He told Roger he would run, and he began gathering people to help him campaign. They started in earnest in June, and Grace did everything she could from licking stamps to shaking hands to going from door to door handing out leaflets. They ran a real "common man's" campaign, and although they never made any secret of the fact that Charles was wellborn and wellheeled, it was equally obvious that he was also caring and sincere and well-meaning. He was an honest man with the country's well-being at heart. The public trusted him, and much to Charles's own surprise, the media loved him. They covered everything he did, and reported fairly.

"Why shouldn't they?" Grace was surprised that Charles was so amazed by his good press, but he knew them better than she did.

"Because they're not always that fair. Wait. They'll get me sooner or later."

"Don't be such a cynic."

She stayed pretty much out of the campaign, except to stand by him when he needed her with him, and to do as much legwork as she could, even if she had to take the children with her. But she had no desire to push herself forward. Charles was the candidate and what he stood for was important. She never lost sight of that.

She hardly had time for her own projects anymore, and "Help Kids!" had to struggle without her most of the time during the campaign. She still took shifts on the hot line whenever she could, but she worked for Charles more than she did anything else, and she could see that he loved what he was doing. He was excited about it, and they went to picnics and barbecues and state fairs, he spoke to political groups and farmers and businessmen. And it was obvious that he really wanted to help them. They believed him, and they liked everything he stood for. They liked Grace too. Her work with "Help Kids!" was well known, yet it was clear that her husband and children were her first priorities, and they liked that about her.

In November he won by a landslide. He put his partnership in the firm in trust, and they gave a huge party for him at the Pierre before he left. And then he and Grace and the children went to Washington to find a house. They were going to be moving there after

Christmas. The children were going to change schools, and they were scared, but excited. It was a big change for them. And they found an adorable house in Georgetown, on R Street.

Grace enrolled the children in Sitwell Friends. And in January, Abigail and Andrew entered third and fourth grades, and Grace found a play group to join with Matthew. He was just two then.

They went back to Connecticut on holidays and for vacations, and whenever Congress wasn't in session and the children were out of school. Charles stayed close to his constituents and in touch with old friends, and he enjoyed every moment in Congress. He helped pass new legislation whenever he could, and found the endless committees he was on fascinating and fruitful. And during their second year there, Grace started an inner city "Help Kids!" in Washington modeled on the two in Connecticut and New York. She manned the phones a lot of the time, and made several appearances on television and radio shows. As the wife of a congressman she had more influence than she'd had before, and she enjoyed using it for worthwhile causes.

They also entertained a great deal, and went to political events. They were invited to the White House regularly. For them, the quiet years were over. And yet they were still able to lead a quiet life in Connecticut. And although he was an elected official, their life remained remarkably private. They weren't showy people. He was a hardworking congressman who stayed in close touch with his roots at home, and Grace was discreet and hardworking in her own arena, and with her children.

They had been in Washington for nearly three terms, five years, when Charles was approached again, and this time with an offer that interested him greatly. Being congressman had meant a lot to him and it had been a valuable experience, but he had also come to understand that there was more power and more influence on the country's destiny in other quarters. The Senate held a great lure to him, and he had many friends there. And this time he was approached by sources close to the President, anxious to know if he was willing to run for the Senate.

He told Grace about it immediately, and they talked about it endlessly. He wanted it, but he was also afraid to pursue it. There was more pressure, greater demands, tougher responsibilities, and far greater exposure. As a congressman, he had been well liked, and in many ways, one of the people. As a senator he could be viewed as a source of envy and a threat to many. All those anxious for the presidency would be looking at him, and anxious to throw him out of his traces.

"It can be a vicious job," he explained candidly, and he worried about her too. They had left her alone so far. She was known for her good works, her solid marriage, and her sense of family, but she was rarely in the public eye. As the wife of a senator, she would be much more in the spotlight, and who knew what that would bring. "I don't ever want to do anything to hurt you," Charles said, looking worried. She, and their family, were always his first concern, and she loved him all the more for it.

"Don't be ridiculous. I'm not afraid. I don't have anything to hide," she said, without thinking, and he smiled, and then she understood. "All right, I do. But no one's said anything yet. No one's ever come forward to talk about my past. And I paid my dues. What could they say now?"

It was all so long ago. She was thirty-eight years old. Her troubles were all so far behind her . . . twenty-one years . . . it was all over, and in many ways, to Grace, it seemed like a distant dream.

"A lot of people probably don't realize who you are, you have a different name, you've grown up. But as the wife of a senator, they could start delving into your past, Grace. Do you really want that?"

"No, but are you going to let it stop you? Is this what you want?" she asked him, as they sat in their bedroom talking late into the night, and slowly he nodded. "Then don't let anything stop you. You have a right to this. You're good at what you do. Don't let fear take over our lives," she said powerfully. "We have nothing to be afraid of."

They believed it too, and two weeks later he announced that in November he would be running for the Senate.

It was a tight race, and he would be fighting a tough incumbent. But the man had been in the Senate for a long time, and people thought it was time for a change. And Charles Mackenzie was very appealing. He had a great track record, a clean reputation, and a lot of friends. He was also very good-looking, and had a family people liked, which never hurt in an election.

The campaign began with a press conference, and right from the beginning, Grace saw the difference. They asked him questions about his history, his law firm, his personal worth, his income, his taxes, his employees, his children. And then they asked about Grace, and her involvement in "Help Kids!" and St. Andrew's before that. Mysteriously, they knew about the donations she'd made. But in spite of their probing, they seemed inclined to like her. Magazines called her up to do interviews, and photograph her, and at first she refused them. She didn't want to be in the forefront of the campaign. She wanted to do what she had done for him before, work hard, and stand just behind him. But that wasn't what they wanted. They had a fifty-eight-year-old candidate for senator with movie star good looks, and a pretty wife who was twenty years younger. And by spring they wanted to know everything about her, and the children.

"But I don't want to do interviews," she complained to him one morning over breakfast. "You're the candidate, I'm not. What do they want with me for heaven's sake?" she said, pouring him a second cup of coffee. They had a housekeeper who came in halfway through the day, but Grace still liked being alone with Charles and the children and cooking breakfast for them herself every morning.

"I told you it would be this way," Charles said calmly about the press. Nothing seemed to ruffle him, even when the stories about him were unflattering, which they often were now. It was the nature of the political beast, and he knew that. Once you entered the ring, you belonged to them, and they could do anything they wanted. Gone the peaceful congressional days when he only had to worry about the constituents he represented, and the local press. Now he was dealing with the national press, and all their demands and quirks, love affairs and hatreds. "Besides," he smiled at her and finished his coffee, "if you were ugly, they wouldn't want you. Maybe you should stop looking like that," he said as he leaned over and kissed her.

He took the kids to school as he always did. Matthew, their baby, was in second grade now. And Andrew had just started high school. They still all went to the same school, and they had gotten to the point where most of their friends were in Washington and not Connecticut, but they were at home in both places.

Things rolled along smoothly until June, the campaign was going well, and Charles was pleased with it. And they were just about to go back to Greenwich for the summer, when Charles appeared at the house unexpectedly in the afternoon, looking pale. For a sick moment Grace thought something had happened to one of the children. She heard him come in, and hurried down the stairs to the front hall just as he put down his briefcase.

"What's wrong?" she asked without pausing for breath. Maybe they had called him first . . . which one was it . . . Andy, Abigail, or Matt?

"I've got bad news," he said, looking at her unhappily and then taking two quick steps toward her.

"Oh God, what is it?" She squeezed his hand without thinking, and when she took it away again she'd left a mark from the pressure of her fingers.

"I just got a call from a source we have at Associated Press . . ." then it wasn't the children, "Grace . . . they know about your father and your time at Dwight." He looked devastated to have to tell her, but he wanted to prepare her. He was only desperately sorry to have put her in a position where she could have gotten so badly hurt. And he realized now that he never should have done it. He had been foolish and selfish and naive to think they could survive the campaign unscathed. And now the press were going to devour her.

"Oh," was all she said, staring at him. "I . . .

okay." And then she looked at him worriedly, "How badly is this going to hurt you?"

"I don't know. That's not the point. I didn't want you to have to go through this." He led her slowly into their living room with an arm around her shoulder. "They're going to break the story at six o'clock, on the news, and they want a press conference before, if we'll do it."

"Do I have to?" she looked gray.

"No, you don't. Why don't we wait and see how bad it is, and then deal with it afterwards?"

"What about the kids? What should I say to them?" Grace looked calm, but very pale, and her hands were shaking badly.

"We'd better tell them."

They picked them up from school together that afternoon, and took them home, and sat them down in the dining room around the table.

"Your mom and I have something to say," he said quietly.

"You're getting divorced?" Matt looked terrified, all of his friends' parents had been getting divorced lately.

"No, of course not," his father said with a smile in his direction. "But this isn't good either. This is something very hard for your mom. But we thought that we should tell you." Charles looked very serious, as he held Grace's hand firmly.

"Are you sick?" Andrew asked nervously, his best friend's mom had just died of cancer.

"No, I'm fine." Grace took a breath and felt the first tightening of her chest she'd felt in a long time. She didn't even know when she'd last seen her inhaler. "This is about something that happened a long time ago, and it's very hard to explain, and understand. It's very hard unless you've been there, or seen it happen." She was fighting back tears, and Charles squeezed her hand.

"When I was a little girl, like Matty's age, my dad used to be very mean to my mom, he used to beat her," she said calmly but sadly.

"You mean like hit her?" Matthew said in astonishment with wide eyes, and Grace nodded solemnly.

"Yes. He hit her a lot, and he really hurt her. He beat her for a long time, and then she got very, very sick."

"Because he beat her up?" Matthew asked again.

"Probably not. She just did. She got cancer, like Zack's mom." They all knew Andrew's friend. "She was very sick for a long time, four years. And while she was sick, sometimes he'd beat me . . . he did a lot of terrible things . . . and sometimes he still beat my mom. But I thought that if I let him hurt me . . ." Her eyes filled with tears and she choked as Charles squeezed her hand still harder to give her courage. "I thought that if I let him hurt me, then he wouldn't hurt her as much . . . so I let him do anything he wanted . . . it was pretty terrible . . . and then she died. I was seventeen, and the night of her funeral," she closed her eyes and then opened them again, determined to finish the story that she had never wanted her children to know. But now she knew she had to tell them, before someone else did. "The night of the funeral, he beat me again . . . a lot . . . very badly . . . he hurt me terribly, and I was very scared . . . and I remembered a gun my mom had next to her bed, and I grabbed it . . . I think I just wanted to scare him," she was sobbing now and her children

stared at her in stupefied silence, "I don't know what I
thought . . . I was just so scared and I didn't want
him to hurt me anymore . . . we fought over the gun
. . . it went off accidentally, and I shot him. He died
that night." She took a big gulp of air, and Andrew
stared at her, stunned.

"You shot your dad? You *killed* him?" Andrew
asked, and she nodded. They had a right to know. She
just didn't want to tell them about the rapes, if she
didn't have to.

"Did you go to jail?" Matthew asked, intrigued by
the story. It was sort of like cops and robbers, or something on TV. It sounded interesting to him, except for
the part where he beat her.

"Yes, I did," she said quietly, looking at her daughter, who so far, had said nothing at all. "I went to
prison for two years, and I was on probation in Chicago
for two years after that. And then it was all over. I
moved to New York and met your dad, we got married
and had you, and everything's been happy ever since
then." It had all been so simple for the past fifteen
years and now it was going to get difficult again. But it
couldn't be helped now. They had taken the chance of
exposure along with Charles's political career, and now
they had to pay the price for it.

"I can't believe this," Abigail said, staring at her.
"You've been in *jail*? Why didn't you ever tell us?"

"I didn't think I had to, Abby. It wasn't a story I
was proud of. It was very painful for me."

"You said your parents were dead, you never said
you killed them," Abigail reproached her.

"I didn't kill them both. I killed him," Grace explained.

"You make it sound like you were defending yourself," she argued with her mother.

"I was."

"Isn't that self-defense? Then how come you went to jail?"

Grace nodded miserably. "It is, but they didn't believe me."

"I can't believe you've been in prison." All she could think of were her friends and what they would say now, when they heard the story. It was worse than anything she could imagine.

"Did you kill Dad's parents too?" Matt asked, intrigued.

"Of course not." Grace smiled at him. He was really too young to understand it.

"Why are you telling us this now?" Andrew asked unhappily. Abigail was right. It wasn't a pretty story. And it wouldn't sit well with their friends.

"Because the press has found out," Charles answered for her. He hadn't said anything till then, he wanted to let Grace tell them in her own way, and she had done well. But it wasn't easy to absorb, for anyone, least of all for children to hear about their mother. "It's going to be on the news tonight, and we wanted to tell you first."

"Gee, thanks a lot. Ten minutes before it goes on. And you expect me to go to school tomorrow? I'm not going," Abigail stormed.

"Neither am I," Matt said, just for good measure, and then he turned to his mother with a curious expression. "Did he bleed a lot? Your dad, I mean." Grace laughed in spite of herself, and so did Charles. To him, it was all like a TV show.

"Never mind, Matt," his father scolded.

"Did he make a lot of noise?"

"Matthew!"

"I can't believe this," Abigail said, and burst into tears. "I can't believe you never told us all this, and now it's going to be all over the news. You're a murderer, a jailbird."

"Abigail, you don't understand the circumstances," Charles said. "You don't have any idea what your mother went through. Why do you think she's always been so interested in abused children?"

"To show off," Abby said angrily. "Besides, what do you know? You weren't there either, were you? And besides, this is all because of you, and your stupid campaign! If we weren't here in Washington, none of this would have happened!" There was a certain truth to that, and Charles felt guilty enough without having Abby rub it in, but before he could answer her, she ran upstairs and slammed the door to her bedroom. Grace stood up to go, but Charles pulled her into her seat again.

"Let her calm down," he said wisely, and Andrew looked at them and rolled his eyes.

"She's such a little bitch, why do you put up with her?"

"Because we love her, and all of you," Charles said. "This isn't easy for any of us. We have to work it out in our own ways, and support each other. This is going to be very hard once the press start tearing your mom apart."

"We'll be there for you, Mom," Andrew said kindly, and got up to give her a hug, but Matthew was thinking about what she'd said. He kind of liked the story.

"Maybe Abby will shoot you, Dad," he said hopefully, and Charles could only laugh at him again.

"I hope not, Matt. No one is going to shoot anyone."

"Mom might."

Grace smiled ruefully as she looked at her youngest son. "Remember that the next time I tell you to clean up your room or finish your dinner."

"Yeah," he said with a broad grin, showing that his two top front teeth were missing. Surprisingly, unlike his siblings, he wasn't upset. But he was too young to really absorb the implications of what had happened.

Eventually, Grace went upstairs and tried to talk to Abigail, but she wouldn't let her mother into her room, and at six o'clock they all gathered downstairs to watch the television in the den. Abby came down silently and joined them, and sat in the back of the room without talking to her parents.

The telephone had been ringing off the hook for two hours by then, but Grace had put it on the machine. There wasn't a soul alive they wanted to talk to. And there was an unlisted emergency line where Charles's aides called him. They called several times, and warned that they had been advised again that the story was ugly.

It was presented as a special bulletin, with a full screen photograph of her mug shot from prison. What startled Grace above all was how young she looked. She was barely more than a baby, only three years older than Andrew, and she looked younger than Abigail in the picture.

"Wow, Mom! Is that you?"

"Shhh, Matthew!" they all said at once, and watched in horror as the story unraveled.

The story was definitely not pretty. It opened with the news that Grace Mackenzie, wife of Congressman Charles Mackenzie, candidate for a Senate seat in the next election, had shot her father in a sex scandal at seventeen, and had been sentenced to two years in prison. There were photographs of her going into the trial, in handcuffs, and of her father looking very handsome. They said he had been a pillar of the community, and his daughter had accused him of rape, and shot him. She had claimed self-defense and a jury had not believed her. A two-year sentence for voluntary manslaughter was the result, followed by two years' probation.

There were more photographs of her then, leaving the trial, again in handcuffs, and as she left for Dwight, in leg irons and chains, then another photograph of her at Dwight. She sounded like a gang moll by the time they were finished. They went on to say that she had been at Dwight Correctional Center in Dwight, Illinois, for two years, and was released in 1973 for two years of probation in Chicago. There had been no further problems with the law subsequently, to the best of their knowledge, but that possibility was currently under investigation.

"Under investigation? What the hell do they mean?" Grace asked, and Charles silenced her with a gesture, he wanted to hear what they were saying.

They explained that people in the community had not believed the sex scandal story at all. And then they followed it with a brief interview with the chief of police who had charged her. Twenty-one years later, he was there, and he claimed to have total recall of the night she was arrested.

"The prosecutor felt she'd been trying to . . ."

he smiled wickedly and Grace wanted to throw up as she listened, ". . . I'd say, tantalize her father, and she got angry when he didn't take the bait. She was a pretty sick girl, back then, I don't know anything about her now of course, but a leopard don't change his spots much, does he?" She couldn't believe what she was hearing, or what they'd encouraged him to say.

They explained again, for all who hadn't caught it the first time, that she was a convicted felon, convicted of murder. They showed her mug shot yet again. And then a photograph of her looking like a moron, with Charles, as she stood next to him when he was sworn into Congress. And they explained that Charles was now running for the Senate. And then it was over, and they moved on to something else, as Grace fell back in her seat in horrified amazement. She felt completely drained of all emotion. It was all there, the mug shots, the story, the attitude of the community as expressed by the chief of police.

"They practically said I raped him! Did you hear what that bastard said?" Grace was outraged by what the chief of police had said about her, he had called her "pretty sick" and said she had "tantalized" her father. "Can't we sue them?"

"Maybe," Charles said, trying to sound calm, for hers and the children's sake. "First we have to see what happens. There's going to be a lot of noise over this. We have to be ready for it."

"How much worse can it get?" she asked angrily.

"A lot," he said knowingly. His aides had warned him, and he knew that from his experience with the press years before.

By seven o'clock there were television cameras outside their house. One channel even used a bullhorn to address her, and urge her to come out and talk to them. Charles called the police, but the best they could do for them was get the reporters off their property, and force them to stand across the street, which they did. They put two camera crews in the trees so they could shoot into their bedroom windows. And Charles went upstairs and closed the shades. They were under siege.

"How long is this going to last?" Grace asked miserably after the children went to bed. They were still out there.

"A while probably. Maybe a long while." And then as they sat in the kitchen, looking at each other in exhaustion, he asked her if she wanted to talk to them at some point and tell them her side of the story.

"Should I? Can't we sue them for what they said?"

"I don't know any of the answers." He had already put in calls to two major libel lawyers, but he also realized that their phones could be tapped by the press, and he didn't want to talk to the attorneys from the house, or even from his office. For the moment, at least, it was a genuine disaster.

The next morning, the press were still there, and Charles and Grace were tipped off again about new coverage on local and national talk shows. She was the hot news of the hour all over the country.

Two guards were interviewed at Dwight, who claimed they knew her really well. Both were young and Grace knew for certain she'd never seen them.

"I've never laid eyes on them," she said to Charles, feeling sick again. He had stayed home with her, to lend her support, as she was stuck in the house, and Abby had refused to get out of bed. But a friend had offered to take Andrew and Matt to school, and Grace was relieved they'd gone. It was hard enough dealing with Abby, and herself.

The two prison guards said that Grace had been a member of a real tough gang, and they implied, but didn't actually say, that she'd used drugs in prison.

"What are they doing to me?" She burst into tears and put her face in her hands. She didn't understand it. Why were these people lying about her?

"Grace, they want a piece of the action. A moment of glory. That's all it is. They want to be on television, they want to be a star just like you are."

"I'm not a star. I'm a housewife," she said naively.

"To them, you're a star." He was a lot wiser than she was.

On another channel, they were interviewing the chief of police again. And in Watseka, a girl who claimed to have been Grace's best friend in school, and whom Grace had also never seen before, said that Grace had always talked to her a lot about how much she loved her father and how jealous she was of her mother. The impression being created there was that she had killed her father in a jealous rage.

"Are these people crazy, or am I? That woman looks twice my age, and I don't even know who she is." Even her name was unfamiliar.

They interviewed one of the arresting officers from that night, who looked like an old man now, and he admitted that Grace had looked really scared and she was shaking really badly when they found her.

"Did she look like she'd been raped?" the interviewer said without hesitation.

"It was hard to tell, you know, I'm no doctor," he said shyly, "but she didn't have any clothes on."

"She was *naked*?" The interviewer looked straight into the camera, shocked, and the policeman nodded.

"Yeah, but I don't think the doctors at the hospital said she'd been raped. They just said she'd had sex with her boyfriend or something. Maybe her father walked in on them."

"Thank you, Sergeant Johnson."

And then came the pièce de résistance on yet another channel. A moment with Frank Wills, who looked even worse and sleazier than he had twenty years before, if that was possible, and he said bluntly that Grace had always been a strange kid and had always been after her father's money.

"*What*? He got everything there was, and God knows it wasn't much," she shouted at Charles, and then laid her head back in despair again.

"Grace, you have to stop going crazy over everything they say. You know they're not going to tell the truth. Why should they?" Where were David Glass and Molly? Why wasn't someone saying anything decent about her? Why didn't anybody love her? Why hadn't they? Why had Molly died, and David disappeared? Where the hell were they now?

"I can't stand this," she said hysterically. There was no getting away from it, and it was unbearable. There was no relief and in this case, there was no reward for this kind of pain and torture.

"You have to stand it," Charles said matter-of-factly. "It's not going to disappear overnight." Charles knew better than anyone that it could take a long time to die down once the flames had grown to such major proportions.

"Why do I have to stand this?" she asked, crying again.

"Because people love this garbage. They eat it up. When I was married to Michelle, the tabloids crawled all over her constantly, they told lies, they snuck stories, they did everything they could to torture her. You just have to accept that. That's the way it is."

"I can't. She was a movie star, she wanted the attention. She must have wanted what went with it." Grace was refusing to see the similarity in their lives.

"And the presumption is that I do too, because I'm a politician."

She sat in the den with him for an hour and cried, and then she went upstairs and tried to talk to Abby. But Abby didn't want to hear any of it from her. She had been flipping the dial, and hearing all the same things in her mother's bedroom.

"How could you do those things?" Abby sobbed as Grace looked at her in anguish.

"I didn't," Grace said through tears. "I was miserable, I was alone, I was scared. I was terrified of him . . . he beat me . . . he raped me for four years . . . and I couldn't help it. I don't even know if I meant to kill him. I just did. I was like a wounded animal. I struck out any way I could to save myself from him. I had no choice, Abby." She was sobbing as Abby watched her, crying too. "But most of the other things they said on TV aren't true." Grace hated them for what they were doing to her daughter. "None of those things was true. I don't even know those people, except the man who was my father's partner, and what he said wasn't true either. He took all my father's money. I hardly got anything, and what I got I gave to charity. I've spent my life trying to give back to people like me, to help them survive too. I never forgot what I went through. And oh God, Abby," she put her arms

around her, "I love you so much, I don't ever want you
to suffer because of me. It breaks my heart to see you
so unhappy. Abby, I had a miserable life as a kid. No
one was ever decent to me until I met your father. He
gave me a life, he gave me love and all of you. He's one
of the few human beings who's ever been kind to me
. . . Abby," she was sobbing uncontrollably, and her
daughter was hugging her, "I'm so sorry, and I love
you so much . . . please forgive me . . ."

"I'm sorry I was so mean to you . . . I'm sorry,
Mommy . . ."

"It's okay, it's okay . . . I love you . . ."

Charles was watching them from the doorway with
tears running down his face, and he tiptoed away to
call the lawyers again. But when one of them came to
see them that afternoon, he didn't have good news.
Public figures, like politicians and movie stars, had no
rights of privacy whatsoever. People could say anything
they wanted to about them without having the burden
of proving whether it was true. And if celebrities
wanted to sue, *they* had to prove that what was being
said about them were lies, which was often impossible
to do, and they also had to *prove* that they'd suffered a
loss of income as a result, or the impaired ability to
make a living, and they had to *prove* yet again that what
had been said had been said in actual malice. And the
wives or husbands of politicians, particularly if they had
either campaigned, or appeared in public with them,
as she obviously had, had the same lack of rights as the
politicians. In fact, Grace had no rights at all now.

"What that means," the attorney who'd come to
see them explained, "is that you can't do anything
against most of what people are saying. If they claim
that you killed your father and you didn't, that's a dif-

ferent story, although they have a right to say you were convicted of it, but if they say you were in a gang in prison, you have to *prove* that you were not, and how are you going to do that, Mrs. Mackenzie? Get affidavits from the inmates who were there at the time? You have to *prove* that these things have been said intentionally to hurt you, and that they have affected negatively your ability to make a living.''

"In other words, they can do anything they want to me, and unless I can prove they're lying, and everything else you mentioned, I can't do a damn thing about it. Is that it?''

"Exactly. It's not a happy situation. But everyone in the public eye is in the same boat you are. And unfortunately these are tabloid times we live in. The common belief of the media is that the public wants not only dirt, but blood. They want to make people and destroy people, they want to tear people apart, and feed them to the public bit by bit. It's not personal, it's economic. They make money off your corpse. They're vultures. They pay up to a hundred and fifty thousand dollars for a story, and then treat it as news. And unreliable sources who're being paid that kind of money will say anything to keep the spotlight on them, and the money coming. They'll say you danced naked on your father's grave and they saw you do it, if it gets them on TV, and makes them a buck. That's reality. And the so-called legitimate press behave the same way these days. There's no such thing anymore. It's disgusting. And they take innocent people like you, and your family, and trash them, for the hell of it. It's the most malicious game there is, and yet 'actual malice' is the hardest thing of all to prove. It isn't even malice anymore, it's greed, and indifference to the human condition.

"You paid a price for what you did. You suffered enough. You were seventeen. You shouldn't have to go through all this, nor should your husband and your children. But there's very little I can do to help you. We'll keep an eye on it, and if anything turns up we can sue for, we will. But you have to be prepared for the fallout from that too. Lawsuits only encourage the feeding frenzy more. The sharks love blood in the water."

"You're not very encouraging, Mr. Goldsmith," Charles said, looking depressed.

"No, I'm not," he smiled ruefully. He liked Charles, and he felt sorry for Grace. But the laws were not made to protect people like them. The laws had been made to turn them into victims.

The feeding frenzy, as he had called it, went on for weeks. The children went back to school, reluctantly. Fortunately, they got out for summer vacation after a week, and the family moved to Connecticut for the summer. But it was more of the same there. More tabloids, more press, more photographers. More interviews on television with people who claimed to be her best friends, but whom she had never heard of. The only good thing that came of it, was that David Glass emerged from the mists. He had called, and was living in Van Nuys, and had four children. He was desperately sorry to see what was happening to her. It broke his heart, knowing how much pain it caused her to go through it. But no one could do anything to stop the press, or the lies, or the gossip. And he knew as well as she did that even if he talked to the press on her behalf, everything he said would be distorted. He was happy to know that other than the current uproar in the press, she was happily married, and had children. He apologized for staying out of touch for so long. He was now the senior partner of his late father-in-law's law firm. And then he admitted sheepishly that Tracy, his wife, had been fiercely jealous of Grace when they first moved to California. It was why he had eventually stopped writing. But he was happy to hear her now, he had felt compelled to call, and Grace was happy he'd called her. They both agreed that the press didn't want the facts. They wanted scandal and filth. They wanted to hear that she'd been giving blow jobs to guards, or sleeping with women in chains in prison. They didn't want to know how vulnerable she'd been, how terrorized, how traumatized, how scared, how young, how decent. They only wanted the ugly stuff. Both David and Charles agreed that the best thing was to step back and let them wear themselves out, and offer no comment.

But even after a month of it, the furor hadn't died down. And all the principal tabloids were still running stories about her on their covers. The tabloid TV shows had interviewed everyone except the janitor in jail, and Grace felt it was time to come forward and say something. Grace and Charles spent an entire day talking to Charles's campaign manager, and they finally agreed to let her do a press conference. Maybe that would stop it.

"It won't, you know," Charles said. But maybe if it was handled well, it wouldn't do any harm either.

The conference was set for the week before her birthday on an important interview show, on a major network. It was heavily advertised, and television news cameras started appearing outside their house the day before. It was agony for their children. They hated having anyone over now, or going anywhere, or even talking to friends. Grace understood it only too well. Every time she went to the grocery store, someone came over to her and started a seemingly innocuous conversation that would end up in Q&A about her life in prison. It didn't matter if they opened with melons or cars, somehow they always wound up in the same place, asking if her father had really raped her, or how traumatic had it been to kill him, and were there really a lot of lesbians in prison.

"Are you kidding?" Charles said in disbelief. It happened to her the most when she was alone or with the children. Grace complained to Charles about it constantly. A woman had walked up to her that day at the gas station, and out of the blue shouted "Bang, ya got him, didn't you, Grace?" "I feel like Bonnie and Clyde." She had to laugh at it sometimes. It really was absurd, and although people mentioned it to him sometimes too, they never seemed to ask as much or as viciously as they did of Grace. It was as though they wanted to torment her. She had even gotten a highly irritated letter from Cheryl Swanson in Chicago, saying that she was retired now, and she and Bob were divorced, no surprise to Grace, but she couldn't understand why Grace had never told her she'd been in prison.

"Because she wouldn't have hired me," she said to Charles as she tossed the letter at him to show him. There were lots of letters like that now, and crank calls, and one blank page smeared with blood spelling out the word "Murderess," which they'd turned over to the police. But she'd had a nice letter from Winnie, in Philadelphia, offering her love and support, and an-

other from Father Tim, who was in Florida, as the
chaplain of a retirement community. He sent her his
love and prayers, and reminded her that she was God's
child, and He loved her.

She reminded herself of it constantly the day of
the interview. It had all been carefully staged, and
Charles's P.R. people had reviewed the questions, or so
they thought. Mysteriously, the questions they'd approved for the interview had disappeared, and Grace
found herself asked, first off, what it had meant to her
to have sex with her father.

"Meant to me?" She looked at her interviewer in
amazement. "*Meant* to me? Have you ever worked with
victims of abuse? Have you ever seen what child abusers do to children? They rape them, they mutilate
them . . . they *kill* them . . . they torture them, they
put cigarettes out on their little arms and faces . . .
they fry them on radiators . . . they do a lot of very
ugly things . . . have you ever asked any of them what
it *meant* to them to have boiling water poured on their
face, or their arm nearly ripped out of its socket? It
means a lot to children when people do things like that
to them. It means that no one loves them, that they're
in constant danger . . . it means living with terror every moment of the day. That's what it means . . .
that's what it meant to me." It was a powerful state-
ment, and the interviewer looked taken aback as Grace
fell silent.

"Actually I . . . we . . . I'm sure that all your
supporters have been wondering how you feel about
your prison record being revealed to the public."

"Sad . . . sorry . . . I was the victim of some terrible crimes, committed within the sanctity of the family. And I in turn did a terrible thing, killing my father.

But I had paid for it before, and I paid for it after. I think revealing it, in this way, scandalizing it, sensationalizing the agony that our family went through, and tormenting my children and my husband now, serves no purpose. It's done in such a way as to embarrass us, and not to inform the public." She talked then about the people giving interviews, claiming to know her, whom she had never even seen before, and the lies they told to make themselves important. She didn't mention the tabloid by name, but she said that one of them had told shocking lies in all of their headlines. And the interviewer smiled at that.

"You can't expect people to believe what they read in tabloids, Mrs. Mackenzie."

"Then why print it?" Grace said firmly.

The interviewer asked a thousand unfortunate questions, but eventually she asked Grace to tell them about "Help Kids!" and her work with the victims of child abuse. She told them about St. Mary's and Saint Andrew's, and "Help Kids!" She made a plea for children everywhere that they never had to go through what she had gone through. Despite their probing and the lack of sympathy with which they had handled much of it, and the spuriousness, she had turned it into a deeply moving and very sympathetic interview, and everyone congratulated her afterwards. Charles was particularly proud of her, and they spent a quiet evening after the cameras had left, and talked about all that had happened. It had been a terrible time for Grace, but at least she had said her piece now.

They spent her birthday at home, and Abigail had friends over that night. But only because her parents had insisted. It was her birthday too. And Grace was very quiet as she sat at the pool with Charles. She was still feeling shaken and withdrawn, and she hated going anywhere. People were still harassing her, even in bank lines and public rest rooms. She was happier at home, behind her walls, and she dreaded going out, even with Charles. In spite of his campaign, it was a very quiet summer.

But by August, finally, everything seemed to be back to normal. There were no more photographers camped outside, and she hadn't been on the cover of the tabloids in weeks.

"I guess you're just not popular anymore," Charles teased. He actually managed to take a week off to be with her, and he was glad he had. Her asthma had gotten bad again, for the first time in years, and she was feeling ill. He was sure it was stress, but this time she suspected what it was before he did. She was pregnant.

"In the middle of all this furor? How did you manage that?" He was shocked at first, but he was happy too. Their children were what brought them the most joy in all their years together. He worried about her during the campaign though. The baby was due in March, and she was two months pregnant, which meant that she'd be campaigning all through the early months. She'd be five months pregnant at the election. He wanted her to take it easy, and try not to wear herself out too much, or get too upset over the press when they went back to Washington. And then he groaned as he thought of it. "I'll be fifty-nine years old when this baby is born. I'll be eighty when he or she graduates from college. Oh my God, Grace." He smiled ruefully, and she scolded him.

"Oh shut up. I'm starting to look like the older woman in your life, so don't complain to me. You look

like you're thirty.'' He nearly did too. Not thirty, but
forty easily. He had barely been touched by the hands
of time, but at thirty-nine she didn't look bad either.

In September, they moved back to Washington. In
spite of his campaign, they had had a quiet summer.
They had only gone out with close friends in Greenwich, and because of the furor she'd caused in June,
and her early pregnancy, he had done all of his campaigning without her.

Abigail started high school that year. Andrew went
into his second year, and he had a new girlfriend, her
father was the French ambassador. And Matt started
third grade with all the usual commotion of new
backpacks, school supplies, whether to have hot lunch
or bring his own. For Matt, every day was still a big
adventure.

They hadn't told them about the baby yet, Grace
thought it was too soon. She was just three months
pregnant, and they had decided to wait until after
Matt's birthday in September. Grace had planned a
party for him. And little by little, she started going out
with Charles again. It was hard being seen again, knowing that her ugly past had become part of everyone's
dinner conversation. But there hadn't been anything
written about her in weeks, and she was feeling guilty
about not campaigning with her husband.

It was a hot September Saturday afternoon, the day
before Matthew's party, and Grace was buying some
things they needed at Sutton Place Gourmet, like ice
cream and plastic knives and forks and sodas. And as
she stood at the checkout stand, waiting to pay, she
almost fainted when she saw it. The latest edition of
the tabloid *Thrill* had just been set out, and Charles
hadn't been warned this time. There was a photograph

of her nude, with her head thrown back and her eyes closed, right on the cover. There were two black boxes covering her breasts and her pubic area, and other than that, the photograph left nothing to the imagination. Her legs were spread wide, and she looked like she was in the throes of passion. The headline read "Senator's Wife Did Porno in Chicago." She thought she was going to throw up as she gathered them up, and held a hundred-dollar bill out with a trembling hand. For a moment she didn't know what she was doing.

"You want *all* of them?" The young clerk looked surprised as she nodded. She was almost breathless. But her inhaler was her constant friend now.

"Do you have more?" she said hoarsely to him. And he nodded.

"Sure. In the back. You want them too?"

"Yes." She bought fifty copies of *Thrill,* and the groceries she needed for Matt, and ran to her car, as though she had just bought the only copies in existence and she was going to hide them. And as she drove home, crying behind the wheel, she realized how stupid she had been. You couldn't buy them all up. It was like emptying the ocean with a teacup.

She ran into the house as soon as she stopped the car, but Charles was sitting in the kitchen looking stunned, holding a copy of the tabloid in his hands. His chief aide had just seen it and brought it to him. They had never warned them. The aide saw the look on Grace's face, and left immediately, and Charles looked at her with real shock for the first time. She had never seen him look as betrayed or as weary, and seeing him that way almost killed her.

"What is this, Grace?"

"I don't know." She was crying as she sat down next to him, shaking. "I don't know . . ."

"It can't be you." But it looked like her. You could see her face. Even though her eyes were closed, she was completely recognizable. And then suddenly, she knew . . . he must have taken off her clothes . . . he must have taken them all off. . . . The only thing she was wearing was a black ribbon around her neck. He must have put it on her, for sex appeal, while she was sleeping. The credit for the photograph said Marcus Anders. She went even paler than she was when she first saw it. And Charles had seen her look. He knew there was something to it. "Do you know who took this?"

She nodded, wishing that she could die for him. Wishing, for his sake, that she had never met him, or borne his children.

"What is this, Grace?" For the first time in sixteen years, his tone was icy. "When did you do this?"

"I don't know for sure that I did," she said, choking on her own words as she sat down slowly at the kitchen table. "I . . . I went out with a photographer a few times in Chicago. I told you about him. He said he wanted to take pictures of me, and they wanted me to at the agency . . ." She faltered and he looked shocked.

"They wanted you to do porno? What kind of agency was this?"

"It was a modeling agency," the life was going out of her. She couldn't fight this anymore, she couldn't defend herself forever. She would leave him if he wanted her to. She would do anything he wanted. "They wanted me to model, and he said he'd take some shots, like for a portfolio. We were friends. I trusted him, I liked him. He was the first man I'd ever gone out with. I was twenty-one years old. I had no experience. My roommates hated him, they were a lot smarter than I was. He took me to his studio, he played a lot of music, he poured me some wine . . . and he drugged me. I told you about it a long time ago." But he no longer remembered. "I guess I must have passed out. I was completely out of it, and I think he took pictures of me when I was asleep, but I was wearing a man's shirt, it was no worse than that. I never took my clothes off."

"How do you know that for sure?"

She looked at him honestly. She had never lied to him, and she didn't intend to start now. "I don't. I don't know anything. I thought he had raped me, but he hadn't. My roommate took me to a doctor and she said nothing had happened. I tried to get the negatives from him, and he wouldn't give them to me. My roommates finally said I should just forget it. He needed a release to use them, if I was recognizable, and if I wasn't, who cared anyway. I would have liked to get them back, but I knew I couldn't. At one point, he tried to make it sound like I'd signed a release, but then he gave me the impression that I hadn't. I don't see how I could have anyway. I was so stoned from what he gave me, I could barely see when I left.

"He showed the pictures to the head of the agency afterwards, and the head of the agency made a pass at me. He said the shots were pretty hot, but he said that I had a shirt on, so I figured nothing really terrible had happened. I never saw the pictures. I never saw him again. I never thought we'd be in this position, that I'd be married to someone important and we'd be vulnerable." Now he could do anything he wanted. And they looked terrible. They looked like real porno. All she was wearing was a black ribbon she'd never seen before tied at her throat. And as she stared at the photograph, she saw that she looked drugged. She looked completely out of it, to her own eyes. But to a stranger, intent on seeing something lewd, it was everything they could have wanted. She couldn't believe anyone could do something like that. He had destroyed her life with a single picture. She just sat there, looking at Charles, her whole body sagging with grief as she saw the pain on his face. Killing her father in self-defense was bad enough, but how was he going to explain this to his constituents, the media, and their children?

"I don't know what to say. I can't believe you'd do such a thing." He was overwhelmed, and his chin was quivering with unshed tears. He couldn't even look at her as he turned away and cried. Nothing he could have done to her could have been worse. She would have preferred it if he had hit her.

"I didn't do it, Charles," she said weakly, crying too. She knew for a certainty that their marriage had just ended over Marcus's pictures. "I was drugged."

"What a fool you were . . . what a fool . . ." She couldn't deny that. "And what a bastard he must have been to make you do that." She nodded through her tears, unable to say anything in her own defense. And a moment later, Charles took the paper and went upstairs alone to their bedroom. She didn't follow him. She was beside herself, but she knew that on Monday, the day after Matt's party, she would have to leave him. She had to leave all of them. She couldn't keep putting them through this.

The photograph itself was on the news that night, and the story broke so big that every network and wire service in the country were calling. His aides were frantically trying to explain that it was probably all a mistake, the girl only looked like her, and no, Mrs. Mackenzie was not available for comment. But even worse, there was an interview with Marcus the next day. He had white hair, and he looked seedy in the interview, but he said with a lascivious smile that the photographs were indeed of Grace Mackenzie, and he had a signed release to prove it. He held it up for all to see and explained that she had posed for him in Chicago eighteen years before. "She was a real hot mama," he said, smiling. And from the photographic evidence, she certainly looked it.

"Was she in great financial need at the time?" the interviewer asked, pretending to look for a sympathetic reason why she had done it.

"Not at all. She loved doing it," he said, smiling. "Some women do."

"Did she give you the release to use the photographs commercially?"

"Of course." He looked insulted even to be asked. They flashed the photograph again, and then moved on to another topic, as Grace stared at the screen in unconcealed hatred. She had never given a release to him, and when Goldsmith the libel attorney called back at noon, she told him point-blank that she had signed no release to Marcus Anders.

"We'll see what we can do, Grace. But if you posed for that photograph, and gave him a release, there isn't a damn thing we can do."

"I did *not* sign a release to him. I didn't sign anything."

"Maybe he forged it. I'll do my best. But you can't unring a bell, Grace. They've seen it. It's out there. You can't take it back, or undo it. If you posed for it eighteen years ago, you've got to know it's out there, and it'll come back to haunt you.'' And then, in a worried tone, "Are there any others? Do you know how many he took?"

"I have no idea." She almost groaned as she said it.

"If the paper bought them from him in good faith, and he represented to them that he had a release, and presented one to them, then they're protected."

"Why is *everyone* protected except me? Why am *I* always the guilty party?" It was like getting beaten again, and raped. She was a victim again. It was no different from getting raped night after night by her father. Only her father wasn't doing it anymore, everyone else was. And it wasn't fair. It wasn't fair that just because Charles was in politics they had a right to destroy her and their family. They had had sixteen wonderful years, and now it had all turned into a nightmare. It was like coming back full circle, and being put back in prison. She was helpless against the lies. The truth meant nothing. Everything she'd done, everything she'd lived, everything she'd built had been wasted.

And by that afternoon she'd seen a copy of the release, and there was no denying that she had signed it. The handwriting was shaky, and the forms a little loose, but even to her own eyes, she recognized the signature. She couldn't believe it. He had obviously made her do it when she was barely conscious.

Matthew's party was subdued, everyone had either heard about or seen the tabloids. All the parents who dropped their children off gave Grace strange looks, or at least she thought so. Charles was on hand to greet them too, but the two of them had barely spoken since the night before, and he had spent the night in their guest room. He needed time to think, and to absorb what had happened.

They had talked to the children about the photographs that morning. Matthew didn't really understand what they were about, but Abigail and Andrew did. Andrew looked agonized, and Abigail had burst into tears again. She couldn't believe all that her mother had put them through. How could she do it?

"How can you lecture us about the way we behave, about morality, and not sleeping with boys, when you did things like that? I suppose you were *forced* to do it, just like your father forced you? Who forced you this time, Mom?" Grace had lost control this time, and she had slapped Abigail across the face, and then apologized profusely. But she just couldn't take it anymore. She was tired of the lies, and the price they all had paid.

"I never did that, Abigail. Not knowingly, at least. I was drugged and tricked by a photographer in Chicago when I was very young and stupid. But to the best of my knowledge, I never posed for that picture."

"Yeah, sure." But it was all more than Grace could take. She didn't discuss it with them any further. And half an hour later, Abigail left to spend the evening with a friend, and Andrew went out with his new girlfriend.

Matthew enjoyed his party anyway, and Grace cooked dinner for him afterwards. Abby called to say she was spending the night with her friend, and Grace didn't argue with her. And Andrew came in at nine, but didn't disturb them.

Charles was in the library working again, and Grace knew what she had to do. When Charles came into their bedroom to get some papers, he pretended not to be concerned, but he was startled to see her packing a suitcase.

"What's that all about?" Charles asked casually.

"I figure you've been through enough, and rightfully so," she said quietly, with her back to him. She was packing two big suitcases and he was suddenly worried. He had been hard on her, but he had a right to be upset. Anyone would have been shocked. But he was willing to let her past die quietly behind them. He hadn't told her that yet, but he was slowly coming around. Some things were harder than others. He just needed some time to himself to absorb it. He thought that she'd understand that, but apparently, she didn't.

"Where is it you're going?" he asked quietly.

"I don't know. New York, I think."

"To look for a job?" He smiled, but she didn't see him.

"Yeah, as a porno queen. I've got a great portfolio now."

"Come on, Grace," he moved closer to her, "don't be silly."

"Silly?" She turned on him. "You think that's what this is? You think having stuff like that out is silly? You think it's silly to destroy your husband's career and get to the point that your children hate you?"

"They don't hate you. They don't understand. None of us does. It's hard to understand why anyone wants to hurt you."

"They just do. They've done it all my life. I should be used to it by now. It's no big deal. And don't worry, without me, you should win the election." She sounded hurt and angry and defeated.

"That's not as important to me as you are," he said gently.

"Bullshit," she said, sounding hard. But at that moment she hated herself for everything she'd done to him, for ever loving him, or thinking that she could leave the past behind her. She couldn't leave anything behind. It had all come with her, like clanking tin cans tied to her tail, and they reeked of all that was rotten.

Charles went back downstairs again, thinking that she needed to be alone, and they both spent a lonely night in their separate quarters.

She made breakfast for him and Andrew and Matt the next day, and Charles made a point of telling her again not to go anywhere. He was referring to the night before and the suitcase, but she pretended not to understand, in front of the boys. And then they all left. Charles had a lot of important meetings, and press fires to put out, and he never had time to call her till noon, and when he did there was no answer.

Grace was long gone by then. She had written to each of them the night before, sitting up in bed, crying over the words until her tears blurred her eyes and she had to start again and again, just to tell them how much she loved them and how sorry she was for all the pain that she had caused them. She told them each to take care of Dad, and be good to him. The hardest one to write was to Matt. He was still too young. He probably wouldn't understand why she had left him. She was doing it for them. She was the bait that had brought the sharks, now she had to get as far away from them as possible, so no one would hurt them. She was going to New York for a few days, just to catch her breath, and she left the letters for Charles to give them.

And after New York, she thought she'd go to L.A.

She could find a job, until the baby came. She would give it to Charles then . . . or maybe he'd let her keep it. She was upset and confused and sobbing when she left. The housekeeper saw her go, and heard her wrenching sobs in the garage, but she was afraid to go to her and intrude. She knew what she was crying about, or so she thought. She'd cried herself when she'd seen the tabloids.

But Grace didn't take the car. She had called a cab, and waited for it outside the house with her bags. The housekeeper saw the cab pull away, but she wasn't sure who was inside. She thought Grace was still in the garage, getting ready to do some errands before she picked up Matthew. In fact, she had called a friend to pick him up, and she had left a long, agonizing letter for Charles in their bedroom, with the ones for her children.

The cabdriver drove as fast as he could to Dulles Airport, chatting all the while. He was from Iran, and he told her how happy he was in the United States, and that his wife was having a baby. He talked incessantly and Grace didn't bother to listen to him. She felt sick when she saw that he had the picture of her on the cover of *Thrill* on the front seat of the cab, and he was looking over his shoulder to talk to her, when he ran right into another cab, and then was rear-ended hard, by two cars behind him. It took them more than half an hour to get unsnarled. The highway patrol came, no one appeared to be hurt, so all they had to do was exchange all their numbers, driver's licenses, and the names of their insurance carriers. To Grace, it seemed endless. But she had nowhere to go anyway. She was taking a commuter flight, and she could always catch the next one.

"You all right?" The driver looked worried. He was terrified that somebody would complain to his boss, but she promised she wouldn't. "Hey," he said, pointing to *Thrill* as she felt panic rise in her throat, "you look like her!" He meant it as a compliment, but Grace didn't look pleased. "She's a pretty girl, huh? Pretty woman!" He gazed admiringly at the photograph that was supposed to be Grace but somehow didn't seem right whenever she looked at it, "she's married to a congressman," he continued. "Lucky guy!" Was that how people looked at it, she wondered. Lucky guy? Too bad Charles didn't think so, but who could blame him?

He dropped her off at the airport, and she felt a little twinge in her neck from when they'd been hit, and she felt a little stiff, but it was nothing major. She didn't want to make any trouble for him. And she just managed to catch her flight. It wasn't until after they landed in New York that she realized she was bleeding. But it wasn't too bad. If she could just get to the hotel and rest, she'd be fine. She'd had a few incidents like that with Matt and Andrew when she was pregnant, the doctor had told her to rest, and the bleeding had always stopped quickly.

She gave the cabdriver the address of the Carlyle Hotel on East Seventy-sixth Street and Madison. She had made the reservation from the plane. It was only half a dozen blocks from where she used to live, and she liked it. She had stayed there once with Charles, and she had happy memories there. She had happy memories everywhere with him. Until June, their life had been idyllic.

She checked in at the desk. They were expecting her, and she had registered under the name of Grace

Adams. They gave her a small room filled with rose-covered chintz, and the bellboy put down her two bags. She tipped him, and he left, and no one had said how remarkable her resemblance was to the porno queen in the tabloids.

She wondered as she lay down on the bed if Charles had come home by then and found her letter. She knew she wouldn't call. It was better to leave like this, if she called and talked to them at all, especially Charles, or Matt, she knew she couldn't do it.

She was exhausted as she lay on the bed thinking of them, she felt drained and utterly worn out, and her neck still hurt, and she had little nagging cramps low in her abdomen and in her back. She knew it was nothing. She didn't have the strength to go to the bathroom. She just lay there, feeling weak and sad, and slowly the room began to spin around, and eventually she drifted off into the blackness.

She woke again at four a.m., and by this time the cramps she'd felt earlier were really bad. She rolled over, and moaned in pain. She could hardly stand them. She lay there curled up for a long time, and then she looked down at the bed underneath her. It was soaked with blood and so were her slacks. She knew she had to do something soon, before she passed out again. But standing up was so painful, she almost fainted. She grabbed her handbag, and crawled to the door, pulling the raincoat she'd brought tight around her. She staggered out into the hall, and rang for the elevator. She rode downstairs huddled over, but the elevator operators said nothing.

She knew the hospital was only half a block away, and all she had to do was get there in a hurry. She saw the bellmen watching her, and the clerk at the desk, and when she got outside into the warm September air, she felt a little better.

"Cab, miss?" the doorman asked, but she shook her head and tried to straighten up, but she couldn't. A flash of pain made her gasp, and suddenly a cramp of unbelievable strength buckled her knees, as he reached out and caught her. "Are you all right?"

"I'm fine . . . I just have . . . a little problem . . ." At first he thought she was drunk, but when he saw her face, he could see that she was in pain. And she looked vaguely familiar. They had so many regulars and movie stars, sometimes it was hard to know who you knew and who you didn't. "I was just going . . . to the hospital . . ."

"Why don't you take a cab? There's one right here. He'll take you right across Park Avenue and drop you off. I'd take you myself, but I can't leave the door," he apologized, and she agreed to take the cab. She could hardly walk now. The doorman told him Lenox Hill, and she handed the doorman and the driver each five dollars.

"Thanks, I'll be fine," she reassured everyone, but she didn't look it. After they'd crossed Park Avenue, and pulled into the space for the emergency room, the driver turned to look at her, and at first he didn't see her. She had slipped off the seat, and she was lying on the floor of his cab, unconscious.

Chapter 15

As they wheeled Grace into the emergency room, she saw lights spinning by overhead, and heard noises. There were metallic sounds, and someone called her by her first name. They kept saying it over and over, and then they were doing something terrible to her, and there was awful pain. She tried to sit up and stop them. What were they doing . . . they were killing her . . . it was terrible . . . why didn't they stop . . . she had never felt so much pain in her life. She screamed, and then everything went black, and there was silence.

The phone rang in the house in Washington. It was five-thirty in the morning. But Charles wasn't asleep. He had been awake all night, praying that she would call him. He'd been such a fool. He had been wrong to react the way he had, but they were all worn down by the constant attack of the tabloids. And it had been a shock. But the last thing he had wanted to do was lose her. He had told the kids she'd gone to New York for a conference for "Help Kids!" and would be back in a few days, which would give him a little time to find her. He wasn't sure where she was. He had tried calling the house in Connecticut all night and she wasn't there. He'd called the Carlyle in New York and there was no one registered by the name of Mackenzie. He wondered if she was at a hotel in Washington somewhere, hiding. And when the phone rang, he hoped it would be her, but it wasn't.

"Mr. Mackenzie?" The voice was unfamiliar. His name was on an I.D. card in her wallet, simply as Charles Mackenzie. And her driver's license read Grace Adams Mackenzie.

"Yes?" He wondered if it was going to be a crank call, and was sorry he had answered. The letters and calls had started again in full force after her photos.

"We have a Grace Mackenzie here." The voice seemed totally without interest.

"Who are you?" Had she been kidnapped? Was she dead? . . . Oh God . . .

"I'm calling from Lenox Hill Hospital in New York. Mrs. Mackenzie just came out of surgery." . . . oh God . . . no . . . there had been an accident . . . "She was brought in by a cabdriver, hemorrhaging very badly." Oh no . . . the baby . . . he felt a hand clutch his heart, but all he could think about was Grace now.

"Is she all right?" He sounded hoarse and frightened, but the nurse was slightly reassuring.

"She's lost a lot of blood. But we'd rather not give her a transfusion." They did everything they could now to avoid it. "She's stabilized, and her condition is listed as fair." And then for a moment, the voice became almost human. "She lost the baby. I'm sorry."

"Thank you." He had to catch his breath and figure out what to do. "Is she conscious? Can I talk to her?"

"She's in the recovery room. I'd say she'll be there

till eight-thirty or nine. They want to get her blood pressure up before they send her to a room, and it's still pretty low right now. I don't think she's going anywhere till later this morning.''

"She can't check out, can she?''

"I don't think so.'' The nurse sounded surprised at the question. "I don't think she'll feel up to it. There's a key in her bag from the Carlyle Hotel. I called there. But they said no one was with her.''

"Thank you. Thank you very much for calling me. I'll be there as soon as I can.'' He jumped out of bed as soon as he hung up, and scrawled a note to the kids about an early meeting. He dressed in five minutes, without shaving, and drove to the airport. He was there by six-thirty, and caught a seven o'clock flight. A number of the flight attendants recognized him, but no one said anything. They just brought him the newspaper, juice, a Danish, and a cup of coffee, like they did for everyone else, and left him alone. For most of the flight, he sat staring out the window.

They landed at eight-fifteen, and he got to Lenox Hill just after nine o'clock. They were just wheeling Grace into her room when he got there. He followed the gurney into the room, and she looked surprised to see him, and very groggy.

"How did you get here?'' She looked confused, and her eyes kept drifting shut, as the nurse and the orderly left the room. Grace looked gray and utterly exhausted.

"I flew,'' he smiled, standing next to her, and gently took her hand in his. He had no idea if she knew yet about the baby.

"I think I fell,'' she said vaguely.

"Where?''

"I don't remember . . . I was in a cab in Washington and someone hit us . . ." She wasn't sure now if it was a dream or not . . . "And then, I had terrible pains . . ." She looked up at him, suddenly worried. "Where am I?"

"You're at Lenox Hill. In New York," he said soothingly, sitting down in the chair next to her, but never letting go of her hand. He was frightened by how bad she looked and was anxious to speak to the doctor.

"How did I get here?"

"I think a cabdriver brought you in. You passed out in his cab. Drunk again, I guess." He smiled, but without saying anything, she started to cry then. She had touched her belly and it felt flat. At three months there had been a little hill growing there and it was suddenly gone. And then she remembered the terrible pain the night before, and the bleeding. No one had told her anything yet about the baby. "Grace? . . . sweetheart, I love you . . . I love you more than anything. I want you to know that. I don't want to lose you." She was crying harder then, for him, for the baby they'd lost, and their children. Everything was so difficult, and so sad now.

"I lost the baby . . . didn't I?" She looked at him for confirmation and he nodded. They both cried then, and he held her.

"I'm so sorry. I should have been smart enough to know you'd really go. I thought you were bluffing and needed some space that night. I almost died when I read your letter."

"Did you give my letters to the children?"

"No," he said honestly. "I kept them. I wanted to find you and bring you back. But if I'd been smart enough to keep you from going in the first place, you wouldn't have had the accident, and . . ." He was convinced it was all his fault.

"Shhh . . . maybe it was just from all the stress we've been through . . . I guess it wasn't the right time anyway, with everything that's happened."

"It's always the right time . . . I want to have another baby with you," he said lovingly. He didn't care how old they both were, they both loved their children. "I want our life back."

"So do I," she whispered. They talked for a little while, and he stroked her hair and kissed her face, and eventually she fell asleep and he went to locate the doctor. But he wasn't encouraging. She had lost a dramatic amount of blood, and the doctor didn't think she'd be feeling well for a while, and he said that while she was certainly able to conceive again, he didn't recommend it. She had a startling amount of scarring, and he was actually surprised she'd gotten pregnant as often as she had. Charles did not volunteer an explanation for the scarring. The doctor suggested that she go to the hotel and rest for a couple of days, and then go home to Washington and stay in bed for at least another week, maybe two. A miscarriage at three months with the kind of hemorrhaging she'd experienced was nothing to take lightly.

They went from the hospital to the hotel that afternoon, and Grace was stunned by how weak she was. She could hardly walk and Charles carried her into the hotel, and to her room, and put her right to bed, and ordered room service for her. She was sad, but they were happy to be together, and the room was very cozy. He called his aides in Washington and told them that he wouldn't be back for a couple of days, and then he called the housekeeper and told her to explain to the children that he was with their mother in New York, and would be back in two days. She promised to stay with them until he returned, and drive Matt to school. Everything was in order.

"Nice and simple. Now all you have to do is get well, and try to forget what happened."

But after they left the hospital, the nurse at the front desk had commented to the doctor, "Do you know who that was?" He had no idea. The name had meant nothing to him. "That was Congressman Mackenzie from Connecticut and his porno queen wife. Don't you read the tabloids?"

"No, I don't," he said, barely amused. Porno queen or not, the woman had been very lucky not to bleed to death. And he wondered if her "porno" activities had anything to do with the scarring. But he didn't have time to worry about it, he had surgery all afternoon. She wasn't his problem.

At the hotel, Charles made her sleep as much as she could, and the next morning, Grace was feeling better. She ate breakfast and sat up in a chair, and she wanted to go out for a walk with him, but she didn't have the strength to do it. She couldn't believe how rotten she felt. He called her former obstetrician in New York, and he was nice enough to come to see her. He gave her some pills and some vitamins, and told her she'd just have to be patient. And when they went out in the hall, Charles asked him about what the doctor at Lenox Hill had said about the scarring. But her own doctor wasn't impressed. She'd had it for years and it had never given her any trouble.

"She's got to take it easy now though, Charles. She looks like she's lost a lot of blood. She's probably very anemic."

"I know. She's had a rough time lately."

"I know. I've seen. Neither of you deserves that. I'm sorry."

He thanked him and the doctor left, and they curled up on the couch and watched old movies and ordered room service, and the next day, he bundled her up in a limousine, and took her to the airport, and put her in a wheelchair. He had thought about driving her back to Washington, but that seemed too tiring too. Flying was quicker. They flew first class, and he got another wheelchair for her when they arrived, and he wheeled her quickly through the airport. But she waved frantically for him to stop as they passed a newspaper stand. And they both stood there, dumbfounded by what they saw.

A new edition of the tabloid had come out with a raging headline. "Senator's Wife Sneaks off to New York for Abortion." Grace burst into tears the minute she saw it, and he didn't even bother to buy one for them to read. There was a huge picture of her on the front from a congressional party months before. He just wheeled her through the airport at full speed and took her to where he had left his car two days before. She was still crying when he opened the door for her with a strained expression. Were they never going to give her a break and leave them alone? Apparently not.

He helped her into the car, and walked around and got in himself, and then he turned to her with a look that touched her very soul. "I love you. You can't let them destroy us . . . or you . . . we have to get through this."

"I know," she said, but she couldn't stop crying.

At least this time, the six o'clock news did not dignify the story with a comment. This was strictly tabloid material. And they told the children about it that night but said it wasn't true. They said that Grace had gone to New York and been in an accident in a cab, which was almost true. She had, but it had been in Washington, and she had lost a baby. But Grace didn't think they should know that, so they didn't tell them about the miscarriage.

She was still feeling very weak the next day, but the children were being very good to her, even Abby brought breakfast to her room, and at lunchtime Grace went downstairs for a cup of tea, and happened to look out the window. There were pickets lined up outside carrying signs of "Murderess!" "Baby Killer!" "Abortion Monger." There were photographs of aborted fetuses, and Grace had an asthma attack the moment she saw them.

She had Charles paged, and when he called her he was horrified, and told her he'd call the police immediately. They came half an hour later, but the pickets only moved across the street, in peaceful demonstration. And by then, a camera crew had arrived, and it became a circus. Charles came home shortly after that, and he was beginning to wonder if they would ever have a normal life again. He refused to comment to the camera crew, and said that his wife had been in a car accident and was ill and he would really appreciate their leaving, after which there was a lot of hooting and jeering.

But that afternoon, when the children came home, the pickets were gone, and only the camera crew remained, and Grace, looking deathly pale, was fixing dinner.

Charles tried to force her to go upstairs, but she flatly refused. "I've had enough. I'm not going to let

them ruin our lives anymore. We're going back to normal." She was determined, although she was visibly
shaky, but he had to admire her, as he pushed a chair
under her and suggested she sit down while he made
dinner.

"Could you maybe wait a week before this show of
strength?" he suggested.

"No, I can't," she said firmly. And much to everyone's surprise, they had a very pleasant dinner. Abby
seemed to have calmed down again while Grace was
gone, and if anything, she seemed helpful and sympathetic. It was hard to know what, but something had
turned her around. Maybe there had just been so
much grief, that she had figured out they all needed
each other. And Andrew commented on the ghouls
outside, and said he was tempted to moon them from
his bedroom window, which made everyone laugh,
even Grace, although she told him not to.

"I don't think we need to see any more Mackenzie
flesh in the tabloids," she said ruefully.

And afterwards, while she straightened up, Abby
asked her quietly. "That wasn't true about the abortion, was it, Mom?" She looked a little worried.

"No, sweetheart, it wasn't."

"I didn't think so."

"I would never have an abortion. I love your father
very much, and I would love to have another baby."

"Do you think you will?"

"Maybe. I don't know. There's an awful lot going
on right now. Poor Dad is under a lot of pressure."

"So are you," she said, sympathetic for the first
time. "I was talking to Nicole's mom about it, and she
said she felt really sorry for you, that most of the time,
they tell lies and ruin people's lives. It made me realize

how awful for you all this must be. I didn't mean to
make it worse." There were tears in her eyes as she said
it.

"You didn't." Grace leaned over and kissed her.

"I'm sorry, Mom." They hugged for a long time,
and had a quiet moment, and then they walked upstairs arm in arm, and Charles smiled as he watched
them.

Life was peaceful again, for the next few days, with
the exception of hate letters about her alleged abortion. But by the weekend, another of Marcus's photographs had been printed in *Thrill* again. She wore the
same black velvet ribbon around her neck, and the
same lack of clothes. It was essentially the same photograph they'd seen before, just a slightly different position, and only slightly more suggestive. It didn't shock
her anymore, it just made her angry. And, of course,
his supposed "release" from her allegedly covered this
one also.

"What are we supposed to wait for here? An entire
album?" Grace said in fury. But Goldsmith told them
again that they had no legal recourse, all the same conditions existed as before. There was supposedly a
signed "release" with her signature, and the fact that
Marcus owned the pictures and she was a so-called celebrity because of whom she was married to allowed
him to publish whatever he wanted. As celebrities, they
had no right to privacy anyway, so they could not be
"invaded," and they couldn't prove loss of income, or
actual malice. "Do you suppose we should call that
bastard Marcus and try to buy the rest of what he has?"
she asked Charles, but he shook his head.

"You can't. That would be like paying blackmail,
and he might not sell them to you anyway. He might

keep some of them back, there's no way of knowing. *Thrill* is probably paying him a pretty penny for this. Pictures like that of someone like you are worth a lot of money."

"Nice for him, maybe we should get a commission."

She was so angry, but there was nothing she could do. And the following week she went to some campaign events with Charles. It was hard to determine how much damage the tabloids had done, people still greeted her warmly. But it was certainly unsettling for all of them, and very distracting.

A third photograph was released two weeks later, and this time when Matt came home from school, he was crying. And when Grace asked what had happened, he said that one of his friends had called her a bad name. She felt as though she'd been slapped when he said it.

"What kind of a name?" She tried to sound calm, but she wasn't.

"You know," he said miserably. "The 'H' one."

She smiled sadly at him. "It doesn't start with an 'H.' Unless you mean harlot."

"It wasn't that one," he said miserably. He didn't want to tell her.

"Darling, I'm so sorry." She put her arms around him, and wanted to run away again. But she knew she couldn't run away anymore. She had to face it with them.

It happened again at his school, and again the day after. And Charles and Grace got into a fight over it that night. She wanted to take the children back to Connecticut, and he told her she couldn't run away. They had to stand and fight, and she told him she refused to destroy her family over his "damn campaign." But that wasn't what it was about, and they both knew it. They were just frustrated at their own helplessness, and needed to scream at someone, since they couldn't do anything to stop what was happening.

But Matthew didn't understand that, and when Grace went to tuck him in, she couldn't find him. She asked Abby where he'd gone, and she shrugged and pointed to his room. She was on the phone with Nicole and she hadn't seen him. And Andrew hadn't seen him either. She went downstairs to Charles in the den, still annoyed at him, and asked if he'd seen Matthew.

"Isn't he upstairs?" They exchanged a look and he suddenly caught Grace's concern, and they started looking for him in earnest. He was nowhere. "He couldn't have gone out," Charles said, looking worried. "We'd have seen him."

"No, we wouldn't necessarily." And then in an undertone, "Do you think he heard us fighting?"

"Maybe." Charles looked even more upset than she did. He was worried about kidnapping if Matt was wandering the streets somewhere. Washington was a dangerous city after dark. And when they went upstairs again, they found the note he had left in his room. *Don't fight over me anymore. I'm leaving. Love, Matt. Mom and Dad, I love you. Say bye to Kisses for me.* Kisses was their chocolate Lab, because when they'd gotten her Grace had said she looked like a little pile of Hershey Kisses.

"Where do you think he went?" Grace looked panicked as she asked him.

"I don't know. I'm calling the police." Charles's whole face was tense, and his jaw was working.

"It'll wind up in the tabloids," she said nervously.

"I don't care. I want to find him tonight, before anything happens." They were both frantic and the police reassured them that they would find him as soon as possible. They said that kids his age wandered off all the time, and usually stayed pretty close to home. They asked for a list of his best friends and a picture of him, and they set out in the squad car. Charles and Grace stayed home to wait for him, in case he came back. But the policemen were back with him half an hour later. He had been buying Hostess Twinkies at a convenience store two blocks away and feeling very sorry for himself. They had spotted him at once, and he didn't resist coming home. He was ready.

"Why did you do that?" Grace asked, still shaken by what he'd done. She just couldn't believe it. None of their children had ever run away. But they'd also never been under that kind of pressure.

"I didn't want you and Dad fighting over me," Matt said sadly. But it had been scary outside, and he was glad to be back now.

"We weren't fighting over you, we were just talking."

"No you weren't, you were fighting."

"Everybody fights sometimes," Charles explained, and pulled him down on his knee as he sat down. The police had just left and they had promised Charles not to tell the papers. There had to be something private in their lives, even if it was only their eight-year-old running away for half an hour. Nothing else was sacred.

"Mommy and I love each other, you know that."

"Yeah, I know . . . it's just that everything has been so yucky lately. People keep saying stuff in school, and Mom cries all the time." She looked guilty as she thought about it. She did cry a lot these days, but who wouldn't?

"Remember what I told you the other day," Charles explained. "We have to be strong. All of us. For each other. We can't run away. We can't give up. We just have to stick together."

"Yeah, okay," he said, only half convinced, but happy to be home again. It had been a dumb idea to run away and he knew it.

His mother walked him upstairs and tucked him in and they all went to bed early that night. Grace and Charles were exhausted and Matthew was asleep almost the moment his head hit the pillow. Kisses was lying at the foot of the bed, and snoring softly.

But the following week, another photograph was released and this one showed Grace full face, staring into the camera, with glazed eyes and a look of surprise on her face, with her eyes wide-open as though someone had just done something really shocking and deliciously sensual to her. They were the most erotic series of photographs she had ever seen, and little by little, bit by bit they were driving her crazy.

She called information then, and wondered why she had taken so long to do it. He wasn't in Chicago. Or in New York. He was in Washington, they told her finally at *Thrill*. It was perfect. Why hadn't she thought of it sooner? She knew she had absolutely no choice. It didn't matter what happened to her anymore. She had to.

She opened the safe and took Charles's gun out, and then she got in her car and drove to the address she'd jotted down on a piece of paper. The kids were at school, and Charles was at work. No one knew where she was going, or what she intended to do. But she knew. She had it planned, and it was going to be worth whatever it cost her.

She rang the bell at his studio on F Street, and she was surprised when someone buzzed her in without asking who she was. It meant either that they were very big and busy, or extremely sloppy. Because with a lot of valuable equipment around, they should have been more careful, but fortunately, they weren't.

It was all so easy, she couldn't imagine why she had never thought of it before. The door was open, and there was no one there, except Marcus. He didn't even have an assistant. He had his back to her, and he was bending over a camera, shooting a bowl of fruit on a table. He was all alone, and he didn't even see her.

"Hello, Marcus." Her voice was unfamiliar to him after all these years. It was sensual and slow and she sounded happy to see him.

"Who's that?" He turned and looked at her with a surprised little smile, not recognizing her at first, wondering who she was, he liked her looks, and . . . then suddenly he realized who she was and he stopped dead in his tracks. She was pointing a gun at him and she was smiling.

"I should have done this weeks ago," she said simply. "I don't know why I didn't think of it sooner. Now put down the camera, and don't touch the shutter or I'll shoot you and it, and I'd hate to hurt your camera. Put it down. Now." Her voice was sharp and no longer sensual and he put the camera down carefully on the table behind him.

"Come on, Grace . . . don't be a bad sport . . . I'm just making a living."

"I don't like the way you do it," she said flatly.

"You look beautiful in the photographs, you have to give me that."

"I don't give you shit. You're a piece of slime. You told me you never took my clothes off."

"I lied."

"And you must have had me sign the release when I was practically unconscious." She was icy cold with fury, but she was in complete control now. It was entirely premeditated. This time it really would be murder one. She was going to kill him, and looking at her, he knew it. He had driven her too far, and she had snapped. She didn't care what they did to her this time. She'd survived it before. And it was worth it.

"Come on, Grace, be a sport. They're great pictures. Look, what's the difference. It's done. I'll give you the rest of the negatives."

"I don't give a damn. I'm going to shoot your balls off. And after that, I'm going to kill you. I don't need a release for that. Just a gun."

"For chrissake, Grace. Give it up. They're just pictures."

"That's my life you've been fucking with . . . my children . . . my husband . . . my marriage . . ."

"He looks like a jerk anyway. He must be to put up with you . . . Christ, I remember all that prudey bullshit nineteen years ago. Even on drugs, you weren't any fun. You were a drag, Grace, a real drag." He was vicious, and if she'd been less wound up she'd have seen that he was coked up to the gills. He'd been using the money from *Thrill* to support his habit. "You were a real lousy piece of ass even then," he went on, but at least she knew the truth about that.

"You never slept with me," she said coolly.

"Sure, I did. I've got pictures to prove it."

"You're sick." He started sniveling then, whining about how she had no right to come in here like that and try and interfere with how he made his living.

"You're a rotten little creep," she said as she cocked the trigger, and the sound of it startled both of them.

"You're not going to do it, are you, Grace?" he whined.

"Yes, I am. You deserve it."

"You'll go back to prison," he said in a wheedling tone, as his nose ran pathetically. The past nineteen years had not been good to him. He had stooped to a lot of things in the meantime, few of them legal.

"I don't care if I go back," she said coldly. "You'll be dead. It's worth it." He sank to his knees then.

"Come on . . . don't do it . . . I'll give you all the pictures . . . they were only going to run two more anyway . . . I've got one of you with a guy, it's a real beauty . . . you can have it for free . . ." He was crying.

"Who has the photographs?" What guy? There had been no one else in the studio, or had there been while she was sleeping? It was disgusting to think of.

"I have them. In the safe. I'll get them."

"The hell you will. You probably have a gun in there. I don't need them."

"Don't you want to see them, they're gorgeous."

"All I want to see is you dead on the floor, and bleeding," she said, feeling her hand shake. And as she looked at him, she didn't know why, but she suddenly thought of Charles, and then Matthew . . . if she shot Marcus, she would never be with them again, except in prison visiting rooms, probably forever. . . . It took her breath away, thinking about it, and all she sud-

denly wanted to do was hold them, and feel them next
to her . . . and Abby and Andrew. . . . "Get up!"
she said viciously to Marcus. He did, crying at her
again. "And stop whining. You're a miserable piece of
shit."

"Grace, please don't shoot me."

She backed slowly toward the door, and he knew
she was going to shoot him from there, and all he
could do was cry and beg her not to.

"What do you want to live for?" she asked angrily.
She was furious at him now. He wasn't worth her time.
Or her life. How could she have even thought he was?
"What does a miserable piece of slime like you want to
live for? Just for money? To ruin other people's lives?
You're not even worth shooting." And with that, she
turned around, and hurried down the stairs, before he
could even think of following her. She was out the
door and back in her car, before he could even cross
the room. All he did was sit down on the floor and cry,
unable to believe she hadn't shot him. He had been
absolutely certain she was going to kill him, and he'd
been right, until the last five minutes. Just seeing him
again, standing there, sniveling, coked out to the gills,
had brought her to her senses.

She drove home and put the gun away, and then
she called Charles. "I have to see you," she said ur-
gently. She didn't want to tell him on the phone, in
case someone was listening, but she wanted him to
know what she'd almost done. She had almost gone
crazy. She had, for a while, but thank God, she had
come to her senses.

"Can it wait till lunch?"

"Okay." She was still shaking from what had happened. She could have been in jail by then and on her

way back to prison for life. She couldn't believe she
had almost been that stupid. But that's what it had
driven her to, all the lies, and the agony, the humilia-
tion, and the exposure.

"Are you all right?" he sounded worried.

"I'm fine. Better than I've been for a while."

"What did you do?" he teased, "Kill someone?"

"No, I didn't, as a matter of fact." She sounded
vaguely amused.

"I'll meet you at Le Rivage at one o'clock."

"I'll be there. I love you."

They hadn't had a lunch date in a while, and she
was happy to see him when he walked in. She was already waiting. He ordered a glass of wine, she never
drank at lunch, and rarely at dinner. And then they
ordered lunch. And when they had, she told him in an
undertone what had happened. He literally grew pale
when she told him. He was stunned. She knew how
wrong it was, but for a moment, just a moment, it had
seemed worth it.

"Maybe Matt's right, and I'd better behave myself,
or you'll shoot me," he said in a whisper, and she
laughed at him.

"And don't you forget it." But she knew she would
never do anything like that again. It had been one moment of blind madness, but even in the height of her
fury, she hadn't done it, and she was glad. Marcus Anders wasn't worth it.

"I guess that kind of takes the wind out of what I
was going to tell you." It had been quite a day for both
of them. He couldn't even begin to imagine the horror
it would have been if she had shot Marcus Anders. It
didn't even bear thinking, though he could understand the provocation. He wasn't sure what he'd have

done himself if he'd ever seen him. But thank God she had come to her senses. It was just one more confirmation to him that he was doing the right thing. It wasn't even a tough decision. "I'm withdrawing from the campaign, Grace. It's not worth it. It's not right for us. We've been through enough. We don't need to do this anymore. It's what I said to you in New York. I want our life back. I've been thinking about it ever since then. How much more are we supposed to pay for all this? At what price glory?"

"Are you sure?" She felt terrible to have caused him to withdraw from politics. He wasn't running for his congressional seat again, and if he didn't persist in the senatorial race he'd be out of politics, for a while at least, or possibly forever. "What'll you do with yourself?"

"I'll find something to do," he smiled. "Six years in Washington is a long time. I think it's enough now."

"Will you come back?" she asked sadly. "Will we come back?"

"Maybe. I doubt it. The price is too high for some of us. Some people get away with it quietly forever. But we didn't. There was too much in your past, too many people were jealous of us. I think just the relationship we have and the kids get plenty of people riled. There are a lot of miserably envious, unhappy people in the world. You can't worry about it all the time. But you can't fight it forever either. I'm fifty-nine years old, and I'm tired, Grace. It's time to fold up our tents and go home." He had already called a press conference for the next day, while she was threatening to kill Marcus Anders. The irony of it was amazing.

They told the children that night, and they were all disappointed. They were used to his being in politics, and they didn't want to go back to Connecticut full time. They all said it was boring, except in summer.

"Actually," he admitted for the first time, "I've been thinking that a change of scene might do us all good for a while. Like maybe Europe. London, or France, or maybe even Switzerland for a year or two."

Abby looked horrified and Matthew looked cautious. "What do they have in Switzerland, Dad?"

"Cows," Abby said in disgust. "And chocolate."

"That's good. I like cows and chocolate. Can we take Kisses?"

"Yes, except if we go to England."

"Then we can't go to London," Matthew said matter-of-factly.

They all knew Andrew's vote would have been France since his girlfriend was going back to Paris for two years. Her father was being transferred to their home office on the Quai d'Orsay, and she had told him all about it.

"I can work in the Paris branch of our law firm, or our London branch, if I go back to the firm, or we can live cheaply and grow our own vegetables in a farmhouse somewhere. We have a lot of options." He smiled at them. He'd been thinking about making a change ever since the attacks by the tabloids. But whatever they did after that, it was time for them to leave Washington, and they all knew it. It was just too high a price to pay for any man, or any family that stood behind him.

He had called Roger Marshall and apologized, and Roger said he understood completely. He thought there might be some other interesting opportunities in the near future, but it was too soon for Charles even to want to hear them.

The next morning, Charles was gracious and honorable and he looked relieved when he told the gathered members of the press that he was retiring from the senatorial race for personal reasons.

"Does this have to do with the photographs your wife posed for years ago, Congressman? Or is it because of her prison record coming out last June?" They were all such bastards. A new era had come to journalism, and it was not a pretty one. There had been a time when none of this would have happened. It was all muckraking and lies and maliciousness, actual or otherwise, provable or not. They went for the gut every time with a stiletto, and they didn't even care whose gut it was, as long as the stiletto came back with blood and guts on it. They had the mistaken impression that that was what their readers wanted.

"To the best of my knowledge," Charles looked them in the eye, "my wife never posed for any photographs, sir."

"What about the abortion? Was that true? . . . Will you be going back to Congress in two years? . . . Do you have any other political goals in mind? . . . What about a cabinet post? Has the President said anything if he gets reelected? . . . Is it true that she was in porno films in Chicago? . . ."

"Thank you, ladies and gentlemen, for all your kindness and courtesy over the past six years. Goodbye, and thank you." He ended like the perfect gentleman he had always been, and he left the room without ever looking back. And in two more months, at the end of his congressional term, he would be gone, and it would be all over.

Chapter 16

The last photograph was released in *Thrill* two weeks after Charles resigned, and it was an anticlimax then, even to Grace. Marcus had sold it to them a month before, and he couldn't withdraw it, even with all his whining. A deal was a deal, and he had sold it and spent the money. But he was terrified that Grace would come back with the gun again, and this time maybe she'd get him. He was afraid to leave the studio, and he decided to leave town. He decided not to sell them the photograph of her with the guy that he'd spoken of. It was a great shot too, and they really looked like they were doing it. But she'd shoot him for sure over that one, and *Thrill* didn't really care anymore. Mackenzie had resigned and he was old news. Who cared about his old lady?

But three days after the picture came out, the wire services got a call. It was from a man in New York, he ran a photo lab, and Marcus Anders had burned him for a lot of money. Anders had made half a million bucks thanks to him, and he'd put it all up his nose and cheated the man who was calling. And besides, the lab man knew there was something rotten about what Anders was doing. At first, it had seemed all right, but then the photographs had just kept on coming. They had beaten her to death, and then the poor guy quit. It wasn't right, for a lot of reasons. So he blew the whistle.

His name was Jose Cervantes, and he was the best trick man in New York, probably in the business. He did beautiful retouching for respectable photographers, and some funny stuff when he was paid enough by guys like Marcus Anders. He could take Margaret Thatcher's head and put her on Arnold Schwarzenegger's body. All he needed was one single tiny seam, and you had it. Presto! Magic! All he'd needed for Grace's photos, he explained, was the tiny black ribbon he'd added at her neck and he could join her head to any body. He had chosen some really luscious ones, in some fairly exotic positions, but at first Marcus had told him it was for fun. It was only when he'd seen them printed in *Thrill* that he really knew what the photographer was doing. He could have come forward then, but he didn't want to get involved. He could have been charged with fraud, but there was nothing illegal about tricking photographs. It was done constantly for ads, for jokes, for greeting cards, for layouts. It was only when you did what Marcus had done that it became illegal. Therein lay the malicious intent, the actual malice everyone looked for and never found. But they had it this time.

Marcus Anders had set out to ruin her. He had had nothing to do with exposing her prison record, he hadn't even known about it, and he had forgotten his pictures of her completely. But once he saw the pieces on her in *Thrill*, about killing her father and going to jail, he unearthed his old pictures of her and set Jose working on them. Jose hadn't even recognized her till he read the first article in *Thrill*, and realized what Marcus was doing. But Marcus had all his work by then.

And they were entirely faked. The original photographs were as she had remembered them, in Marcus's white shirt, many of them even in blue jeans. What had worked so well for their purposes was the expression on her face, as she lay back against the fur, drugged and only semiconscious. It made her look as though she were having sex at the time they were taken.

The story made a lot of news, and *Thrill* was wideopen for a major lawsuit. Mr. Goldsmith, the attorney, was delighted, and charges of fraud and malicious mischief were brought against Marcus, but he had disappeared by then, and word was he'd gone to Europe.

Marcus and *Thrill* had done it for fun, and for profit, and just to prove they could, each one not really caring, not taking responsibility, the artist, the photographer, the forger, the editor, and in the end, the Mackenzies were the victims.

But they all looked whole in body and soul again, as they packed their house in Washington, and went to spend Christmas in Connecticut. And then they went back to close the house on R Street. It had sold immediately to a brand-new congressman from Alabama.

"Will you miss Washington?" Grace asked, as they lay in bed on their last night in the house in Georgetown. He wasn't sure if she was sorry to leave or not. In some ways, she wasn't. In others she would miss it. She worried that Charles would always feel that he had left unfinished business. But he said he wouldn't. He had accomplished a lot in Congress in six years, and learned innumerable important lessons. The most important one he'd learned was that his family meant a lot more to him than his job. He knew he had made the right decision. They'd been through enough pain to last a lifetime. It had made the children stronger too, and brought them all closer together.

He had had other offers too, from corporations in the private sector, an important foundation or two, and of course they wanted him back at the law firm, but he hadn't made up his mind yet. And they were going to do exactly what he'd said. They were going to spend six or eight months in Europe. They were going to Switzerland, France, and England. He had already made arrangements with two schools while they were there, in Geneva and Paris. And Kisses was going to stay with friends in Greenwich until they came home for the summer. He'd have made his mind up by then about their future. And maybe, if she was up to it, Grace might have another baby. And if not, they were happy as they were. For Charles, all the doors were open.

The next day Grace was already in the car with the kids when the phone rang. Charles was making a last check of the house to make sure they hadn't left anything behind, but he had only found Matt's football, and a pair of old sneakers under the back porch, otherwise everything was gone. The house was empty.

The call was from the Department of State, from a man Charles knew only vaguely. Charles knew he was close to the President, but he had had few dealings with him, and he knew mainly that he was a good friend of Roger Marshall's.

"The President would like to see you sometime today, if you have time," he said, and Charles smiled and shook his head. It never failed. Maybe he just wanted to say goodbye and thank him for a job well done, but it seemed less than likely.

"We were just about to drive to Connecticut. We're out of here. The kids are already in the car."

"Would you all like to come over for a few minutes? I'm sure we could find something for them to do. He has fifteen minutes at ten forty-five, if that suits you." Charles wanted to say "Why?" but he knew that wasn't done, and he didn't want to slam any doors behind him, surely not the one to the Oval Office.

"I suppose we could do that, if you can stand three noisy kids and a dog."

"I've got five," he laughed, "and a pig my wife bought me for Christmas."

"We'll be right over."

The kids were vastly impressed that they were stopping off at the White House to say goodbye.

"I'll bet he doesn't do that for everyone," Matt said proudly, wishing he could tell someone.

"What's that all about?" Grace asked, as he drove the station wagon to Pennsylvania Avenue.

Theirs was the least distinguished vehicle to drive up to the White House in quite a while, he was sure, and he had told Grace honestly that he had absolutely no idea what they wanted.

"They want you to run for president in four years," she grinned at him. "Tell him you don't have time."

"Yeah. Sure." He laughed at her as he left them in the car, and an aide came to invite them inside. They were going to give the kids a mini-tour, and a young Marine volunteered to walk Kisses. There was a nice friendly atmosphere that was typical of the current administration. They liked kids and dogs and people. And Charles.

In the Oval Office, the President told Charles that

he was sorry he had withdrawn from the Senate race, but he understood it. There were times when one had to make decisions for one's own life, and not the country. And Charles told him that he appreciated the support, but would miss Washington, and hoped they'd meet again.

"I was hoping that too." The President smiled at him, and asked him what his plans were, and Charles told him. They were leaving for Switzerland that week, for two weeks of skiing.

"How do you feel about France?" the President inquired conversationally, and Charles explained that they were going to Normandy and Brittany, and they had made arrangements to put the kids in school in Paris. "When do you plan to arrive?" He was looking pensive.

"By February or March probably. We're going to stay till school lets out in June. Then travel around England for a month, and come home. I figure we'll be ready by then, and I'd better go back to work one of these days."

"How about in April?"

"Sir?" Charles didn't quite understand and the President smiled.

"I was asking how you felt about going back to work in April."

"I'll still be in Paris then," he said discreetly. He had no intention of coming back to Washington before a year, or even two, and not back to the States till that summer.

"That's not a problem," the President continued. "The current ambassador to France would like to come home by April to retire. He hasn't been well this year. How would you feel about a post as ambassador

to France for two or three years? And then we can talk
about the next election. We'll need some good men in
four years, Charles. I'd like to see you among them."

"Ambassador to France?" He looked blank. He
couldn't even imagine it, but it sounded like the
chance of a lifetime. "May I discuss this with my wife?"

"Of course."

"I'll call you, sir."

"Take your time. It's a good post, Charles. I think
you'd like it."

"I think we all would." Charles was bowled over.
And the back door to Washington was open for him
whenever he wanted.

He promised to let the President know in a few
days. The two men shook hands, and Charles went
downstairs looking excited. Grace could see that something had happened upstairs, and she was dying to
know what it was. It took them forever to get the kids
and the dog back into the car, and finally they did and
everyone asked at once what the President had said to
him.

"Not much," he teased them all and strung it out,
as they drove away from the White House. "The usual
stuff, you know, so long, have a great trip, don't forget
to write."

"Dad!" Abby complained, and Grace gave him a
friendly shove.

"Are you going to tell us?"

"Maybe. What am I bid?"

"I'm going to push you out of the car, if you don't
tell us soon!" she threatened.

"You'd better listen to her, Dad," Matt warned,
and the dog started to bark furiously as though she
wanted to know too.

"Okay, okay. He said we're the worst-behaved people he's ever met and he doesn't want us back here." He grinned and they all shouted at him in unison and told him he wasn't funny. "So bad, in fact, that he thinks we should stay in Europe." In truth it had been hard enough to say goodbye to their friends in Washington after six years, but they were excited about their adventure abroad and Andrew could hardly wait to see his friend in Paris.

Charles was looking at Grace then, with a curious glance. "He offered me the ambassadorship to Paris," he told her quietly as the kids continued to make a ruckus behind them.

"He did?" She looked stunned. "Now?"

"In April."

"What did you say?"

"I said I had to ask you, all of you, and he said to let him know. What do you think?" He was looking at her as he drove through Washington, and headed north to Greenwich.

"I think we're the luckiest people alive," she said, and meant it. They had come out nearly unscathed from the fires of hell, and they were still together. "You know what else I think?" she asked, leaning close to him as she whispered.

"What?"

She said it so the kids wouldn't hear. "I think I'm pregnant." He looked at her with a grin, and answered back in a whisper just loud enough to be heard despite the din in the backseat.

"I'm going to be eighty-two when this one graduates from college, maybe I should stop counting. I suppose we'll have to name him François."

"Françoise," she corrected, and he laughed.

"Twins. Does that mean we're going?" he asked politely.

"Sounds like it, doesn't it?" The kids in the back-seat were singing French songs at the top of their lungs and Andy was beaming.

"Do you mind having a baby over there?" he asked her quietly again. It worried him a little.

"Nope," she grinned. "I can't think of anyplace I'd rather be than Paris."

"Does that mean yes?"

She nodded. "I think so."

"He said he'd like me back here in two or three years to talk about the next elections. But I don't know, I'm not sure I'd ever want to go through all this again."

"Maybe we wouldn't next time. Maybe they wore themselves out."

"After the stunt that jerk pulled with his photographs, we may end up owning *Thrill* by then," he smiled ruefully. Goldsmith was going to be busy.

"We could burn it to the ground. What a nice idea." She smiled evilly.

"I'd love to." He smiled and leaned over and kissed her. In some ways, listening to their children laugh and sing in the backseat, and looking at her, made it seem as though the nightmare of the past months had never happened.

"*Au revoir*, Washington!" the kids shouted as they drove across the Potomac.

Charles looked at the place where so many dreams were born, and so many died, and shrugged his shoulders. "See ya." Grace moved closer to him, and smiled as she looked out the window.

Introducing
a new way to learn more about Danielle Steel

Visit the Danielle Steel Web Site at:
http://www.daniellesteel.com

Finally, a Web Site completely devoted to Danielle Steel and her books.
Log on, and you'll find:

- **The Danielle Steel Bookshelf**, featuring all of Danielle Steel's novels, with excerpts from each one and a 4-6 minute audio sample from audio editions

- **Hot off the Press**, featuring a chapter excerpt from Danielle's latest bestselling book

- **The Danielle Steel Screening Room**, featuring information on movie and TV tie-ins

- **The Danielle Steel Trivia Contest**: win a signed edition of her latest book!

- **The Danielle Steel Guest Book**: add your name to Danielle's electronic mailing list or send her an e-mail letter

- **Plus, the Danielle Steel Scrapbook**—never-before-aired audio and video interviews and more, available only on the Danielle Steel Web Site

http://www.daniellesteel.com

D • 11

Just fill in the coupon below, return it to us, and you will receive exciting information on the author who enriches your life with the most unforgettable characters in contemporary fiction.

JOIN THE

DANIELLE STEEL

FAN CLUB

Mail to:

DANIELLE STEEL FAN CLUB
Dell Publishing
Publicity Department
1540 Broadway
New York, New York 10036

Dell

Yes, enroll me in the Danielle Steel Fan Club.

Name _____

Address _____

City _____

State/Zip _____